MRS. GULLIVER'S TRAVAILS

By Cynthia Lee Winford

Patti,
Blessings,
Cindy

All characters in this book are fictitious, and any resemblance to real persons, living or dead, is coincidental.

ISBN-13: :978-1500892753
ISBN-10: 1500892750
Printed by CreateSpace,
An Amazon.com Company

Available on Kindle and other devices

In memory of my mother Astrid, who fulfilled her lifelong dream by moving to Florida

Acknowledgements

I would like to thank Jackie Nicholson for her valuable information concerning the culture of the Gullah/Geechee people on the Sea Islands off the coast of South Carolina; Diana Herman, RuthAnn Ridley, Lori T. Sly, and Donna Wesley for their much needed critiquing; my friends, who continue to encourage me to write; and my husband, Bob, who bore with me in the writing of this second novel.

Credit is also given for the use of an excerpt from *September Song,* written by Kurt Weill and Maxwell Anderson, 1938.

PART I

ROSEWILLOW

CHAPTER ONE

Nothing as hurtful as this had ever happened to Annah before.

For a long while, she watched the sky darken along the horizon and counted debris-laden waves roll toward and away from her as she sat upon the beach. The harsh, salty South Carolina winds burned her face, but the pain didn't match the ache burrowing into her soul. She grasped the end of her silk scarf as it fluttered around her head and brushed sand off her linen slacks.

As the wind howled, she screamed, "Jackson, why did I have to find out about this now?" No one heard her through the roaring sound of waves hitting boulders along the shore. "How can I confront a dead man?"

Once she gained her composure, she forced herself to stand up and climb the slope toward the veranda of her antebellum home. As she jostled her way through marsh grasses and fallen, weathered fence posts, she turned to view the murky clouds heading her way and defiantly said, "No man will ever hurt me again!"

—

Delsey opened the French doors to the veranda at the rear of the house when she spied her approaching. "Annah, where did you go? I've searched all over for you. What happened to you? You're covered in sand."

Annah brushed the front of her blouse, pulled the scarf from her neck, and swept her hair back with both hands. "I'll be fine. I needed time to be alone, so I walked down to the beach."

"I have never seen you so distressed."

Annah put her hand on Delsey's arm. "I'm fine. Don't worry about me."

Delsey crossed her arms over her white apron. "You're fine? I shouldn't worry about you? Annah, I know you better than that. What's upsetting you?"

"Nothing." She wiped the grit off her arms.

"Nothing?" Delsey uncrossed her arms and stood firmly in front of her.

Annah couldn't pass her without answering. She gripped her scarf. "How can I confront Jackson, now that he's dead?"

Delsey eyed her. "Confront him about what? Is it because Charlotte came into the house just as the
phone was ringing and talked with a strange woman who wanted her letters back? What's in those letters?" Annah returned her stare. "Well, you don't know her, and you don't have to give her anything."

Annah relaxed. "Delsey, you're more like my mother than my maid."

Delsey put her fists on her hips. "Well, someone has to keep you straight."

"You're right, as usual. Now I'm going upstairs to clean up."

"Miss Annah," Jerome interrupted. "Custer and I finished tying down chairs and tables so they wouldn't blow away with the strong winds, and we covered your flowers."

"Yes, missus. Lordy, it's blowin' like the dickens out there," Custer said, as he wiped his brown face with a handkerchief pulled from his back pocket. "Looks like the storm is a comin'."

"Thank you," she said. "You've both done a fine job." She was more concerned over Jackson's betrayal and the knowledge that his mistress wanted their letters than the outside furniture and flowers blowing away in the winds.

Annah strode upstairs to her bedroom to change out of her sand-covered clothes. She was glad that her older daughter had talked to that woman. It prompted her to search Jackson's desk. She pressed her hands over her forehead to relieve the tension. Storm winds rattled the shutters on the outside of the house, so she covered her ears to block out the noise.

Delsey was right. She was distressed. Why shouldn't she be? She found his neurological research papers and data on diseases, but one folder stood out differently from the others. Travel Receipts. It was in there that she found the personal letters written in a woman's handwriting.

At first, she was too hurt to read them, but decided if she didn't read them, she'd always wonder what the woman wrote. Finally, she chose the first one and read that she and Jackson had planned a trip to Cancun before Christmas and that he would be home for the holiday. The letter, dated in November, was right before he died. On her way out of the office, she determined not to allow anyone in there.

With tears streaming from her face, she decided to shred all the letters later when she was of a better mind. *She won't get the letters if I have anything to say about it.*

—

Kat opened the front door without knocking. She rushed toward Annah, who was descending the stairway toward the entryway.

"Hon, your daughter called me and said you haven't been yourself lately. You know you can always count on me to be here for you." She grabbed both of Annah's shoulders and held her backward to look at her. "My goodness sakes, hon, you look like death is a stompin' at your doorstep." She led her to two antique chairs in the hallway, and they sat together without speaking for a minute or two.

"Kat, thank you for coming over," Annah said. "You can't imagine what's happened. I can't talk about it now. It's too painful."

Kat clucked her tongue. "Sugar darlin', you've got both my ears and you can tell me about it later. You know that." She reached over and patted Annah's shoulder. "Now, please take care of yourself. I've never seen you so awful looking. Why, your face is ashen, you've lost weight, and you look like you've been dragged through a turnip patch. This is not like you."

Exhausted, Annah leaned back against the chair. "Kat, the phone doesn't stop ringing. I don't want to talk to anyone. Charlotte answered the phone this morning and told me a woman called to ask me to return her letters from Jackson."

Kat looked at her questionably. "What letters? Forget whatever she said if it's that awful." In one quick moment, Kat rushed through the hallway to the telephone recorder and said, "Oh, Annah, I'm not even going to tell you how many messages you have on this dang thing. I'm going to wipe them out, and you forget about them."

"Wait," Annah said, as she stood and followed her to the phone. "I should at least hear them."

"Nope. You just go sit your little bottom down and I'll take care of them." Kat pressed a button and erased all forty-nine messages at once. "There. Now you don't worry yourself about any of them anymore."

Annah gasped. "I guess I won't have to now."

"Hon, I don't have any more time to stay here with you. Spencer and I have a meeting to go to and I'm almost late. Let's get together for lunch tomorrow and talk." She grabbed Annah's hand with both of hers. "Have Renaldo make you a good hot meal now." Then, she hurried to the door and left.

Annah decided she would do so. She wanted to know if Kat had heard any gossip.

Hurricane force winds blew in from the Atlantic that afternoon. Annah directed Jerome and Custer to close the shutters over the outside windows. Heavy winds and rain rattled the house. Jerome picked up a battery-operated radio to take down to the cellar with them. Delsey, Renaldo, her cook, and Lucia, her housekeeper, joined them. One by one, they walked down the narrow wooden stairs to the cellar as the smell of mold and damp concrete rose up to them. Annah pulled a cord attached to a hanging light bulb, while Jerome and Custer unfolded rusty chairs stacked against the wall for them to sit on.

"We may be lucky," Jerome said. "The weatherman said the storm may blow northward and away from us. Right now, we only have to worry about the heavy winds blowing down trees and maybe a shutter or two."

Annah breathed a sigh of relief. Damage to the house would have been one more worry.

For over two hours, Jerome listened to the radio waiting to hear the forecaster tell them the danger had passed. The others kept busy eating snacks that Renaldo had packed for them and talking. Delsey sat with Annah still hoping to calm her. When the storm cleared, everyone climbed to the main level. Delsey with the others walked out back to check on their newly remodeled servants' quarters. The storm had blown limbs and leaves across much of the front driveway, and a shutter on the east side of the house had broken off, but there appeared to be little damage to the house.

CHAPTER TWO

Jimmy Nealy, a reporter from the local newspaper, *Shoreline Times*, in Rosewillow drove his car up the driveway canopied by low oak branches and hanging moss. As he drove toward the Gulliver's antebellum home, its magnificence overwhelmed him.

He rounded an ornate fountain still covered in protective plastic to keep the flowers safe from the storm. He parked his car behind a black Jaguar. Someone was visiting, and he thought with disappointment that his interview would not be possible this day.

He shut off the engine and heard a loud conversation coming from the open front door.

"Mrs. Gulliver," the visitor said. "I'm the person who called this morning. I've come to collect my letters."

Mrs. Gulliver eyed her. "What letters are you talking about?"

The reporter saw that the visitor was obviously years younger than Mrs. Gulliver. She was attractive and a woman of class.

"For your information, your husband and I were lovers for ten years. I wrote him many letters over that time, and he told me he kept them in an undisclosed file in his office."

Mrs. Gulliver gritted her teeth, "You're too late. I shredded them."

"Excuse me?" she paused. "They were my and your husband's property, not yours."

"I said I shredded them. They were my property, and I had the right to destroy them. Now, please leave immediately."

The reporter watched the woman's shoulders rise with hostility.

"I said leave, or I'll call the police."

"You wouldn't dare do that. You already know what would happen to your reputation if I let this be known to the Rosewillow community."

Mrs. Gulliver moved backward to slam the door shut. "Get

off my porch and property right now!"

The woman moved forward and pushed the door with her hand. "I don't believe you shredded them. Your husband is dead, so all I have now are my letters. Give them to me."

The reporter rested his arms on top of his car and continued to watch while two other women from the inside the house came to stand by Mrs. Gulliver.

The visitor turned and smirked at the reporter and then turned back to Mrs. Gulliver. "I'll leave, but I have more to tell you. You may or may not have destroyed my letters, but you will never destroy the love we had for each other." With a swift rotation and a contemptuous look on her face, she sashayed down the steps, but stopped and looked back at Mrs. Gulliver again. "Would you like to know that he told me he never loved you?"

Mrs. Gulliver slammed the door as hard as she could.

The visitor walked toward the reporter in a provocative manner, entered her car, raced her engine, and drove away.

Jimmy slid into his car and wrote a few notes. His hands shook as he wrote. Did he have a story from what he witnessed? *Mrs. Gulliver is one of the most influential women in Rosewillow*, he thought. *Should I expose this disgrace to the public?* He waited not knowing if he should go ahead with the interview or drive away and come back at another time.

—

"Mom? Who was that woman, and what's this about wanting her letters back?"

Annah faced the door, unable to look at her daughter, Emily. The entire incident was too shameful, and now she, as well as Delsey, would know about Jackson's affair. Worse still, that man outside heard it all. "Oh, my god," she said. She spun around and stared at them unable to speak. All she wanted now was a shot of Jackson's whiskey.

Annah moved away from them toward the parlor where her husband had kept his liquor. She found the bottle and a crystal glass in an antique walnut cabinet. She poured whiskey into the glass and downed it all at once.

"Annah," Delsey asked, as she followed her into the room. "Calm down."

Annah held back her tears as she returned to the hallway and sat down on the lower step of their spiral stairway. She covered her face with her hands.

Emily sat down on the floor in front of her and crossed her legs.

"Here, Annah, take this tissue," Delsey said, sitting down beside her on the step. "Don't let that woman rob you of the life you had with Jackson. You had three children with him, which she didn't have. You have four grandchildren and one on the way, and you have this beautiful, historic home, which is the envy of many. Don't think for once that he didn't love you. You were his wife, and he was proud to show you off to his friends and associates. That woman had to hide her relationship with him for all those years and could only see him once in a while."

"Thank you, Delsey." Annah dabbed her face and eyes. "What more can I say? You both now know that Jackson was unfaithful to me. I was stupid. I didn't see the signs. What I'd like to ask from you is that you never mention this to Charlotte or Morgan, or to anyone else. I don't need any more grief."

"Okay, Mom," Emily said. "Don't worry. We won't say a word to anyone about what we heard. I'm so sorry for you, but you're going to have to explain those letters to Charlotte."

"No, I don't. I'll think of something to tell her, but not what the letters actually said."

"Another thing," Delsey said. "Men of Jackson's status have all kinds of women running after them until they give into their charms, and then they turn stupid."

"What? Men turn stupid?" Jerome and Custer asked in unison as they walked toward them.

Delsey gave Annah a look of consternation. "Never you mind," she said to them and waved for them to leave.

"This is women's talk," Jerome said, as they shook their heads and left.

Delsey began to hum as she wrapped her arms around Annah's shoulder. "Annah, I know things. Where evil be, good be also."

Stunned, Annah asked, "What do you mean?"

Delsey stood and raised her arms high. "Because," she said, "Sectembtuh come'yuh."

"September is coming?" she asked. "Delsey, sometimes you are so mysterious."

Nervous, Jimmy walked up the steps, straightened his tie, and stuffed his shirt deeper into his slacks. He cleared his throat, shifted his camera and notepad to his left hand to free his right, and knocked on the immense oak door. Minutes passed, which seemed like hours. He glanced sideways at the porcelain vases and stands strategically placed on the porch floor.

As he watched the handle turn on the door, the face of an older black woman dressed in the uniform of a maid appeared. "Hello, I'm Jimmy Nealy. I work for the *Shoreline Times*. May I speak to Mrs. Annah Gulliver?"

The maid stood back and said, "I'm sorry, she's not available right now."

His composure changed. He stuttered, "When can I come back later to talk with her?"

"If you'll leave me your number, I'll have her call you."

He reached into his shirt pocket, pulled out a business card, and handed it to her. "Here's my number. I've left several messages, but she hasn't returned my calls."

She studied his face and took the card. "I'll tell her you came."

The reporter looked over her shoulder and saw Annah strolling toward them. "Mrs. Annah Elisabeth Gladstone Gulliver?" he asked.

Looking startled, she said, "Yes, I'm Mrs. Gulliver. You've just said my names like you're reading an obituary."

He flushed. "Mrs. Gulliver, I'm Jimmy Nealy. I work for the *Shoreline Times.*"

Mrs. Gulliver studied his face. "Delsey, I'll take care of this," she said, as Delsey left.

"What did you say your name was?"

"Jimmy Nealy. Mrs. Gulliver, I'm sorry if I've disturbed you. I've been assigned by my editor to ask you a few questions about the history of your plantation."

She held the door open. "Mr. Nealy, this is no longer a plantation. Today, we simply call it Gladstone."

In front of him stood the most attractive woman, he had ever seen. He felt he was looking at a goddess. She emanated refinement, dignity, gracefulness, and elegance.

He stuttered again, as he said, "My editor told me to come over here since you haven't returned my calls."

She gave him an exasperated sigh, closed her eyes, and shook her head. "Mr. Nealy, I don't have the energy to answer your questions at this time." A moment later, she walked over to the phone in the entryway to view the number of calls, but Kat had deleted them. "Indeed, Mr. Nealy," she called to him, "there are no messages listed. You may have left a message, but we've deleted them since I haven't had the time to listen to them."

He admired the way she spoke in the slow dialect of South Carolina. "Mrs. Gladstone, I'm sorry, Mrs. Gulliver, please excuse my nervousness. This is my first assignment as a reporter. I wanted to catch you at home before you went out someplace."

Mrs. Gulliver's gaze caused him to blush more. He cleared his throat. "I'll only take ten minutes. I just have a few questions," he said, as he clasped his camera and notepad to his chest. He knew he had blown the assignment. "I'm sorry. I'll come at another time," he said, as he reeled around and headed for the porch steps.

"Young man, like everyone else, I have a busy schedule. If you want to interview me, please call again, and I'll look at my calendar to see when I'm free. Now, is not good."

"Okay," he said, as he looked sideways over his shoulder wishing he could run away. "I'll do that. Thank you."

"Mom, who is he?" a young woman asked, as she walked toward her.

"He's a reporter wanting to interview me, of all things."

When he heard her, he turned to see Emily standing beside her mother. He couldn't help but be mesmerized by the chandelier's golden light overhead reflected on her face and blonde hair, making her glow. He noticed her hazel eyes glistening and her shoulder length hair swinging as she talked.

Suddenly, his notepad fell to the ground. Small pieces of paper slid out, flying around and behind him while he ran to collect them. He looked up at them apologetically.

"Good-bye," Mrs. Gulliver said, as she closed the door.

Jimmy walked toward his car, threw his camera and pad through the open window, sending it onto the passenger's seat, and crossed his arms over the car top. Spellbound by the meeting with the mother and daughter, he hoped to return. *Mrs. Gulliver's daughter is just as elegant and captivating as she,* he thought.

CHAPTER THREE

As usual, Charlotte barged into the house with her children in tow. "Grandmamma," Cherry cried, as she ran to her. Annah's six-year-old granddaughter wrapped her arms around Annah's waist and hung on. Daphne and Douglas, the twins, hurried to catch their hugs also.

"How did your lessons go the other day?" Annah asked, returning their embraces.

"Good, Grandmamma, I learned to butterfly in the swimming pool," Cherry said.

"I learned how to ride horses on a pretty saddle," said Daphne.

Protruding his lips, Douglas asked, "What's so pretty about them? They're just saddles."

Charlotte crossed her chubby arms and began to lecture. "Mother, for goodness sakes! You never listen to your messages. I called this morning to warn you of the weather. The news reporter said that the tail end of a hurricane was coming your way, and that Kat was coming over here to talk to you. I told her all about your behavior lately."

Annah held her breath for a moment. Charlotte's behavior was always disrespectful. She led them into the parlor. "Charlotte, you needn't worry about me. I have my help to keep me informed of the weather and such, so you don't have to come over every day to check on me. Kat came by this morning and we talked."

As the children headed out to play, Annah said, "Come, let's have a chat."

"A chat would be good, Mother, because I have something to ask you anyway." Charlotte paused. "Um," she said, as she cleared her throat and raised her fist over her mouth to force a cough.

Annah positioned herself in the chair intent on listening to her.

Charlotte surveyed the bookshelves, which covered one wall from the floor to the ceiling.

"Yes? You wanted to say something?"

"Well, Mother," she began. "Morgan and I have discussed how big this house is and that you now live in it all by yourself."

Annah gazed at her. She knew Charlotte and Morgan squabbled over who would inherit the house. "Yes?"

She squirmed. "But we haven't talked to Emily yet."

"Is this what you came over to tell me that I'm all by myself in this big house?"

"Ah, Bradford and I would like…." Her lips quivered as she lifted her right hand to the top of her eyelid to stop a nervous twitch.

"Yes, Charlotte, go on." Annah maintained a questionable expression.

"Mother, you know we wouldn't do anything that wasn't in your best interest."

Annah held her pose. "Go on."

She stammered. "We think that maybe one of us, one family, should move into this house and help you out. I mean, now that you're getting older and Father's gone, you will need more help here, and we thought we'd let you choose which of us you'd like to move in here with you." Breathless, she continued. "Emily's in college and Morgan and Patricia need more room with another baby on the way."

Annah studied the rug pattern. After a long silence, she tossed her head back. "I'm fifty-five, able-bodied, still attractive, and healthy, and all of you think I need help."

Her grandchildren's voices grew loud as they reentered the house and a fight ensued. The twins, at ten years old, never ceased to create havoc.

"Mother! We know how old you are and you're still healthy, but the house wouldn't be so empty for you if one of our families lived here with you."

Annah thought about her grandchildren running up and down the stairs, in and out of the parlor, and throughout the other rooms in the house fighting and leaving toys all over. She knew she would be under duress when it came time for birthday parties in her elegant dining room, and she envisioned the problems her adult children would be, disrupting her life.

Charlotte continued. "Bradford and I love this old house. I mean we would really adore living here, and the children would be able to spend hours on the beach in the summer. Also, Bradford, if you let us live here, would be able to help you fix things."

Annah's eyes widened. "Dear, I have five people here to help me around the clock. You know that. Jerome and his cousin, Custer, take care of maintenance, and I can call my property manager to fix larger problems, which they cannot do. I don't need Bradford to fix things."

Instantly, Charlotte rose and rushed out of the parlor to discipline the children.

Annah leaned comfortably back in her chair. After Charlotte returned, she said, "My dear, I have a lot of company with Delsey, Jerome, and Custer. Renaldo is a wonderful cook, who makes scrumptious meals for all of us, and Lucia is an excellent housekeeper. Don't worry about me. I'm fine living with them here. I couldn't ask for more help."

Charlotte's face flushed as she attempted to speak, but stopped. Finally, she leaned over and gave Annah a swift hug. "Children," she yelled. "It's time to go home."

Annah looked out the parlor door toward Jackson's office. She thought about the papers on Jackson's desk. He had been an esteemed neurologist and his papers should be preserved and archived for future reference by researchers in his field. If only she had more interest in doing so. She had lied to that woman about shredding them, but now it was important to do so before Charlotte found them.

Yes, she was lonely without him, especially in the evenings. They had been married for thirty-five years and usually spent time together reading or talking in the parlor after dinner while the help cleaned the dishes. Now, she spent that time alone in her bed reading.

She considered Rosemary, a friend of hers in the Rosewillow Women's Club. She entered a rehab for an addiction to prescription drugs, which her husband didn't learn about until then. She wondered how she acquired refills. Was she having an affair with her doctor?

She thought about Helena, who shot her husband's lover when she found them in bed together. She doubted she would have shot Jackson's lover if she had found her in bed with him, but she certainly would have divorced him. Annah decided there were too many clandestine love affairs going on in Rosewillow. She knew she was raised to be better than that.

Charlotte returned to the parlor. "Mother, we're leaving. Take care of yourself and answer my phone messages."

Annah felt relieved she was leaving. "I will."

The children ran to Annah's side and pushed each other to be the first to hug her.

"Now, scoot," she said to them, as she glanced at Charlotte.

Charlotte's heavy frame slowed her as she tried to catch up with the children who raced out the front door. "Mother," she yelled as they descended the wide outside steps. "I'll be calling you again. Please answer your phone."

Annah waved as she stood by the front door. "I said I will do so," she called. As she watched them speed away in Charlotte's SUV, she whispered, "Where can I go to find peace?"

Delsey came behind her. "Annah, if you'd like, I could have a word with Charlotte. She's too controlling and rude to you."

Annah turned. "Delsey, she has always tried to control me, but I'm not going to let her. Thank you for offering to help, but I'll have to handle this myself."

"Give me a switch and I'll take her out to the tool shed," Custer said, laughing. He and Jerome, Delsey's husband, had just entered through the back door.

Delsey put her fists on her hips. "Hush."

"Just thought I'd help. That girl is spoiled and nothin's goin' to change her. I've seen how she treats her sister and brother. You'd think she was their boss or somethin'."

"Custer, Charlotte has her own problems trying to take care of three unruly children and a husband who won't lift a hand to help her," Annah said.

"She treats him the same way she treats her kids, pushin' him around and tellin' him what to do; and, Miss Annah, if you'd let her, she'd take over this house and you, too," he added.

"Now you mind your own business," Delsey said. "Annah, like I said, if you need help keeping Charlotte away for a while, I'll be here to do it."

Annah looked from Delsey to Custer and saw the smile on Jerome's face. She could always count on them to help her in any situation. They had raised her and helped with raising her three children. They were in their seventies.

"Now, Annah, you go and get some rest, and forget about Charlotte's bad manners. Call me when you need me," Delsey said, as she followed the men out.

"That, I will certainly do," she said. She took in a deep breath, glad that Charlotte did not inquire about that woman's request for her letters.

CHAPTER FOUR

At a secluded table in the Rosewillow Tea Room several days later, Annah and Kat enjoyed a quiet lunch together.

"Hon, how are you doing? Mercy sakes, I wouldn't even know how to handle what you've had to do with Jackson's death and all. You've gone through tough times. Lord knows you've been bombarded with one thing after another."

Annah poked at her salad with her fork and twirled a tomato around the edge of the plate. She put her fork down, wiped the corners of her mouth with a pink napkin, and sighed. "I just don't know. I feel like the whole world has swept out from under me. That's why I called you to have lunch. You're my dearest friend, and you always give me a lift."

"Gracious." Kat said, as she reached over and took Annah's hand in both of hers. "You know what I've always said; you can count on me to be here for you." Suddenly, she gave Annah a look of surprise. "Hon, I have something to tell you, but you have to keep this a secret for now. Hear?" She removed her grasp, reached into a large brocade purse by her feet, lifted several colorful brochures in her hands, and fidgeted with them.

Annah sat up with rapt attention. She knew Kat seldom revealed secrets, even to her best friend. "What are those?"

"Look at the pictures on these brochures." She held three in front of her and fanned them toward Annah's face. "Aren't these the prettiest you ever did see?"

Annah squinted, endeavoring to look at one, but Kat wouldn't stop moving them. Finally, she reached across the table and plucked one out of the bunch. The cover displayed pictures of palm trees, a sandy beach, and stucco ranch houses covered with red terra cotta roofs. Yachts docked at piers dotted the waterfront, and farther out, small sailboats skimmed the horizon.

"Are you going on a holiday?"

"Spencer and I have planned our retirement. We're moving to Ionia, Florida in a month. It's on the Gulf of Mexico, south of Tampa. You know me. I've always loved Florida anyhow."

Annah could see her scanning her face for a response as she waited for more information.

"Hon, Ionia is a new retirement community, just so perfect for people like Spencer and me. We've signed a contract on a custom Spanish model house, which is almost completed there." She paused and held a brochure over her nose. Her eyes peered over the top of it, above a picture of a pelican.

Annah suddenly felt weak. She glanced at Kat and then to the brochure in her hand.

"We've put our house up for sale. You know, I've never liked living all squeezed together like toads on a lily pad in our little old house. We bought it so many years ago, but it was never for me, no ma'am." She beamed at Annah. "Gracious sakes alive, I don't know how you can live in that humongous house you've got. It's so big."

She's right, Annah thought. *It certainly is big, and it's empty without Jackson.*

"Sugar plum, at least you and Jackson were able to renovate your house to keep with the times. I mean imagine not having all the modern conveniences like you have. Why, he even converted that old coach house into a garage for his Corvette, his Mercedes SUV, and your gorgeous car. Mercy me."

"Yes, he saw to everything."

"And what would your servants do without a remodeling of their little old shacks? Goodness, I mean their quarters in the back of your house."

"Cottages, Kat, not quarters. They are now pleasant houses for our help, and they have all the amenities of private homes. Besides, I don't like to call my domestic help servants." She continued. "Years ago, Jackson had the shacks, as you call them, torn down. There were ten all together, but we rebuilt four of them into wonderful living places. We use one for guests."

"Didn't Spencer tell me he recently updated your home? Last summer, he took out all those ceiling fans and installed a state-of-art air-conditioning system."

"Yes, because he couldn't stop the heat from boiling his body into a shriveled prune."

Annah closed her eyes. She could not imagine Spencer turning purple. Still holding the brochure, she said, "I'm happy for you. Ionia must be a dream to you."

"It is. You know, I couldn't tell you about this until we decided on everything. Spencer would have shot me dead. I mean, he would have had my hide!" To emphasize the threat, she slapped her rear side.

Annah opened the tri-fold in her hand and saw more pictures. One showed white-haired retirees golfing. Another displayed them waving from their boats, and another viewed couples dining in a fine restaurant overlooking the harbor. They posed with healthy suntans and broad smiles on their faces. She lifted her face to see the joy on Kat's face.

"So, you're really moving? You're serious about this?"

"Yes, ma'am! Isn't it wonderful?" She held two brochures close to her chest and with both hands patted them with her fingers. "But, hon, now I feel so bad. I mean, I hope I haven't hurt you by telling you this. Gracious sakes, who would have known Jackson was going to depart the earth like he did?" She paused. "You know, you will always be welcome down there with us, don't you?'

Annah cleared her throat. "How will you leave your family and friends in Rosewillow? You've lived here half your life."

Kat mischievously shrugged her shoulders. "Now, did you hear what I said? Huh? *You* of all people will always be welcome at our house, and our family and other friends are welcome to visit anytime, too. We'll have plenty of room. You, especially, can come down whenever you want to get away. Why, we could lie on the beach, go swimming, and go yachting. You know, all the fun things retirees do."

"But what about your commitments to the Rosewillow Women's Club and to all your volunteer work?" Annah put the brochure on the table and laid her hand over it. "Kat, what is your family going to think? What about your grandchildren? Have you told them yet?"

"That's why I want you to keep this little secret for a while longer. After today, I'm going to round up my kids and grandbabies and tell them about this over a good supper, and when Spencer and I are ready to move, we'll have the *Times* print a notice. Of course, I'll let everyone else know about our move before the notice appears." She squeezed her hand. "My babies will be fine. They'll come visit me during holidays and summer vacations. Don't you worry now, Annie-girl, I will expect you to be the first to visit."

Troubled, Annah couldn't think of anything more to say. She rubbed her neck and looked away, struggling to hold back tears. She couldn't bear the loss of another significant person in her life. She straightened her shoulders and regained control of herself. She studied the numerous brochures Kat laid on the table and asked, "May I take these home and read them?"

"Oh, please do." Kat reached into her purse again and piled more brochures on the table. "Here's a real estate magazine and tourist information from the Chamber of Commerce."

Annah couldn't bear the happiness in her voice, the idea that their friendship would end hurt too much, so she didn't question her anymore. She gazed at her with intensity. Kat was so different from her, even in her looks. Kat's reddish blonde hair swung long and casual. Her eyes were an alluring green. In the summer, her skin would turn a golden tan from the sun. She was outgoing. Kat liked crowds and mingling with the common folks, and yet she was influential in the elite circles of the Rosewillow society because of her husband's status.

They finished the last of their lunch as Annah poked her fork into her banana cream pie and mashed the crust with it, and as Kat stirred two sugar lumps around in her teacup. Their conversation ended with neither knowing what more to say about Kat's future.

Instantly, Kat looked up. "Sugar, I'm so excited about our move and new house, I forgot to ask you what you wanted to tell me during our lunch."

Annah listened to her as she gathered the brochures in her hands and straightened them in front of her. She gave Kat a warm smile. "Dear, it's not that important anymore. I want you to know I'm happy for you and Spencer, and I hope you have a wonderful life in Florida."

"Well then, hon, I want you to know that whatever it is, you'll be in my prayers."

Annah pushed her chair back, reached for her purse, and stood. "Thank you. You needn't worry about me. I'll be fine."

Kat eyed a slice of lemon in her water glass, picked it out with two fingers, and then squeezed the juice into her drink. "Goodness, look at the time! We must be going."

The lunch over and paid for, Annah gripped the brochures and advertising material tightly in her hand and followed Kat out the door.

"Now, hon, keep my little secret." Kat said, as she pulled the straps of her big purse over her shoulder.

"Of course I will. You know me."

With quick hugs, they headed for their cars.

Annah's hands trembled as she pressed the button on her remote key to unlock the door. She dumped her purse and brochures on the seat beside her and gripped the steering wheel. "Be calm," she said to herself as she started the engine. She backed her car out of her parking spot and drove it onto the cobblestone street. She looked into her rearview mirror and saw Kat waving at her. She was going to miss their lunches together. She wondered if she would ever have a chance to visit her in Florida. She thought widowed women our age lose their married friends because wives think that they're out to get their husbands. Then she chastised herself. "Come on Annah, you're in a self-pity party again."

She had planned to tell Kat about Jackson's mistress, but the occasion never occurred. Anyway, to tell her such a thing in a public restaurant wouldn't have been a good idea anyway. *Well, that's for the best. Why spoil Kat's announcement and her idea of Jackson as a faithful husband and father?*

She drove on for several miles, holding back a rush of tears. *Tough times? Yes, I've been through tough times.* She continued toward the winding road that led to her grand home along the Atlantic shore.

Annah wondered if *she* would be able to move away from Rosewillow and the home she had lived in all her life. She gripped the steering wheel and thought about the steamy South Carolina summers, the brilliant blue skies she so often bragged about, the warm hospitality of southern people and acquaintances she so long enjoyed. All this would make leaving difficult.

She guided her car along her driveway. This view of the live oak trees draped with hanging moss always gave her the feeling she was entering a lofty garden. She steered her car toward the carriage house and pressed the button on her remote to open the door. Once parked, she walked the stone path toward the house and entered through a side door off the kitchen. Inside, she dropped her purse and brochures on the table and spread them out. Renaldo had not started dinner yet and no one was around. Curious about Kat and Spencer's desire to move to Florida, she couldn't wait to read the information. Annah chose one colorful brochure, sat down on a tall stool, put on her reading glasses, and began to read.

Welcome to Ionia, Florida

> *We invite you to visit Ionia, a charming new community for seniors, nestled in a quiet cove off the Gulf of Mexico with waterfront views, sandy beaches, and a lush tropical landscape. Leisure activities in the surrounding area include sunset sailing excursions, a golf course, nearby shopping, and fine restaurants. For greater cultural satisfaction, Ionia is an easy drive to the Tampa-St. Petersburg Airport for convenient travel to other destinations. Join people your age in this community, designed for comfort in your choice of condominiums,*

> *townhouses, and custom homes at affordable prices. Make your reservations today for a free tour and dinner: Call 1-800-555-1113.*

Annah laid the brochure down. *Should I?* She seriously considered dialing that number. Overcome with giddiness, she began to laugh. She lifted the edge of her hand and pressed it against her lips. *I could, you know. I could drive there by myself.* She dropped her hand. *Why not? I need a vacation anyway.* She looked around to see if anyone had seen her with the brochures, but no one appeared. As she studied the colorful cover in front of her, she found herself drawn to the happy faces of couples pictured on them, and remembered Kat's joy. With a loud voice, she said, "Yes, I could."

She also knew that for such a decision, it was time to visit Grandma Wilmont.

CHAPTER FIVE

Grandma Wilmont's house stood with elegance upon Magnolia Lane, near the Rosewillow town square. Built in the early 1900s, it brought charm to the community well into the twenty-first century. True to its nature, magnolia blossoms brightened the landscape, along with cascades of azaleas and variegated flowers tenderly grown and cared for over many years. As Grandma Wilmont grew older, she hired a gardener to tend to them.

Annah parked next to the wrought iron gate, where a winding stone sidewalk led toward the house. She looked forward to spending time with her cherished grandmother, a woman of faith. She always looked to the moments as a special treat. On the way, she had stopped at the bakery to purchase Grandma's favorite lemon cakes.

Maybelle, Grandma Wilmont's dedicated live-in nurse, peeked through the lacy chiffon curtains on the door. Her grandmother, at ninety years old, was afflicted with rheumatoid arthritis, and she required round-the-clock care. Maybelle, at seventy-two years old, had worked hard most of her life and her aged body had taken its toll on her. She hobbled over to the door and opened it as Annah approached. Annah noticed her gray hair pulled back in a bun and her patterned apron tied over her housedress. She had lived with Grandma Wilmont for almost twenty years and the Gulliver family considered her a family member because of her loyalty.

"My dear," Maybelle said. "Your grandmamma has been looking forward to seeing you ever since you called."

Annah handed her the pastry. "I've been eager to see her, too."

Maybelle led Annah into the parlor where Grandma Wilmont

sat in a wheelchair, her hands folded in her lap. A crocheted handkerchief laid neatly over one leg and her well-read, Bible over the other. A smile crossed her aged face, and she lifted her arm revealing a shaky arthritic hand ready to grasp Annah's hand.

"Grandma, how I've missed you," Annah said as she leaned over, wrapped her arms around her frail shoulders, and clung to her.

"I have missed you too, Annie. Come sit down by Grandma and keep me company." She pointed to the sofa next to her. Across the back laid a white crocheted afghan.

Annah sat close beside her and turned the wheelchair toward her. "How have you been?"

"I'm doing well as can be. Got me the good Lord to care for what ails me and my Maybelle to keep me company." She reached out her hand to touch Annah's cheek. "But you look like you've got something on your mind, baby girl. Tell me what's wrong."

Maybelle entered the room carrying a silver tray with a dish of the cut-up pastry, napkins, three china teacups, and a pot of hot tea. She set the tray down and prepared to serve them.

"Nothing's wrong. I mean a few things are. I...." Annah's eyes watered, and her throat closed, and she put her head on her grandmother's lap, who placed her hands over Annah's head.

Maybelle sat across from them, rubbing her arms, watching, and waiting to serve the much desired refreshments.

Annah always came to her grandmother's home for comfort and counsel. She lifted her head as her grandmother handed her the handkerchief to wipe the tears from her eyes. "I'm sorry. Everything seems to be coming down on me since Jackson died."

Grandma Wilmont waited with her hands clasped together.

"I feel so distressed at times. The telephone never stops ringing, which I can't bring myself to answer. I know there are requests for speaking engagements from the members of the Women's Club and from Henry St. James on the museum committee." She put her hands on her lap. "I feel totally alone now that Jackson is gone. I have my help, but they can't take his place. Plus, I have a reporter knocking on my door to interview me; and, would you believe, my children want to move in with me and take care of me."

She reached for Grandma Wilmont's hand. "Grandma, worst of all, I found out that Jackson had a mistress. So, with all this, I just have to get away from Rosewillow for a while."

Grandma Wilmont's eyes watered. She lifted her bifocals, wiped a tear away, and listened.

Maybelle set a cup of hot tea with a sugar bowl and a bowl of cream on the coffee table in front of Annah and offered her a spoon. Annah took the spoon and fixed her tea while Maybelle carefully attended to Grandma Wilmont by serving her tea already prepared.

Grandma Wilmont sipped her tea. She bent her frail head, letting her silver hair fall slightly forward on her face. Then, she put down her teacup and said, "Shush, Annie, let me pray with you, and we will read what our dear Lord has to say to you."

The three bowed their heads and Grandma Wilmont led them in prayer. Annah listened quietly and Maybelle rocked her head up and down in agreement.

Finally, she opened her Bible to Jeremiah 29:11-12 and commenced to read. "*For I know the plans I have for you, declares the Lord, plans to prosper you and not to harm you, plans to give you a hope and a future.*" She finished reading the entire verse and closed the book, smiling and peering above her wire-rimmed glasses at Annah. "Annie, take a trip. It will do you good and leave your worries at home while you're there. Wherever you go, enjoy yourself."

Annah looked into her grandmother's faded gray eyes and saw love. She whispered, "Thank you," she said. "I think I know where to go. Kat and her husband are moving to Ionia, Florida and have invited me to stay with them once their house is built. In the meantime, I think I'll ask her to drive down there with me and show me the area. We could have a short vacation. It should be fun."

"Yes, Annie, and while you're there, let the Lord give you clear eyes to see your future and give you hope."

She rose to hug her delicate shoulders again and sat down.

For another hour, they shared stories, listened, cried, and laughed together.

"Grandma, I remember all the times you let me stay overnight on weekends, and we'd sneak over to the islands and visit Delsey's Geechee family. I had so much fun as a child being with you."

Her grandmother gave her a whimsical look. "Yes, Annie, you were my co-conspirator."

During those times, Delsey's family sang old spirituals while clapping and shouting in rhythmic translation like drums beating, and they would invite them to eat the catch of the day.

One day, an old man handed Annah a strange piece of wood. It was a piece of driftwood shaped like a cross. "Yo hol' dis' now, chil', it sca' da' debble 'way," he said, for which Annah became so frightened she ran as fast as she could to find her grandmother.

Annah's two girlfriends, Sallie Mae and Crystaline played with her when her grandmother spent time with Auntie Josie. Auntie Josie, being only twenty-five years old, knew more about cooking than she did, so Grandma would watch and learn from her because someday, Grandma would say, she might have to cook her own food, too. Sallie May and Crystaline always had fun things to do, like fishing for crawdads along the muddy flats.

Annah could still taste the foods she grew to love there, shrimp salad, crab, fried rice, turkey wings, collard greens, and pecan cookies, all the foods her mother would have been appalled to know she ate. Respectful young ladies of her caliber never ate "down home cooking" like that. Annah once asked Delsey if she would make Gullah foods her Geechee family made, but she would always say, "Annah, no one would like them. I let our cook prepare the foods here," with which Annah would reply, "Please?" Delsey knew of her secret retreats with her grandmother because she would come back from one of her stays telling her stories of all the things they did.

Once, she peeked into a sacred Praise House to listen to the elders speak in a language she didn't know and heard the members shouting. When she asked her grandmother what they were saying, she would tell her they were praying. "That's not the way you pray, Grandma, their hands are raised to the sky," and her grandmother would say, "God hears our prayers with hands folded or with hands raised to the heavens."

Annah also remembered a very special time when she was twelve. She asked a lady, named Clara, to teach her how to weave a sweetgrass basket. As the women gathered around her and her teacher, they all exploded with shouts of laughter at her attempts to make one. She couldn't help herself, she laughed with them when her hands fumbled from one straw to another.

Most of all, their storytelling fascinated her, especially the many stories of Bruh Rabbit, tales of a conniving rabbit. When it was time to return home, she would always ask, "Grandma, please take me back soon because I had so much fun." Then, when they prepared to leave, the people would follow them to their boat, singing and clapping, and waving them off with shouts.

Finally, when they pulled their boat to shore on the mainland, her grandmother would always whisper, as if someone would hear her say it, "My little Annie, don't tell your mother where we were today. Okay?" For which she would answer, "Cross my heart and hope to die if I do." *Today*, she thought, *there would be no secrets because the times are different. I can speak of my friendship with these people with boldness and love.*

Annah sipped the last of her tea. "Yes, Grandma, I was your co-conspirator. The island people were the most interesting people I have ever known," she said.

Grandma Wilmont nodded in agreement.

"And how is Uncle Rufus?" Annah asked.

Uncle Rufus Milford Gladstone, Grandma Wilmont's twin brother, told hilarious stories. He enjoyed letting everyone know about his travels around the world. In his ancestor's, Captain Gladstone's, footsteps, he spent his adult life sailing and working on ships, hoping one day to become a captain, which never happened. After he retired from seafaring, he married Beatrice and found a little bungalow along the seashore where they remained until they both entered a nursing home.

"He's just fine. He and Beatrice share a room together, but she doesn't remember him. His heart is broken, since he still loves her so."

"I know, and I'm sorry. I should visit them both some time."

"Yes, Annie. You should some time."

Annah put her teacup down, gazed warmly at her grandmother, and rose. After they said their farewells, she opened the outer door and turned to wave a final good-bye, just as she saw her grandmother yawn, slump into her wheelchair, and fall instantly to sleep. She watched Maybelle cover her shoulders with a knitted shawl and wheel her toward her bedroom. As she closed the front door, she knew it had been a special time for them all.

CHAPTER SIX

The sound of a slammed door Wednesday morning caused Annah, still in her robe and slippers, to peer over the upstairs railing to see who had come into the house.

"Hi, Mom! Michael's here." Emily called, seeing her. Michael dropped his backpack and suitcase. "He caught the bus late last night at college and called me early to pick him up downtown. He finished his finals and didn't want to stay on campus."

Annah saw a tall, skinny man. Michael's black hair hung over his forehead and eyes as he looked at her through round, steel-rimmed glasses.

"Mom," Emily said, as she grabbed his arm. "This is my Michael." She giggled and held him close to her.

With a questioning look, Annah eyed the young man, and then descended the winding stairway to greet him in the entryway.

"Mom," Emily said. "Michael and I are serious about each other."

The three of them faced one another for a long period without talking.

Emily cleared her throat. "Mom, I should have told you about Michael, but when I came home from college last week after my finals were over, you looked so distraught that I decided to wait to tell you about him." She paused. "We're living together."

"Mrs. Gulliver, it's nice to meet you," Michael said, as he held his hand out to shake hers.

Emily drew her fingers through the top of her hair.

Annah didn't know what to say. Her impression of Michael was that he was not what she had wanted for her daughter.

"Mom, do you mind if Michael and I stay with you for the summer to help you? We can both sleep in my room and out of your way."

She lifted her eyebrows in a questioning response. "Do what, dear?"

"You know, we could help you clean out Papa's closet, or his office, or take his Corvette and Mercedes for drives to keep them running."

Annah didn't reply. They didn't answer her question.

"Michael, Mom's been through a lot with Papa's death," Emily said, as she took his arm again. "She'll be okay with you here. You wait and see."

Annah saw him smile. "I'm sorry Michael. Please forgive my bad manners. I'm glad to meet you." She reached over and patted Emily on the arm. "Come, let's talk a minute. I want to hear about school. We haven't had much time this week to talk and I haven't seen you since November."

Emily glanced at Michael and nodded as Annah led them to the parlor.

Michael and Emily sat in a loveseat across from her. A large black marble table stretched lengthwise between them.

In the midst of their silence, Michael put his arm over Emily's shoulder.

Annah started. "Emily, I'm glad you came home right after your finals; and, Michael, tell me about yourself. I assume you two met at college. What's your major?"

Michael removed his arm from Emily's shoulders, leaned forward, and clasped his hands together. "No, ma'am, we met at a bar. Emily caught my eye from across the pool table, and we drank a couple of beers together, decided we were madly in love, and, well, you know the rest of the story."

Emily elbowed him.

"My major is being a career student."

Annah frowned at Emily.

"Oh, Mom, Michael's teasing you." She elbowed him again. "That means he loves school. Michael is going on for a doctorate, just like Papa, but he has to work while going through college, and it might be years before he ever earns that degree. He wants to teach at a large university."

"Yes, ma'am, but a career student is probably what I'll end up being," he said, laughing.

Annah continued to stare at Emily and then back to Michael. "Well, Emily is attending college to be a photo journalist." She thought about the implications of what she said. "She will be struggling for some time to be on her feet and support herself after four years of college tuition and fees."

As the air grew tense, Emily added, "Mom, you know I won't be struggling to pay my tuition and fees." She turned to Michael. "I think Mom believes everything you say."

Annah leaned forward to match Michael's posture. She decided to be as bold as they were. "Michael and Emily, dear hearts, I don't appreciate you thinking you can sleep together here. I understand by what you've told me that you're living together. I know times have changed and couples live together before marriage, but it is not acceptable to me." She glanced from one to the other. "But, you *do* plan on being married soon?"

She waited for a response and saw Michael avert her eyes. She continued. "Michael, you may sleep in our guest cottage. I'll have Jerome and Delsey prepare it for you." She paused seeing their expressions. "I'm sorry, but this is the only suggestion I have for you." She stood and left the parlor, leaving the two young people frozen in their seats.

As she started up the stairway toward her bedroom to shower and dress, she heard muffled laughter. She stopped in mid step, but decided to ignore them. They heard her request and now it was up to them to follow it.

After their discussion about Michael staying in her room, Emily felt troubled. At twenty-two, she thought she should be able to live with a man. She could hardly ask him to sleep in a servant's cottage.

"Michael, I'm so sorry," she said, as she snuggled her head into his neck.

He held his head close to hers. "That's okay. We'll work things out." He reached his arm around her and wiped a tear from her eye with his finger. "Come on. It'll be okay."

"I don't want you to stay in a cottage. You're not a servant."

"Hey, baby, I wouldn't mind staying in one. Didn't she say it was a guest cottage? We'd be close and could still spend time together. It'll be okay."

"Maybe we'd better go back to my apartment. We've hurt my mother's feelings."

"My folks think the same way," Michael said. "They don't believe we should live together without being married." He tickled her sides and sent her laughing off the loveseat. "Don't you think they did it before they were married?"

"Of course not!"

"Bull. You don't know what they did before they married. You think they were angels."

Emily pushed him to stop. "Let's go look at the cottage and make sure one is fit for you to stay in," she said. "I don't want bugs or mice crawling out while you sleep."

"Emily," Delsey said, hearing her remark. "Now, you know better than that. We keep all the cottages clean and the guest cottage is always ready."

Emily felt Delsey's rebuke. "Let's go see it anyway."

—

To keep her mind off Emily and Michael, Annah spent time dumping Jackson's clothes out of his dresser drawers and closet and sorting them to give them away. She had been unable to bear the task of ridding the bedroom of his effects. It was too soon. Keeping his suits and shirts hanging beside her clothes meant he was still with her, but she knew she would have to face this reality eventually.

"Jackson, Jackson, what a clotheshorse you were," she said. She filled three large boxes and five good-sized plastic bags that she had stored in the closet for a time like this, and kept the suits on their hangers.

"Michael," she yelled over the banister from the upper floor when she heard them return to the house. "Would you be so kind as to help me carry a few boxes, bags, and loose clothing and set them near the foyer door? I'll call the Friendship Society to pick them up."

"Yes, ma'am." Michael peered up from the bottom of the stairway.

"Mom, you mean you're just now throwing away all Papa's clothes?" she asked, seeing the number of boxes and bags.

Michael carried several items down the stairway as Emily helped him. They stacked all the items against the wall by the front door.

"Thank you," Annah said, as she twirled around and reentered the bedroom. The closet, empty of Jackson's belongings, pronounced what was in her heart…empty of Jackson's nearness. She sat down on the edge of the bed. *God, how I want to get away from here.*

She reached for the phonebook and called the Friendship Society. They agreed to pick up her donations the following day. Then, she lay down on the bed, overwhelmed by loneliness.

—

"Mom? Papa's friend is here," Emily called up the stairs as she spied Delsey opening the front door to greet him. Delsey let him in and left.

Annah could hear Randall's voice from the doorway and stepped downstairs to meet him. He held a bouquet of flowers and a box of candy. "Randall. How nice to see you. What brings you here?"

"Didn't you hear my message?" he asked, straightening his back and adjusting his bow tie. He handed her the flowers and candy.

"Are you ready?"

"I'm sorry, Randall, there have been a lot of things on my mind lately, forgive me for not returning your call. She took the gifts and added, "Thank you. How lovely."

Her mind raced to think of how to respond to his question. "Where are we going?"

"Annah, my lady friend, you didn't return my call, so I assumed you were busy, but I knew, because we're old friends, it would be all right for me to come over here and you would be ready to go with me in a jiff."

Annah didn't know what to say.

"Oh, Mom, how sweet. Just like in the movies. Here, let me put the flowers in water for you," Emily said, as she reached for them and gave Annah a sly smile.

Randall looked at Michael and held his hand out to shake his. "How do you do? I'm Randall Spotswood, a friend of the family."

"How do you do, Sir. I'm Emily's roommate."

Randall turned to look at Annah with surprise.

"Randall, Emily has invited her friend here for us to get acquainted with him."

Annah watched Emily leave to look for a vase. Michael followed her.

"Ah, Randall, why don't we sit a moment in the parlor and talk?" Annah asked.

"Excellent! I would like that; but, Annah, are you ready to go? It's late, and we have quite a drive ahead of us."

Annah took his arm in her hand, led him toward a chair, and sat in the chair opposite him. "Refresh my memory, Randall. I'm having too many lapses lately with all that's been going on." She leaned forward. "Where are we going?"

Randall brushed lint off his left suit sleeve. "My dear, I would like to take you to a splendid, secluded restaurant, just the two of us. Surrounded by stately oaks, bathed in magnolias and lovely fauna, and set on a cliff overlooking the azure blue ocean, it is delightful. We will dine on the finest china and sip wine or drink cinnamon tea. We could watch the seagulls and pelicans dance in the air, have a quiet, romantic dinner, and spend the rest of the evening together."

Annah didn't move. The formality of his words stunned her. She studied his posture. It reminded her of an era long past when men knelt to ask the hand of his future bride. Her premonition confirmed, he had 'come calling'.

"I've looked so forward to being with you, Annah, my dearest." He reached for her hands and moved his head closer to hers.

Of all the things she needed right now, it wasn't another man in her life. Annah moved away, clasped her hands on her lap, and looked for help from Emily as she returned to the room.

"One moment, Randall. I have to take care of something," Annah said, as she stood and hurried away taking Emily down the hall with her.

"Emily, please help me. Randall has invited me to spend the day with him, driving north, and having dinner at a restaurant along the shore. I have no intention of encouraging a romantic relationship with him."

Emily giggled. "Oh, Mom. It would be good for you to have a boyfriend. You know someone to go out to dinner with and stuff." She shrugged. "Randall's okay. He may be an old dinosaur, but he's been around the family forever. We're okay with him hanging around you."

"A boyfriend? Emily, he's almost seventy and I'm fifty-five."

"What's that mean? Aren't you a senior citizen, too?"

Annah did not want a reminder of the gray hair appearing on her head. "Dear, would you tell him we have plans for this evening?"

"Mom! Now you want me to lie for you?"

"Emily." Annah put her hands on her hips. "I need you to help me cancel this engagement."

"You mean date, Mom. It's called a date."

Date? Would she want a date with a man she never liked in all the years she had known him? "Dear, I don't care for Randall. He's, well, he's not my type. Let's put it that way."

Emily put her arms around her mother. "Okay, whatever your type is. I'll tell him Michael and I have already made plans with you for dinner, but *you're* going to have to deal with him later. He has a crush on you, and I don't think he's going to take no for an answer."

Annah glowered at her. "We'll see about that."

They strolled into the parlor as Randall rose to meet them. "Randall, gosh, it's good to see you. I've been away at college since Papa died and haven't had a chance to come home since then," Emily said, as she gave Randall a radiant smile.

Randall stood and reached out to take Emily's hand. "Thank you, Emily. Good to see you looking so chipper."

Emily let his hand go. "Randall. Mom forgot you were coming today." She gave Annah a nod. "We made plans to spend the evening together. Michael and I would like to take her out for dinner and have a long talk."

Randall's shoulders slumped.

"Oh, you know. Like, we haven't talked for ages. Just ages, and we have so much to catch up on." She watched Randall move slowly away from them. "I hope you understand."

"Yes, my little bunny bear," he said, referring to the name he called her when she was little. "I understand." Randall left the parlor, walked past Annah without looking at her, and headed toward the front door.

"Randall, I'm so sorry this happened. I appreciate your invitation, flowers, and candy." Annah watched him reach for the doorknob. "Would you like a cup of tea before you go?"

"Annah, my dear, I'll give you a call at a later time. I really would like to visit with you and spend the day. We can do something at another time," he said, as he opened the door.

Emily and Annah watched him leave.

"I've hurt him deeply, haven't I?" Annah asked, seeing the door close. "What else could I have said or done? I'm not interested in him or a date with him."

"Mom, there's nothing you could have done. He's smitten with you."

Annah put her hands on her face. "That's all I need," Annah said. "He'll be back and I'll have to figure out how to say no without hurting him again. Emily, I've been out of the dating scene since I was twenty."

Michael moved toward them. "We guys don't stop at one rebuff. He'll be back. I saw the look in his eyes. You're going to have to come up with some fancy stories to stop him."

"Yeah, Mom, just wait and see. This is going to be fun."

"You two! This is not going to be fun at all. He's a whiskered old man with dirty thoughts."

Emily and Michael broke out in laughter. "You mean he's a dirty old man? Randall? Mom! Randall's a puppy dog."

Annah stormed away. Over her shoulder she yelled, "Emily and Michael, you behave yourselves tonight. I expect you to respect my rules. Michael is to spend the night in his cottage and, you, Emily will remain in your room."

They turned away and faced the door, cupping their hands over their mouths.

CHAPTER SEVEN

More and more Annah longed to go away. She remembered the brochures she had hidden in the top drawer of her dresser, and she was anxious to go over them again. She pulled them out, sat on her bed, read about Ionia, Florida, and then decided to call Kat.

"Kat, would you consider driving down to Ionia with me?"

"Hon, I sure would," Kat answered. "Why, I sure would! Wouldn't that be just the funnest thing to do? My goodness, I'm going to start packing right now."

Annah's heart raced with anticipation. It would be the 'funnest' thing to do.

"Sweetie, are you interested in seeing our new home?"

Annah thought about what excuse she would give her family for taking the trip. Maybe Kat would let her tell her secret to them. "Yes. I'd love to see your new home."

"Spencer would be so pleased to know that. He's been showing our pictures to the kids, and they can't wait to come visit us already. Can you believe it? I thought we'd get, my goodness gracious, a screamin' and a hollerin' and no end of their talk about it."

That's what I would expect from my children, "a screamin' and a hollerin'," she thought.

"We'll take my car, and we'll stay at a nice hotel. What day is good for you to go?"

"Why, hon, I could leave tomorrow. Spencer is doing most of the packing to move. He's just been precious through this whole thing. He really wants to move away from Rosewillow. My goodness, we've lived here for twenty-five years and nothing's changed, except the gossip that's gotten outlandish. I mean, did I tell you about Mae?"

"No, but I don't want to hear it now." She didn't want to hear any gossip about Mae. She was concerned that gossip was circulating Rosewillow about Jackson having an affair. Annah picked up a brochure and studied it. "Dear, how many miles is it from here to Ionia, and how much time will it take to drive there?"

"Let me ask Spencer. He knows all that stuff. I just watch the palm trees, just a' swayin' in the wind, and tell him to watch out for those rude upper east coast drivers. Yes, ma'am. That's what you're going to have to watch out for, too."

"Please ask him if he has a map of Florida, so we'll know what roads to take."

Kat howled. "Hon, Spencer and I have been driving down there for, oh my, at least five times and I've been observant to the tee. I know my landmarks. There's this big resort, my goodness sakes, it's…."

"Kat, you can point that out to me as we drive past it. Let's take, maybe, a four or five day vacation, and you can show me around Ionia. I'd love to see it. Is Friday too soon?"

"Sweetie girl, I'll be ready with bells on my feet."

"Kat, it's 'bells on my toes'."

"Heck, who cares--feet, toes, fingers? You know what I mean."

Kat always misused her clichés. Her humor would be one of the reasons why Annah would miss her when she moved. She put the receiver down and stared at the brochure. Oh, how she needed this time away. She had two days to pack.

—

Delsey knocked on the door. "Annah, Pastor Burnham is here."

Bewildered, Annah dropped the brochure on the bed. Why now? "Delsey, please take him into the parlor. I'll be right down." *That's all I need now, the pastor visiting me.* She left the room and went to meet him.

"Pastor Burnham, welcome to our home," she said, as she reached out her hand.

"Annah, it's nice to see you. I thought it would be okay to come over even though you didn't return my call."

Another missed call. "Pastor Burnham, please forgive me. I'm beside myself with so much going on. I haven't listened to my messages in a day or two."

"I understand," he said, warmly. "That's why I came to see how you're doing and to pray with you. Your grandmother told me you're a little upset right now."

There were many others upset with her recently, too. "My grandmother is always worried about me. Won't you have a seat and we'll talk."

The minister found a chair to sit in.

"Pastor Burnham, I'm doing fine. I have my immediate family and my help around me. I'm just fine." Annah noticed his sad look.

"I'm so sorry about the loss of your husband. I didn't have much time to talk to you at the memorial or the funeral with so many people taking up your time and knowing you were grieving. I liked Jackson very much."

If he only knew about him, she thought. "Thank you. Jackson had many friends."

"On a side note, Annah, if you'll let me be more personal, I haven't seen any of your family in church for quite a while. Your grandmother comes to church faithfully every Sunday. Maybelle brings her, and they sit close to the front so they can both hear well."

Annah sat down across from him. "Yes, I know," she said. "I've been so busy and involved in so much here I haven't had time to attend church." He folded his hands together. "I know, God is more important than a schedule, but I never seem to get my priorities in order."

"Annah, I would love to see you and your other family members attend next Sunday."

She knew her children and grandchildren would not attend church on any given Sunday. "Pastor Burnham, I can't. You see, I'm taking a trip to Florida for an extended weekend with Kat. You remember, Kat Holister? She and her husband, Spencer, have visited with us at church occasionally."

The minister lifted his glasses higher on the bridge of his nose and said, "No, I'm sorry, I don't remember, but where in Florida are you going?"

"We're taking a trip to Ionia on the Gulf south of Tampa. Kat and her husband enjoy visiting there. I asked her if she would drive down with me and show me around, and we could take a short four or five day vacation." She paused. "It'll be a chance to get away for a while. It'll be a quick trip, and I so desire rest."

He took her hands in his and held them. "Annah, that's good. You go away for a little time and enjoy yourself. I'm sure there are many things you still have to do here. When you return, I would like to see you again in church. Will this be something you could do?"

Annah hesitated. Attending church seemed undesirable to her. How could she tell him that she was angry with God? Why didn't God give her a hint of Jackson's unfaithfulness? God only left her with Jackson's trickery and no way to confront him now that he's dead. "I'll see," she said.

Delsey entered the room. "Annah, Mr. Henry St. James is on

the telephone for you. Should I tell him you'll call him back or would you like to take the call?"

Annah felt her face flush. "Thank you, Delsey, tell him I'll call him right back."

Delsey turned and left the two of them alone again.

"Annah let me pray with you, for strength to carry on, for safety on your trip, and for your walk with the Lord."

Good. Then maybe he would leave, and she wouldn't have to give him any more excuses. "That would be very nice."

The minister bent his head and prayed.

Annah could only count the seconds. "I'm sure my grandmother would be happy to see me sitting at her side again," she said, once he finished and let go of her hands. "Pastor Burnham, thank you so much for coming over. I'll tell my grandmother you came."

He rose, put his hand on her shoulder, and said, "Have a good trip."

"Delsey," Annah called, "please see Pastor Burnham to the door."

Delsey led him out and returned to the parlor. "Annah, you might just do what your pastor says. You've been so depressed that all of us think you need to get your spiritual strength back. You're acting like someone's been hitting you over the head with a hammer."

"Yes, Miss Annah," Jerome said, coming to Delsey's side. "That's not like you. We'd like you to be your old self again."

Annah stood. "And, just what is that old self you're both talking about?"

Custer interrupted. "That old self rushed around givin' us so many chores to do, we couldn't keep up. Now, you're either sittin' in the parlor, or on the veranda, or disappearin' into your bedroom to be by yourself. If you asked me, I'd say it's scary to see you this way."

Annah pursed her lips and gave them a glum look.

"We don't want you to think we're criticizing you, Annah. We care for you. Your husband is not coming back," Delsey said. "We're all praying you'll start living again."

She took in a deep breath. "That's why I'm going away."

"Just where are you going and how long will you be gone?" Delsey asked.

"Oh, Delsey, I'm sorry. You are the first person I tell when I'm planning to do something. Kat and I will be leaving Friday to go to Ionia, Florida, and we should be back Monday or Tuesday. I know all of you will be fine here."

Delsey clasped her hands over her waistline and grimaced, and Jerome walked away.

"Now what are you thinking?"

"That the two of you always get yourselves in trouble. Every time you plan something with Kat, you end up having to be rescued."

"Delsey, when have we needed to be rescued before?"

She dropped her arms. "Remember when you two decided to drive over to the islands and visit with my family? You ended up getting lost, and you drove your car into the marsh. You called Jerome and Custer to pull you out and, because it was almost evening by the time they found you, you had to turn around and go home without seeing anybody."

"Well, that was only one time."

"Then another time, you two decided to drive down to Savannah for the day and go shopping, but you both drank so much at lunch, you couldn't drive home; so once again Jerome and Custer had to go and help you drive your car home."

She studied Delsey's face. "Delsey, we were not drunk. We were having a good time and laughing so much over our lunch, that we may have had one drink too many. That's all."

"Uh huh."

"Okay," Annah said. "So we have good times together. We'll be careful driving to Florida. No one will have to rescue us from ourselves."

Delsey put her fists on her hips. "Annah, I'll know when you two are in trouble. If I have to, I'll have Jerome drive down to help you." Then she turned around to walk away.

Annah heaved a sigh, returned to her room, and packed the brochures into her suitcase.

CHAPTER EIGHT

Annah switched the receiver from one ear to the other as she dialed Henry's number. Talking to him always gave her apprehension. "Henry, you called?" she asked after hearing his voice.

"My dear Annah, how are you? I can't sleep at night thinking about you."

Annah suppressed a laugh. "Henry, I'm fine. How are you?"

"I'm missing my dear friend Annah. You are always on my mind. I called to tell you that I would love to take you to dinner. When would be a good time?" He continued. "Would tomorrow at seven be okay? There's a new restaurant downtown called Glover's Cove that I hear is wonderful."

Annah held the phone tightly to her ear. This wasn't a good time. "Henry, thank you for your invitation, but I can't tomorrow night. Kat and I are planning a trip to Florida and I haven't started packing yet. We'll be away for at least a week."

"My sweet, you never go away. I'll be worried about you. Kat is…I mean, Kat is a good friend of yours, but is she the right person for you to travel with?"

Annah stared at the ceiling. "Yes, Henry. She and I get along very well. I feel safe with her, and she knows the way." She could hear his heavy breathing on the other end. "She and Spencer have driven to a little town called Ionia several times together. She knows how to get there." Annah heard the sound of a huff on Henry's end. "Henry?"

"Yes. I was thinking. I could drive the two of you there."

She lingered a moment before speaking. "Henry, this is a girl's weekend…you know, to go shopping, get our hair done, nails done, things like that." He didn't answer. "You know, girl stuff, Henry.

Would you like me to hang around with you and your men friends?"

"Annah, my dearest, I would prefer to be the one to travel with you more than anyone else on earth."

She searched for the right words. "Henry, thank you for your help, but I don't want to inconvenience you."

"Hmm, I know you girls like to go gallivanting, so I won't intrude. Now listen to me, sweetheart, if you have any, and I mean any trouble, you call me immediately and I'll come down right away. This is an order."

She thought a moment about his words. Maybe it was because of his domineering nature that she often felt intimidated by him. "I'll keep this in mind. I'll talk with you next week."

"Good-bye my sweetheart. Have a pleasant trip."

"Good-bye Henry." She hung up the phone with a sigh of relief. Henry seldom took no for an answer.

To keep her mind off him, she decided to start packing. She knew she would have to purchase a new swimsuit and cover. It had been a long time since she had sunbathed on the beach, and she hoped to spend time getting a tan.

About an hour later, there came a knock on the front door. Delsey opened the door to see Henry standing there. "Annah, your friend, Henry, is here to see you," she called. Annah peered down the stairway and saw Henry standing in the entryway.

"Why, hello ladies," he said.

Annah gasped and walked down to greet him. "Henry, what a surprise!"

He swooped her up into his arms, and then let her go.

"Henry, I thought we had just talked?" she asked, shaking.

"I wanted to see you, Annah, not just talk to you on the phone. You look worn out. Are you okay?"

"Yes, of course," she said, shutting the door behind him. Delsey nodded and left them alone.

"Henry," she said, "I probably look worn out from dealing with seven months of legalities and paperwork to complete caused by Jackson's death. It seems to never end."

He placed his hands on his sides. "Well, I came over because I had forgotten to remind you about the meeting tomorrow. I thought I would come and read the report you've prepared, so I could present it to the committee since you won't be there."

"Oh." Annah covered her mouth with the palm of her hand. "I haven't started it yet."

"No? Annah, you, and your report are the reasons for the meeting. Remember, you were to finalize fundraising ideas on the museum so we can begin the process. We've invited the county commissioners, city personnel, and about twenty-five people to hear your report."

"I'm so sorry. I've been distracted."

He examined her face. "I know, but you've had over a month to prepare your report. Didn't you put this date on your calendar?"

"Yes, of course I did." She hadn't looked at her calendar.

"Well, it's too late to do anything about it. We'll have to call the meeting off."

"I think so, Henry." Annah cringed, thinking she had to call over thirty people. That meant she would be on the phone all afternoon.

"Annah, I'm concerned about you. This is not like you at all. This report should have kept your mind off the loss of Jackson and onto more positive issues." He coughed. "Okay, I'll have to round up the girls in the office and have them make calls to cancel and reschedule the meeting," he said, as he chastised her.

"Thank you," she said with relief. Henry, being the director, had the authority to change the meeting to another time.

"You look like a ghost, and you've lost a lot of weight. Are you eating right?"

She was getting irritated at his overbearing behavior. "Yes, I'm eating right. I'm sorry for forgetting."

He started to reach for her, but she stepped sideways. "Sweetheart, I'll check on you later. Maybe we can find someone else to prepare the report. Take care of yourself." He moved to the door, turned the handle, and said good-bye.

"Thank you for canceling the meeting."

"I'll call you in a day or so to give you another date."

"No. I'll be gone. Remember? Kat and I won't be back for several days."

He stopped and gave her a critical look. "Yes, that's good then. You'll be rested up to continue your work with the committee when you come home."

As she closed the door, she saw him grin and heard him whistle as he walked away. She didn't want to think about the museum or the committee, and the fact that he intruded upon her disturbed her. The smell of his cologne lingered on her face and clothes; and she knew if she had given him the chance, he would have kissed her. The thought both excited and frightened her. She knew his affections for her were more than a crush. She had known him for years and always held him at arm's length when he approached her, even with Jackson next to her. Randall's affections were stiff and exaggerated. Henry's were intense and sexual.

Several minutes after she shut the door, one of the board members from the museum called. She looked at the I.D. and picked up the receiver. "Hi, Muriel."

"Annah. I want to tell you that Henry just called me on his cell phone and has given me the responsibility to write your report and present it to the committee and to the officials who are interested in seeing this project through."

Irritated at Henry giving Muriel the job, Annah said, "That's wonderful. I know you were as involved in researching this presentation as I was. Good luck."

"I was wondering if I could have your notes to help me."

Annah held the phone tightly to her ear. Muriel always demanded credit for work she never accomplished and always wanted to be the one in charge. "Muriel, I would give them to you, but I don't have the time to look over them. I'm going on a trip for a few days. I'm sorry. Can you wait?"

There was silence on the other end. "Muriel?"

"Well, I guess so. I'll have to come up with fundraising ideas all by my little old self then."

"Like I said, if you'll wait a week, I'll give you what I have."

Again, there was silence for a few seconds. "No thank you. Toodle-oo," she said.

"Goodbye," Annah said, as she pressed the button on her machine and erased the remaining messages. She didn't want to be bothered by anyone else's request. She knew she had lost her position on the museum committee, and it was her fault. *Well, Muriel competed with me for the job anyway, and I really don't care.*

Jimmy Nealy parked his Chevy behind another car and shut off the engine. He wished the person in the car would leave quickly. He checked his shirt pocket for a pen and opened his notebook in his lap, dating the top page. Emily had answered his call and said her mother would probably be home and, if he was nice, she might give him an interview. What he didn't know was Emily forgot to tell her he was coming.

Out of the corner of his eye, he saw the man who owned the vehicle, standing beside his door, holding his head sideways, and peering at him. He put his hands on the edge of the open window and faced him.

"And who are you?" the man asked.

Jimmy threw the note pad and pen on the seat beside him.

The man's eyes surveyed the inside of his car. "I asked you who you are. I don't recognize you."

"Um, I'm a reporter, and I'm here to interview Mrs. Gulliver."

The man leaned against the open door. "Mrs. Gulliver doesn't need to have reporters interviewing her. Please leave."

Jimmy cleared his throat. "Sir, I only have a few questions to ask her." He fidgeted with his key, undecided about what he would do next; but then, located the ignition switch, and started the engine.

The man moved away from the door as Jimmy began to move the car forward.

"Reporters!" the man said with disgust.

Jimmy desperately needed to interview Annah, so he slowly drove from her home and parked behind a large hedgerow to wait. His career depended on this assignment, and he was determined to get it. He watched the man's car pass him and disappear around the street corner.

Once again, Jimmy parked his car in front of Annah's front steps, picked up his note pad, pen, and camera, left the car, and walked up to the front door. Annah opened it just before he knocked, thinking Henry was returning. She was in the entryway and heard footsteps.

"Young man," she said, seeing it was Jimmy. "Didn't I tell you I don't give interviews?"

"Ah, yes," he stammered. "Mrs. Gulliver, I talked with your daughter, and she said it would be okay to come today."

"Well, she told you wrongly." She paused. "Did my daughter also ask you not to print what you saw and heard the other day?"

"Yes." He backed up to leave, but tripped, fell face forward, and bumped his nose on the porch floor. His nose dripped blood onto his shirt.

Horrified, Annah pulled a clean tissue from her pants pocket. "Here," she said, as she handed it to him.

Jimmy held onto his nose with one hand as he lifted himself up and took the tissue from her. "Thank you," he said, holding his head skyward.

"Well, I should be the one to thank you for not printing that horrible episode here."

Jimmy hadn't yet told his editor about what he witnessed. He was unsure how to handle the story. "Mrs. Gulliver, please," he said with a muffled voice beneath the tissue. "I'll only ask you a few questions."

Annah clasped her hands together. "I don't think you're in any condition to interview anyone," Annah said, staring at him.

Jimmy held the tissue tightly to his nose, searched the ground for his notepad and camera, and then walked back to his car. Sitting in the seat for a long while, dejected and tired, he knew he had blown the assignment again.

As he drove away from Annah's house, he held a blood-soaked tissue over the lower part of his face. A woman passed him and sped up. Through his rearview mirror, he could see the car screeching to a halt as it rounded the water fountain. He didn't know who she was, but he could bet Annah would answer all *her* questions.

—

Charlotte shut the engine off, slid out of her car, and rushed into Annah's house. "Mother," Charlotte called from the front door. "Are you all right?"

Annah saw the frightened look on her face. "Yes, I'm all right, Charlotte. Why do you think something's wrong?"

"Mother, I was afraid you were hurt. There was a crazy man driving away with blood all over his face. What happened to him?" She walked over to Annah and eyed her for blood stains.

Annah put her hand to her forehead. "Charlotte, the man is a reporter, and he's trying to interview me. He fell and suffered a bloody nose. I'm fine."

"Oh, I was afraid he had hurt you," she said, nervously grasping her pudgy hands. "Mother, I came back here to talk to you." She peered around the room. "Where are Emily and that boyfriend of hers? Are they here?"

"Yes, but I don't know where they are at the moment. They might be on the beach."

She ran her hands through her hair. "Mother. Everything's going wrong."

"What's going wrong?" Annah asked. "Charlotte, I don't have time for this. I have to get ready for a trip."

"A trip? Where are you going?"

Exasperated, Annah explained that she was taking a trip with Kat to Ionia, Florida. "We're taking a short vacation to get away."

"A short vacation? With Kat of all people? What are you getting away from?"

Annah was tired of explaining things, especially to Charlotte, who had to know everything she did. "Problems. I want to think things out."

Charlotte stood back and gaped at her. "Mother, you belong here with us where we can help you with any problems you have? You have too much to do here."

"I'll only be gone for a few days. Whatever I have to do here can wait until I get back."

"Mother, what do you know about Ionia, Florida? I've never heard of it."

Annah felt very tired with all the questions. "It's a new community for seniors on the Gulf. Kat and her husband enjoy visiting there. We're leaving Friday."

"Well, you should have consulted me. I'm always worried about you, and I would have told you, you shouldn't go."

"Stop right now. Stop trying to control me, Charlotte. Mind your own business. What I do should not affect you in any way. I need time away and whatever I have to do here can wait until I get home."

She dropped her arms. "What does Emily think of this?"

Annah turned away in disgust. She was bored with the whole conversation. "I haven't discussed it with her, but she knows I'm planning this trip."

Charlotte's face flushed with anger. She turned to walk out, but then changed her mind. "We'll talk later since you're too busy right now," she said and quickly left the house.

Annah watched her go. In exhaustion, she sat down on the bottom stairway step in the entryway, her elbows on her knees and her hands on her head. "I can't wait to leave."

—

Charlotte called her brother. "Maybe he can put some sense into her," she said.

"Hello. Morgan here," he answered.

"Morgan, Mother is going on a trip for a few days with Kat."

"I can't hear you. Speak louder. I'm on my sailboat and the winds are picking up."

Charlotte cupped her hand around the mouthpiece. "I said Mother is going on a trip with Kat. You know she can't do that. She has too many responsibilities here, and we need her. Please call her and tell her not to go. She'll listen to you more than me."

She couldn't hear his response through the background noise. "What did you say?"

"I said I can't call her. I'm going to be out here for another day. You tell her."

She heard static on the line. "What?"

"You tell her," he yelled. "What the hell is she going on a trip with Kat for anyway?"

"That's what I asked her. She said she had too many problems and needed to get away."

"Speak louder."

"Oh, Morgan, just forget it. I'll talk to you later." She hung up and stomped her foot. "I can't depend on Morgan or Emily." *I'll speak to Bradford. Someone has to stop her.*

CHAPTER NINE

In desperation to stop Annah from going to Florida, Charlotte told Renaldo to plan an early meal with the whole family the next day. Renaldo suggested that the meal would be nicer if everyone would bring a favorite family dish. She called Annah to announce her plans.

"Mother, I've arranged with Renaldo and the others to make dinner for you tomorrow evening. Patricia will make fried chicken, honey biscuits, and will bring her homemade peach preserves. I'm making potato salad and a marinated cucumber dish." She thought a moment and added, "Oh, and Morgan said he would bring the wine for us. Renaldo and Delsey will provide the sweet tea and dessert." Charlotte waited for Annah's acknowledgement.

Astounded, Annah couldn't respond.

"Mother, aren't you happy?"

Annah felt numb. Finally, she said, "Dear, I wish you had consulted with me first. Food is the last thing on my mind right now, and I might have had other plans for the evening."

"What could that possibly be? You haven't gone out very much, since you've been getting ready for your trip. I assumed you would be pleased that we all want to spend time with you and have a nice dinner together. We don't do this often enough."

Annah could only feel herself getting angry. Whenever her children and grandchildren get together, they always squabble. She craved peace and quiet, not an evening of disorder and noise. "Sometimes you assume too much, Charlotte. It will be nice to have dinner with all of you; but, remember, I'm leaving early Friday morning, and I don't want to be up too late."

"We'll only stay for dinner."

Annah hung up the phone in disgust.

—

Annah closed her bedroom door. She surveyed the portraits of her family hanging on the walls. The pictures bore witness of happier times. The one that held her attention most was with Jackson and her seated with their three children. It was taken at a time when they were younger and the children small. She entered the master bathroom to freshen her face with a damp washcloth. As she peered into the mirror, she whispered, "What did that other woman have that I don't have? That seductress!" Then, she threw the washcloth into the sink and exited the room.

At least tomorrow, she would have time to finish packing.

—

Charlotte recovered from her shock at having Annah hang up so abruptly, but it didn't stop her determination to hold the dinner party the next evening. She called Emily.

"Why are you rushing to have all of us together? Michael and I were looking forward to seeing a movie tomorrow night. Can't this dinner wait until Mom comes back from her trip?"

"No. We have something very important to discuss with her before she goes."

"What's so important that it can't wait until she comes home from her trip?"

"Emily, mother needs to be here with us and not running off on a silly trip with that Kat. We have to stop her from going." Her voice became hoarse. "So, what are you going to make? It better be good because we want this to be a special meal for Mother."

After some hesitation, Emily said, "Michael and I will go downtown and order a pizza."

"Pizza? Don't you have more respect for your family?"

"There you go again, never appreciating my contributions."

Charlotte growled. "You'd better not cause trouble. Mother needs our help. Thank the good heavenly Lord you're away at school most of the year,"

Emily snickered. "Thank the good heavenly Lord that I don't have to put up with you all year. Michael and I don't cook much. We eat out and pizza is just fine with us."

Charlotte shouted, "You're lazy, you know that?" and hung up.

—

Thursday evening, Annah entered the kitchen in time to see Renaldo slicing a praline pie and Lucia gathering dishes to carry to the dining room. Delsey came in to help them.

Renaldo glanced up at Annah. "Ma'am, we'll take care of the meal and call you to come to the dining room when we're finished."

"Thank you," she said with relief, but it was short-lived. Charlotte stomped into the kitchen behind her with the twins. She placed her two dishes in the center of the table.

"I'm gonna get you," Douglas squealed, as he reached to grab Daphne.

"Mommy, stop him," Daphne cried, as she ran around the long kitchen table and knocking into Delsey, who gently pulled Daphne from her.

Behind them came Morgan, Patricia, and Mandy. Patricia held her tray of fried chicken up and looked for space on the table to set them. Delsey moved Charlotte's dishes aside for her to put them down.

"Renaldo, where are your napkins," Morgan asked, as he yanked each drawer open and angrily closed them. "Charlotte told me to take them into the dining room."

"Delsey, would you help him?" Charlotte asked, taking Daphne by the hand.

Morgan groaned and indicated by his facial expressions he was above such work. Patricia went to his side to help.

Suddenly, Cherry, Charlotte's five-year old daughter, shrieked from the dining room as the sound of crashing plates stopped everyone from what they were doing. Charlotte ran to see shattered china spread all over the wooden floor. "Cherry? Why did you touch Grandma's fine china? Lucia is setting the table, not you."

Annah followed her, mentally counting the number of broken plates and cringed at the loss. "Charlotte, please watch your children."

She didn't answer Annah. Instead, she glared at Morgan. "Morgan, please help me clean up the broken dishes."

"You pick up the pieces yourself. Cherry is too little to handle china, and you should have known better."

"Morgan, I didn't know Cherry had her hands on the plates." She pouted at him and labored to bend down to pick up the fragments, while Jerome walked in with a trash can, broom, and dustpan to sweep up the smaller pieces.

"Cherry needs a good spanking. You spoil her," Morgan said.

In the midst of the confusion, Lucia brought in more plates to finish setting the table. Renaldo lit the candles while everyone found his or her seat, and Delsey and the men brought the food dishes in from the kitchen.

"Mother, it's time to eat," Charlotte called, standing again.

Annah brushed the hair away from her face and slowly walked around the table to sit at the far end. "Let's have no more arguing," she said.

"Where's Emily," Charlotte asked in a huff.

"I'm sure she'll be here in a few minutes with her friend," Annah responded.

"Yeah, I'll bet. I haven't met him yet, but he's probably a winner," Morgan said. "Emily really knows how to pick her boyfriends."

"He might be a very nice man," Patricia said, as Morgan gave her a spiteful look.

Michael came through the door holding a large pizza. "Where do you want this?"

"In the kitchen," Charlotte said with disgust. "Emily, you could have helped us. You should have cooked something instead of buying it."

"Oh, well," she answered. Michael found an empty area on the table to place the pizza, and Emily pointed to Michael to sit in the chair next to hers.

"Charlotte, where's Bradford this evening?" Annah asked. She shifted to make herself more comfortable on the silk, gold-corded chair.

"Mother, I forgot to tell you, he's running a bit late. He had something special to do." Charlotte's eyes sparkled, and she held her lips pursed together.

Annah picked up her white, linen napkin and smoothed it on her lap. She glanced around the table and felt pleased to see everyone dressed so nicely. She had put on her favorite gray slacks and lacy white blouse for the occasion.

Daphne punched Douglas in the arm, and in turn, she kicked him under the table.

"Twins! Stop this. Grandma does not want you fighting. She reached over and swatted their heads. "Stop punching each other," she yelled, as they glared at each other.

"Dears, let's be cordial. I am not in the mood for this fighting," Annah said, as she placed her hands beside her plate and waited for the children to settle down.

Charlotte and the three children sat to the right of Annah with an empty chair for Bradford. Emily and Michael sat to the left, with Patricia, Morgan and their daughter, Mandy next to them. Everyone noticed, but did not mention Jackson's empty seat at the end of the table.

"Shall we pray?" Annah began, after all the noise subsided.

"Yes, Mother, who shall say the prayer for Father?" Charlotte asked.

Suddenly, Bradford burst into the room carrying an enormous bouquet of red roses in a tall, green vase. "Here we go," he said. "Roses for a grand lady. We wanted to cheer y'all up."

"Sweetheart, how lovely," Charlotte said with unconvincing surprise. She beamed at Annah. Annah watched Bradford shove two dishes aside to place the vase in the center of the table. He rushed over to Annah, kissed her on the cheek, and returned to Charlotte's side to plop down in his chair.

Emily rolled her eyes and gave Morgan a weary look.

"Hey, Bud, just what we need, more flowers." Morgan grimaced.

"Charlotte, were you in on this little secret?" Patricia asked. "What a thoughtful idea."

"No. It was all Bradford's idea. Wasn't it, sweetie pie?" She patted his hand.

Bradford lifted her hand and kissed it.

"They smell," Douglas said, as he held his nose.

Daphne kicked him under the table again. "They do not, stupid."

Douglas smashed her foot with his, making her scream and causing Charlotte to swat both of the children again.

"Stop it," Charlotte said, as she swatted them again.

Bradford raised his voice. "Hey, Morgan, what y'all been up to lately besides sailin' that yacht of yours 'round Blister Island? Your face looks like y'all smashed it into the mast."

Morgan glared at him and played with his fork "I work, like you. My face is sun burnt."

Bradford folded his arms. "Oh, yeah, let's see. Y'all work on a sailboat and drink martinis all day."

Morgan held his breath. "One of these days you'll stop making a jackass of yourself and be a man. You're kissing the butt of that jerk you work for."

Bradford started to stand up, but Charlotte yelled, "Stop it you two!"

Emily shoved her shoulder against Michael. "See what I mean about my family?"

Annah closed her eyes momentarily. "Thank you for the flowers Bradford. They're very lovely. We were just about to pray before we started eating." Delsey, Renaldo, and Lucia, along with Jerome and Custer, entered the room to be a part of this time.

Jackson always felt it an obligation to pray at such dinners, so now it was her turn. "Let us pray before our food turns cold," Annah said. "God, we thank you for this family time and bringing us together. Bless this food and those who have helped to prepare it. Amen."

As the others left the room, Delsey asked, "Annah, would you like me to turn on music?"

"Thank you, Delsey that would be fine." *Maybe the music will calm everyone down.*

Bradford glared at Michael. "Hey, Em, who's your girlfriend?"

"Brad, you twerp, this is my fiancé Michael." Emily took Michael's arm and held it.

Bradford leaned back and roared. "Fiancé'? Y'all are kiddin', Em. He looks like y'all dragged him out of a cave with that head of hair."

Michael looked at him with surprise. "Sir, for your information, your sister likes my hair this long, and I don't feel I have to make excuses to anyone for my choices in life. Your hair, however, needs updating." He winked at Emily. "Yours was popular in the nineteen seventies."

Bradford glowered at him and said to Emily, "I don't like your choice of friends, dear sister-in-law."

"Brad, you're a horse's ass," she responded. "*You* of all people shouldn't criticize others. You always look like you need a haircut."

"Mother, please have them stop criticizing and swearing at each other," Charlotte said, as she stood up and covered Cherry's ears with her hands. "This has to stop."

Annah observed the table of empty plates. "Charlotte, would you please sit down and begin to pass the dishes around? No one has eaten yet." She motioned with her hands to Bradford and Michael. "Bradford, meet Michael. Michael, meet Bradford, my rude son-in-law."

Morgan piped up. "Yeah, our nitwit family member."

Bradford slid his chair away from the table and started to lift his oversized body out of it, but Charlotte stopped him. "Who do y'all think y'all are, callin' me names? At least I don't cover my brain with a woman's blonde wig like y'all do?"

"What? Stick it up your rear end."

"Bradford and Morgan, stop it. We have a guest here, and you're being disrespectful of him and the rest of us," Annah said.

Except for Bradford and Morgan glaring at one another, the others passed the dishes and stayed quiet except for Cherry, who made slurping noises.

"Well, since this is going to go on forever, I'm going to eat a piece of pizza. I hate cold pizza." Emily reached over the pan to pick up two pieces, giving one to Michael and one to her.

"Delsey and Lucia," Annah called. "Would you come here? We need your help to pass the dishes."

"Yes, Annah," Delsey said. Renaldo followed them in and started to pass plates of food from one end of the table. The help were dressed in dressy clothes other than their usual work clothes, even though Charlotte had ordered all the help to wear their uniforms for this momentous occasion. Delsey had intervened without her knowledge and told the others to ignore her.

The gathering grieved Annah and sapped her strength as the heated discussions and tensions continued. The children repeatedly hit, kicked, or punched each other, and the crying and screaming peppered whatever decent conversations anyone attempted.

As the noise escalated, Annah gazed at Jackson's empty chair. She missed him. He would have stopped the demeaning conduct in an instant. All Annah could do was try.

The scent of the roses on the table permeated the air. It brought memories of Jackson's wake back to her. Within four days of his death, Dr. Jackson Morgan Gulliver's ashes lay buried forever in the family plot, next to her parents and ancestors, in the Rosewillow Cemetery.

"Mother," Charlotte began, bringing Annah back to reality. She placed her silverware and napkin upon her plate. "We hope we can have more family get-togethers like this."

"Charlotte," Annah said. "Next time you plan a get-together with all of us, please let me know first."

Charlotte's cheeks turned red. "We hope our getting together keeps you from being lonely and lets you know how much we love you."

What my children don't know about loneliness, she thought.

"Mom, that's why Michael and I are going to spend the summer with you," Emily said.

"Mother, what we *all* hope is that you will invite us to live here with you." Charlotte's words came in rapid fire. "You know we love you and want to help you and take care of you. I mean like, do things for you that may become a burden for you as you enter your elderly years. Didn't Father handle the business and financial affairs for you? Bradford could help you with Father's papers. You know, like sorting, filing, discarding, and I could help you with your bank accounts and such. I took bookkeeping in college."

"Ha! You? *You* take care of Mom's bank accounts? Give me a break, Charlotte. You're nosy and want to know how much she's got," Emily said.

"Emily," Charlotte said, her voice growing hoarse. "You mind your own business."

"This *is* my business. You always want to control everybody. Well, this time you let Mom decide what she's going to do. Besides, what did you mean by *all* of us wanting to live here?" She turned to Annah. "Mom, what do you think about this? Do you really hear what Charlotte is saying?"

It seemed to Annah that her entire life was crumbling around her. Now her children were saying she couldn't handle her own business and arguing about who would take over the house.

"Hey, you two," Morgan said. "No one asked me about this either. Patricia and I might like to live here, too."

"See!" Emily said. "Who do you think you are, Charlotte, deciding for all of us?"

"Well, Bradford and I have been talking about helping Mother out. She's all by herself now. Besides, who are you to talk? You've invited yourself and this…this boyfriend of yours to spend the whole summer here. Did Mother say it would be okay or did you just assume you could do whatever you wanted to do?"

Annah interrupted. "Girls, this is appalling. No one is taking over your father's business affairs, or my bank account, and I don't need anyone to care for me." Annah forced her chair back. "This get-together was thoughtful. I love all of you, and now it's time you left."

"Wait, Mother. We also want you to know that this trip to Florida with Kat is a terrible idea. You're needed here with us so we can help you."

She stood and hurried from the room, startling them.

"Mother! We haven't eaten our dessert yet," Charlotte called.

As she quickly disappeared from their presence, she heard Charlotte say, "Mother's not herself lately, she's tired all the time, and she's losing too much weight. She needs us to help her."

Annah slammed her bedroom door and stood facing her bed for several minutes seething with anger. *Tomorrow, I'll be out of this house and away from them all. Yes, Charlotte,* she thought, *I'm not myself lately, and you had better get used to it. I'm about to change many things, including myself.*

—

Still seething with anger, Annah waited as everyone but Emily and Michael had left the house, and stepped downstairs holding her purse. Spying Emily, she said, "I'm going to take a little drive. I need fresh air. I'll be back in a while."

"Where are you going?"

"Out for a drive."

Once in her car, she brushed her straight hair smoothly over her ears and noticed in the rearview mirror that she was more gray than usual. *No wonder,* she thought.

As she drove away from the house, she rolled down the windows to allow the fresh air to blow into the car. Late summer evenings in South Carolina are hot and humid. After several miles, she turned into the Rosewillow town square and decided to stop at the small restaurant for dessert. With all the arguing at the table, she had told them to leave before the help served the desserts. Once she parked in front of the restaurant, she changed her mind. Going in alone depressed her.

On her way out of town, the possibility of Randall and Henry becoming suitors abhorred her. She shuddered at the thought. She was not ready for such relationships. Besides, she had no inclination to become more than a friend to either one of them, and she realized she had grown numb to the thought of wanting a man, any man. Jackson took care of that. For years, she had felt him grow distant to her. Why didn't she see the signs?

Annah reflected on Emily and her boyfriend. They are young and love is exciting. They have no inhibitions. What a difference from when she was their age.

She thought of Charlotte and Bradford. They had been childhood sweethearts, and they're still married after eleven years. Well, she and Jackson were married for thirty-five years. What does time have to do with a relationship when a marriage goes sour?

She considered her son's marriage. Morgan rules his household just like Jackson ruled ours. Is Patricia truly happy under his strict control? Would he be unfaithful to her some day?

She drove for over an hour, going around town several times. Once she stopped at a point overlooking the ocean, she stepped out of her car and leaned against the door. The air was cool and crisp. She took a deep breath and let it out slowly, more to release stress than to breathe in the fresh air.

Remembering Charlotte's disturbing words, she became indignant again. "Who does she think she is? I'm the owner of that house and no one is going to take it away from me or move in without my permission. Not Charlotte or anyone else.

"And, to think that I can't take care of myself or that I need help is an abomination!" She seethed. "Of course I'm getting older, but I'm far from being elderly. The nerve of her to suggest that!"

"This business of them not wanting me to go to Florida is intolerable. I will go if I want to and nobody is going to stop me!"

Peering out over the ocean, she knew her trip to Florida would be the best thing she could do now. It would give her relief from the tensions at home and time to reflect on her present life.

It was late when she returned home. She walked through the entryway to the parlor, found the bottle of sherry in the bar, and pulled out a small glass.

"Annah, we've been worried about you, where did you go?" Delsey asked, seeing Annah.

She held the bottle to her side and gripped her glass. "I needed to take a long, quiet drive so I could think."

"Well, I'm glad you're home. I sometimes think you're going to run away."

"What? Delsey, why on earth would you think that?"

"*You* think about it now." She started to leave, but then stopped. "Annah, we've told you before that since Jackson died, you haven't been yourself. You've been stuck in your own little world, making the rest of us worry about you, especially since that woman showed up."

She stood clutching the bottle and her glass, wanting nothing more right now than to have that drink. "I know I've been down, but I didn't realize it was affecting everyone else."

Jerome came up beside Delsey, after hearing the conversation, and put his arm around her. "Miss Annah, we've been praying for you."

Annah looked from one to the other. "Thank you, but I'm fine." She paused. "God didn't help me when I've needed him the most, so I'm sure He doesn't care to do so now."

"Annah, that's not true," Delsey said. "You know better than that. He's been with you all your life and taken care of you."

"Oh, sure He has. Is that why I spent ten years naively thinking I had a faithful husband? I had no clue. God had nothing to say to me about it."

Delsey dropped her arms, took Jerome's hand, and turned to walk out of the parlor. "By the way, Renaldo said he would cook up an early breakfast if you'd like it." Then, they left.

Annah watched them leave; knowing Delsey was upset at her. She always felt Delsey's rebukes, but this time she didn't want to accept it.

Once in her bedroom, she undressed and put on her satin pajamas, poured sherry into the small glass, and sipped it. Then, she slipped under the covers in her bed, lifted the book from her nightstand, which she had half finished reading, and snuggled into her pillow.

Does Delsey think I'm running away because of this trip to Florida?

She opened her book, but found herself reading and rereading one page. *This is ridiculous*, she thought. She sat up to finish her drink, placed her book back on the nightstand, turned off her light, and went to sleep.

—

Delsey and Jerome walked up the steps to their cottage porch. They sat down in the glow of the light beaming from their kitchen window. The moon was full, casting a gray light over the rear of the house. She pushed her rocker back and forth, making creaking sounds.

"What was all that fuss about in the dining room tonight?" Jerome asked, leaning toward her in his wicker chair.

She stopped moving her feet. "It's beginning," she said.

He clasped his hands over his knees. "What's beginning? What do you see?"

Delsey placed her elbow on the chair arm, and looked straight at him. "Changes. I feel changes are coming to this family. They're breaking apart."

Jerome listened intently.

"This trip is Annah's destiny, and we'll be a part of it." She rocked harder. "I'll ask her if we can visit our families on the island while she's away. I know she'll agree and say it will be good for us to go." She stopped rocking. "It's time for us to prepare for whatever lies ahead."

Jerome stood and moved his wicker chair up against the house. "I'll gas up the pickup in the morning and tell Custer to be ready to go as soon as Annah leaves for her trip."

CHAPTER TEN

Annah rummaged through her jewelry box looking for her favorite gold ringed earrings and bracelets. She was in a hurry. She had finished packing, and Spencer and Kat would soon be coming so she and Kat could leave on their trip. In frustration, she finished packing and decided on other pieces to wear. She carried her case downstairs.

When Spencer and Kat arrived in front of Annah's house, Emily met them at the door. "Come in. Mom is ready to go."

"Yes, I am," Annah said, walking toward them. She pointed to her suitcase and the basket of food that Renaldo prepared for their trip and called for Custer to take them out to their car. Then she turned to Emily. "Emily, did you borrow my gold ring earrings and two gold bracelets that I usually wear?"

"No. Why, did you lose them?"

"I can't find them. I'll have to look for them when I get home."

"Darlin', is that all you're taking with you? One suitcase?" Kat asked. "I brought two. I wanted to have enough clothes so I wouldn't have to worry about washing them."

Annah shook her head. She wouldn't worry about washing clothes. They would be washed when she returned home.

Spencer did you bring a map?" Annah asked, even though Kat said she knew landmarks.

"Yes, let me show you the map, since you'll be driving." He walked into the parlor, sat down on the sofa, and spread the map out. Annah sat across from him and watched him draw an imaginary line along the route they were to take. Kat stood and listened, and Emily peered over her mother's shoulder.

"Now, dear, you will have to take I-95 south through Savannah. I think you and Jackson have traveled that way many times. Haven't you?"

"Yes, of course, we've spent a great deal of time in Savannah together."

"Good, from there, you'll continue on down until you reach Jacksonville and go west on I-10 until you see the sign for I-75. From there, you'll go south all the way to Ionia. Kat knows the landmarks, and you shouldn't get lost."

"Count on me, hon. I know my landmarks."

Spencer nodded. "Now, Annah, if you drive the speed limit, you should be there in a little less than eight or nine hours. Of course, you'll want to stop and eat along the way, which will make your trip longer."

"Yes, we will, but I think we'll have enough food with two baskets full," Kat said, smiling. "We can stop and have a picnic and eat our hearts out."

Annah looked up at her with curiosity. She didn't address her saying they would eat their hearts out, but she questioned that they had two baskets. "Kat, did you prepare a basket of food for the trip?"

"Did I! You're going to just love; I mean, just love what I packed."

Spencer held his finger on the place that he stopped on the map. "Now, ladies, if you spend too much time eating and stopping for gas, you will probably have to consider your trip to take nine to ten hours, depending on the traffic. I think the whole trip is a little over 550 miles."

"Spencer, baby, you're making it too difficult for us. Me oh my, all those instructions make my head spin," Kat said.

He folded the map and handed it to Annah.

"Spencer, I'm looking forward to driving this trip," Annah said. "I can't wait to get away and see Ionia where you both enjoy visiting. Of all the states we've traveled through, Florida is one of the prettiest."

Kat gave Annah a playful smile, which Annah took as an acknowledgement of not giving away her secret of their retiring there.

"Hon, we'll open our windows and feel the wind in our faces as we go."

Annah stood and said, "Kat, I don't want to be blown from the Atlantic to the Gulf in one hundred pieces. I just got my hair done yesterday."

"Annah, do you have any questions about your trip?" Spencer asked.

"You know what I think?" Emily interrupted, pointing to the map.

"What?" Spencer and Annah asked in unison.

"I think you ought to use a yellow pen to mark the route, so they won't get lost."

"Emily, I've driven that way with Spencer many, I mean *many* times. Don't you go worrying about us now," Kat said. We'll be all right."

Spencer leaned over and kissed Kat on the cheek, and touched Annah's arm. "I have work to do. I have to go." he said, as he left them to drive home.

"Missus, y'all are packed and ready. I had to squeeze all the bags into the trunk. There wasn't any room for the baskets, so I set them on the back seat." Custer said.

Annah looked at Kat. "That's fine," she said to Custer. "We'll certainly want our food within reach."

"Yes, ma'am. I have some totally delicious cookies in mine. I mean, they're scrumptious. Let's go, Annie-girl. I'm so excited."

As soon as they were ready, they said their goodbyes and walked out to the car.

"Emily, dear, Delsey and the men are going to visit their families on the Island while I'm gone and Renaldo and Lucia will take care of the house." She hugged her. "Don't worry about us, we'll be all right. I'll give you the hotel phone number where we'll be staying in Ionia."

"Okay." Emily said, looking from one to the other as they climbed into the car. "Mom, did I hear you say you would give me the hotel phone number when you get there? You mean you didn't make reservations at one?"

"No. Kat said there are many hotels there and they're never full. We shouldn't have any trouble finding a room."

Emily looked serious. "Well, you and Kat have a good time and be careful."

Annah waved to Delsey as she stood on the porch, started the engine, and drove around the fountain toward their destination. Once on the street, she turned to Kat. "I am so looking forward to getting away and having a restful time."

"Yes, ma'am."

Annah's cell phone rang, and she struggled to pull it from her purse. "Yes?"

"Mother," Charlotte said. "You left without even saying goodbye to me."

Annah held her phone to her chest for a moment, hesitating to answer. "Charlotte, I was just thinking about that," she said. "I'll see you Monday or Tuesday, depending on what happens. Oh, and would you please call Morgan and tell him I've left on our trip?"

She heard Charlotte groan. "I already told him, Mother. I don't think you've made a very good decision going off at this time. If I were you, I'd turn around right now and come home."

Annah glanced sideways at Kat. "No, we're not turning around. We've planned a wonderful weekend and I don't want to spoil it. You'll be fine, and I can finish whatever I need to when I come home." She heard Charlotte groan again.

Annah realized she hadn't told her grandmother when she was leaving, so she wanted Emily to do so. "Sweetheart, would you call Grandma Wilmont and tell her I've left for Florida with Kat and will call her when we get there? I'd appreciate you doing this."

"Okay, Mom. Like I said, be careful and have a good trip."

"We will," she said. "Kat, I'm going to turn off my phone so no one will call me until we get to Ionia."

"I'm glad. That's the only way you'll find peace."

Within an hour, they had driven through Savannah and were heading down to Jacksonville. "What route did Spencer tell me to go? Was it 90?" Annah asked as she read an upcoming sign."

Kat squinted at it. "That doesn't sound right. Look at the map."

She threw her hand instantly to her mouth. "Kat, I left the map on the table."

"Annah? How are we going to know the way?"

She glanced at her. "Kat, you said you knew the way. Let's try to remember. Do you recognize any landmarks? Look at that exit over there."

"Um, yes. I recognize that exit, but I don't remember if we took it or not. Let me see." She lifted her sunglasses and pointed her chin in that direction. "Hon, I just don't know. I do remember him saying a number with a zero at the end. Do you think we'd better take it?"

Annah hesitated. "If it goes west, I guess we won't have any problem. Let's take it." She drove off the interstate and onto a road heading west. "Ah, this does not look like a major road, Kat. I think we should have stayed on 95."

"Hon, it goes west. Just keep going."

After several miles of seeing small, run-down houses, heavily forested areas, and swamp on both sides, Annah said, "This is not the way. We should have gone another mile or two."

Eventually, they came to a major road that crossed 90. "This is the road. See? Take it. I remember now. We should have taken the road with the number 10."

Annah sighed with relief and turned the car to go west on 10. "Now how far do we go before we turn south?"

"I'm not sure. It has a zero in it, so it must be the way." She scratched her head. "Now, you just let me see if I remember these landmarks." Only bushy trees and a sandy ground surrounded them. A vulture circled overhead. "Goodness, look!"

Annah gazed at the big bird circling over the tree tops. "I don't think he's coming after us." She turned to examine Kat's shocked face. "Okay, I'll drive a little farther west. Maybe you'll remember more."

Kat frowned. "Let's see if we can find the road that goes south."

Annah snapped her head sideways at Kat. "Well, then, do I take any road that goes south, for heaven's sake?"

"Annah, *You* left the map at home."

"Okay, let's take this next road south. They passed a small sign indicating 51 South.

"That does not sound familiar to me at all. It gives me goose pimples."

"Goose bumps, not goose pimples."

Kat folded her arms over her chest. "Goose bumps, okay?"

"What's wrong with driving 51? It goes south."

She folded her arms tighter. "I don't know anymore. I just know Ionia is along a highway numbered 75, which you just crossed. That's where we should have turned."

"Then why didn't you stop me from going past it?" Annah asked with frustration. Suddenly, she noticed the swampy landscape. "Oh, I don't think we should have turned on 51."

"You're probably right, and I have to pee."

"What? Kat, what a vulgar word. I've never heard you say such a thing."

She rocked her head back and forth. "It doesn't matter. I have to go pee."

Annah slowed the car down. "Here? In this place?"

"Yes, here in this place, right now."

Annah pulled the car over to the side of the gravel road. "Hurry. It's starting to rain."

Kat opened the door and her foot slipped on the slimy bank. She screamed as her body slid down the slope and into the water.

Annah bolted out of the car after seeing her disappear and ran around it to rescue her. "Kat, are you all right?"

She grabbed a thick root and pulled herself up. "Lord have mercy, I've never felt so much like a dirty old toad in my life. I'm covered in muck."

Annah held onto the door handle and reached for her hand, helping her up.

"I could croak I'm so green and slimy."

Annah scrunched her nose. "You smell awful, too."

Kat's feet slid as she grabbed onto the car. "I smell? You mean I stink! My Lord!"

Annah couldn't help but say it. "Now you don't have to worry about your hair. It's not only messed up, it's stuck to your head."

Kat bent to wipe mud off her slacks. "Annie girl, just wait, you're going get yours."

"I'm sorry," she said in between howls.

As Kat slapped the mud off her hands, she said, "Well, one good thing happened."

"I can't imagine what."

"I don't have to pee anymore."

"What?"

"Here, grab my hand again and help me into the car," Kat said.

Annah's eyed her. "Don't pull me down with you. You said I was going to 'get it'."

"Oh, I'm only kidding." Kat reached for her hand and pulled Annah's foot into the mud. It sank up to her ankle, covering her new sandal.

Annah screamed. "Kat, that was not nice."

"Hon, didn't you say we're going have fun on this trip?"

"For goodness sakes, let's clean off this muck. This is not fun."

They dragged themselves out. "You'd better change out of your dirty clothes," Annah said. "So you don't get mud all over the seat."

Kat looked up at the dark, threatening clouds. "I may be clean in a change of clothes, but maybe not dry. It's going to start pouring."

Annah moved around the car to press a button on the dashboard to open the trunk. "Which suitcase do you want to open?" she asked, looking at the two Kat brought.

"Right now, I don't care. Pick one." She unbuttoned her blouse and took off her slacks as the rain fell harder.

Annah struggled to pull the case out and lay it across the bumper.

"It's locked. I'll have to get my key."

"Why in the world would you lock your suitcase when it's only the two of us?"

"Because that's what people do." She pouted. "Annah, would you look in my purse and find my keys?"

"Yes, and I'm going inside while you dress. It's raining, and I don't want to be wetter than I am," Annah said, as she wiped her feet and shoes clean with a rag from her trunk. She crawled back into her seat to find Kat's keys and handed them to her through the open window. She waited while Kat dressed. "Please leave your muddy clothes in the trunk."

"Hon, I don't want to see these clothes ever again," she said, as she threw them into the creek.

"Kat! You're not supposed to throw trash and clothes out along the road or into creeks. You're being a litterbug."

"Let the alligators eat them," she said, as she climbed into her side of the car.

"What do you mean by alligators?"

"I just saw one slither into the water with another eyeing me as I dressed."

Horrified, Annah started the engine. "Let's go," she said. "I can't believe this is happening, alligators and swamps. Where in the world are we?" She pressed on the gas pedal, but the rear right tire slid sideways sending mud flying backwards.

"Maybe they want us to stay for dinner," Kat said.

"Dear me, don't frighten the both of us."

"Hon, you know little ole' me, I'm only kidding. Do you know how to rock?"

Annah pursed her mouth. "What in the world are you talking about?"

"I mean to rock a car out of the mud."

"Of course I don't know how to rock a car. How do people learn to do that?"

"Silly, when a car is stuck in snow, you have to try to rock it out."

Annah beat her hand on the steering wheel. "That's it. You said I'm going to get mine and this is it. My clothes are dirty, I'm stuck in a swamp, and going to be eaten by reptiles, and now you're talking about rocking my car out of snow."

"See?" Kat said. "We're having fun."

"Sure we are. "What would we be doing if we had stayed at home?"

"We'd be going to lunch, going to meetings, and doing some shopping like we always do," Annah answered with exasperation. "Tell me how to rock."

"It's like this. Put it in drive, step on the gas, let up, put it in reverse, step on the gas, and then let up. It'll rock itself."

"Okay." She tried it, but the wheel only spun deeper into the mud and wouldn't go forward or back. "We're done for."

The rain splattered more heavily on the windshield and the sky drew gloomier, as they sat alone in the car. Neither one knew what to do, nor did they speak to each other.

"And, on top of everything, now *I* have to go to the bathroom," Annah said.

Kat put her hand on Annah's shoulder. "Hon, remember, there's no bathroom here. You just have to go wherever."

Disgusted, Annah stepped out of the car. "Wherever? If only my family could see me now…."

Kat looked out the windshield and waved her hand and head around, making the clumped strands of her hair swing. "Look around you. No one's watching."

"Oh God, this is just humiliating."

She looked all the way around. No alligators. No people. She pulled her slacks and pants down and let go behind the car.

Kat looked through her side window at the swamp and mossy trees. The damp smell of moldy vegetation wafted up at her. She scanned the river's edge obviously looking for alligators, snakes, and other creatures.

"I have never been so ashamed of going to the bathroom in my entire life," Annah said, as she returned to the car.

"Hon, we women have to do what we have to do. Men have it easier. Just think…."

"No! I'm not going to think about that, Kat. Now, forget what I just did. Okay?" She glared at her. "I mean, if I ever hear you speak of this embarrassing experience to anyone, I'll die, and then you'll die."

"Yes, ma'am," Kat answered, holding her hand over her mouth to cover her grin until she burst out in squeals of laughter.

"Kat! I mean it. You'll die."

"Yes, ma'am," she said, as she held her head straight, turned her eyes sideways, and peeked at her.

Annah laid her head back on the seat and closed her eyes. "On top of it all, we have no cell signal. If we get out of here alive, we should just turn around and go home."

"No, ma'am. We've gone too far. Besides, we may not ever get out of here."

Suddenly frightened by two men standing outside their car, Annah turned to her and whispered, "Look. Two men are standing there glaring at us."

Kat studied their clothing. They wore waders and overalls with large suspenders. One man held a rifle pointing down under one arm and the other man held a long, sharp pole in his hand. The first one spit on the ground and shuffled his foot. He opened his mouth to smile, showing two front teeth missing. The other nonchalantly picked at his teeth with a toothpick.

The rain stopped and the sky began to clear. Rays of light

poured through the clouds.

Annah pressed the button to let the window roll down a few inches. "May I help you?"

The second man dug his pole into the ground and leaned on it. "Y'all need help?"

Annah glanced quickly at Kat. She felt too afraid to speak anymore.

"Yes, sir. Our tire is stuck in the mud," Kat said, as she leaned toward the window. "Can you push us out?" She clasped her hand against the steering wheel in front of Annah.

One man shifted his head sideways and stared, while the other leaned further forward.

Annah looked in her rear-view mirror and through her steamy back window to see that they had parked their pick-up behind them.

"S'pose we could," one said. "Billy Joe, what'cha make of this?"

The other spit tobacco juice on the ground and put his hand on the door. "Hmm, what'cha two doin' here on this swamp flat?" he asked.

Annah's heart pounded. "We lost our way and took a wrong turn. Is this 51?"

One lifted his baseball hat and scratched his head while the other spit again. "Nope."

They didn't move from outside Annah's window. They continued to stare.

"Do you think you can you push us out of the mud?" Kat asked.

The men ambled around the car, peered at the tire in the mud, and the man with the pole rubbed his chin, appearing to assess the problem. Finally, he said, "Missy, start ya'll engine and step on the gas. We'll push ya'll out."

Annah's hand trembled as she turned the key to start the engine. She pressed the gas pedal and sent mud into their faces. "Kat, they're going to kill us," she whispered.

"Whoa there, not so hard." They wiped their faces with the sleeves of their shirts and pushed again. In an instant, the car came free.

Annah grabbed Kat's hand and squeezed it. "Let's get out of here."

One man came around to the car window before they could drive away, "Where'd ya'll say yer a goin'?" the man with the rifle asked. He now held it flat against his waist with one hand on the barrel and the other next to the trigger.

"Ah," Annah started. "We were on I-10, and I think we

wanted to go south on I-75, but couldn't find it. We found a sign indicating 51 South. If we went south, we thought we'd see another sign indicating route 19." She eyed one man and then the other.

The man with the pole grasped his suspenders. He squinted at her as he spoke. "Missy, as much as I can tell, you've missed 51 and this here road is just a swamp track for us alligator and hog hunters." He glanced at the other man. "Billy Joe, what'cha think? Where should these ladies go?"

Billy Joe scratched his belly. "Don't know. Guess they should turn around and head back to where they come from." He scratched his ear. "Let's see, if they go north, they'll end up on 90, but they can take.... No, they'll be on 250. Maybe they should take 250 to 10.... No, maybe 252 to 129 to...let me see now. No...."

"Ya'll been chewin' too much tobaccy," R.J. said. "Missy, go back where ya'll come from and go that away," he said, pointing east. "Billy Joe, ya'll is telling them to go east when they want to go south. Now, I know ya'll don't get out to these swamps much." He looked back at Annah and Kat. "Best ya'll better get a map. There's a station straight up that way," he said, as he waved. They walked back to their truck, climbed in, and drove away.

Annah could hardly breathe. She closed her eyes and trembled.

"Annah baby, we just escaped death. I mean, we could have been thrown to the alligators, for goodness sakes." She breathed a sigh of relief. "You know? Oh, heavens to Betsy. Why, we're in cracker country, and my Mama always told me to stay out of these parts." She swooned. "Annah, do you remember seeing the movie *Deliverance*?"

"Kat, stop. You're scaring me. Let's get out of here."

Annah waited until she couldn't see the men's truck, and then turned her car around on the narrow, muddy road.

"Whew, where'd you learn to do that?" Kat said, looking astonished.

"It's what my uncle taught me. He used to let me drive his tractor."

"Good night, girl. You, on a tractor?" She leaned back and howled.

"Yes. What makes you think I've never even ridden on a tractor?"

"Hon, you've always dressed up. I can't imagine you driving a tractor."

Annah looked sideways out the window and made a face. "Thanks for the compliment, but we didn't know each other when I was a child. When I visited my Uncle Rufus, he let me drive his tractor around his farm. My parents never knew about it."

Eventually, they returned to where they started.

"I guess we'll have to find that gas station and pick up a map."

"Hmm, I've been thinking. I've changed my mind. After that experience, I'd like to go home. "I'm a bundle of nerves," she said, as she gripped the steering wheel and watched for highway signs.

"Huh? No way, hon. We're going to have our vacation. Now, you just keep driving north, and we'll find that old gas station."

Annah stewed, but kept driving. They reached a familiar road. "Okay, we're back on 10. Let's find that gas station."

They kept driving until an old weather-beaten building appeared with two rusty, antique gas pumps sitting in front of it.

"Let me see if they have a map," Kat said, as they stopped beside a gas pump. She ran into the building, screamed, and ran out again. "Quick. Get going," she said. "There's a horrid woman in there that looks like, you know some creature from the dark lagoon."

A tired looking, hunched-back woman, with two canes wobbled slowly toward their car. Her face held tiny rolls of wrinkles from living and working outdoors in the sun for most of her life. Her matted gray hair hung behind her ears in long strands. The woman leaned on the edge of her window, and in a scratchy voice, she asked, "Ya'll want gas?"

"Yes, please," Annah said, horrified at the appearance of her.

The woman backed up and stood beside the car. "Well, get yo'self out and pump it."

Annah looked at Kat as she slid out to fill the tank.

After filling the tank, Kat paid the lady and climbed back into the car. "Annah girl, you have a lot to learn."

They watched the woman stagger toward the station house as they drove away.

"Do you know that old woman never questioned my muddy hair?" Kat asked.

Annah thought a minute. "She probably sees people looking like you all the time. This is swamp country." She thought again. "Besides, she didn't look like a creature from the dark lagoon, it's called black lagoon, and she's isn't a creature."

Kat folded her arms. "I don't want you to ever; I mean *ever* to correct my words again. If I want to say dark lagoon, I'm going to say dark lagoon. You can call it a black lagoon if you want to, but I don't want to." Kat gave her a look of disgust and settled into her seat. "Hon, we forgot to ask for a map. Where are you heading?"

"I'm going home," Annah said.

"No, you're not. I don't want to go home. Mercy me, we're halfway there. What are you going to do with me? Leave me on the side of the road?"

"Maybe," she said. "Oh, I'm sorry. I'm lost and don't know what to do."

"Annah, we're going to Ionia and that's it."

Annah gave her a look of resignation and drove the car off the road, twisted the steering wheel around, and directed the car toward I-75 going south. Ionia loomed in their future.

After some thought, she said, "And, Kat, if you ever, *ever*, tell anyone I had to pee beside the car, baring my behind to the whole world, you'll never see the light of day again."

"How do you know those crackers didn't see you?"

"Kat!"

PART II

IONIA

CHAPTER ELEVEN

A brilliant orange and amber sun slipped below the horizon as Annah and Kat arrived in Ionia. "Here we are," Kat said, as she pointed to a grand sandstone marker announcing the way to the seaside development. A tall wooden sign beside it listed various scenic attractions.

Annah exhaled. "Yes, this is absolutely wonderful. I'm already feeling better."

"Spencer and I stay at the *Cabeza de Playa Motel.* It's absolutely, and I mean absolutely the best. It's off the beach, and we spend our evenings on the small balcony just watching the sun go down and sipping Margaritas."

"How lovely. Direct me to it."

Kat directed her to the street where a modern Spanish adobe hotel came into sight. A blinking sign indicating the *Cabeza de Playa Motel* lit the way, and beneath it, flashed "No Vacancy." Annah stopped the car.

"Darn! Look at that sign," Kat said. "Well, that shouldn't stop us. There are more motels along this strip. Let's go see."

They continued along the main street searching for a motel with a vacancy sign, but didn't find one until they reached the town's outer limits.

"There," Kat said, as she pointed to a bright yellow sign with the word "Vacancy" under the motel's name, *Delilah's Palace.* "See, we're lucky."

"Yes." Annah parked the car under a stripped canvas awning, which hung sideways off its frame, and which covered the double doors of the entrance. It was difficult to see the exterior because of the lack of lights.

"Now, you wait here. I'll get us the best room."

Annah stretched her neck against the headrest and took a deep breath. She delighted in finally being able to rest and be away from Rosewillow. Times were different now. Without Jackson, the demands upon her at home had become unbearable. Right now, she could forget about everything.

"Hon," Kat said, when she returned to the car, "we've got our room." She slid into her seat. "Why so glum?"

Annah sat up. "I'm just mulling over a few things." She started the engine and parked the car in a vacant spot. "Let's go see."

"Guess what? I have a surprise for you."

"What kind of surprise?" Annah asked, as she walked around to the trunk to open it.

Kat lifted the three cases and placed them on the ground. "My surprise is that we have adjoining rooms on the upper level. Won't that be just perfect? We can sit on the balcony, watch the sunset, and talk 'til we're green in the face."

"Blue. Blue in the face," Annah corrected.

Kat turned her back to her and gritted her teeth. "Blue, then."

Rolling their cases to the elevator, Annah pressed the up button. The sounds of clanging startled her when the elevator door opened. A woman's computerized voice said, "Going up."

When they reached their floor, the door opened for them to view crushed pop cans and debris along the walls. The voice said, "Second Floor."

Stunned. Annah asked, "How long has it been since they've cleaned this hall?"

Kat held the elevator door open. "Well, let's hope the rooms are clean." They rolled their cases toward their rooms. "Here's your door key. Our rooms are 201 and 202." She handed Annah a plastic card and slid her card into the key holder in her door. "Isn't this the most exciting thing since eggnog pie?"

Annah raised her eyes. "This is not only going to be exciting, it may be traumatic."

Kat pushed her door open, flipped the light switch, and glanced around her room. Spying an inside door, she unlocked it to reveal the adjoining room. "See," she said, poking her head around the door. "We have connecting rooms."

Annah laid her case on the bed. The room suggested an outdated Mediterranean motif. She saw a soiled bedspread, a spotted carpet, and no alarm clock, refrigerator, microwave, or any bathroom amenities. There were two lamps with evidence of greasy fingerprints. She walked to the bed to check the sheets to see if they were clean and if there were bed bugs.

Kat went into her own room and screamed. "I just saw a bug crawl under my bed!"

Annah stomped her foot. "This is unsatisfactory. I'm getting your money back. Don't unpack," she said. She returned to her room and grabbed her purse. "Watch my case."

"But, Annah, this is the only motel we've found open."

"I'm going downstairs and tell them how disgusted I am at the lack of cleanliness in our rooms and the hallway. I can't believe these people stay in business." She instantly left and entered the elevator once more. It rattled until she reached the first floor. With determination, she headed toward the front desk. "Madam," she said to the clerk. "My friend and I are very disappointed with the condition of our rooms. We want our money back, so we can find another place to stay."

A bleached blonde clerk with heavy makeup and long red fingernails sat on a high stool smirking at her. She took a long drag on her Camel cigarette and blew the smoke into the air above her. "Who do y'all think you are stormin' over to me like that?"

Annah glared at her. "Madam, my friend and I have the right to get our money back because we don't like the condition of our rooms or your motel."

"Lady, whoever y'all are, we run a respectable place here. See?" She raised her arm and waved it around the lobby. Two men seated at a small round table playing cards looked Annah up and down and sneered. At another table, an elderly couple sat reading magazines and drinking coffee. They stopped what they were doing and watched. A cleaning lady leaned on the handle of her mop and placed one hand on her hip in a sign of disgust.

Annah could not believe the scene going on in front of her. "Well, we are not satisfied with your establishment. We would like our money back."

The clerk took another long drag, pinched a piece of tobacco off the corner of her lip with her fingertips. "So?"

"So?" Annah asked. "What does *so* mean?"

She snickered. "So, y'all want yur money back? Y'all never gave me no money."

Annah stood still for a moment. "Just a minute, I'll be right back with my friend. Please have *her* money ready." She turned away from the desk and walked quickly to the elevator. "Of all things," she said, impatient for the elevator to reach their floor.

"Kat, let's grab our suitcases. We're not staying here, and you have to go the front desk with me. You have to ask for your money back so we can leave this horrible place." She took the handle of her suitcase and led Kat to the elevator.

Once again, they endured the rickety elevator and the computer voice saying, "First Floor," and returned to the front desk.

"Ma'am, I would like my money back," Kat said. "I gave you my credit card and paid for two adjoining rooms that came to one hundred dollars."

The group of people, which had now grown to ten, gathered in the lobby along with the clerk and broke out in uproarious laughter.

"What's so funny?" Annah asked. They stopped laughing and continued to watch.

"I'm sorry, but our little-bitty computer just broke down, and I can't return yur money," the clerk said, mimicking a little girl and being as obnoxious as she could.

The people roared even louder as the clerk sat down on her stool, wheeled it in a circle, and dramatically lit another cigarette with a pink plastic lighter.

That did it. Annah seized Kat's arm and pulled her out with her.

"But they have my money," Kat said.

"That's what they think. When we get away from here, you can call your credit card company and refuse the charge. Come on; let's figure out where else to stay."

"Hon, I'm so sorry; I should have thought ahead and gotten us a place. It's getting late, and what are we going to do now?"

Unable to find a decent motel, Annah guided the car to the side of the road and cut off the engine. She slumped back in her seat, exhausted from the long drive, and turned her head sideways to look at Kat, who was leaning on her elbow against her door.

Kat dug her cell phone out of her purse and called Spencer. "Holister here," he answered. "Honey, we're in Ionia and can't find a motel."

He was silent for a few moments. "Sweetheart, the only other option is to drive to another location. Look at your map and see what's around."

She tapped the phone on her ear with her fingernails. "Honey sweets, we don't have a map. Annah forgot it at home." She heard long sigh.

"I can't believe you two made it down to Ionia without a map," he said. "Then drive up to Tampa. I'm sure there're loads of motels there. You're only about twenty or thirty minutes away from it."

"Okay, I'll call you when we find one. I love you."

"Love you, too. Watch the signs and stay out of trouble."

She looked apologetically at Annah. "Hon, Spencer suggested we drive to Tampa, it's a big city, and we should find a motel there."

"Great," was all Annah could say. She was so tired; she could hardly lift herself up. She started the engine and guided her car back on the highway. "I hope it's not another roach motel."

The muggy night air and the echoing sounds of heavy waves washing over driftwood in the Gulf waters on the Ionia shore matched Annah's mood. She wasn't pleased to learn she had to drive up to Tampa. She preferred to stay in the area, close to their destination.

As she returned her car to the highway, she realized they needed to stop for gas, so she pulled her car into a station next to a pump and shut the engine off. Kat stepped out and filled the tank with gas.

Annah stretched her arms and back to relieve some of her tension.

"I'll see if they have a map of Tampa and ask them if they know of a decent motel up there." When she returned, Kat said, "Annah! We have a place here. It's a Bed and Breakfast nearby and there's a vacancy. The man gave me directions. He says it's owned by very nice and hospitable people."

"Show me the way," Annah said, much relieved.

After they left the station, they drove a mile to a gravel road, turned, and spotted an elegant three-story house with its porch lights on and a sign, which read *Pulley's B&B.* Annah found a place to park and shut down the engine. Kat left the car first, and then walked toward the front steps. A tall dark-haired woman opened the door and greeted them.

"Welcome ladies. I knew you were comin'. Bobbie called from the station and told me you were on your way."

"Oh, my. Word gets around fast here," Kat said

"Come on in and make yourselves at home," she said. "Roy, we have guests."

Kat waved to Annah. "They have a room here. Let's look at it."

"Welcome," Lola said to Annah as she approached her. "I'm Lola Pulley and this is my husband, Roy. You're lucky; we have one room open with twin beds."

Annah surveyed the interior and took notice of its cleanliness. "Yes," Annah repeated. "We would like to stay here very much."

Lola led them up a wooden staircase, which creaked from age and use, toward the bedroom. She unlocked the door and held her hand out to invite them in.

The pictures on the walls were reminiscent of another time and place. White, cotton-fringed bedspreads covered the beds and fine linen curtains hung neatly over two windows. A hand-painted lamp between the beds glowed softly. Everything appealed to Annah.

"I'm sorry, but there's no bathroom in here. You'll have to share one with two other guests and it's down the hallway to the right." Lola walked them to it.

As they entered the bathroom, Annah examined the light blue, plush towels hanging exquisitely over racks, and various soaps and lotions lay beautifully positioned in ceramic trays. An attractive, cloth shower curtain with another plastic curtain behind it hung over the tub and shower. She was pleased with it all.

"I'm going to enjoy being here," she said. "This is exactly what I was hoping for."

"This is wonderful!" Kat said, scanning the room.

Lola clasped her hands. "Well then, ladies, let's get you registered and work out the number of days you'll be stayin' with us. Usually, our check-in time is three the first day and the check-out time is eleven the day you leave. Since it's past eight o'clock and you've missed supper, I won't count this day." Closing the bathroom door, she led them downstairs.

"Roy," Lola called, "would you help these ladies unload their car while I register them?" "Okee dokee," he said, heading outside the house after Annah handed him her car keys.

Annah stayed with Lola as Kat followed Roy out. "Thank you for helping us," Annah said, as she rubbed her stiff neck. "What are your rates?"

"Fifty eight dollars a day," Lola said, as she opened a registry book to sign them in.

Annah felt they had found a gold mine.

"Annah, come see," Kat said, as she rushed toward the counter.

She led her to the sliding glass door leading to the back patio. "We have a view of the beach and the ocean from here. See the lights? There's a cruise ship out there. That's what I would love to do someday with Spencer. Why, we could sail around the Gulf of Mexico and the Caribbean, just like pirates." She bent over and held her hand over her mouth, restraining a laugh. "I mean, we wouldn't be pirates, but we could see where the pirates sailed their ships. There's a lot of history here."

Lola put her elbows on the counter and listened. "Yes, and we have a long strip of private beach where you'll enjoy sunbathin'."

"It's a good thing we couldn't find a motel," Annah said. "This is better here." She put her hand on Kat's shoulder. "You are definitely going to have a different life here than in Rosewillow." The mention of Kat and Spencer sailing together left Annah longing to do the same.

"I know. Let me get unpacked and showered. I still have mud all over me. She rushed from Annah's side while Annah finished filling out their information.

"How long will you two be here?" Lola asked.

"Well, we planned a four-day vacation, so I think, probably Tuesday. If we decide to stay longer, would that conflict with other reservations?"

"Oh, dear, no. You're welcome to stay as long as you wish. Our B&B is so far out that many people don't know we're here. We usually get reservations by referral from people who have stayed here before."

That suited Annah. "Thank you," she said, as she left the counter, walked toward the staircase, and headed for their room.

"Darlin', this room is charming. Look!" She opened the top drawer of the dresser. "Why, we even have extra towels." She looked around and stooped to look under the bed. "Thank the good, heavenly Lord. No bugs!"

Annah moved over to the window and drew back the curtain. She watched the lights of the cruise ship pass by. Once, she and Jackson had taken a cruise to Jamaica and the Bahamas. No, she would not spoil this trip thinking about it. She dropped the curtain, twisted the long plastic rod to close the shades, and moved to the bed to sit down.

"Hon, why are you suddenly so sad? This is a happy trip. Come on, now." Kat sat next to her. "I know you're missing Jackson again. Remember, we're on vacation, and we have lots to do tomorrow. I can't wait to show you our house." She leapt from the bed and opened one of her cases. "Let's hang up our clothes," she said, as she dashed to the closet.

Annah reached for a tissue to blow her nose. She rose from the bed, unpacked her case, and found several tops to hang. The activity would do her good, and it would keep her mind off her loneliness.

"Annah, I'm hungry," Kat said. "It's eight thirty, and we can probably find a good restaurant open. Want to go?"

Annah felt grubby from the long, hot drive, but agreed. "Lola," she called as they walked past her downstairs. "We're going out. Do you know of a good restaurant nearby? We missed supper and we're famished."

Lola called back. "Yes." She gave her the name of a local restaurant and directions to it. "We lock the doors at eleven, so ring the doorbell if you come back later than that."

"I don't think I can stay out that late. I'm too tired."

After a dinner of salad, shrimp, crusty bread and glasses of wine, they returned to the B&B and their room. It had been a long drive, a bad experience in the swamp, a few arguments, but a warm, tasteful meal to end the day. Tómorrow would be an adventure.

CHAPTER TWELVE

Dressed in shorts, a summer halter-top, and sandals the next morning, Annah was ready to go for their tour of Ionia.

"Hon, my goodness, how you snored last night. Why, I thought you would be blown out of your bed and shattered to smithereens."

"Kat, that's silly. What time did you get up?" she asked.

"I always wake up with the songbirds, but this morning I woke up to the sound of a foghorn."

Annah gave her a look of dismay. "Oh, stop it. You're making it all up. I don't snore like a foghorn."

"Let's go see my house," Kat said, opening the bedroom door and beckoning her on. "Let's go. You're just going to be bowled over with how pretty Ionia is."

"I'm already bowled over just being here."

Annah noticed a large platter of sweet breads, small cakes, and donuts as they passed through the downstairs dining room. She chose a slice of lemon cake and poured tea into a Styrofoam cup as they headed out the door. "I hope I don't gain weight on this trip," she said.

"Good. You look like you've lost over twenty pounds."

"Look. I'm going to eat every single bite of this. Watch me."

Annah and Kat canvassed the Ionia development. They viewed small cottages, high-rise condominiums, elegantly designed timeshares, custom homes, and the overall community.

"Let's go off the beaten path and see other areas around here. I have something in mind that I hope to find," Annah said.

"In your mind? Whatever are you thinking about?"

"It's just something I'd like to find, maybe a small cottage for a retreat."

Kat glanced sideways at her. "For rent, or to buy?"

"I haven't decided yet."

"Okay, but I want you to see our home first. It's still being built, so we can't go inside."

They turned onto an asphalt road bearing the road sign *Coral Lane.* They surveyed homes in various stages of completion lining the road. Several needed stucco siding and tile roofing. Others stood exposed like skeletons showing only their framework upon concrete pads.

"There." Kat pointed. "There's our house. Keep driving. It looks like they're getting ready to finish the outside. We asked for sandy-colored stucco and a burnt orange tiled roof."

They parked on the street in front of it, and Annah turned off the engine. Bits and pieces of construction materials lay haphazardly around.

"Come on, let's walk around the property, and see the inside through the windows. Spencer will be so happy to hear they're almost finished with it."

"When is the house going to be ready for you to move in?"

"We told them we wanted to move into it by mid-July."

Kat walked through the front court yard and peered into the picture window. "You'd better come look at this. I can see through the living room to the Florida room on the other side."

As she strode up beside her, Annah pressed her face against the glass to look in.

"Let's walk around to the back. I want you to see our pool and back porch."

She followed her around the house to the back yard where they peeked again into the windows and examined the screened-in pool and porch. She wanted to say so much to Kat about the difference between this house, even though it would soon become a beautiful home, and their elegant house in Rosewillow, but kept quiet.

"Sugar, we're really going to be happy here."

"Yes, I'm sure you will be."

"Now you've seen it. We'll have three bedrooms and two baths, and you know you can come visit us any time you wish."

"Thank you. I may just take you up on it."

"Now, when you get back to the highway, turn left at the light, and we'll drive through the forest area. Hon, I know there's cottages mingled in the trees. When Spencer and I were out touring this area, we found a couple of small ones. Tell me if you see something that looks like what you imagined. We'll have to drive a little eastward into the forested area." She watched for a road. "Turn here."

Annah slowed down at a corner near a fruit stand where several people stood in line to buy fresh produce. As she turned on the road, she heard her car tires hit sand amassed with sea shells. "Here?"

"Yes, just keep going."

As they drove, they found themselves surrounded by uprooted palm trees and piles of rotting vegetation. Soon, two wind damaged houses appeared within the trees.

One of the houses caught Annah's attention. "Let's go look at that place." She drove into the driveway, stopped, and stared through the windshield. "This is it."

"My gosh," Kat said, shocked at the sight of it. "You've got to be kidding. Sweetie, this is a big house not a small cottage."

Annah's sandals crushed through a conglomerate of sand and small stones as she stepped outside the car to get a better view of the house.

Kat came over to her. "Whatever are you looking for?"

"This is what I would like as a retreat from my family."

Kat placed her hand on Annah's shoulder. "Darlin', this place is frightful."

"No, no. This is it. I could spend time alone, reading, resting, and fixing it up."

Kat gave her a disgusted glance. "You've gone off your roller."

"Rocker, Kat."

Kat clucked her tongue. "Rocker, whatever. Hon, you have never fixed anything in that mansion of yours. How do you expect to know how to fix anything in this place?" She walked in front of her and picked up her hands. "Look at your manicured nails. How are you going to get down and dirty?"

Annah let go. "I hope to make changes in my life and this would be a start."

"Well, if you want to do that, then pick a better house. This one is too damaged."

As they walked up the driveway, Annah imagined what she could do with the house to have the quiet she craved. There would be only one phone, one small television to catch up on the news, a stereo system to play classical music, and specially chosen books to read.

She would have the house to herself, no more large parties, no large groups to entertain, no weeklong guests. She would see to that. Except she knew her family would want to visit, but she would put a limit on how long. This time, she would be in charge. Not Charlotte. Not Morgan.

Here she would be able to heal. She had so much hurt. Here she would not be lonely because she wouldn't have memories of

Jackson surrounding her at every turn. She would learn to do things on her own. She had always stood in his shadow and let him take charge.

She would make new friends and would have Kat and Spencer nearby. Kat cared little about Annah's status, and they enjoyed their times together. They had met at a local community event in Rosewillow twenty-five years ago, talked through their dinner together, and soon became fast friends. Annah loved her for her realism. She always brought her back to earth with her humor when pride of position got in her way.

"Darlin', look at this house. It would take you a fortune to fix up. You would have to clean up all the debris, the palmetto bugs, the mice, and Lord knows what else. Mercy sakes, you'd have snakes crawling in your bed at night."

Annah peeked sideways at her. "Yes, wouldn't that be fun?"

"Girl, you've gone mad. Maybe you drank some of that swamp water when I wasn't looking."

Annah clasped her hands. "I could be so happy here. Really. And it would be a retreat for me to come to when I feel overly stressed."

"Hon, with all your wealth and comfort, why do you feel overly stressed?"

Annah shook her head. "Kat, I'm tired of it all. Wealth doesn't give happiness. I don't have to worry about money, but I have struggles like everyone else. You have your husband and a wonderful family. I'm lonely." She continued. "I have three adult children who are continually fighting for control of me and my assets. I want a new life. I want changes. If I could give away my fortune to a worthy cause, or to make someone else happy, I would. Then I would be free."

Kat fixed her eyes on her for a long moment, and said, "I'm sorry. I never realized you felt that way. You have always been so proud and reserved."

"Kat, inside, I'm a bundle of nerves. I want out of the role of mistress of Gladstone. It's become a heavy burden." She gazed at the house before her. "This could be my way out."

Suddenly, they heard the sound of someone hammering.

"It sounds like someone beat you to fixing this house."

Annah felt her heart drop. "Let's go see," Annah said, leading the way.

Broken limbs and palm fronds covered the sides of the driveway. The house and property had survived a storm sometime in the near past.

The hammering continued.

"Someone is working on a house nearby," Annah said, as she stopped to listen again.

The hammering stopped and started again.

She walked through trees surrounding the house to get a better look. "There," she said, as she pointed to where the hammering sound came from.

Kat squinted. "Yes, ma'am. Someone's fixing the neighbor's house."

"Let's see who it is."

"No. Who knows who it is? It might be dangerous. We're trespassing."

Annah gave her a quick smile. "Okay. Stay here. No one knows we're here. I want to look through the window of this house."

"You bet your sweet bottom I will."

Annah walked up the broken steps toward the porch to peek through the front window. The house was empty. She held her hand up against the pane and saw into the living room. She moved over to the front door and worked at opening the knob, but the door wouldn't open.

"Can I help you?" A man's voice bellowed over to her.

Annah jumped away from the door and turned to see a large man standing next to a tree. He wore work clothes and held a hammer. She left the porch to go back to her car and Kat's side. "We were in the neighborhood and wanted to see this house," she called back, not knowing whether to trust him or not.

He walked toward them, lifted his baseball cap, and ran his hand through his hair. Sweat poured down the side of his cheek. Slipping the hammer into a loop on the side of his overalls, he took out a handkerchief and wiped his face. "This is Mrs. Puckett's place. She died of a heart attack six months ago. She was eighty-five and too sick to care for the house. Then, a storm hit this area and tore it apart." The man looked from her to Kat. "I hope to work on her house after I finish her neighbor's."

Annah thought she saw a twinkle in his eye, as he looked her over.

"Name's Floyd," he said, without moving his eyes off her.

"We were just looking at the house," Kat said.

Annah gazed at Floyd as he continued to examine her.

"Isn't this an interesting house?" he said.

"It looks like it was once a beautiful home," Annah said, returning his stare.

"Yes, ma'am. After Mrs. Puckett died, the house sat empty. She lived here most of her life. Now her family owns it and wants it repaired."

Annah watched him pull a half-smoked cigar out of his top pocket and put it between his lips. He took a book of matches from his other pocket, struck a match, and lit the cigar. He sucked into it and blew out smoke, all the while watching Annah watch him. "Hope you don't mind my cigar," he said, chuckling.

Annah couldn't stop looking at him. There was something about him that attracted her, and she didn't know why. To break the tension, she asked, "So, you remodel houses?"

"Yes, ma'am," he said, as he took another drag, held the cigar between his teeth, and grasped the straps of her overalls.

For an uncomfortable moment, Annah could not discern why he kept his eyes on her. He looked her up and down with obvious great interest, and she felt embarrassed.

"Hon, we should get going now," Kat said. She took Annah's arm and forced her toward the car. "Thank you. We have to go."

Annah pulled her to stop and asked the man, "Floyd, may I call you Floyd? My name is Annah." She hesitated, feeling Kat pulling at her again. "And, this is my friend, Kat. We're visiting from South Carolina."

"Annah, stop, we don't know anything about this man. Let's go," Kat whispered and pushed at Annah a little harder.

She wouldn't budge. "No, I want to ask him a few questions." She pulled her arm away.

Floyd lifted his face and blew smoke away from them. It looked like he was enjoying their discomfort. "Ladies, you don't have to be afraid of me. My friends call me a teddy bear because I'm such a nice guy," he said.

Annah decided she liked the man. Trust him? She wasn't quite sure yet, but there was something about him that made her warm up to him. "Is Mrs. Puckett's family living nearby?"

"No, they live in Pennsylvania."

She tried to avoid his magnetic eyes. "How often do you communicate with them?"

"Seldom. Their trustee handles the family's business, and I work with him." Floyd spit out a piece of tobacco.

Kat pulled her arm. "Hon, let's go."

Annah turned to look at the house. She envisioned it remodeled and restored. She turned back to Floyd. "Floyd, how much would it cost to restore this place? I mean, do you have an idea?" She wasn't quite sure yet if she wanted to buy the place, but threw the question to him.

He smiled, crossed his arms over his stomach, and held his head back. "Well, now, let me see."

Kat elbowed Annah, who elbowed her back.

"Let me see." He surveyed the area and the house. "Now, let me see. I'll bet it would be too much for you lady. He glanced at her BMW and said, "But, maybe not. I don't know. I'll have to give you an estimate after I look inside. Besides, the repair cost is the responsibility of the estate and insurance company."

"Can we get inside the house to look it over?" Annah asked.

"Not yet. If you're that interested, I'll have to check with the bank and get a key."

"How do I get a hold of you to find out?"

"Hmm, there's Lucky over at The Albatross you could call. I spend a lot of time there after work. Where are you ladies staying?"

"We're staying at the…."

Kat swift-kicked her. "Don't tell him," she said sternly.

As they scuffled, Floyd put his cigar in his mouth and then took it out. "Ladies, like I said, you don't have to be afraid of me. I'm just a hard-working guy who needs money for food and beer, and maybe a cigar or two. I'm not going to hurt you in any way." He pulled a piece of scrap paper from his pants pocket, a short pencil, and began to write his name and number. "Here, if you're really serious about this place, call me." He handed it to Annah, winked at Kat, and quickly left after saying, "Call The Albatross, I usually stop there on my way home."

Annah waved back, knowing that's just what she was going to do.

"Annah, I'm ashamed at you. You're ogling him. I'm beginning to think you're more interested in him than the house. Don't you even think what I think you're thinking. If you really want this place, call the local bank like he said."

Annah felt a tug at her heart. That's what she should do; but first, she wanted to see the inside of the house, and she would meet him at The Albatross. She wanted to know when the repair work would be finished, and if she could buy it from the family. Besides, there was something very captivating about him.

Kat stomped her foot. "You're going to do it, I know. I can see it in your eyes. Quit it, darlin'. You're going to get yourself in a heap of trouble, just like a hummingbird heading for a thorny bush at high speed. There won't be life left in you."

"Kat, that's ridiculous. Do I look like a hummingbird to you?"

"Yes, ma'am. Raised to be a respectable South Carolina woman, your eyes are on a cigar-smoking man with a beer belly. He's a northerner, and you know how crass those northerners are."

Annah squinted at her. "Are you prejudiced? He looks and sounds like a very nice man. Just ignore his cigar, which is what many men smoke. I never thought to hear that kind of talk come from you."

"I'm telling you, I saw a gleam in your eye." She paused, pointing her finger at Annah and jabbing her arm. "You don't have to go into any bar and get in trouble. I mean it, girl." She jabbed her harder.

Annah averted her eyes. "Let's go see where The Albatross is, just out of curiosity."

"Just out of curiosity, huh? That's an excuse to see him again."

"Maybe." Annah grinned and strolled back to the car. "Let's go."

Kat punched her hands into her pockets and followed her.

After they left, Annah drove two miles along an asphalt highway to another sandy road. Off the pavement, a sign announced the town of Packard and below it a small sign advertising "The Albatross." She turned at the signs and headed toward the town. In the center stood a weather-beaten building with the faded name of the bar above the door. Annah pointed, "There it is."

"Yes," Kat said, as she heaved a deep sigh.

She noticed trucks and beat-up cars parked in front of the bar. She knew Floyd wasn't in there, since they had left him at the house. Beer signs and flashing Christmas lights hung from one end of the building to the other. Broken shingles hung over the roof and paint blackened the windows.

"This town gives me the creeps. Now, what are you doing?" she asked, seeing Annah guide the car through town, turn around at the end of the road, and drive through it more slowly. A stray dog crossed the road, barked at them, and headed toward the back of a building.

"Kat, if I bought that house, I should know what kind of a community is nearby."

"It's a community all right, a dingy bar with twenty-five drunks in it, ten mothers worn to a frazzle raising fifty kids, who are knee-high in swamp mud, and a hundred dogs."

"Kat, please. Just because I met a man does not mean I'm going to get serious about him. Floyd seems honest and that's about it. I'm only interested to meeting him again so I can look inside that house."

"Uh, huh."

"Uh, huhhhh." She pressed the gas pedal to go faster out of town. "It's time to get back. I'm hungry and you probably want lunch. I hope Lola hasn't stop serving yet."

They left Packard and The Albatross and headed back to Ionia in silence. Kat pouted, but Annah was caught up in her own thoughts. What could she do with such a place?

When they returned to their B&B, Kat said, "Hon, I don't want you to get hurt again. I hope you're not using this idea of having Floyd remodel that cottage just to be with him."

Annah threw her arm over Kat's shoulder. "Kat, don't worry. I know better." But, she couldn't keep her mind off that fascinating man.

CHAPTER THIRTEEN

Charlotte stormed into Annah's home and rushed through the rooms looking for Emily. She found her in the family room cuddled beside Michael in a loveseat. They were watching a movie. "Emily, Mother is not checking her voicemails. I know something's happened."

Michael looked away from the film. "I'm sure she's all right. If something's happened, you would have received a call from the police."

"I'm not talking to you. Emily, let's drive down and find her."

Emily sat up. "I'm sure she's fine, Charlotte. Quit worrying about her."

"Well, I'm going to call Spencer to learn if he's heard from them, and if I should drive down there to help," Charlotte said, giving her a look of disgust.

"For crying out loud. Leave Mom alone. She said she wanted to have a little vacation. Don't drive down there and interfere with her fun. You're always trying to control her."

Charlotte folded her arms and glared at her. "I don't want to control Mother. Why does she need a vacation anyway? She has too much to do here." She swung around and stomped out of the room.

The loud slam of the front door caused Delsey to come to the hallway and walk into the family room. "Emily, what's going on now?"

Emily and Michael sat back in their seat. "Charlotte is just being Charlotte. Through all that crap with my sister, we've missed the best part of the movie."

First, she called Morgan. His response was, "Sis, why worry? She'd call you if something was wrong."

"Morgan, Mother has never, and I mean never, gone away on a trip like this before, and she's with Kat, that batty woman." She heard him groan.

"First of all, Pudge, she's an adult, and second of all, Kat is very smart. She has a degree in renaissance art. You don't like her, and I think you're jealous of her."

"Morgan, stop calling me Pudge. I hate that name. I am not jealous of Kat. I just don't like Mother running off with her."

She could hear him speak to Patricia. "Pat, would you please talk to my sister. I'm tired of her complaints." She didn't answer.

Taking the phone back, he said, "Sis, I'm busy right now. I'll call you later." He hung up before Charlotte could respond.

She gritted her teeth. "Damn."

Since no one agreed with her, she dialed Spencer. "Spencer, have you heard from Kat since they left?"

"Hello Charlotte. Why, yes. She called me as soon as they reached the outskirts of Ionia. Said they were fine, a few missteps, but on their way to find a motel."

"What missteps did they have?"

"I don't know. Nothing serious, I'm sure, or Kat would have told me about it. Why, are you worried about them?"

"Yes. Mother has not been herself lately."

"Charlotte, don't worry about them. Kat knows her way around Ionia."

"I'm thinking about taking my family and driving down there. Maybe we need a weekend away, too."

"If you do, give them my love."

"That, I will certainly do. Thank you. Good-bye," she said.

At home, she told Bradford they needed to drive to Ionia and see if her mother was okay. "I'm worried about her."

What? Ya'll are crazy. That's a whole day's drive and I have to work tomorrow. Besides, your mother is probably fine. She'll be lyin' on a beach somewhere gettin' tan and drinkin' a margarita every day."

"Bradford! I don't want to drive down there with just me and the kids."

He jumped up from the kitchen chair and walked over to her. "Geez, let your mother run her own life." He reached to kiss her, but she moved her face away.

"What am I going to do? Let her be irresponsible?"

Shaking his head, he left her. "I have never seen your mother be irresponsible."

"Then we'll go by ourselves."

Kat heard the ringer in her pocket and pulled out her phone. She stopped, looked at the I.D., and answered it. "Hi, sweetheart."

Spencer had news. Charlotte was on her way to Ionia. That

she was worried about them.

"Why?" she asked, frowning at Annah. "We're just having fun and touring Ionia. Did you tell her where we're staying?" She heard him cough. "Spencer did you?" she asked with exasperation."

"Yes, sweetheart, I did. She wanted to know."

Turning toward Annah, she said, "Okay, I'll have her call Charlotte."

"You don't have to tell me, I heard the whole thing," she said. "Do you see why I have to get away from Rosewillow? My daughter won't mind her own business."

"Annah, don't let her rule your life. Don't let her destroy your trip. Maybe she'll change her mind and not come after all."

"You know Charlotte as well as I know her. If she says she's on her way here, she won't turn back. I'll just have to figure out how to evade her."

"You're right. We don't have to spend time with her if she comes."

—

"Annah," Lola said when she spied her in the dining room the next morning. "Your daughter and her three children arrived late last night. They were all very tired from drivin' all night, so I sent them upstairs to one of our rooms to get some sleep. I put them near you so you could all be together."

Annah knew there was nothing she could do now. "Lola, I wish I had told you to tell them that there was no room here, but my daughter beat me to it."

"Oh, gosh. Your daughter said they drove up and down the main street and stopped at Bobbie Ray's station to get directions to our place." She tapped her pen on her knuckles. "Bobby Ray gave them to her and told her you were here." She paused. "We couldn't let her and those babies stay out in the cold when we had room, especially when she said she was lookin' for her mother and friend here. That's when I knew she was your daughter."

"That's very nice of you," Kat said. "Hon, it'll be okay. Remember, we're taking a boat tour today. They can spend time on the beach."

Annah thought a moment. "Yes, good idea. We'll see them when we return."

Roy walked into the room. "Well, did you ladies see the sights yesterday?"

"Did we," Kat said. "We visited Packard and met the locals."

"Packard?" Lola and Roy asked in unison.

"My nephew, Floyd, lives near there," Lola said, walking closer to them.

Surprised, Annah said, "We met him. We heard him hammering on a house when we stopped to look at a small cottage."

"Good," Lola said. "Lord knows, he's a fine man. He lost his wife over a year ago and came down to live here to be with us and start his own business."

Roy added, "Came from upstate New York. Was a contractor, but he gave it up to live here. Couldn't take the memories anymore."

"We stopped at Mrs. Puckett's cottage. Annah is thinking about buying a small retreat; and, after talking with him, she asked him if he would be interested in fixing that house for her," Kat said.

Roy raised his eyebrows. "Annah, if you have Floyd do it, be prepared for him to take a lot of time," he said. "It might take him a year or two to do it because he'd rather be fishin'."

Kat smirked at Annah.

"I didn't want you to broadcast that," Annah said to her.

"He's a craftsman," Lola said. "He does good work."

Charlotte entered the room. "Mother, did I just hear Kat mention that you're buying a house down here?"

Annah turned quickly to see her come in. "You're mistaken, Charlotte, we were discussing what Lola's nephew is doing for a living. He likes to fish and fix up houses. That's all." She paused and gave Kat a look of despair. "Charlotte, why in the world did you feel you needed to come down here? Kat and I are simply taking a few days of vacation."

"Mother, I was concerned about you two. You always seem to get yourselves in a fix, and we have to help you out. I came down to be with you just in case."

"That was unnecessary, Charlotte," Kat said. "Your mother came here to rest and have a little vacation away from all of you."

"Mother! Kat is not very nice. Aren't you glad to see us here?"

Neither Annah nor Kat answered her.

"Okay, we're here, and I hope we can spend time with you two today." She gave Annah a swift hug and ignored Kat. "The children are still in bed, and I should get back up there." She spun around and climbed the stairs.

Kat followed Annah toward the dining table.

"The food dishes are hot," Lola said. "So, be careful pickin' them up from the middle of the table. We serve our meals family style."

"Thank you," Annah said. "We'll talk more about Floyd later."

"That was a close one. You're going to have to explain to Charlotte what I said about you buying a house," Kat said.

"And you're going to have to tell her you're retiring and moving here."

They pulled out two chairs and sat down. Kat picked up the bowl and dished a spoonful of scrambled eggs onto her plate. "Let's eat and get the hell out of here," she said.

"Yes. Let's hurry and eat, so we can slip away without being noticed."

Having eluded Charlotte and the children, they drove toward Mrs. Puckett's house. On the way, she couldn't stop thinking of Charlotte. *The nerve of her! She rudely invited herself and intruded on us. In times like this, I just want to slap her.*

"I think we turn here," Kat said, as she pointed to the fruit stand on the corner of the road as her landmark. "Wouldn't you think that storm would have blown the fruit stand to smithereens?"

When they reached the house, Annah stepped out of the car. She noticed problems she hadn't seen before. Green mold covered the underside of the eaves and along the foundation. She wondered what else she would discover. She listened for hammering and watched for Floyd, but it was quiet, and he was nowhere.

Kat came to her side. "I know you were hoping to see Floyd. We'll have to go into that bar to see him; but let me warn you, you're going to be in for a shock. That bar is a different world than what you're used to. It'll be full of beer drinkin', cigar spittin', porno-gawkin' men, and you'd better be prepared."

"Oh, you're exaggerating. It can't be that bad."

"Hon, you have two choices. Floyd can restore the house and wait a long time for it to be finished, or you can look for another one that's in good condition."

"I know, but I'd still like to talk to him."

"I just thought I'd give you a piece of advice. You've only looked at one house."

"Thank you for that." She leaned against her car. "How do you know about such things as raunchy bars?"

Kat folded her arms and leaned next to her. "You and I grew up differently. I know about bars because, as a kid, I used to play the slot machines while my parents drank beer and played cards or pool with their friends in the local bar. It was their hang-out. On weekends, they went dancing there, and we kids went along with them because they didn't have a babysitter. When I think about those times, I realize it was the town's community center."

"I'm surprised. I've never heard you speak of your childhood."

"I grew up in a rural community. My Daddy struggled to put food on the table for the six of us. He worked in a metal shop and was paid only when he and the owner sold one of their finished works. My Momma took in ironing for extra money. I was the baby of the family, so I had privileges that my two sisters and brother had. My Momma died when I was fifteen."

"I'm sorry. That must have been hard for you."

"Yes, it was. I met Spencer when I turned eighteen and fell madly in love with him. Gosh, he was handsome, and I learned to be a proper lady by imitating the fine ladies of his town, which was twenty miles from ours. I always thank the Lord that I was accepted by him and his family because I wanted to be like them. Once we were married, Spencer helped me through college. I have been blessed, and I owe it all to him that I fit into the Rosewillow community."

"You fit very well."

"I wanted to change. You ladies let me see a privileged side of life, and I enjoy being Mrs. Spencer Holister, a woman of respect and dignity. I never let on where I came from."

"Well, I have a lot to learn to change things, too. My life has been too superficial. Kat, wealth doesn't bring happiness. I want what you have, a purposeful life, a family that truly loves one another, and the freedom to be myself."

Kat stood and surveyed the area around Mrs. Puckett's property. "My, oh my. I hope you make the right choices. At our age, life is too short for us to make mistakes. You can either be a flamingo or a sandpiper. It's your decision."

"Oh, for goodness sakes, Kat. Flamingoes and sandpipers, I swear."

Kat nudged her side. "Come on." She walked around the car and climbed into it.

Annah followed. "So, Kat, you ran with the flock and became a flamingo, and I'm a flamingo who desires to become a sandpiper."

CHAPTER FOURTEEN

As Annah and Kat drove toward The Albatross, a dingy bar in a dusty, deserted town where local workmen hung out after long hours in the hot Florida sun, Annah eyed Floyd's truck in front of the bar. She parked across the road, slid her purse under the seat, as did Kat, and said, "Okay, bird of many feathers, show me the way."

"Yes, ma'am. By the way," Kat said, as she stepped out of the car, "do you like beer?"

Annah locked the car door. "Why? Can't I order a martini?"

Kat howled. "Annah, you're going to ask for a martini in a dumpy bar? They'd laugh you right out the door."

Annah opened her mouth to say more, but instead said, "Okay, I'll try one, just for you."

"Let's go. Oh, and one more thing, the bar's going to smell, so don't make a funny face when you enter."

Annah stopped, pulled her hair away from her eyes, and looked around the town. The soft wind picked up dust from the dirt road creating a slight haze over the buildings. Two dogs fought beside an old storefront next to the vacant bank, and she noticed yellow curtains hanging over an unwashed picture window in an empty antique store. The town reminded her of another time and place. From where she stood, she could already smell the faint order of beer and heavy smoke. "Anything else I should know about?"

"Yes. Don't get mad when you get pinched on the ass. Just slap the guy's arm, smile, and walk away as if nothing's happened."

"Oh, my god."

"Come on, this should be fun."

Just as Kat said, the room reeked. The sour aroma of sweaty

armpits and dirty bodies made her gasp for breath. She tapped Kat on the shoulder and said, "Let's get out of here. This is more than I can bear. It's so dark in here, I can't see to walk."

Instead, Kat took her hand and led her to the counter, pointing to a stool, and motioning for her to sit down. Annah attempted to sit, but slipped on something greasy on the floor making her look clumsy.

"Wow, pretty lady, watch your step," a man in a paint-splattered t-shirt said to her. He came over and ran his hand down Annah's arm.

"Please take your hand off my friend," Kat said, as she pushed him away.

"Okay, okay," he said, raising his arms as if to ward off evil.

Annah felt sick. She scanned the room looking for Floyd.

"You ladies want a drink?" the bartender asked, as he wiped a beer mug with a wet towel.

"Yes, what do you have on tap?"

He grinned and gave her three names. Kat chose the lightest beer knowing Annah wouldn't be able to handle the heavier brews.

"Annah, I see Floyd over at the corner table. Let's go over and talk to him," she said, as the bartender placed two mugs on the counter and waited for Kat to pay. She reached into her shorts pocket and pulled out the needed funds. "Come on, let's go."

Annah grabbed the handle of her beer mug and followed Kat to a dark corner booth, where she could see a swirl of smoke above the table.

Floyd looked up at them as they came near. "Well, if it isn't my two tourist friends. I wondered if I'd see you again. He patted the seat next to him. A man on the seat across from him belched and excused himself as he motioned for them to sit. They both slid in on the other seat and faced Floyd.

"Excuse him. He shouldn't have burped in the presence of such fine ladies," he said, as he looked hauntingly at Annah.

"Floyd, we came to see if you would give me the name of the bank and the phone number so I can inquire about that house?" she asked. "Have you talked with the family to see if they would like to sell it?"

Floyd took a long swig from his beer bottle and set it down. "As a matter of fact, I did talk with them, and they would like to contact you about it." He placed his cigar in the ashtray and looked from one to the other.

Annah squirmed under his gaze. "How do I contact them?"

"When you're ready to leave, I'll go out with you. The number's in my book in the truck."

Annah cleared her throat. "Have you been inside the house

yet?"

He crossed his arms on the table. "No, but I've been told that there's a lot of mold inside the house. It's been shut up for six months. Are you sure you want that house?"

"Floyd, I would like a place of my own away from crowded developments. After touring the area, this is the house that's caught my attention." She glanced from Kat to Floyd and went on. "If the house needs too much work, I may want to look at a different house." She paused, watching his expression. "I don't have much time here. We're leaving Tuesday or Wednesday."

He grinned. "Well, that house you like is going to take a great deal of work and time to repair. When do you want to buy a house in this area?" he asked, uncrossing his arms and taking another long swallow of beer.

Annah sat forward. "As soon as I can."

Floyd scratched his head. "Just as an estimate, I think it would take me over a year to repair and the family may want to put it up for sale for maybe, I'm guessing $250,000. He sat back in his seat and watched her response.

"A year?" Kat asked.

"Yes, if you want me to repair it. I'm still repairing the house next to it."

"I don't know if I could wait that long," Annah said. "But, $250,000 seems like a good price." Her eyes were transfixed by Floyd's gaze. She had no idea what a house like that would sell for."

"You know, ma'am, I want to discourage you, because there's really too much cleaning up to do with that house and the cost of repair and remodeling might too high." He reached to hold Annah's hand.

His hand felt warm and gentle, even though its roughness caught Annah by surprise. She didn't want to let go. He enclosed her hand with his other one and squeezed them together.

Kat tried to get Annah's attention. Finally, she pushed Annah sideways out of the booth. "Let's go back to the house. It's lunch time."

Annah stalled. "Yes, we should go. I'll think about what you said and get in touch with you again. I assume you'll be here."

"I'll be looking forward to that." He looked at their glasses as he dropped Annah's hand. "You gals haven't finished your beer yet," he said, as they stood up. "By the way, where are you staying?"

"We're staying at Pulley's B&B," Annah said, remembering he was the couple's nephew.

"Well, first, you two are staying with my aunt and uncle and, second, you can call me on my cell or home phone. They can give you both."

"They're wonderful hosts."

"Yeah, they're great people. They've run that place for many years." He winked at Annah. "Give me a call."

Floyd put a fresh cigar in his mouth and chewed the end of it. He asked, while Kat pulled her away from the table, "Married?"

Annah held her breath for a moment. "I just lost my husband."

"Hey, Floyd, you gonna keep those purty women all to yourself?" a man asked, leaning across the bar counter. "You gonna share?"

"Nope, they're all mine," he said, grinning.

"Heck. Just thought I give them a try, but with you there, I'm outta luck."

Kat hooked onto Annah's arm and pulled her away. "Let's go," she said. "Thank you, Floyd. She led her away before he could stop them."

Out the door they went, with Kat dragging Annah sideways as she pushed their way through a gathering crowd of workmen.

"Y'all come back now," said a man wearing overalls. "We sure like purty women here."

As they drove away, Annah thought about Floyd, and how she would love to be wrapped up in those burly arms and put her head on his shoulder. *How could I think of such a thing?* She grimaced. *He's not my type. Besides, I've only talked to him for a few times.*

Turning to look at her, Kat said, "Annie girl, I just know what you're thinking. We've been friends for too long. You stop this now. That man will only get you in trouble."

"Kat," Annah said, as she pulled onto the highway. "I don't know what *you're* thinking. He's not anyone I would ever get serious about, you know that?" Then she remembered the twinkle in his eyes and the feeling she had being near him and that he was to give her the name of the bank and the phone number before they left.

"You can't fool me. I see the look on your face."

Close to lunchtime, they were back at the B&B. "Hon, let's get into our swimsuits and go lie on the beach if Charlotte and the children aren't there."

"Yes, let's do," Annah responded. "We can take a couple of sandwiches with us and lemonade to drink."

Once they were dressed and had gathered two cotton bags filled with their necessities and a basket with lunch, they headed down the path to the private beach. A gentle breeze, a warm sun, and a cloudless sky welcomed them.

"Here's a spot," Kat said. She dropped her bag, adjusted her large brimmed hat, unfolded a long towel, laid it on the sand, and sat down.

Annah spread her towel next to hers."

"Hon, you're as white as a ghost. You never get out in the sun."

Annah opened her bag and pulled out a bottle of sunscreen. "Well, that's because I don't want to burn my skin. I don't tan very well. I burn. Besides, I always wear sunscreen and a hat." She adjusted her hat to cover her face.

"No, I think you don't want to wrinkle."

"Of course I don't want to wrinkle. Do you?"

"I'm fifty-one and I already have wrinkles. You're older and your face is smooth."

"Then, why do you want to get out in the sun, get burnt, and get more wrinkles?"

Kat applied moisturizer to her arms and legs. She lowered her hat over her face. "I don't get wrinkles from the sun, I get it from experience. The sun gives me a lovely tan."

Annah sat down. "With experience you get wisdom. The sun gives you wrinkles and dries out your skin, plus it makes you look old."

Kat lifted her hat. "I hope I don't look old. Gray hair makes women look old, too. At least I color my hair to make me look younger. You don't. You look like you've let yourself go, girl."

Annah threw a handful of sand on Kat's legs. "Well, I've had my mind on many things, which is why I'm turning gray faster than I should." She paused. "But, thanks. You just made me realize I've been letting my appearance go, so when I get home, I'll have my stylist color my hair."

Kat brushed the sand off her legs. "Annah, I didn't mean to hurt your feelings. I hope you to get over your depression and start having fun again."

"That's what I'm here for, getting over my grief and family feuding and having fun."

Kat rummaged through the basket of food. "I'll be truthful with you. You did not belong in that bar with those people, and you do not belong in any kind of relationship with a man like Floyd. He's not of your class. Just as you said, with experience comes wisdom. If you continue this fascination with Floyd, you'll get hurt, and I don't think you want to gain that kind of wisdom."

Annah heaved a sigh. "I told you, I'm not interested in him."

"Okay, you have my advice. Let's eat."

They ate their lunch in silence.

Finally, Annah gathered her towel, bag, and basket, and led Kat up to the house.

As they entered the parlor area, Kat met other guests and began a conversation with them while Annah went back outside and sat down on a patio chair. She wanted to be alone. She had to digest Kat's words. She was determined not to let any man hurt her again. Jackson's deceit was too much to bear. Kat was right. Any involvement with Floyd would only bring heartache, especially since they really didn't have anything in common. How would she ever explain to her family, the Rosewillow community, and her help that she had been smitten by a blue collar worker?

When Kat noticed Annah outside, she left the guests and walked out to be with her. "Hon, these precious people are giving us information on the area. Are you interested?"

"I'm sorry. What were they talking about?"

"Mrs. Cray told me about interesting tourist spots. If we drive north, we'll find a quaint little town with oodles of shops to buy sponges and souvenirs. It's a pretty little Greek town known for its Greek food and history. I guess it was once one of the most prolific fishing areas for sponges. Its Greek origin is displayed in its architecture and the local culture." She continued. "Mr. Townsend told me there are other tourist areas we might want to see. We could pick up more brochures at the information center in Ionia tomorrow morning."

Annah thought she'd rather see Floyd, but quickly chastised herself for the feeling that came over her. Her face flushed. "Kat, that sounds like something I would like to do. Now, please excuse me. You carry on with your discussions," she said. She entered the house and walked up the stairs to their room. Once there, she sat down on the end of the bed.

"Annah, what's going on? Floyd again?" Kat said, entering the room after her.

"No. Yes. Oh, Kat, what's the matter with me? I know you're right about him, but I don't know what to do. Am I leading him on?"

Kat sat down next to her. "I don't think you're intentionally leading him on, it's just your mannerisms when you're with him. You look like a teenager on her first date."

"Oh, come on."

"I mean it. He's aware of your infatuation with him, and he with you."

"Then help me stop acting that way. Help me to stay away from him. I don't know what's come over me."

Kat thought a moment. "The only thing I can think of is that you tell him you're no longer interested in that house and then never see him again."

"You're so right again."

"Mrs. Gulliver, we only have a little more time here. Let's get away from Ionia, Floyd, and that house, and remember who you are in Rosewillow. Let's take a drive to that Greek town Mrs. Cray told us about."

Annah slapped her leg. "You bet." The next morning, Annah and Kat hurried from the B&B to spend a day sightseeing and shopping in Tarpon Springs, the little Greek town north of Tampa.

CHAPTER FIFTEEN

In Rosewillow, Jimmy Neely faced his angry editor. He knew he was about to receive a sharp reprimand.

"Young man, just what has been the problem with you interviewing Mrs. Gulliver? It should be as simple as one, two, three. Not two, five, nine. How many times do you need to knock on her door, talk to her, and write a story?" The editor ran his sweaty hand over his partially bald head and straightened little tufts of gray hair in the process.

Jimmy squirmed in the leather chair in front of his boss's desk. Piled on one side of his desk lay a stack of papers one foot high; and, on the other, an electric typewriter with a sheet of paper rolled into the carriage. The editor preferred to write his work on a typewriter and have his assistants retype and edit it on their computers.

Jimmy gazed at him through the messiness of his desk. "Sir, every time I call her to make an appointment, she doesn't return my calls, and when I go to her house, something happens."

"Something happens?" The editor took a cigarette out of a pack in his shirt pocket, and stuck it unlit between his lips, all the while staring at Jimmy.

"Ah, like, first, a woman showed up, obviously unannounced, and she and Mrs. Gulliver got into an argument; and, when she left, I talked to her maid. She said she wasn't available, that I could come back, so I handed her my card. But then, Mrs. Gladstone, I mean Mrs. Gulliver came to the door and told me to call back to make an appointment. But then, her daughter came up beside her." He lifted his leg, laid his foot on the other knee, and played with the shoestring on his shoe.

The editor swirled his unlit cigarette around in his mouth with his hand. "So? Her daughter came up beside her and then what?"

"Then I left." He didn't want to sound like a bumbling fool so he didn't explain dropping his papers and seeing them fly away."

"Then, when I drove over there at another time, a male visitor told me to go away, so I drove away, but I hid and went back after he left. That's when I met Mrs. Gulliver at the door again, but I fell and got a bloody nose. See? That's why I haven't been able to get any information from her."

The editor leaned his elbows on the desk, took his twisted his soggy cigarette out of his mouth, and examined it. "This time you got a bloody nose?"

Jimmy slouched down in the chair.

"Let's see. She doesn't answer your calls, shuts the door in your face, tells you to make an appointment to speak to her but you can't make an appointment because she never has time, and then leave and go back and then you fell and got a bloody nose." He breathed deeply.

"Yes sir, I fell on my face."

"You fell on your face." The editor picked up a pencil and tapped it on his desk. "Yet, she doesn't have a problem arguing with some woman who shows up unannounced, however, and visits with a man who probably also showed up without an appointment like you did."

"Yes, sir. This man told me Mrs. Gulliver doesn't need reporters asking her questions."

He leaned on his desk. "You got balls, boy?"

Jimmy felt his face flush. "Balls, sir?"

"Yes, balls." He sighed. "You numbskull. Are you a man or a whimp?

"Oh, yes, I mean, no. I mean, I'm a man, a journalist. Sir, give me another chance and I'll get that interview."

He put the pencil down, rolled his cigarette between his thick, hairy fingers, and rested it in a dirty ashtray. He folded his hands on top of several pieces of typed paper, and said, "Jimmy, I hired you to be a journalist. This was your first big assignment. If you don't perform, I'll have to either let you go or send you off to work in the classified ads department. Hear me?"

Jimmy shifted in his chair, crossed his legs, uncrossed them, and said, "Yes, sir."

The editor unfolded his hands. "What were those women arguing about?"

"Ah, I can't remember, sir."

"You can't remember? Did you hear them?" The editor

tapped his fingers waiting for a reply. "Jimmy, if you're holding something back on me, I want to know about it."

"Ah, I was too far away to hear it all."

"To hear it all? What did you hear then?"

Jimmy knew he was not good at lying, but he wanted to see the daughter again, and he didn't want to create a scandal.

"Well?" The editor waited. "Hmm, secrecy, huh? Boy, you might be holding a story that could earn you a few more bucks." He continued to tap his fingers. "However, I want you to write an interesting story about the history of Gladstone. We have many new people moving into our town, and I hope to increase our readership with it."

Jimmy thought about his beat up '95 Chevy and, oh, how he would like a new car. Earning more money would surely help. If he couldn't get the interview, he might lose his job. "Ah, I will sir."

"Okay, get that article or you're fired."

Jimmy's heart leapt. Instantly, he jumped up from his chair, nearly falling forward onto the editor's desk. He crossed his arms over his chest, uncrossed them, put his hands in his pockets, and took them out again. "Sir, I'll get on the interview right away."

"You bet your sweet butt you will. Here are some facts to verify with her. Annah's ancestor, Captain Rupert T. Gladstone, owned a fleet of schooners, which hauled freight up and down the Atlantic Coast during the mid-1800s. When the Civil War broke out, he used two schooners as privateers to capture enemy vessels. Being a lucky bastard, he forced a Union cargo ship aground off the Florida coast on its way to Key West holding substantial payments going to Union troops stationed at Fort Zachary Taylor. According to his Letter of Marque, the fortune was his to keep."

"How much of a fortune?" Jimmy asked, awed by the story.

"That's something for you to find out. Anyway, the captain built the Gladstone Plantation when he retired right after the Civil War. Now it's for you to obtain the rest of the story. How many generations owned the house? How many descendants of servants stayed on? What are their stories? What other historical facts can you add to the article? How much remains of the original structure?"

"Sir, I should be taking notes."

"Use your imagination," he said. "I would also like to know who will inherit the house after Mrs. Gulliver is no longer living there. Will she hand it down to the kids or grandkids? Do they even want to live in the house, since it's so old and expensive to keep up? Is this enough?"

"Ah, yes, sir. I mean no, it's not enough. I'll get the information."

"Balls, boy. Remember you have to have balls. Your fiery red hair should whip you into action. Go knock on her door and talk to her, and I don't want to see your freckled face until you have a complete and good story. Get the facts."

"Yes, sir," he said, as he spun around and hurried toward the door. As he reached for the handle, someone opened it and slammed it into his nose.

Startled, the editor's pretty, blonde-haired assistant looked at him holding his nose. "Jimmy! Are you okay?"

"I'm okay," he said, lifting his nose in the air to stop another nosebleed. In embarrassment, he rushed out the door.

His big worry wasn't his banged up nose. It was if he would be able to remember all those questions. *I feel like I've just had a history lesson*, he thought.

Jimmy knew as soon as he left his editor's office that he had better go back to Mrs. Gulliver's house. As he approached it, he wheeled his car up the driveway canopied by overhanging trees toward her home. He couldn't help but be overwhelmed again by the magnificent antebellum mansion coming into view. Stark black shutters contrasted with the bright white of a freshly painted exterior. Two grand levels adorned with Romanesque pillars stood guard over long porches bedecked with rockers, small round tea tables, and oversized pots of flowers and plants.

He rounded an ornate fountain, which spilled water into an imposing basin encircled with white magnolias and bold, red geraniums. Lime-green algae and rusty stains lay crusted over the basin giving a sense of it having flowed continuously forever. As he parked his Chevy close to the broad front steps, he thought he should have parked it out of view on the other side of the fountain, but he changed his mind. She had obviously seen it the first time he met her, and she would know he was a reporter with average wages and not a man of wealth.

Taking a deep breath and straightening his tie, Jimmy stood on Annah's front porch and knocked on her door. He hoped to get a chance to talk with Mrs. Gulliver or her daughter. He pressed his notepad and camera against his chest. Emily answered.

"Ah, Miss, you know I've been trying to get a story together about the history of your place, and I only have a few questions. Is your mother home?"

She held the door open, appearing to hesitate whether or not to let him into the house. "No, my mother is away." She stared at him. "Oh, heck. Come on in. Maybe I can answer them."

Jimmy bumped his foot against the door jam as he entered and leaped into the entryway.

Startled, Emily said, "Be careful. You could fall and hurt yourself." She led him into their parlor, pointed to a chair, and curled up on the sofa facing him. He asked questions and scribbled notes on his pad.

Emily looked him over, making him uncomfortable. "Jimmy, I think you'll get more information for your article if I gave you a tour of our house and property. Follow me." She stood and led him back to the front door.

"Let's start here," she said. She waved her arm around alerting him to view the walls and furnishings. "The large picture on your left is my great-great-great grandfather, Captain Rupert T. Gladstone."

They walked over to it so Jimmy could study it. He snapped a picture. The captain sat sideways in a chair, facing away from the photographer. He wore his gray Confederate Navy uniform and sported a handlebar mustache. He held his head upward with a serious expression.

"Your grandfather was a distinguished and handsome man, Emily."

"Yes, I know, thank you. Let me show you a portrait of his wife, Sarah."

Jimmy followed her a few feet down the grand hallway.

"This is my…oh, you know, Sarah. They had her painted instead of taking her picture. I think she was beautiful, especially in her blue brocade dress. I think she was much younger than Rupert."

Jimmy took a picture of her portrait and made notes on his pad of paper.

On the other side of the long hallway was a lengthwise sketch of a schooner. "This was an artist's rendition of the captain's ship."

Jimmy laughed. "I think I'm going to get enough pictures for an album."

"That's good. If you'll notice, we have pieces of furniture from his era still in good condition that we display throughout the hall. We also have a sizeable book with signatures of guests going back to the 1870s.

Jimmy gently lifted the cover to the first page and noticed the scrolled lettering. "Looks like they used a quill and ink then."

"Yes, they did. Now, let me show you our family room, which he used to entertain his male friends." She led Jimmy through double doors into a large room enhanced with polished paneled walls. She pointed to a rectangular glass case about five feet long. Within the glass, lay a model of the schooner resembling the picture in the hallway.

"Gosh, I feel like I'm in a museum," he said, snapping another picture and jotting notes.

"Our family has tried to maintain the integrity of Rupert's life and his achievements."

"Emily, one of his grand accomplishments is your historical home. I'm impressed."

"Thank you. I have more to show you. We have another glass case in the parlor area. Let's go there."

She led him back down the hallway to the parlor and pointed to the display case. "Here are some of the artifacts from his ship and seafaring days, a sextant, the ship's bell, his log book, a compass, and various other pieces, which he brought home from his travels."

Fascinated, Jimmy studied the items in the case. He wished he could take them out and hold them.

"If you'll look at the bookshelves, you'll see many books, some of which are over a hundred and fifty years old and first editions that Rupert coveted. We don't let many people touch them because a few of them are deteriorating. We've tried to preserve them in airtight covers."

"I won't go near them, trust me."

"I'd also like to point out that every room in the house has a fireplace, but we don't use them. The house is too old and the risk too great. The only fireplace we use is here in the parlor. My father liked to have this one burning. It helped him relax after his busy days."

"Let me show you the ballroom where my family has entertained many elaborate parties and our kitchen, which was fashioned after the galley on the ship. We also have a gorgeous dining room, which my mother has restored to its original state, and upstairs we have six bedrooms. The main bedroom still has the four-poster bed, which Rupert and Sarah used. My parents had it remodeled into a king-size bed for more comfort."

"Well, it's good that your family was able to change what needed to be changed over the years to make the house more livable." As they walked from room to room, he continued to take pictures and make notes.

"Yes, if you'll look up the stairway, we have portraits and pictures of the generations of family members who have lived here."

Jimmy looked up to view them. "I know we don't have time today, but I would like you to tell me the stories of their lives. I think I could continue the history of your house in a series in our paper. Many readers will be inspired by them," he said.

Emily scanned the faces of her ancestors. "I'm sure they would be." After Emily gave Jimmy the grand tour of the house, she took him outside to see the carriage house, which now housed their vehicles, and the four servants' quarters, which were brought up to date and expanded to have all the modern conveniences.

Through the tour of the house and property, Jimmy enjoyed himself and began to care more for Emily. "Emily, what can I say? You've made my day! Thanks for your help. I can go back to my desk and work up a good article."

She took his hand and led him out the door. "Jimmy, if you need any more information, please come back. I'll take the time to answer more questions for you."

He stood in the open doorway not to wanting to leave, but then, on impulse, reached out and hugged her, dropping his pen and paper. "Oh, sorry. I'm clumsy. I'll call you if I need more information…and I hope I can see you again."

Looking a little shaken by his impulsive hug, Emily said, "Yes, please call first, and I'll try to think of more things to tell you."

Behind her, he noticed a young man with long dark hair and wire-rimmed glasses looking angry. He didn't know who he was, but he knew Emily was about to have an argument.

He quickly left, not wanting to be involved with the argument. Once in his car and driving away from the house, he felt excited that he was able to gain so much information, but one thing remained. He had not been able to interview Mrs. Gulliver. He hoped his meeting with Emily would be enough and his editor would be pleased with the article he planned to write.

CHAPTER SIXTEEN

As Annah and Kat traveled north toward Tarpon Springs, Kat said, "Annah, we're going to find you a t-shirt with Greek sexy words to wear so you can start being the real you."

"Oh, my," she responded. "I can't wait." Just then, her phone rang.

"Mom," Emily said, crying. "Michael and I got into a horrible argument and he packed up and went back to school."

Annah heard her blow her nose. "Whatever for?" she asked.

Emily sobbed. "Just a minute," she said, blowing her nose again. "You see, it's that newspaper man, Jimmy Nealy. He came over to get information about the history of our house to write an article for his paper. Michael misunderstood his intentions when he hugged me. He got jealous." She cleared her throat. "Mom, it was a friendly hug. It didn't mean anything to me."

Annah exhaled. "Sweetheart, it'll be okay. If Michael loves you, you can still talk it out, and he'll understand what happened. Give him time to think about it."

"I don't think so. He's too hard-headed." She paused. "Well, there goes my summer. I thought we would have had fun together here instead of talking about our studies all the time."

Annah glanced at Kat with a look of motherly concern. "Emily, you can still do all those things. You can ask Morgan to take you sailing."

"I know, but it won't be the same. Morgan's no fun."

"I'm surprised at you."

"Mom, he acts like a doting father and husband, but when he's on his boat, he drinks like a fish. You and Papa spoiled him, just like you did Charlotte."

"Emily, I don't want to hear this criticism. Is everything else okay up there?"

"Everything's okay. Renaldo and Lucia are keeping me company."

"Don't worry about Michael. It may be for the best. You have another year of school to go through, and that's what you should be thinking about right now."

"Oh, Mom, I have half the summer to kill. What do I do now?"

"Hmm, why don't you invite Jimmy back and help him with his article. It seems to me that he likes you."

"Geez!"

"Think about it. Kat and I are on our way to Tarpon Springs today to visit a small Greek town. I'll take pictures and show them to you. Take care of yourself and don't let Michael spoil your summer."

"Mom," Emily added between sniffles. "I love you."

"Love you, too," she said. She kept her eyes on the road ahead and thought about Emily. Her relationships with young men always ended in tearful scenes. How many boyfriends has she brought home? Six? Ten? She wondered about Jimmy. Maybe, just maybe, he would be the one to help Emily grow up. He didn't have the refinement of a young man of their culture, but he seemed honest and caring.

"Is Emily okay?" Kat asked. "You look so serious."

"Yes. I think Emily will be just fine. Now, let's go shopping."

As they drove, Annah said, "Do you realize that if the ladies in the Rosewillow Women's Club could see me dressed in ragged shorts, a sexy t-shirt and sloppy sandals, I'd be ridiculed?"

Kat leaned on the console between them. "Annie girl, you shouldn't worry about them. Didn't you say you wanted to wear more comfortable clothes?"

"Yes." Annah heard her phone ring again and reluctantly answered it.

"Mother, are you trying to ignore me and your grandchildren? You are being very rude. We came down to spend our vacation with you, and you don't even bother to wait for us to get up or to look for us when you were here at breakfast so we could talk."

Annah gave Kat a long look. "Charlotte, Kat and I have several things to do today, and we had to hurry out. Take your children to the beach, and I'll see you tonight."

"Mother! We went to the beach yesterday. What else could we do? The children found it difficult to walk on crushed shells." She huffed. "Where are you?"

Annah didn't respond. She was watching for road signs along highway 19 going north.

"Mother, I'm talking to you. Where are you going? Can we meet you some place?"

Annah looked at Kat, who took the phone from her.

"Charlotte, your mother and I have plans that do not include you today. Take your children to the carnival outside Ionia. They'll love to go there rather than go with us." Then, she turned the phone off and handed it to her. "I'm sorry, hon; I had to do that to get her off your back."

Annah agreed with her. "You know, I'm thinking that I'm about to make that decision. I'm about to welcome a *total* change in my life, and I won't turn back."

She spotted an old sign pointing the way to Tarpon Springs. "We're here," she said. She drove the one mile and turned at the light. Signs with Greek letters and caricatures of fishes and sponges dotted the road on their way into town. It appeared to be alive with tourists and vendors selling from wooden tables along the sidewalk. Open doors to shops down the narrow streets invited people in as well.

"This looks like fun," Kat said, as she peered out the window.

Annah found a parking spot behind one shop and locked the car doors.

"Let's go find a set of clothes to fit my new personality," Annah said. "But, I don't see anyone wearing jeans; they're all in shorts and capris."

"You may have to settle for one of those flimsy cotton pants, but you'll love them."

They walked up and down the street entering and exiting little gift shops, examining trinkets and shells, and trying on clothes. Kat found a long muslin skirt and top, and she helped Annah try on pants and a loose-fitted top with a small nylon rope tied around it.

"Why, hon, you look just fine in clothes like that."

"These are comfortable," she said, as she searched through a table of t-shirts and held up a yellow one. "That's because I never had a need for them. You can't get dirty in $500 slacks and $300 tops."

Kat picked up the price tags on the clothes Annah was holding. "Do you think you can afford these? Seven dollars for the shirt and twelve for the pants? Just wait until you see the price of my flip-flops."

They walked over to the shoe table and Annah tried several on. Her final choice was a pair of open-toed sandals with burlap laces for $10. "These are so expensive; I'll have to sacrifice my lunch for them." This made them laugh.

"Annah, you're learning fast."

Annah felt extremely happy for the first time in years. She took her clothes and walked to the register to pay for them, but realized she had never used cash before to buy clothes. She only used credit cards. "Kat, do people charge for items as inexpensive as these?"

"What? Of course, they do. Just give her your card."

Annah opened her purse and pulled out her wallet. The cashier told her the total, and she the handed her the credit card. The woman took her card, ran it through the register, and handed it back to her without comment.

"See?" Kat asked. "No problem." Then she paid for her clothes.

Annah waited for the transaction and glanced around the shop. All through her life, she had purchased clothes in high-quality shops. Everything in this shop was inexpensive.

"I'm hungry. Let's go to that Greek restaurant, and have gyros for lunch. Have you ever eaten a gyro?"

"No, but I'm willing to try."

"They're delicious. They're made of lamb, with tomatoes and onions, and the most scrumptious yogurt sauce. You'll love it."

Annah clutched her bag of new clothes and hurried along the street toward the restaurant with Kat. By the time they finished shopping and eating, it was nearly evening. "Let's go," she said. "I can't tell you how much fun I've had today."

They drove for several miles without speaking.

"I don't know about you," Kat finally said. "But I'm ready to go back to the B&B and sit. My feet ache and my back's out of whack."

"Me, too, and a tall, cold Margarita will top the day off."

As soon as they returned to the B&B, Floyd phoned Annah with news. "Mrs. Puckett's great-grandson wants to keep the cottage and fix it up," he said. "Seems he's getting married and wants to move to Florida."

"I guess that's it then," she responded.

"I wonder if you'd like to take a drive with me tomorrow and look at another place. It's within the Ionia city limits, and it's almost move-in ready."

"Almost?" she asked. "What does it look like?"

"Well, it's fine inside. It's much like the style of Mrs. Puckett's cottage, but a little smaller. It needs a new roof. That last storm did damage to it, but I think you'd like it better than Mrs. Puckett's old cottage."

"Grandmama," Cherry said, running up to her and grabbing her around the waist.

"Ah, Floyd, can I call you back? I have my family here and I can't talk."

"You can't talk? Who's Floyd?" Charlotte asked.

She heard him say, he'd call back in fifteen minutes and hung up. "Charlotte, Floyd is the nephew of the lady who owns this B&B." She glanced up at her. "He was wondering if we wanted a tour of Ionia," she lied.

"Oh," Charlotte said. "Come on children, let's go take our baths. It's getting late. Daphne, you go first, and then Douglas, and then I'll help Cherry with hers. Shush, let's go." She turned away from Annah, but stopped short and looked straight at her. "Mother, where have you and Kat been, and why are you wearing those cheap clothes?"

Annah put her fists on her waist and glared at her.

"Okay, Mother, tomorrow you and I have a lot to discuss," she said, as she turned and followed the children up the stairs.

Annah watched them go. She didn't want to think about what Charlotte wanted to discuss. "Kat," Annah called, seeing her engrossed in a conversation with two ladies. "May I have a word with you?"

She lifted her head to see Annah hurrying toward her. "Yes, I saw Charlotte and the kids running up the stairs. Is everything okay?"

"Everything's fine, but I need to talk to you."

"Okay." She turned to the ladies. "I have to go now, we'll talk later." They nodded.

Moving her over to a corner, Annah said, "Floyd just called. It looks like I won't be able to buy that house. Anyway, he wants to show me another house tomorrow that needs a little restoration. Do you want to go?"

Kat gave her a funny face. "Annah! Didn't you say you wanted to stay away from him? Didn't we talk about forgetting him and the house?"

"Yes. Yes, we did, but I'd like to see another house. I would still like to buy a retreat away from home. I'll try not to encourage him or let him think I'm interested in him."

Kat shook her head no.

"Oh, come on. It'll be fun. Tomorrow is Tuesday, so we'll have to leave for home Wednesday if it's all right with Lola."

Kat walked toward the sliding patio doors and scanned the dark clouds and the rough waves on the ocean.

"He's going to call in a few minutes, and I'd like you to go with us."

Kat gawked. "I would love nothing more than to watch you both lusting after each other all morning."

Annah lifted her eyes to the ceiling. "Didn't I say there's nothing between us?"

She walked up to her. "Hon, think this over. It's nice that he wants to help you find a house here, but I think you had better go on home and really, and I mean really, think this whole relationship through before you get yourself in so deep you won't be able to climb out."

Annah sat down on an armchair and didn't answer her. Yes, she had better ask herself how she really felt about Floyd. Why was she being drawn to him? Was she so lonely she would fall for a man of his station? She had better take a long look at what the result of such a relationship would mean.

Then, the phone rang. "It's Floyd for you again, Annah," Roy said.

She gave Kat an uncertain look and returned to the counter to answer the phone. "Hello. Floyd, I've been thinking that I should go home and think seriously about buying a house here. Thank you for your help, but Kat and I are leaving in the morning for Rosewillow." She waited for his response, but only heard his breathing until he finally said, "Okay, doll. I hope to hear from you soon and I wish you a safe trip home."

Roy looked solemnly at her and said nothing. He left Kat and Annah alone in the parlor and went to bed.

—

Annah tossed all night. Finally, she peered at the clock radio. It read seven o'clock, two hours before nine. She could smell coffee brewing in the downstairs dining room and decided to go down there. She didn't want to wake Kat, so she quietly slipped out of the room.

Lola and Roy were preparing breakfast for the guests.

"Annah, you're up so early," Roy said, as he changed the tablecloth on the long, wide table. "Couldn't sleep?"

Annah watched him carefully straightening out the edges. "Yes, but I wanted to get up and have coffee."

"You're just in time. It's ready. By the way, I've wanted to tell you I'm glad you met Floyd. He's been a lonely man for over a year. Now, he spends too much time in that bar drinkin' when he's not workin' or fishin'." He brushed the top of the tablecloth. "He loves to fish. Why, he goes out every chance he gets and takes his boat up and down the river. Sometimes, he catches a baby alligator for fun and throws it back into the water. It's illegal to keep them."

"Just for fun?" Annah asked, holding her hot cup of coffee with both hands.

"Yep, down here anyway. People catch them for their meat and skins, but they have a license to do so. Some people do it illegally, but there are so many alligators around that I'm glad they're gettin' rid of them legally or illegally."

"I'm learning a lot about alligators recently," she said. "I'm glad you told me about Floyd. I know what it's like to lose a spouse. I lost mine about eight months ago, and it's taking me a long time to adjust being alone."

Roy stopped. "I'm sorry to hear that. You know, you kinda look like Teresa, she had long dark hair and pretty blue eyes like you, and she was as slim as you, too."

Annah lifted her cup to her lips, but stopped and asked, "I do?"

"Yep, you do." Roy gathered a fresh bouquet of flowers from a plastic bag and arranged them in a small vase with water in it. "You sure do."

She picked up the cup again and sipped the coffee.

Lola walked into the dining room with a number of plates. "Good mornin'," she said.

"I'm sorry to hear you're leavin' today. We'll miss you, and you know you're always welcome to stay here when you're visitin' Kat and her husband."

"Thank you. We've enjoyed getting to know you two." She picked up a frosted, sweet roll and took a small bite.

"Are you still thinkin' of buyin' a house here?" she said, setting the plates.

"I might. I like the area, but I'm going to think things over."

"Floyd knows the houses in this area. He's restored and remodeled many of them."

Charlotte came into room. "Mother, I heard you and Kat are going somewhere. Where are you going? Don't you see that we want you to do something with us today?"

"Dear, Kat and I are driving home. Kat has to be home to pack for their move."

"What? You're leaving already. Kat is moving? Why didn't you tell me all this and so we could follow you home?"

"We don't want you to follow us," Kat said.

"Mother, that's a terrible thing for her to say to me. Why do you let her butt in our conversation all the time?" She faced Kat. "Stay out of our conversations!"

Lola finished her chore and looked up at Charlotte. "My dear, I understand that they didn't know you and your children were comin' down here in the first place."

"So what! We're here and we're family. Families do things together."

Roy interrupted. "If you gals are goin' to drive home, you'd better get started. It's gettin' late and you'll hit rush-hour traffic."

Kat moved quickly. She ran up the stairs to grab their suitcases and purses.

"Of all things! You two are incorrigible," Charlotte said, as she stomped her foot.

Kat pulled Annah toward the front door. "Let's go."

"Sorry, dear, have fun with my grandchildren," Annah said as she gave Charlotte a quick hug and took Lola's hand in hers. "Thank you so much for your hospitality. I do hope we can return soon."

Kat rushed her out of the house glancing sideways at Charlotte, who looked infuriated.

CHAPTER SEVENTEEN

Annah could barely see the road ahead. She pulled the visor down over her windshield to cover the bright Wednesday morning sunshine as they traveled east on the drive to Rosewillow.

She and Kat had said their good-byes to Lola, Roy, Floyd, and the guests, as well as to Charlotte and her grandchildren. Charlotte decided to stay another day so the children could spend more time on the beach. Annah was glad for that. They wouldn't be following behind her on the highway. Before they left the B&B, Annah left a message on Emily's phone that they would be late getting home and to not worry about them.

"Hon, you look like you just saw a ghost. What's wrong?" Kat asked.

"I don't know. Maybe I'm being foolish." She looked over at her. "When you said you were moving to Florida, I became envious. I decided I could move, too, or find a retreat. I've never needed to make a decision to buy a house before, and I don't know how to go about doing it. That's why I thought I could talk to Floyd and see if he could help me."

Kat turned to her. "Excuse me, who are you again? Annah Gulliver, the woman that everyone looks to make important decisions, or Dr. Gulliver's stay-at-home wife?"

Annah leaned toward her. "Kat, I've been sheltered all my life, but I have never been a stay-at-home wife." She continued. "That bar scene was quite an experience, and yet I want to thank you for it. It was an eye-opener for me. That was the first time I've engaged with blue-collar people."

"I know it was scary for you, but I'm surprised at you. You've told me numerous times about your trips over to the islands with your grandmother when you were a child to visit Delsey's family. They were not wealthy, so you should have had the experience of being with ordinary folks."

"Yes, you're right, but that was different."

"No ma'am. Those people were honest and hard-working. You once said you wished you could live there forever with them."

"Yes. I pretended they were my family."

"See. People are the same inside regardless of how they look on the outside. They laugh, cry, love, and hate the same way everyone else does." See paused. "I'll put it a different way. Everyone puts their pants on the same way."

Annah shook her head. "Kat, do you really know what I'm saying? Maybe I don't belong in a middle class community. Maybe I wouldn't fit in…and it's that man."

"What about that man?"

"Floyd. He fascinates me, and I can't stop thinking about him. Am I crazy?"

"There you go again. We've already talked about you two not being compatible even though he's a decent individual."

"I know I don't fit into his crowd, but I can't stop wondering about him."

"Hon, you know why? You spent thirty-five years living with a man who was cold to you and never showed you much love. You're hungry for affection. Didn't you once tell me Henry used to give you those strong feelings even when Jackson was alive?"

Annah looked out the side window. "I have wanted to tell you a secret about Jackson."

Kat gave Annah her full attention.

"Jackson had an affair. He had a mistress for ten years. I saw her at the funeral, but didn't know who she was until recently when she called and stopped over to pick up her letters to him. She said some nasty things to me. Charlotte took her call and warned me about the letters she wanted. I searched Jackson's desk and found a folder with the letters in it. I only read one because it hurt too much to read any more."

Kat slumped back in her seat. "Oh, no."

"That's what I said." She rubbed her forehead. "I'm going to shred all of them without reading them as soon as I get home."

Kat didn't say anything for quite a while, and then asked, "Did she say she'd come back again for them?"

"No, thank God. I think she felt she had had her say. She wanted to hurt me and she did. Very much." Annah continued. "I guess I knew something was different with Jackson years ago when he stopped wanting sex, but I shoved the possibility of him having an affair away so I wouldn't be hurt. What I should have done was confront him and, if he admitted having another woman, I should have divorced him. After all, he was living in my family home, not his."

Kat shook her head negatively. "It's over, Annah. Just remember the good times when you were first married and you shared a good life together. I know it'll take time for you to forget and forgive, but do it."

"I'm not going to let another man hurt me again."

"I can understand your feelings. I hope for your sake, that'll never happen to you again."

"Another thing," Annah said. "That woman told me that the people of Rosewillow knew about his affair, and I was a laughing stock. Did you ever hear this gossip?"

"No. If any of the women in our club knew, they wouldn't have told me since we know each other too well."

They drove on in silence watching the scenery and highway signs, and then Kat said, "Well, hon, once you're away from Ionia, you'll know what you want to do. Try to forget Floyd and buying a house for now. Whatever you decide, the hurt Jackson caused you will never leave, but time will help you face it. You have to go on with your life."

Annah stepped on the gas pedal. She wanted to forget Floyd and getting home sooner would make it easier.

—

Seemingly out of nowhere, a car slammed into theirs, causing Annah to lose control and race across the on-coming lane. Her car rolled once and landed upside down in a creek bed. Water roiled in from Annah's open window, while she and Kat hung upside down helplessly strapped in their seats.

Kat screamed hysterically. "Help. Someone help us. Please." She struggled with the seat belt and finally dropped into the muddy water growing deeper over the ceiling, which was now upside down. "Annah, are you okay?"

Annah hung beside her, her hair and arms dangling.

"Help," Kat yelled as loudly as she could, terror stricken and fearful of Annah's condition, but the sound of rushing cars muted her voice and they didn't stop. Kat pulled at Annah's arm to waken her, but she hung there unconscious. With muddy hands, she lifted Annah and unlocked her seatbelt while bracing her body to catch it when it fell. Using all her strength, she turned her upright. She tried to roll one window to open it and climb out, but mud pressed against it keeping it tightly shut.

"God, help us," she cried. "Annah, wake up." She gently

positioned her head to see if there were bruises, but only succeeded in greasing her face with her dirty hands. She slapped her several times to wake her up, but she didn't stir. Annah's head and body fell against the window on her side.

In a panic, Kat found her purse, covered in mud, and slipped her cell phone out. It was clean except for her wet fingers on the buttons. She wiped her fingers against her blouse and trembled while she pushed the numbers to call 911 in hopes of getting the Florida State Patrol. Now, she sat in water filling over her lap.

"Hello, this is the…." the voice answered, but Kat stopped the woman from identifying herself.

"Lady, we've been in an accident. We're upside down in a creek bed with muddy water rising in our car, and I can't wake up my friend. She hit her head and is unconscious."

"What are your names? Are you hurt also? What highway are you on? What is the make of your car and the license number? Do you see a mile marker near you?"

Kat began to burst into sobs and could hardly speak. "You're asking me too many questions." Finally, she calmed down, and in gun-shot fashion, said, "I'm Kat Holister and my friend is Annah Gulliver, and we're upside down in our car in a creek bed, and I don't know the license plate number. I don't know what highway we're on, except we left Ionia on 75 and drove a little ways northeast, and I don't know anything about a mile marker. Please hurry. We were driving east on our way to South Carolina, but the sun got in her eyes, and another car sideswiped us and kept on going and knocked us off the road, and...."

"Okay, ma'am, we'll have patrol cars out looking for you along I-75 leading out of Ionia. Are there landmarks nearby that you can identify?"

Kat thought a moment. She had been concentrating so much on Annah's shocking disclosure about Jackson that she hadn't paid attention to what they were passing. "It's been over an hour since we left Ionia. I don't know…, but we were going east and now we're lying in a creek bed."

"Okay, ma'am, please calm down. I'll have an ambulance come for your friend. Help is on the way. Sit tight."

Kat thought that was the most ridiculous statement she had ever heard. What else could she do.?

She waited for what seemed like hours. In the meantime, shaking, she called Spencer to tell him what happened. He said he would get there as fast as he could. "Where are you?" he asked. She didn't know, but she knew they were east of Ionia, and she would call him again as soon as the state patrol came.

Fifteen minutes after her call to Spencer, a motor home

stopped alongside the road next to them. The driver and a teenage boy jumped out and ran toward them.

"God almighty, what happened here?" the man asked as his shoes sank into the muddy slope and creek. "You all right in there? You hurt?"

Kat knocked on her window and moved her head from side to side, and then pointed to Annah. She hollered through the window. "My friend isn't moving. We were run off the road by a maniac driver, and he didn't stop to help us."

"Come on, Josh, let's get these women out of there." They worked their way through the swampy water to open the car door. "It's locked. Can you open it?"

"It's not locked. The door is stuck in the mud."

"Josh, run and get me the shovel, quick like." The teenager made his way back out of the creek and over to the side of the motor home to open a small storage door and retrieve a shovel.

A woman carrying a blanket came out of the motor home. Her two young daughters followed her. "Good Lord, Frank. Can we help?"

"Yeah, lay that blanket down on the ground for these poor women to lay on when we get them out." She and the girls did just that, unfolding and spreading the blanket flat on the shoulder of the road.

With shovel in hand, the man tried to dig the mud away from the car door, but the water kept washing it back. "Man. I won't be able to get these women out of there."

Then a Jeep with two young men stopped behind the motor home. They could see what the people were doing and saw the car upside down, as they peered down at them.

"Hey there, can we help?" one of them asked.

Looking up, the man yelled back, "Yes, come help us roll this car right side up." He tossed the shovel onto the bank.

The young men rushed down to meet them and all four of them rocked the car, but it only dug deeper into the creek bottom. Kat found herself being tossed around inside and banging her body against the door. Annah's body rolled side to side, bumping her head once more on the window.

In a final attempt to turn the car upright, they lifted it enough to open Kat's side. She climbed out covered with mud and silt. Returning for Annah, the men reached inside the car and dragged her out, and then one man wrapped his arms around her body and carried her up the incline to lay her on the blanket.

Minutes later, two patrol cars came careening to a stop along the road.

Kat saw them coming toward her, but her concern was to see if Annah was awake.

"Ma'am, are you okay? How's the other woman?" the officer asked, seeing Annah lying on the blanket.

Kat couldn't stop herself from trembling in order to speak to them.

An officer approached and knelt down beside her. "You okay?" he asked.

Kat's trembling grew worse. "I'm so sorry. I'm so sorry, Annah," she said to her unconscious body.

The officer stood up. "Does anyone know what happened?" he asked the other people.

"No, sir," Frank said. "We were high enough in our vehicle to see the car turned upside down and decided to stop just in case someone was in it. Well, we were surprised when we saw these two women in there. My son and I tried to help them get out, but couldn't and thanks to these young men, we were able to roll the car enough to pull them out." He continued after waving his hand at the men. "We're sure glad they came along." One young man leaned over and brushed his pants and the other crossed his arms.

"Okay, we'll wait here for the ambulance, which should be here in a few minutes and when this lady," the officer said, pointing to Kat, "calms down, we'll get the report."

"Ma'am," he said to Kat, as he knelt in front of her again, "When you're able, I will have to ask you some questions."

Kat nodded, still shaking. The woman from the motor home sat down beside her and placed her arms around her shoulders.

Soon, a fire truck and an ambulance came roaring toward them. The emergency medical technicians quickly saw the situation. One rolled out a gurney and two of them, along with two firemen, rolled Annah onto a short wooden pallet and walked her over to place her on the gurney. Within minutes, an EMT prepared her for travel to a hospital in Tampa after taking readings of her condition.

Kat steadied herself to give the officer a complete report of the accident. She gave him their names. "I'm Katherine Hollister and my friend is Annah Gulliver." She said the driver who hit them never stopped, and she was thankful there was no on-coming traffic when they skidded across the other side of the road. The people were asked by the officer to stay for a little while longer to be witnesses to what they saw, and Kat was assured a tow-truck would come and haul the car back to the impound lot in Tampa. In the meantime, they said she could ride beside Annah in the ambulance to be with her.

"Please get our purses and suitcases out of the car so we can clean up in the hospital and change clothes," Kat asked.

"Yes, ma'am," the young men responded, immediately heading back down to the car.

Through her tears, Kat thanked all the people who stopped and helped them, and climbed into the ambulance. The siren rang as it turned onto the highway. Sitting next to Annah, she clutched her hand and held it tightly, saying, "Annah, if only I had not told you about Ionia and agreeing to go on a vacation there, all this would never have happened. I'm so sorry." She stared out the back two windows, replaying the accident scene over and over in her mind.

—

Emily heard Annah's message that they were on their way home. She had so much more to talk to her about and she missed her. She strolled over to her father's office, opened the door, and stared into it. It was eerily quiet. Papa would never come back. She scanned his book shelves and felt consumed with despondency at his now clean desk. This wasn't like him. When alive, papers, notebooks, and open research books, laid scattered with his writings. His life was his work and that made it even sadder for her. He was never there emotionally to talk to her, as a father should.

Papa, if you only knew how many times I wanted to just be near you and talk about father and daughter things, she thought. *Was Mom as sad as I am that Papa never had time for her? Was she filling her life with people outside our family because he didn't give her his attention?*

"Emily," Delsey said, as she touched her arm.

"Oh, Delsey, you startled me. I didn't hear you coming. I thought you were still away with you family."

"We came back this morning. Can I help you? You look tired and unhappy."

Emily moved away from the door frame. "I don't know. I guess I still can't get over Papa dying." Her head and posture fell.

"My Emily, your Papa is in a better place. He has Jesus walking by his side."

She walked over to the stairway, sat down on the second step, and wrapped her arms around herself. "I want him to be alive."

Delsey strolled over to her. "We all do, baby doll. We all do."

"You knew that Michael packed up and left here didn't you?"

"No, but it's best that he's gone. That young man was not for you."

"I thought we were going to be married someday, but now it's all over. He was jealous of Jimmy, who came over to get the history of our house for his newspaper article. I didn't even know Jimmy before he came. I showed him around and when he went to leave, Michael saw him hug me. It was all a misunderstanding."

Delsey clasped her hands over her round stomach. Her face

broke out in a wide smile.

Emily frowned and gave her a questioning look. "What?"

"Things are going to be all right."

"Delsey, you always do that. How do you know? You give me the creeps."

"Emily, good Jesus knows best. You forget that man now. He wasn't for you." She let her cry. "I've been here since you were a baby and watched you grow up. Why, you're like my own child. You go on now. He," she said, pointing to the ceiling, "has something better for you." She patted her arm and walked away, but stopped, as if she heard something Emily couldn't. Then, Delsey froze.

"What?" Emily asked, watching her.

Emily went over to her and studied her face. "Do you hear something? What's wrong?"

Her eyes glazed over, and she gave Emily a serious look. "Emily," she said. "Just be glad that man's gone. That's all."

CHAPTER EIGHTEEN

Lola read Charlotte the message stating that Annah and Kat had been in an accident. Kat had called from the Tampa Hospital. Upon hearing the news, Charlotte froze. She seemed not to understand her.

"What? My mother has been in an accident? What happened?"

"Kat said your mother is in the ICU. That's all I know." She handed the small piece of paper over to her. "She gave me a number for you to call."

Lola watched Charlotte as she tightened the towel around her waist to keep her wet swimsuit from dripping on the floor. She and the children had taken a morning swim. She took the message and waved to the children to follow her up to their room. Once she was out of sight, she called Floyd and notified him. "Maybe you could drive there and see her."

He pressed his cell phone against his ear and wiped his forehead with a much used handkerchief. "What happened? Is she okay?"

"You know as much as I do about it." She leaned her elbows on the counter and chewed on the end of a pen.

Roy came through the door. "Lola, I heard what you said. Should we drive to the hospital and see what we can do to help?"

Lola leaned her head to hold the phone on her shoulder. "I'm talkin' to Floyd now. I think he'll go up there to see. We have guests comin' in a half hour. I can't leave and I'll need your help here."

Floyd immediately began to pack his construction tools in the back of his pickup. He had spent the day restoring another house. "Lola, I'm on my way. In the meantime, will you have Roy drive over to my house and take care of Roscoe? He needs to go out and eat his dinner." He didn't have time to go home and change from his sweaty work clothes to a clean shirt and pair of Levis.

"Okay." Lola hung up. "Good Lord, Roy, I hope she's okay. Right now I have to fix lunch for everyone, and you'll have to set the table; and then Floyd wanted to know if you'd drive over to his house and take carc of Roscoc."

Charlotte packed up quickly, settled her account, and called Emily and Morgan to tell them to meet her at the Tampa General Hospital. She would give them directions as soon as she could. Then, she and the children left the B&B, and headed north.

Emily hung up the phone after hearing Charlotte become hysterical, and then called Morgan. He said he heard the news from Charlotte and thought it would be a good idea if they both drove down together. Then, she spoke to Delsey. "Mom's been in an accident. Morgan and I will be driving together to Tampa, just as soon as we're packed and ready to go."

Delsey stood in front of Emily without speaking for a moment. "What else did Charlotte tell you?" she asked. "Did Charlotte say anything about her injuries?"

"Injuries?" Emily ran her hands through her hair and swept it back. "Only that Mom and Kat were at the Tampa Hospital. It must be serious or she wouldn't be in the ICU."

Delsey tightened the bow on the back of her apron. "Emily, your mother needs you. I'll ask Jerome if he'll follow you down there."

Emily shook her head. "No, Spencer will be there for Kat. Charlotte is there already, so I don't think Jerome needs to follow us."

"Then you two be careful driving, and call us if you need him."

Emily took Delsey's arm. "Delsey, why didn't you tell me something had happened? I think you knew something was wrong and you didn't tell me. I would have driven down there sooner."

Delsey put her hand on Emily's. "I didn't want to scare you. Now, how can I help you so you can go quickly?"

Rushing from her side to run up and pack, she said, "I can get everything packed myself, Delsey. Please see if there are snacks for us to take with us."

Overhearing their conversation, Renaldo said to Delsey, "I'll get some food and drinks for the long drive. Lucia, come help me."

Delsey raised her arms and closed her eyes. "Yes, Sir, changes are starting. Please take care of Annah."

Floyd called the Sheriff's Office. They told him the details of the accident and said the woman's car was being towed to the Tampa impound lot. "No," he told them. "Please have the tow truck bring the BMW down to Ionia to Ed's Garage."

Floyd left Ionia immediately. He hoped he wouldn't be held up in traffic. *However long it takes, I'll be there,* he thought. *Wasn't it enough that I lost Teresa and sat in the hospital watching her die a slow death with cancer? Now, I'm rushing to see another woman lying in a hospital bed. Is she all right? How bad are her injuries?*

He took his cap off and placed it on the seat next to him. *What is it about Annah that I care so much about her? I've only just begun to know her. Yes, she looks like Teresa, even her hair and eyes are the same. Well, that shouldn't make me want to get involved with another woman right now,* he thought, but she captivated him. It was more than her looks; she had a quality about her that was deeper than that. She was serene, gentle, polished, and engaging, and since the first day he set eyes on her, he couldn't stop thinking about her.

He knew where the hospital was. He had driven there for medical tests of his own. He stopped at a traffic light, stared up at the tall, sprawling building in front of him, and cringed. He hoped Annah would recover from whatever harm had come to her. Driving into the parking lot, he found a place close to the entrance and shut off the engine.

In the side mirror, he checked his hair, grabbed a comb from his back pocket, and quickly ran it through. He put his cap on, but changed his mind and put it back on the seat. Was he nervous, he asked himself? "Oh, God, let her be okay," he said, as he slammed the door and hurried toward the entrance.

Once inside, he asked the lady at the information desk for directions to the ICU and headed for the elevator. When he reached the room, he saw Kat sitting beside her. Annah's face displayed bruises, and she had cold packs wrapped around the top and side of her head.

"Annah," he said from the doorway, "you're awake." He quickly went over to her and reached for her hand. "I came to see how you're doing."

Annah turned her head slightly and with a hoarse voice said, "Oh, Floyd, I wish you hadn't seen me in this condition."

He pulled a chair over to her and sat down after saying a brief hello to Kat. "Tell me about your accident. How badly are you hurt?"

Kat said she felt partially to blame for Annah's head injury because when the driver hit their car, she flew sideways into Annah and that's what caused her head to hit the side window. Annah hushed her and told Floyd it was not her fault. It was the impact of one car hitting another.

Floyd put his hand up to stop them. "It doesn't matter who did what. It matters that it was a hit-and-run accident and that person should be charged for causing it and driving away."

She put her hand on his arm. "I was knocked out. The emergency room nurse told me they immediately rushed me down to get an x-ray and a CAT scan of my head. I don't remember what happened after the car rolled, and I was surprised to wake up in this room with Kat sitting beside me. She filled me in on most of it. Now we're waiting for the results of my tests."

"The doctor should be in to talk with us pretty soon," Kat said, wringing her hands and remembering to call Spencer. "Excuse me. I'll be right back." She stood up quickly to leave.

"Just a minute," Floyd said to her. "Did *you* get hurt?"

"Mercy me, I'm okay. Just a few bruises," she said, closing the door behind her.

Annah watched her go and, after removing her hand, asked Floyd, "I wonder what happened to my car and all my things in it?"

He reached for her hand, put it back on his arm, and placed his other hand on top. "I had your car towed to Ed's Garage in Ionia, so you could decide what to do with it when you're out of the hospital. The police said it's totaled, but that will be up to the claims adjuster. You'll have to call you're insurance company when you get out of the hospital."

She looked back at him. "It's one more problem I have to deal with."

"When you get back to Ionia, we'll go over and clean the car out. Ed is a friend of mine. He won't touch your personal belongings."

Kat returned to the room and sat down. "Spence is on his way. He says he'll get directions to the hospital when he gets near here, but it may be early tomorrow morning."

The door opened and the doctor came in. "Hello," he said, as held his hand out to shake hers. "I'm the neurosurgeon on call today. Are you family members?" he asked, looking at Floyd and Kat.

"They're not my family," she said, glancing at Kat and looking up at Floyd. "They're my good friends." She closed her eyes and knew she had given in to her feelings toward Floyd. He had come in her time of need and was no longer a stranger. Now, she would have to deal with her emotions and his attention to her.

"Are you willing to have your friends hear my report?" the doctor asked, taking off his glasses. "Or, should I tell them to leave the room?"

Annah looked at them. "They may hear your report."

He put his glasses back on. "Mrs. Gulliver, your pictures look good for now. You had a minor concussion, and I don't see any cracks in your skull. We'll have to continue to watch for bleeding between the skull and the subdural area of your brain. He looked down at his clipboard and scanned the facts written on it.

Confused, the three of them stared at him.

"Bleeding in her brain?" Kat asked.

"I'm sorry," he said, as he looked up at Kat. "I should go over the results with you first, Mrs. Gulliver. The CAT scan revealed that because of your concussion, you have had a very slight unilateral subdural hematoma rise on the left side of your head. Since this happened only today, this shouldn't be serious, but we will have to watch it and give you at least one more CAT scan to see if the blood now forming develops into a major condition that needs surgery."

Horrified, Kat's mouth dropped open as she asked, "Surgery? On her head?" The doctor talked directly to her. "Yes, ma'am, subdural hematomas can be dangerous. If they are left to swell, the pressure from extensive blood forming in that area of the brain may cause an individual to lose the ability to function and possibly to die. I don't want to scare anyone. This can be remedied by surgery and the individual will go on to live a normal life."

Floyd held Annah's hand and squeezed it.

"How long will it be before my next CAT scan?" Annah asked.

"Let's wait a week. For now, I would like you to spend the rest of today and night here in the hospital to rest. It's important for us to watch for any nausea, vomiting, or dizziness." He studied Annah's face and touched her head, gently separating layers of her hair. "You will have a bump on your head for a while. I'll have the nurse report back to me, and if it is still as prominent tomorrow, we'll have you stay another night to keep checking on you. Otherwise, I'll sign a release, and you may go home with instructions to return in exactly one week." He slid the clipboard under his arm and asked, "Any questions?"

Annah glanced at Floyd and Kat and said, "No, I guess not."

"I'll have a nurse make an appointment for you," he said. "Will one of you be available to take care of her at home and make sure she'll be back here for the appointment?"

"I'll be available to care for her," Kat said.

Floyd looked at the doctor. "Of course," he said. "And, I'll make sure she's back here for her appointment."

"Then, I'll check on you tomorrow morning," the doctor said and walked out of the room.

The three of them glanced at each other and up at the television. Floyd moved his chair closer to Annah and took her hand again. Kat blew her nose on several tissues and wiped away on-coming tears.

Annah quietly said, "I never thought that I would one day be the beneficiary of my husband's research in neurology. He gave his life to his work, and I didn't appreciate it, as I should have. Now, it's my responsibility to see that his research continues to add this knowledge for other's sakes. I'll submit his paperwork to the Society when I get home."

Floyd squeezed her hand and turned his head away from Annah's face. She closed her eyes again after seeing his fear.

CHAPTER NINETEEN

Charlotte and the children quietly slipped into Annah's hospital room. She was asleep. "Shhh," she cautioned them. "Let's not wake her." They moved chairs around to sit in, and then waited. Annah appeared to not hear them.

Charlotte sat beside Annah and observed the IV pumping saline into her arm and the cold packs wrapped around the left side of her head and face. Her face glowed with swollen purplish and green bruises.

"Now your grandmother is hurt, but she'll get better, and then we'll drive her home to take care of her."

"But, Momma, I want to go swimming again. You said we were going to stay another day and you broke your promise," Daphne said, pouting.

"Yeah, you promised," Douglas, added. "Take us back to the beach."

"I told you to be quiet. You're going to wake your grandmother, and she'll be mad at you." Charlotte pulled the white sheet and cotton blanket up on Annah's shoulders as she whispered. "I can't always do what you two want me to do."

"But you promised," Cherry said. "I want to go swimming again, too. Grandmama is asleep anyway." She stomped her foot.

Floyd and Kat returned to the room. They had gone downstairs to the cafeteria for coffee and sweet cakes. "Charlotte," Kat said. "I didn't expect you so soon."

"Who's this?" Charlotte asked, scowling at Floyd.

Floyd straightened his back and frowned.

"Charlotte, this is Floyd, a friend of ours," Kat said. "He's from Ionia, and he knows your mother. He's concerned about her after hearing we were in an accident. Floyd, meet Charlotte, Annah's older daughter and these are her children, Cherry, Daphne, and Douglas."

"Nice to meet you," he said to Charlotte with a look of displeasure and nodded to the children.

Charlotte's eyes scanned Floyd's work clothes, splattered with paint, and his hair flattened by his baseball cap. He also smelled of cigar smoke.

Kat broke into the uneasiness between them. "Your mother has had a concussion from the accident and will need a lot of rest. She'll be here at least until tomorrow. We talked with the doctor, and we'll keep an eye on her to see if she experiences any after effects from hitting her head on the side window of her car when we rolled." Kat went on to explain what happened in the accident and how Annah must have another CAT scan in a week.

"A week? Why should she drive all the way back here in a week for one test?" Charlotte asked. "We'll see about that. I'll take her home, and we'll find a good doctor around Rosewillow, even if we have to drive to Charleston."

Kat glanced at Floyd. "No, Charlotte. Floyd and I discussed taking her to Ionia and having her stay at the B&B. She needs lots of rest. I can stay at the B&B while she's there to help her, and he offered to bring her back here for the test."

Charlotte shrieked. "Well, who does he think he is?"

Floyd tightened his arms around his chest and peered at her.

"And," Kat began. "You should know that Spencer and I will be moving within two to three weeks to our new home in Ionia. The house is still under construction, but should be completed by then. I can stay here until she's well."

"Is that why you wanted my mother to drive down here with you? Look what happened!"

Hearing the commotion, Annah woke up, startled to see her daughter, grandchildren, Kat, and Floyd standing in the room. "What's going on?" she asked.

Charlotte fumed. "Mother, I am so worried about you. I heard you were in an accident and I packed up our things from the B&B and brought the children here with me."

Annah looked around the room, not knowing what to say.

"Annah, we've told Charlotte all about the accident and your condition. We also told her Floyd would drive you back to Ionia and take you to the B&B where we stayed, so you could be close to the hospital to get your second CAT scan." She paused. "She is not happy about this."

Floyd slid a chair to the other side of Annah's bed, across from Charlotte, and promptly sat down.

Charlotte looked at him with disgust. "Mother, I can't believe you're hanging around with a man like this," she said, pointing at Floyd.

Kat yanked Charlotte's arm and dragged off her chair and out of the room. The children ran after them. "We need to talk, young lady, and leave the two of them alone."

Annah and Floyd listened to the outcry from Charlotte and the children as they rushed away. A few seconds later, it was quiet, except for the normal sounds of moving hospital carts and staff shuffling monitors through the hallway.

Floyd leaned his face down toward Annah and lifted his brow. "That's your daughter?"

Relieved they were gone, she sighed. "Yes, but she takes more after her father than me."

He rested his arm on the bed. "You say he died eight months ago? If she's like her father, then I'm glad I never met him."

She moved back from him, startled by his discernment. "Yes, in fact, he was a bit domineering. Charlotte does take after him."

"My wife and I never had children. We had hoped to have them."

"Were you happy anyway?" she asked, laying her head sideways on the pillow.

"Sure. We filled our time doing things together. We had fun because we were financially set and were free to travel and do what we pleased. Teresa worked as a secretary in a law firm and loved her job, and I was a general contractor. Life was great until the economy went sour, and I lost my shirt. At about the same time, she died of cancer, and I just gave it all up and moved to Florida to live around Lola and Roy. Lola's the only family I have now."

"I'm so sorry you lost your wife."

"Don't be. I'm living the life of Riley right now. I work when I please and hang around with my friends at the bar whenever I can. We play poker and challenge each other at the pool table. I also like to fish. Yeah, when I'm out on the river, I'm in a world of my own."

Annah listened and smiled. "Would you believe I've never fished a day in my life?"

"What? An all-American woman like you has never fished?"

"That's right. I wouldn't know one fish from another. They all look alike. All I know about are shellfish, like shrimp and lobsters, which were bought off commercial fishing boats along the wharf. Sometimes…" She was going to say, my cook would purchase them at our local fish shop and cook them for us, but stopped herself.

Floyd sat up. "Sometimes?"

She struggled to think of how to continue her sentence. "Sometimes, my son would go fishing and bring in larger ocean fish." She did not want to say he had a rather large sailboat. That would lead to a discussion on how large, what does he do for a living to afford one, and she might let on that they have money.

"Well, lady," Floyd said. "You've got a date. I'm taking you fishing on the prettiest river you ever laid your eyes on." With that, he leaned over, picked up her hand, and kissed it.

Charlotte walked in and saw him kiss her hand. "Mother, what is that man doing?"

Kat stormed in after hearing Charlotte raise her voice. "Charlotte, didn't we just talk about your poor manners? Do we have to go down to the reception area again and discuss this all over again?"

"Grandmama," Cherry said, dancing. "They had a play area and lots of toys. I got to play with them downstairs."

Charlotte pouted and took Cherry's hand. As she ushered all three of them out, she said, "Let's find a motel for the night." She stopped outside the door. "Mother, we'll be back in the morning. If they let you go, I'll drive you home," she said and stormed from the room.

Floyd and Kat held each other's eyes.

"Floyd," Annah began, "don't let her bother you. I want to have you drive me to Ionia, and I'll stay at your aunt's place this week so I'll be close to the hospital for the tests. Would you do a favor for me and call her to reserve the same room that Kat and I stayed in last time? It's peaceful there. Spencer is coming down to be with Kat, so I'm sure they will find a motel of their own to stay in."

"I can't think of anything better I'd rather do," he said. "We have a date in Ionia on a pretty little river, remember?"

Kat watched them as their faces grew close and their eyes met. She swooned as she left the room, and Annah almost died of embarrassment.

Emily, Morgan, and Spencer arrived in the middle of the night and a nurse guided them to Annah's room. They peeked in to see her, but she was sleeping soundly. Kat woke from the recliner in the room to see them standing at the door. She followed Spencer out. They would wait in Ionia to hear further news of Annah.

Emily and Morgan decided to find a nearby motel for the night and found one close to the hospital. They had ridden down to Tampa in Morgan's sports car, and he stated that he didn't want to leave his car parked in that motel parking lot where vandals would break into it and destroy it.

"Oh, Morgan, quit your fussing. Where else do you think you

can park it? This motel is all lit up, and no one's going to vandalize your car," Emily said.

"Well, I don't trust this area or city. There're too many gangs. You can check in and get a room, but I'm going to sleep in my car so I can make sure no one breaks into it."

"Suit yourself, but I think you're stupid. I'm going to have a good night's sleep, and you can stay up all night protecting your car."

"Thanks for that. I'm not stupid for thinking this way. You're too naïve, sis. You've been sheltered all your life. I've seen things you haven't. There're creeps out there that would rather kill you than smile at you."

"Morgan, you're a pain to be with sometimes. Good night then," Emily, said as she grabbed her backpack and exited the car. She looked forward to a good night's sleep in a decent, air conditioned room. The humid air hung heavily over the city and her hair had gone limp. She envisioned clean sheets and a hot shower waiting for her.

Morgan locked the doors of his car, let the driver's seat lay backward, crossed his arms, and closed his eyes. He tried to sleep, but drops of rain turned into a shower so he had to close his windows to avoid getting wet. Soon, the interior of the car heated up until he opened the window on the passenger side to let in some air.

The next thing he saw was a gun barrel sticking through the window.

"Open up or I'll shoot your ass," a man yelled through the window. "I said open this door or I'll kill you, man." He lifted what looked like a tire iron and aimed it at the window.

Frightened, Morgan sat straight up and fiddled to unlock the door. His hand shook as he felt for it in the dark.

Another man pounded on the window on the driver's side and shouted at him. "I'm gonna smash this window if you don't hurry up," he said.

Morgan unlocked the doors and the man on his side yanked at his arm, pulled him out, and dragged him to the ground. He kicked him, dropped the iron, and beat his head and face with his fists until his jaw broke. Then, the two men jumped into the car, revved the engine, backed up, and squealed out of the parking lot.

Morgan lay bleeding on the ground. His head swam making him dizzy and the excruciating pain in his jaw caused tears to run down his face. He opened his eyes but couldn't see well from where he lay, and his ribs ached from being kicked. He laid there for quite some time before a car's headlights shone on him. A woman climbed out of her car and ran to him.

"Are you okay?" she asked. "I'll get help." She ran quickly into the motel and the receptionist called the police.

It took only five minutes for a police car with its red, white, and blue lights flashing to arrive in the parking lot and stop in front of Morgan. Two officers came toward him holding flashlights. One returned to the vehicle to call an ambulance, while the other talked to Morgan.

With great effort, he told the policeman who knelt down beside him that he couldn't identify the men because it was raining and too dark. He said they had stolen his car, laptop, clothes, and everything else he had of value in his car. The officer stood and wrote notes on a small tablet to make his report. "Can you give me a description of the men?"

"It was too dark, but I'm sure they were in their twenties. The one that beat me up was taller than me. I don't know about the other guy," Morgan said as well as he could through his broken jaw and swelling chin. "They wore jeans and t-shirts."

The officer wrote more notes. "Sir, I'm afraid to tell you that you'll probably never see your car again. Thieves steal cars for parts, and it doesn't take long to break them down. As for your other items, forget about them, too. They'll be hocked or pawned before we can recover them." He jotted down a few more notes. "Did they take your wallet?"

Morgan slipped his hand into his rear pocket and found the wallet missing. "Yeah. Those schmucks took that, too." He tried to lift himself up, but the pain in his ribs and jaw caused him to lie down again.

"Well, sir. We've called an ambulance for you, and they should be here any minute. Do you have family or friends nearby to notify of your condition and where you'll be?"

Fatigued, he stretched his arms over the pavement. With difficulty he said, "My sister is in this motel. I'll give you her name, and I'd appreciate it if you'd tell her."

As he spoke, the ambulance came through the parking lot with its siren on. Morgan struggled to sit as the emergency personnel climbed out and headed toward him. They rolled a gurney beside him and lifted him onto it. Once in the back of the ambulance, they drove to the hospital, the same one where Annah lay sleeping.

Emily had heard the sirens, but considered them part of the Tampa scene and ignored them. After all, this was a big city and there was always something happening, either drug busts, car accidents, or crime. It was no concern of hers.

She stepped out of the shower and dried off. Her damp and dusty clothes lay piled in the corner of the bathroom. She looked forward to watching the news on the television, have a cigarette, or two, and going to bed.

Then came a knock on the door.

"Oh! Who's there?" she asked, hoping it was Morgan instead of a stranger wanting into her room.

"Police. We're here to talk with you about your brother."

What if it wasn't the police? What if it was someone to fear? She covered herself with a large towel. "Wait a minute. I have to dress," she said, as she ran to her backpack and pulled out a set of clothes and underwear. She could hardly get her clothes on because of her nervousness.

Five minutes went by and the officer on the other side of the door knocked again. "Miss, we don't have much more time to wait."

"How do I know you're a real policeman?" She heard a loud sigh and another knock.

"Emily Gulliver, your brother, Morgan, has been badly beaten and has had his car stolen. He gave us your name, and we acquired your room number from the front desk. I'm here to give you this information about him."

"What's happened?" she yelled. She opened the door and stared at the officer, who showed her his badge. He held a clipboard with papers attached.

"Miss Gulliver, your brother is a victim of a crime. Two men attacked him, stole his car, and beat him up. We've taken him by ambulance to Tampa General Hospital."

Emily ran her hand through her wet tangled hair. "Is he all right?"

"It appears he has a broken jaw. Other than that, the doctors will know more." He dropped his hand and held the clipboard to his side. "Do what you have to do," he said and walked away.

Emily watched him go down the long hallway. "Oh, God, please help us," she said. "How am I going to get to the hospital?" She shut the door, turned around and stared at the room, and decided to call a taxi. "I've got to see him." She put on her shoes, grabbed her purse, closed the door behind her, and rushed to the elevator to leave the motel. She would worry about her tangled, wet hair later when she returned to the room.

—

The EMTs rolled Morgan through the Emergency Room door. He couldn't open his jaw more than an inch to speak, but he made everyone know how angry he was. "I'm going to make those guys pay for this," he mumbled. "They're not going to get away with this. They're not going to take my car. They're not going to keep my laptop with all my personal information, nor my wallet with my credit cards and license." Then, he remembered they stole his cell phone, too.

"Sir," a male nurse said to him. "Please stop talking. You're only going to make things worse for yourself." He rolled him into the admitting room.

"Do you know how inconvenient this is to me?" he spit through his teeth.

"Yes, sir. We'll take care of you, but you must stop trying to talk."

Morgan felt pain everywhere in his body, from his head to his ribs to his back where they pounded and punched on him. "Ackkkkkk," he cried.

Emily heard his scream as she entered the ER. She went to the nurse's desk. "That's my brother screaming, may I see him?"

"Miss, you'll have to sign in first. What's his name?" Emily gave her his name and looked it up on her computer. "He's still in triage and then the nurse will determine where he should go from there. We'll let you know when you can see him."

Exasperated, Emily asked, "How long will I have to wait?"

The receptionist fingered a few papers. "I can't give you any time. You'll have to wait your turn like everyone else. Please take a seat."

Emily spun around and looked at a room filled with people and only one seat left for her to sit at. She tapped her fingers on the counter. "Lady, I can't wait all night. It's one in the morning now."

The woman hunched her shoulders in a noncommittal response.

"Lady, I'm talking to you."

The woman sighed. "Miss, I can't help you. You'll just have to wait. These people are waiting to see their friends and family, too, and they were here before you."

Emily scanned the people again and realized she could be there for hours. She stormed out of the room, pushed the outer door open, and flagged another taxi. Not knowing that the men had stolen Morgan's cell phone, she tried to call him but didn't get an answer. *I'll come back later after I get some sleep,* she thought, gritting her teeth.

Charlotte made arrangements for her and the children to stay at a motel east of the hospital. The children demanded she take them back to the B&B and the beach, but she insisted their grandmother was more important. They had to see her once more the next morning before they drove home to Rosewillow. For several minutes, their voices could be heard screaming and yelling at each other, until Charlotte slapped Douglas and told him to shut up, making him cry even louder. As she gathered them together, she marched them out to her car, strapped Cherry into her seat, told the twins to sit on either side of her in the back, and slammed the door. After turning on the engine, she headed for the motel for the night.

As they walked the corridor to leave, Floyd told Kat his thoughts about Charlotte's behavior.

"I know," she said. "That young lady is incorrigible. You'll have a fight on your hands when you pick Annah up to take her to Ionia."

Floyd looked sideways at her. "Yeah, I've only spent five minutes with her daughter, and I've already sized her up."

"Goodness, she would shut the mouth of an alligator if she could. I've known that girl since she's born and watched her grow up in the pears of her father's eyes. He spoiled her."

Floyd squinted. "Pears? You mean the apple of her father's eyes."

She put her hand over her mouth. "Of course. Silly me."

"Well, I got your meaning anyway. So, how does Annah handle her?"

"Usually she ignores her and walks away, but sometimes she snaps back at her and tries to correct her bad behavior by discussing it with her. Mostly, when I hear Charlotte getting nasty, I tell her off, like when she criticized you."

Floyd said nothing more, but he thought like Kat. He knew how to handle her.

Floyd left the hospital to return home to his house in Packard. It was time to take care of his dog, Roscoe. Roy looked after him while he was gone. Tomorrow, he would leave early to drive back to the hospital and take Annah back to Ionia. He wanted to make sure Charlotte didn't steal her away to Rosewillow.

He decided he would have enough time to stop at a clothing store in the morning and buy new clothes to wear. Today, he had left home quickly, still in his work clothes. He hoped to give Annah a different idea of him, since all she had ever seen him in were grimy work clothes and cut-off shorts with bawdy t-shirts. In New York, he had looked better. *I'm a bum,* he thought. *No, more like a man who didn't care about himself anymore.*

How my life has changed, he thought. *Annah has given me a renewed sense of purpose.* He grinned. *I can't wait to take her fishing.*

CHAPTER TWENTY

A white-haired lady at the information desk greeted Emily in the hospital the next morning. "I would like the room number to Morgan Gulliver, who checked in last night," she said. The woman smiled, checked her list on a computer, and gave her the information.

Emily hurried to the elevator, pressed the up button, and waited for what seemed a long while. "Come on," she said, as she pressed the button again.

"You have to be patient, dear," a voice said behind her. She turned and saw an elderly woman in a wheelchair. She wore a hospital gown, and a nurse stood holding the handles to it behind her. For an instant, the woman reminded her of her great-grandmother Wilmont.

"You're right, ma'am, I need patience," she said, tapping her foot. "My brother was beat up last night, and I couldn't see him because the Emergency Room was filled with sick people and others looking like zombies waiting…oh, God…probably for hours for someone. I got mad and went back to my motel room. I didn't want to wait until doomsday in a room full of unhealthy people."

The woman's eyes twinkled. "I'm one of those people someone wanted to see the night before," she said. "We all have times of waiting on a loved one. These are times of learning. These are moments to listen to what the Lord wants to teach us."

As the elevator door opened, the nurse rolled the woman in, while Emily held the door open. She didn't know what else to say to her. They were together until the fifth floor.

When they reached their floor and exited, Emily started to walk away, but the woman waved to stop her so she could reach for her hand. "My family couldn't see me right away either. At home, I fell and broke my hip and was rushed to the hospital in an ambulance. My family thought I had died and the staff wouldn't tell them my condition. They were in tears waiting to see me." She squeezed her hand. "The doctors took me into surgery immediately, which is a miracle with what they can do today. Here I am today, alive and well, and many blessings have come out of this experience."

"I can't imagine any blessings coming out of a broken hip."

"My children have not spoken in fifteen years because of disagreements. This emergency has gathered them together, and they're now speaking again. It's a blessing to me to see them forgive each other and become a family again." She paused. "Remember, dear, have patience and you'll be wiser for it."

As Emily watched her being wheeled away, she thought, *What am I to learn? Morgan and Charlotte never get along. Nothing is going to change that.*

She found Morgan's room and peeked in. He lay back with his head propped on a pillow, watching the news on television.

"Morgan, are you okay?" she asked, walking into his room. Purplish, swollen bruises covered his face, neck, and arms.

He turned to see her and struggled to open his mouth to speak. "No! I'm pissed at everything and everyone."

She spied a chair against the wall and sat down. "The police came to my door and told me what happened. I took a taxi to get here last night, but they wouldn't let me see you, so I went back to the motel. Does Mom know you're here? Did you try to call her room?"

He gave her a disgusted look. "How could I tell her I was here? I can hardly talk." He put his hand to his jaw. "The doctor said my jaw is broken and there's not much they can do with it except let it heal. They set it last night, but they can't put a brace on it. I just have to eat by drinking liquids through a straw and be careful what I eat. I also have two broken ribs, so they put a large bandage around my back and chest. I can hardly move."

"Morgan, if you had checked into a room instead of staying out in your stupid car, then this wouldn't have happened. It would have been stolen anyway."

He struggled to answer. "It is not a stupid car."

"Well, I'm sorry for you. I'll call Mom." Emily called for a nurse, who spoke through the speaker phone, she asked her to get Annah's phone number. "Thank you," she responded when she heard the number. She dialed her room, but there was no answer. "I'll have to find her and tell her what happened to you."

Morgan tried to sit up, but he hurt too badly. "They twisted my arm and slammed me on the ground. I have scrapes and cuts all over my arms and legs. I shouldn't have worn shorts and a t-shirt."

"It's your fault."

"I don't care. I'm going to get those guys and get my car and wallet back and all my other stuff. I'll get on those cops' asses to find them." He rubbed his face. "I'm checking out of here at eleven. Ma will be okay. I'm going down to the police station this morning."

"Morgan, first of all, Mom needs to know what happened to you. Besides, I'll bet they won't discharge you today. You're in too much pain. Second of all, how do you expect to get to the police station?"

He changed the channel on the T.V. with the remote and turned up the volume. "I can call for a cab to take me there."

"You're really dumb, you know that? The police are probably working on the case and you'd be wasting your time going there. Just call them and see if they've found out anything."

He turned the volume up higher. "After I talk to them, I'm going to rent a car and go home."

"How are you going to rent a car and drive without a license? Besides, you've lost your credit cards."

"Damn it, Emily. Then I'll steal a car and drive home and the cops can stuff it."

"Now, you're really out of your mind."

He threw his blanket over his shoulder and slid down in the bed.

"Another thing, how did you check in here without an I.D. and an insurance card?"

"Geez! Hospitals take in homeless people without I.D.s and insurance. I winged it by telling them my wallet with all my information was stolen, and I would send them the information when I got home."

Emily shifted in her seat. "Since I came down with you, I'll have to figure out how to get home myself. I may have to fly. I don't want to drive home in Charlotte's car with her kids whining for nine or ten hours."

Morgan struggled to sit up. "I don't blame you. I wouldn't want to spend that much time with Charlotte regardless. When I get home, I'm going to take Dad's Corvette. Ma is supposed to give it to me anyway."

"Have you talked to her about it?"

"No, but it's mine. I'll just take it. Dad said I would inherit it anyway."

Emily stood up. "You disgust me. I'm going to go see Mom and tell her you're here. You can do what you want, but if you don't visit her, you'll hurt her."

"Come on, Em, she's stronger than that."

Emily left him in a huff and shut his door. As she walked the hospital hallway, she viewed the Gulf and the beautiful blue horizon out the large picture windows. It helped her ease her tension. She thought about the old woman's words, that her broken hip brought her children together. Morgan's attitude didn't show concern for Annah or the rest of them. His mind was on his loss of possessions. Will he learn that his family is more important from his experience?

___

The cold packs were off Annah's head, but her face glowed with green and yellow splotches on the left side of her forehead and cheek.

"Good morning," she said, surprised and happy to see everyone. "Did Kat tell you I was here? You didn't have to drive down. I'll be all right."

Emily ran to her and kissed her lightly on the cheek. "Mom, I was so afraid you were terribly hurt. Kat told us the whole story. You're both lucky you didn't get killed."

Annah lifted herself up and settled back against her pillow. "Kat saved my life with her quick response by calling for help and getting us to the hospital. Did she tell you my car is totaled? I can't believe it. All I remember is being hit by another car and knocking my head on the window. I guess I blacked out at that point. I'm shocked she didn't get hurt, too."

Kat pulled a chair close to her bed and sat down. Her face was drawn and tired. "I was banged around, but I didn't get hurt like you."

"I know," Emily said to Kat. "But, Mom, as far as your car goes, you can always drive Papa's Mercedes."

"I'll probably do just that."

"Mom, Morgan had a run in with some thieves last night. They stole his car, beat him up, and left him lying on the parking lot pavement at the motel where we were staying. They've bandaged him and set his broken jaw. He's on the fifth floor, but wants to check out at eleven this morning."

"Oh, no, Emily. Were you there when they attacked him?"

"No, but the police came to my door and told me what happened. I took a taxi to the hospital to see him, but couldn't because of the number of people in the waiting room who were there before me in line."

"Well, that boy had better see his mother," Kat said. "Or, I'll swat his behind."

Morgan staggered into the room, scowling. "Don't talk about me like that, Kat. I'm a grown man and will do as I please." He looked at Annah. "Are you doing okay?" he asked with muffled words.

Annah pulled the covers up to her neck. "I'm fine, dear. Emily told me you have a broken jaw, and I can see you're having trouble talking."

"I sure in hell am, but I thought I'd stop in and see you before I talked with the police about last night. The cruds took everything, my car, my wallet, my laptop, my cell phone, everything!"

"Morgan, do the nurses know you're out of bed and walking around?"

"They weren't around so I just left. Even the nurses at the nurse's station didn't stop me. Some hospital, huh?"

Emily shook her head. "Mom, Morgan is going to rent a car to go home if he doesn't get his car back and then take Papa's Corvette to use."

Annah looked surprised.

"You bet I will. Dad willed it to me," he said with defiance. "Since you smashed your car, you can take Dad's Mercedes. I want my inheritance now." He sat down in another chair and waved to her. "I love you, Ma."

Kat leaned on the arm of her chair and looked him in the face. "Morgan, how do you think you're going to rent a car and drive without a license? Plus, you have to have at least one credit card to rent it."

He stood bent over in pain. "I don't know how the hell I'm going to do that like you said." He glanced around the room. "Someone's going to have to come up for a way to get me home, and I mean today."

The air hung with heavy silence.

Annah pulled herself higher on the pillow. "Morgan, did you ever think of asking me if you could have your father's Corvette? If you want it, you'll have to wait to have me bestow it to you legally, so you can put it in your name and get plates for it. In the meantime, I don't want you to drive it without a driver's license."

Morgan fumed. "I'll drive it anyway."

Annah held her breath for a moment in anger and then changed the subject. "Dears, I asked Floyd to take me to the B&B. We have a lot to discuss. Did Kat tell you I'm looking for a house there for a vacation home?"

"What? Mom, you're not?" Emily asked.

Annah took her hand in hers. "Emily, I was going to tell you this after I got home, but I guess this is the time to do it." She dropped her hand.

"For a vacation home?" Morgan asked, holding his hand to his jaw. "What for? You have a house in Rosewillow. "

She leaned toward him and spoke slowly. "Morgan, I think it would be fun to have a place to go to and have a quiet retreat."

With a look of belligerence, he propped his feet on the top of the foot of her bed. "You have quiet every day at home. What's your problem?"

Annah folded her arms. "Since your father died, I have craved to get away from Rosewillow. I've decided to buy a small house near Ionia and Kat and Spencer. I've also met some wonderful people whom I consider friends. Your father and I have enough assets that I will be able to buy a property of my choice outright. I plan to come down here whenever I feel like getting away."

"That's a stupid idea," Morgan said, as he adjusted his feet, cleared his throat, and covered his jaw to speak. "You've lived in Rosewillow all your life, and you have so much peace at home; I'm surprised you don't go mad." He dropped his feet and leaned forward. "Listen Ma, Patricia hopes you will help her with the new baby. It's due in a week. We've been counting on you."

"He's right, Mom," Emily added. "We don't want you to do something foolish like buying a house to get away from us. Besides, I won't be going back to college for another month, and I planned on doing all those things we've always done together. You know, like going shopping, going out to lunch, and other stuff."

"When do you plan to buy this thing?" Morgan asked. "You'll lay all that money out and not be able to use it and you'll be sorry. The house will sit empty and you'll worry about it. Anyway, I thought Dad left money to share with us. Wasn't it also to be part of our inheritance?" He glanced at Emily.

"Yes. I am counting on that money to pay my tuition for next year's college."

"What's this about our inheritance and tuition?" Charlotte asked, as she walked into the room with the children.

"Pudge, Ma wants to buy a house down here to get away from all of us," Morgan said.

"What? Mother, no!" Charlotte's face contorted with unbelief.

"Yeah, that's what I say, no."

"Mother, you're not serious. You're buying a house? Here, of all places?"

Annah had enough. "Listen to the three of you. I have a will of my own. It's time for me to make my own decisions." She straightened her blanket. "If I find a house here, I'm going to buy it so I can be alone for a while and away from the demands in Rosewillow. You've all been taken care of financially, so you don't need any more money."

"All you have to do for peace is not answer the phone or the door. We don't bother you that much," Morgan said.

Charlotte grimaced. "Don't you love us anymore?"

Annah closed her eyes. "Of course."

"Charlotte, Mom is going to use up all our money. I need

$75,000 for my final year's tuition at college this year," Emily said.

"Yeah, Dad promised to buy me that yacht over in Charleston that I've been looking at. He said there should be enough money to share between all of us," Morgan added.

"Mother, you can't take our money. Your share should be one fourth of it. After Father died, I told Bradford we would get enough to send the children to a private school. You know the one over in Walden? It's $10,000 per year, per child," Charlotte said.

"Excuse me! I am not going to put up with your squabbles about money. I think the three of you are being very selfish."

"We are not selfish, Mother. We're just reminding you of your obligations to us."

Annah gave Charlotte a stern look. "I have been in a terrible accident, and I don't feel well. You should all be more considerate than to discuss money issues right now. In addition, I think it's best for all of you to go somewhere else in the hospital and discuss your problems. I have my own to worry about."

Charlotte huffed and turned to Morgan. "What may I ask happened to you, for god sakes?"

"Some jerks beat me up and stole my car and everything in it, as well as my wallet."

She scanned his face. "What's the matter with your jaw?"

"They broke it." He stopped and looked at her. "Hey, how about renting a car for me to drive home. They took my credit cards and license, and I won't be able to rent one myself."

She stood over him. "You want me to rent you a car and you're going to drive it home without a license? Are you nuts? That's illegal and I'd be the one who'd get in trouble. Go home with us or find another way home."

He put his arms around himself and feigned agony. "I can't depend on *you* to drive me. You're bratty kids would drive me berserk."

"Good! Because I wouldn't want to spend nine hours with you either. That would drive me to insanity."

"Stop it, both of you. I'm not in the mood for these squabbles," Annah said.

"All of you, please leave your mother alone. She has to rest now," a nurse said, as she entered the room to check on Annah after hearing the shouting.

Quietly, they left with Charlotte pushing the children out. They would discuss these issues later with Annah. Right now, they were on their way to discuss them somewhere else.

Morgan struggled to stand straight, but followed the rest of them down the hallway.

"Good luck, Morgan, if the nurses see you walking the hallway, they'll strap you in bed so you won't do it again," Emily said.

"Shut up. You don't know what they'll do. I have a right to go where I want to," he said, coughing and wrapping his arms around his chest.

They walked together down the hallway toward an elevator to take them to a sitting room as the doctor passed them. He headed toward Annah's room and quickly entered it.

"Mrs. Gulliver, how nice to see you looking better," he said. "The nurses have told me you're doing fine this morning and able to be released. I've checked your latest charts, and I agree with them. How do you feel?" he asked, removing the stethoscope from around his neck, putting the ear pieces into his ears, and placing the scope on Annah's chest. He checked her pulse, examined the bruises on her face, and stepped back. "Well?"

"I'm fine. I'm sore on the left side of my face and head, but I think I'll recover."

He pulled at the small beard on this chin and studied her. "Do you have a headache?"

"Yes, but a little one. Mostly, my head hurts where I hit it on the window."

He made notes on a sheet on his clipboard. "Okay," he said. "I'll have your nurse prepare your papers for release and also schedule a CAT scan for you in exactly one week. I don't want you to miss it, young lady," he said, as he took her hand for a brief second. "Understand?"

"Yes, I understand. I'll be here."

The doctor nodded to Annah and rushed from the room.

Within a half hour, the nurse came into the room with signed release papers. "So, Mrs. Gulliver, let's get you dressed to go home. I'll bet you're ready."

"Yes," she answered, slipping sideways out of bed and heading for the small shower and toilet room within her ICU. Once dressed, Annah remembered Floyd was going to come and drive her to Ionia, and she hoped he hadn't forgotten.

The nurse helped her into a wheelchair to take her outside where someone would be waiting to take her home.

"Mother," Charlotte said, entering the room. "You're dressed! Good, now we can go home." The three grandchildren ran to Annah and started fighting.

Annah closed her eyes. Maybe all this was just a nightmare. "Charlotte, thank you for offering to take me home, but I'm planning on staying in Ionia for another week. I have an appointment here for a CAT scan, and it will be closer to the hospital than driving back."

Charlotte straightened up. "Excuse me, but there is no

problem driving you home and looking for a doctor to care for you up there. Don't you think we have labs with CAT scan machines in South Carolina?"

"My dear, it's only about a twenty minute drive from Ionia to Tampa. I prefer to stay here and not travel nine or ten hours to go home right now." She paused. "I can take care of myself, thank you."

"Mom, are you ready to go?" Emily asked, as she walked over to them.

"Like I said to Charlotte, I am going to Ionia to stay for a week, and afterward come back to the hospital for another test. Floyd is picking me up."

"Why, when you can go home with Charlotte?" Emily asked.

The nurse handed Annah her suitcase and purse when they were at the curb.

"You heard me," Annah said, responding to both of them.

Annah scanned the parking lot but didn't see Floyd. She tried not to look disappointed. "Maybe Floyd was stuck in traffic," she said.

"Maybe he forgot," Emily said.

Annah raised herself out of the chair to stand. "I'm going to wait here until Floyd comes to pick me up. All of you can go now."

"Mother, you can't stand here by yourself. I'll drive you to Ionia then, since you're so stubborn."

Annah wrung her hands together. Floyd was nowhere. She turned her head in time to see all her children and grandchildren surrounding her. Was she wrong not letting them take her home? Were they that needy of her? Don't they know better than to expect her to be available to them for every whim? Why should they assume she would take care of Patricia's baby when they could arrange to have a nanny be there when they take their weekend sailing trips? They certainly could afford it.

"Both of you, I'm going to call Kat and Spencer and have them pick me up. I love you and appreciate your concern, but I'm staying here in Florida for now."

"Ma, you're going with Charlotte," Morgan said, walking out the hospital door, dressed in his shorts and t-shirt.

"Morgan, stop right now. You are not going to tell me what to do. I'm calling Kat. Thank you for coming down here, now go back home." Annah's head began to pound from the stress. The arguments were getting too much to bear.

"Mother, I'm staying with you. You're not going to stand here alone," Charlotte said.

Annah pulled her phone from her purse and called Kat. She and Spencer would be there in a half hour, to go inside the hospital, find rest in a comfortable chair, and wait. "Now, everything is fine.

They'll be here to pick me up. Go home."

Charlotte followed her with her children into the hospital and sat down beside her to wait for Kat and Spencer. She didn't say another word.

Annah remained adamant. She looked straight, ignoring the children's whimpering, and thought, *What happened to Floyd?*

CHAPTER TWENTY-ONE

Emily and Morgan waited outside the hospital for the taxi to pick them up and take them to the rental company lot. Emily intended to rent a car to drive to Rosewillow. Morgan changed his plans to stop at the police station. He would call them from home. If they found his car and stolen items, he would know then.

"I can't stand those brats of Charlotte's," Morgan said, holding an ice pack to his jaw with his hand and leaning against a post. "Hell would have to freeze over before I would drive with Charlotte and them."

"That's not very nice. Why don't you two get along for a change?" She leaned against the wall of the building.

"Charlotte thinks she's better than everyone else."

Emily shifted from one foot to the other and looked around for a bench to sit on. She opened her backpack and pulled out a pack of cigarettes and a lighter. Then she lit one cigarette and put the items back into her pack.

"Oh, don't tell me you smoke?"

"So what, I can do what I please." She lifted her head and blew the smoke upward.

Morgan moved away from her. "Don't tell me I'm going to have to put up with your smoke all the way home."

Emily turned to face him. "You could always drive home with Charlotte."

"What choice do I have? Either I have to listen to three screaming kids and a mother who screams back at them constantly, or inhale your smoke." Disgusted, he shook his head. He looked around the parking lot for the taxi, but didn't see it. "Em, just wait until you get kids of your own. They'll be no different."

"Well, that'll be a long time from now. I don't have any plans to marry."

He sat beside her when she finished smoking. "I'm glad to hear that. I thought you were serious about that four-eyed creep. He wouldn't have fit into our family anyway."

"What? Michael is very intelligent, and he's going to go on for his doctorate. I thought he was interesting."

Morgan growled. "Yeah, he was interested in your money and thinking he could afford his doctorate because you would support him."

"You're wrong, Morgan. He told me he was going to get a part-time job to pay for his tuition, and I could continue my education, too."

"Come on, what kind of a part-time job would pay for the tuition at the university you go to?" He slapped her shoulder lightly and said, "Ouch." His right arm still hurt from the beating. "You're afraid Ma won't give you your share of Dad's insurance money to pay for your college. We have to convince Ma to give us our inheritance now instead of waiting for her to die. If she didn't have this silly idea in her head to buy a house in Florida, we'd have more money to split between us. Ma doesn't need Dad's insurance money. We should have it."

"Morgan, I want to just shoot you. Is that what you're waiting for? Mom to die?"

"Of course, not. I mean, hey, we're a rich family. We'll inherit that old mansion she lives in. Isn't that what Dad said?"

Emily sat back. "Morgan, you're selfish and cruel." She crossed her legs and nervously kicked her right leg up and down. "Besides, I'm going out with Jimmy now. Jimmy's the reporter that's been asking for information about the history of our house."

"Oh, cripe! You just don't stop do you? You jump from one guy to another. You can't seem to hang on to any of them for any amount of time."

"Mind your own business."

He was quiet for a few minutes. "Well, we should all think about what we're going to say to Ma. Going off and buying a house hundreds of miles away is pathetic."

"I know, but like she said, she's in charge of her life now."

Just then, the taxi pulled up and they climbed in. Their conversation about their inheritance would continue all the way home in their rental car.

—

After Spencer and Kat left for Ionia with Annah, Charlotte walked toward her car with her three children running ahead of her. Near her car, she noticed a heavy-set man climbing out of his truck. She wondered if that was the same man her mother introduced her to in the hospital. No, he was dressed too well. Why did Kat say he was a friend of theirs? Well, it was no business of hers if Kat wanted to hang around with a low-life. She thought her mother probably doesn't know him very well, but then she remembered him kissing her mother's cheek. *How much of a friend is he?*

"Come on, pick up your feet," she called to the children. "We have a long drive home and the morning's already gone."

Daphne, Douglas, and Cherry pushed each other to sit in the front seat. "It's my turn," Douglas yelled, as the others screamed that it was their turn to sit in front.

"No. I want all of you strapped into your seats in the back, and I don't want any arguing. Hear me?" Charlotte opened the back door. Anyway, she had to think things out. She didn't want to deal with Douglas talking to her for nine hours. *Lord knows, there are decisions to make when I get home, and I have to talk to Bradford about arranging a family discussion with Emily and Morgan, and it had better be soon.*

As the taxi with Morgan and Emily passed Charlotte, she yelled for them to stop.

"Hey, Morgan, do you see that man over there?"

He opened his window and peered at the man. "Yes."

"Is he the man who was in Mother's room?"

He leaned his neck forward to get a better look. "I don't recognize him."

"Well, somehow he looks like him, but maybe it's not him."

Morgan hung his arm out the window and waved. "Pudge, we'll see you at home."

Charlotte shook his fist at him. "Don't call me Pudge."

Morgan watched her children make faces at him as they crawled into the back seat of her car. He signaled to the driver to go on.

As Charlotte headed north toward South Carolina, she whispered to herself between screams at the children to settle down and quit fighting in the backseat. "That man was going to drive Mother back to Ionia, but Spencer and Kat took her. Thank God. Who knows what nasty things were on his mind?"

Soon, she had enough of the arguing behind her. "If you children don't stop picking on each other, I'm going to pull off the road and spank each one of you." At seventy miles per hour, she slapped the nearest head she could find, swerving the car almost into the on-coming lane.

"Mama, Douglas won't stop picking on me," Daphne sobbed.

"I'm not doing anything. She started it first."

"I did not. Douglas won't leave me alone."

"Stop!" Charlotte yelled. "That's it. I'm going to spank you both." She slowed the car, pulled over to the side of the highway, and stormed out. Opening the back door, she unsnapped the shoulder harness over Douglas and yanked him from his seat.

Instantly, she froze. A patrol car drove up behind her, stopped, and an officer stepped out of his car. He walked toward her. "Ma'am, are you having trouble?" he asked.

"Yes," she said, shaking. "You might say that I am."

"What seems to be your problem?"

Daphne sobbed loudly. "Mama is going to beat me up."

"Yeah, she's going to spank us and make us cry," Cherry said.

Charlotte's heart raced. "Sir, I was not going to beat up my children. I am not a bad mother. I've put up with them fighting and screaming for the last one hundred miles and I was going to discipline them. That's all. I was not going to hurt them."

"Yes, you were," Douglas said to the patrolman, sticking his tongue out at her.

Charlotte felt like slapping him, but instead gave him an angry stare.

"Young man, you are being disrespectful to your mother. I don't want to see you doing that again. Do you want to apologize to her?"

Douglas crossed his arms and said, "No, but I guess I have to. I'm sorry."

"Thank you," he said and peered into the back seat at the other two children. He seemed to evaluate the situation for a moment. "Ma'am, would you like me to escort you to the police station nearby so we can calm these children down and settle whatever problem you're having?"

Charlotte's face suddenly blazed red. "Ah, no sir. I think I can handle this. I suppose the children are hungry. I'll stop at the next town so we can eat lunch. They've been cramped up in the car for over two hours," she said, stammering.

The officer listened and watched her. "Okay, I'll follow you into the next town and see that you do find a good restaurant." He nodded and returned to his patrol car.

Charlotte was beside herself. She motioned to Douglas to get back into the car and strap himself in. She trembled as she slid behind the wheel, started the engine, and guided her car back onto the highway. She could hardly see through her watery eyes, or catch her breath for the pounding in her heart. She hoped the next turn-off was only a couple of miles away.

Just wait until I get home. Bradford needs to punish these children for almost getting me in trouble with that officer, she thought. "Now, you behave yourselves in the restaurant. I don't want any more screaming and fighting," she said to them, as she peered into the rearview mirror.

I have to tell Bradford what I suspect is going on with Mother and this…this Floyd.

—

Bradford waited at the door for Charlotte and the children when they returned home. "Well, y'all look bedraggled, but I'm glad y'all are home safe," he said, picking up Cherry and swinging her through the door. "Did my baby have a good time?"

She pouted. "No. Mama's mean. She wouldn't let us do anything, and she made a big policeman mad."

He put her down. "What? Y'all got a policeman mad?" he asked, looking at Charlotte. "What did y'all do?"

Daphne and Douglas answered. "She was going to beat us up, but he stopped her."

"Bradford, they're telling stories," she groaned. "First of all, I asked the children what they wanted to do the whole time we were in Ionia. They swam and played on the beach, and we had wonderful meals and a nice B&B to stay in." She dropped the case she was carrying and put her purse on top of it. "When we were coming home, I couldn't stop their fighting in the car, so I pulled over to the side of the road to spank Douglas first, but a policeman pulled up behind us and got out of his car. He wanted to help me because the children kept screaming and hollering. What else could I do but try to settle them down?"

Bradford placed his hands on the heads of Daphne and Douglas and said, "Haven't I warned y'all not to lie? Haven't I also warned y'all not to fight with each other in the car? Y'all could have caused your mother to have an accident."

The twins pulled their heads out from under Bradford's hands and ran upstairs to their bedroom. Cherry continued to pout. "Mama's mean just like I said."

Charlotte gave Bradford a quick kiss and turned to get more bags from the car.

"Here, let me help." He followed her out to the car.

Charlotte continued her diatribe. "Mother is being silly. We found out she is looking for a house in Ionia to use as a get-away. She wants to have time alone down there. Can you believe it?" She slammed the trunk lid down. "We need her here. What is she thinking? Who's going to run the house?"

He shrugged. "Well, that makes it more reasonable for us to move into the mansion and oversee it whenever she's gone. That is, if she does."

"Yes! I hadn't thought of that."

"But sweetheart, your mother knows she can't pick up and leave anytime she wants to. Anyway, didn't y'all say she's only goin' to use that house for a retreat? We could use that house for our retreat, too."

Charlotte gave him a surprised look. "Why, Bradford, you are surprising. Yes, that would be wonderful, and when she's down there, I could bring the children, and they could go swimming and play on the beach. Mother would enjoy that, don't you think?"

Bradford placed the suitcases on the floor and grabbed her shoulders. "See? We'll have the best of both worlds." Cherry skipped up the stairs toward her bedroom. "And the children will, too," he added.

"I also want to talk to you about a horrible-looking man Mother and Kat have made friends with. I don't like him, and I think he's after her money."

"How much of a friend is he?"

"I have no idea, but it doesn't look good to me. We'll meet with Emily and Morgan for dinner tomorrow evening," Charlotte said. "I'll give them a call."

"Morgan, I'll drop you off at your house and go home," Emily said, as they neared Rosewillow. I'm tired and so are you. It was fun being with you on this trip. Do you realize we've never spent this much time together?"

He shrugged. "I guess I never thought about it. Though, I have to say, this was quite an experience learning about your lost loves and talking about serious matters. You're empty headed most of the time."

As he opened his door and stepped out, she stuffed her pack of cigarettes and lighter into her backpack pocket. "Thanks for the compliment. You've got a screw loose, too, sometimes."

"Hey, let's talk more again."

"Give my love to Patricia and Mandy for me."

"Quit smoking," he called, as he walked toward the front door of his home.

"I'll stop when I want to," she yelled.

When she arrived at her house, Jimmy was standing at the door waiting for her. He grinned. "Hi, honey. I'm glad you're safe and sound." He took her case and backpack from her and then set them down to enfold her in his arms. "I missed you."

Emily soaked in his warmth. "I missed you, too."

"I estimated how long it would take for you to drive home, but you took longer than I thought you would. Delsey made me a quick sandwich and a glass of sweet tea, and I've been watching a movie."

"With Morgan beside me complaining of his pains and having a hard time moving his jaw to speak, I was beginning to think the trip was too long. He's a bore." She picked up her case and pack and headed upstairs. "Let me settle down and clean up, and I'll be right down. I have a lot to tell you." She paused. "And, would you ask Delsey to make me a sandwich, too? Have her make it crab salad on toast and a Coke. I'm starving."

"You bet," Jimmy said, as he strolled to the kitchen to talk with Delsey.

As Emily came into the kitchen, Delsey said, "Emily, you've been on my mind all the time you've been gone. I've been seeing you here and there and everywhere. You've been happy, sad, scared, and angry." She gave her a long, deep stare. "Now, you sit yourself down and eat this sandwich. I'll make you another if you want." She set the plate in front of Emily and handed her the can of soda.

Jimmy sat down beside her, and Delsey poured a glass of tea for him.

"After you called us about Morgan's attack and your mother's condition, I've felt a storm brewing."

With her mouth full of food, Emily asked, "A storm?"

She rolled her eyes. "Heavenly Lord."

Bewildered, Emily held her sandwich half way to her mouth and then put it down. "Delsey, what?"

"Eat your sandwich," she said. "I'm glad you're home, and now I'm going to bed." She walked out the back door toward her cottage where Jerome was resting.

After Delsey left, Emily and Jimmy discussed the events at the hospital. She told him about her mother's desire to buy a small house in Ionia to get away from everyone. "This hurt me, Jimmy, my mother is not herself right now. She's running around doing all kinds of silly things."

"What silly things? All she did was to go on a short vacation with her friend. Maybe she likes the area, and the idea of buying a small house to spend time down there sounds normal to me."

Emily went on. "I mean silly things like…." She stopped. "Oh, we need her here."

"For what? You're all adults and can take of yourselves, and I don't think she's doing anything wrong." He sipped his tea. "And, hey, I like to go on vacation. I can't right now, with my job and all, but I hope to accrue enough time at the newspaper to get me a week or two off."

She placed her elbows on the table and held her head with

both hands. "She met a guy down there and I think she's falling for him."

Jimmy drank his tea in one gulp, emptying the glass. "Sweetheart, you're imagining things. You're hurt because your mom did something she has never done before. Didn't you say, Kat and her husband are moving down there, and your mom wanted to see their new home?"

"Yes, but I think this guy is now the real reason she's willing to stay down there."

After Jimmy left for the night, all she could remember was hearing him say sensible things, and she being a real nincompoop.

CHAPTER TWENTY-TWO

Floyd didn't know that Annah had been released from the hospital. He rushed through the entryway, caught the elevator up to her floor, and eagerly walked to her room. It was empty with the bed already made for another patient. "Damn," he said, chastening himself for shopping for clothes and taking too much time.

As he hurried back to his truck, he hoped she had left with Kat and her husband instead of Charlotte. Maybe he could catch them on the highway. Pounding his fist on the steering wheel, he said. "You better not lose this woman."

As he drove away from the hospital, he looked into every Suburban he passed with three people. Surely, he thought, she would remember his truck and wave, but he couldn't find them.

Finally, he reached Ionia hoping she would be at the B&B.

—

On their drive home, Kat leaned over her car seat to see Annah. "Are you okay back there? You're so quiet."

She folded her hands. "Well, I've been thinking maybe I've been too rash. Maybe I should try to resolve my difficulties with my children instead of rushing into buying a small house in Ionia."

"That's a very good idea, Annah," Spencer said, as he looked back at her in the rearview mirror.

Annah's headache worsened, so she laid her head down and folded her legs up on the seat. If she could sleep the rest of the way to the B&B, she might feel better.

As they approached the B&B, Spencer said, "Annah, sweetheart, we're here."

"My head is throbbing," she answered.

Roy came out of the house and met them at the car. "Why, you gals can sure get yourselves in trouble. I mean, we heard about your accident with your car stuck upside down in the mud and all. You'll have to tell Lola and me all about the details." He looked at Annah's discolored face. "Wow. You really did hit your head."

"She'll be fine," Kat said. "I'm sure she'll tell you about it later."

"Okay. Floyd called us and arranged for you to stay another week here. We're happy to have you back."

Spencer got out of the car. He pulled out a pouch of tobacco and began to fill his pipe. "We have reservations at the Cabeza de Playa in case you need to call us." He pressed his thumb into the bowl, placed the stem in his mouth, and lit the tobacco, sending swirls of white smoke into the air.

"We'll do just that," Roy said. He followed Kat and Annah up the front steps carrying Annah's suitcase.

"Hello, there," Lola called from the front counter. She walked around it and stood in front of Annah. "Mercy, I hope you're not too hurt. We're all worried about you."

"Where is Floyd?" Annah asked, trying not to look too anxious.

"I don't know. I thought he'd be the one drivin' you here instead of your friends."

Kat winked at her. "I think he was delayed. He'll probably be here soon. We didn't see him at the hospital before we left, but he knows Annah is coming here." She took Annah's arm. "Come on, dumplin', let's get you upstairs."

"Let me help," Lola said. She took the suitcase from Roy and followed them.

"Kat led her into her room and helped her settle in.

"Now, don't you go worryin' yourself about Floyd. I'll bet he has a good excuse for not pickin' you up at the hospital. You get some rest, and when you're up and movin', come on down and we'll talk," Lola said.

Annah puffed up her pillow and lay back on the bed. "How can I ever thank the both of you," she said, as she closed her eyes.

—

Once in the B&B parking lot, Floyd stopped the truck, and hurriedly slid out. The lot was empty of cars. He walked quickly up the steps, opened the front door, and spied Roy. "Is she here?"

Lola walked into the room holding a pitcher of iced tea. She set it down on their serving table. "Floyd," she said, smiling. "Annah is upstairs layin' down. Her friend said she needed to take a nap. She has a headache." She looked him up and down. "Why, honey, you look wonderful. I haven't seen you dressed like that before."

"Got a date or somethin'?" Roy asked, grinning.

"You might say so," Floyd said, letting his shoulders fall. "Can I have one of those?" he asked, pointing to the plate of donuts.

"Of course, silly. You can even have two if you want." She looked him over again "My, how handsome you are."

"Thanks." He poured a glass of ice tea and took a long drink. "I stopped at a clothes store in Tampa to buy some decent clothes. I wore my old work clothes to the hospital when I first visited her, and I wanted to look nice to take her home." He placed the empty glass on the counter. "Well, guess I'll see her tomorrow," he said. "I just wanted to know if she made it here okay."

"She's okay," Roy said, grinning even more.

Floyd slapped Roy on the arm. "See you guys later."

Roy whistled. "Geez Louise, you smell like you're on the prowl."

Lola flashed a look at Roy to show her displeasure.

Floyd returned to his house. He was satisfied that she had made it back to Ionia safely and didn't go home with Charlotte. All he could think about was that they had a week to know each other, and he could take her fishing on the river. He thought he'd better go through his gear and find a rod and reel that would be easy for her to use. The fact that she had never fished before surprised him.

After he changed clothes, let Roscoe outside for a break and fed him, he hopped back in his truck and steered it toward The Albatross. He needed a cold beer along with his cigar and the company of his rowdy friends.

Hoots and howls greeted him as he entered the bar. "Hey Floyd, where you been? Heard you were shackin' up with some high-falutin' gal," one man asked.

Floyd first ignored their cackling, then answered, "She's not high-falutin', and we're not shacking up. She's beautiful inside and out." He walked over to the bar and sat down. "Give me a Bud," he said to the bartender. He handed it to Floyd, who downed it and asked for another.

His friend, Jake, sat down beside him. "Hey, man, you're not going get messed up with that woman are you? She'll tear your heart apart and leave you for some slob."

Floyd put his second beer down after taking a long swig. "Not this one. She's a doll." He bit off the end of his cigar and spit it out in his hand."

"We'll see. If she's what these guys say she is, as I said, she'll leave you in a flash when she realizes she won't be able to change you. She'll want you to wear suits and stuff, go to expensive restaurants, and not let you come here."

He struck a match and held it, but then let the match burn out. "Naw, she's already been here herself. She's accepted me for the way I am. Besides, I don't think she's uppity. She's class. Her girlfriend's been around, but that doesn't take anything away from her."

"What about that BMW they drove up in? By the way, is that her car sitting at Ed's?"

"Yeah, that's her car, but she might have had a husband who did business and could afford it for her. You never know. I'd like to drive it. My truck is ready to crap out."

"By the looks of the car, she must have rolled it over."

"Yeah, she rolled off the highway and it landed in a creek bed." Floyd went on to tell him the rest of the story. "She'll be around for a week, and I'm going to take her fishing."

Jake ordered a beer and lit a cigarette. "Okay, man, I'm going to watch you and see how this story ends," he said. He slapped Floyd on the back and left him to play poker.

"Yeah," Floyd said, still smarting from the slap, "this is going to be one hell of a story."

—

Annah woke early. She rolled off the bed and stretched. Her headache had dissipated. She gathered her clothes and toiletries and slipped down to the common bathroom to clean up. She thought Floyd must have driven home instead of picking her up at the hospital. *What did I do to discourage him?* She decided to visit with Lola downstairs,

"Annah, your daughter, Emily, called from home. Says to call her right away. She has somethin' important to tell you."

Annah stopped. "My daughter always has something important to say. Thank you, Lola. I'll go back up and call her from my cell phone." Annah returned to her room, sat down, punched the numbers, and waited for Emily to answer.

Emily answered and started talking rapidly. "Mom, Maybelle says Grandma Wilmont is near death and wants to see you now. Please come home."

Annah felt her heart leap. "Honey, I don't know how that's possible. I'm not supposed to drive with the medications I'm on and my head injury. Besides, my car is totaled."

"But Mom, you have to. She's dying."

She thought a moment. "Well, I guess I could call Kat to see if she and Spencer could drive me home. I'm sure they'll also want to see Grandma Wilmont before she passes."

"I'm sure they'll do it. Grandma is like family to them." She paused. "Mom, how do you feel? Are you able to travel?"

"I'm feeling a little bit better, but my face looks like a rainbow and my head hurts. Did you have any trouble driving home with Morgan?"

"No, he's was okay. I haven't had a chance to spend time like that with him for years, and it turned out to be an interesting trip."

Annah exhaled. "Okay, I'll call you as soon as I talk with Kat. I'm sure there won't be a problem." Her heart sank. She wasn't ready to lose her grandmother. She had always been her strength and given her counsel throughout her life. She loved her too much. Grandma Wilmont was the matriarch of the family, and it was important to be there for her.

"Lola, my grandmother is dying and I must go home as soon as I can," Annah said. She's waiting for me to see her before she goes, so I have to go."

"Oh, Lordy. I'm so sorry. Is there anythin' I can do to help?"

"No. There's nothing anyone of us can do now except go see her." Annah called Kat. When she hung up, Lola asked her how long she would be gone.

"I really don't think I'll be gone long. Could you keep my room for me?"

"Of course, Annah, you are always welcome here."

"Thank you," she said, and then added, "Does Floyd know I'm here?"

"Yes, dear, he came to see you while you were sleepin' and didn't want to wake you. He was glad to hear you made it back okay."

Annah breathed a sigh of relief, but still couldn't understand why he didn't show up.

Roy walked into the room as they were talking and overheard them. "Annah, sweetie, Floyd was all dressed up in fine clothes. He smelled like a rose."

"Roy, keep your mouth shut," Lola said, while gesturing with her forefinger for him to stop. "Annah, he was late gettin' to the hospital because he stopped to get new clothes so he would look nice to take you home." She glared at Roy again. "I love that nephew of mine. He has a good heart, and he's a fine, decent man. He's sorry he wasn't there to meet you."

Annah looked from Lola to Roy. "That's good to know," she said. Turning around, she headed for the stairs with a glass of ice tea in hand, smiling all the way to her room. She wouldn't have much packing to do since most of her clothes were still packed. Muddy water leaking through the case had stained several blouses, but she would worry about that when she got home. In the meantime, she would get ready to go. After calling Kat, she said that they should be there for Grandma Wilmont, too, and they would be ready to leave at eight o'clock the next morning.

"Floyd will want to know that Annah has to drive home to be with her grandmother," Lola said, as she wiped the counter of smudges.

"Yeah, I'll call him," Roy said. "Hey Floyd, Annah's grandmother is dyin', so she asked Kat to take her home to Rosewillow. Do you want to see her tonight before she leaves?"

Floyd slapped his head and pushed the cell phone deeper into his ear. "What a stupe!" Now he smelled of cigars and beer, and he was dressed in a pair of cut-off shorts and a wrinkled gray t-shirt, which he had worn two days before.

"What did you say?"

"Roy, I can't right now. I'm at The Albatross and I look like hell. Please apologize to her for me. Better yet, can you get her to the phone so I can talk to her?" He chastised himself. Why didn't he think he could have driven over to see her that evening?

"Well, sure. I'll go up and knock on her door for you. Hold on," Roy said, as he put the phone on the counter and turned to Lola. "The old boy went to The Albatross. I don't think he's up to seein' her tonight."

Lola looked up at the ceiling. "Missed opportunities," she said. "When is that man goin' to straighten up?"

Roy walked up to Annah's room and knocked. "Annah, Floyd is on the phone. Can you talk to him right now?"

She dropped the clothes she held in her hands. "Why, yes. Give me a minute and I'll be right down."

Roy did an about-face, returned to the counter downstairs, and picked up the phone. "You're a lucky son of a gun. She's on her way downstairs. Give her a minute. What the hell did you do, Floyd, get yourself drunk?"

Of course not," he scowled. "It's that I'm wearing sweaty clothes, and I don't want her to see or smell me this way."

Annah tried to appear calm as she walked toward Roy and took the phone. "Thank you," she said. She held it for a few seconds before speaking. "Floyd?"

He leaned on his elbows on the table in his usual corner booth and sighed. Holding his hand to his forehead and the other hand grasping the phone, he said. "Annah, I'm so sorry I haven't been able to see you since they brought you home from the hospital. Do you forgive me?"

She looked up at Lola, who frowned. "Of course. I understand you're a busy man. Thank you for coming over to make sure I was okay."

"Will you be back before your hospital appointment? Remember you have a CAT scan coming up that you can't miss. I

don't want anything to happen to you."

"I'll make sure I'm back in time. The way my daughter explained to me, my grandmother may die shortly, and it should all be over within the week, and then Kat and Spencer will drive me to Tampa before returning here." She paused. "I have much to do here…don't I?" Annah glanced at Lola, who appeared disgusted.

Floyd tapped his fingers on the counter. "You bet you do, sweetheart. I'm going to miss you. Remember, we have a date for a fishing trip that will change your life."

Annah placed her hand on her heart. "I'll miss you, too," she said.

Lola examined her face and walked around the counter. "Now, you take care of yourself. That man needs to worry about someone else besides himself."

Lola put her arms around her shoulder and led her over to the sofa. "Go ahead and cry. Let it out. You've been through a lot with your husband dying and all, and your daughter bein' so rude." She continued. "I've watched your daughter and her children while they were here," she said. "You've been in a terrible accident, spent time in the hospital, and now your grandmother is dyin'. On top of all that, well, you're getting' a crush on that Floyd of mine, and you two can't seem to get together."

Annah pulled a tissue from her pocket. "How observant you are."

"There, there. Everythin's going to be all right." She continued. "In a week, you can come back here. We'll make sure it's quiet, and you will have more time to yourself and get to know him."

"Thank you, Lola. I'm so grateful I met you. You're a special person." She blew her nose. "I'm looking forward to returning."

"I want you to do me a favor while you're up at your home."

"Certainly. What kind of favor?"

"Well, I kind of feel you let your daughter and her children get to you. Don't let them control you. You're their mother and grandmother and a grown woman. Stand up for your rights and do what you want to do. If you do that, you'll be a much happier person."

Annah wasn't used to displaying emotion. She reached for her hand and held it. It was a moment in a friendship that would continue to grow as time went by.

In The Albatross, Floyd ordered another beer and said to himself, "You jerk, you might as well get stewed. No one's going to care tonight."

CHAPTER TWENTY-THREE

A cool wind blew off the Gulf, driving away the humid summer air as Spencer drove the three of them north toward Rosewillow. Annah closed her eyes, and listened to the hum of the wheels on the highway and occasionally listened to Spencer and Kat's conversation. She covered her shoulders with her sweater in the back seat.

She contemplated on the changes in her life. She was losing people she loved. First, her husband died and a little of herself died with him. One by one, her children have distanced themselves from her emotionally. Charlotte is turning cold and manipulating. Morgan is becoming selfish and rude, and Emily is searching for meaning in her life by seeking relationships with one man after another.

Her best friends, Kat and her husband, are moving, and their friendship would become long-distance. Only time will tell if their relationships to each other would change, too. Now, Grandma Wilmont is dying and she would soon experience an emptiness that only her grandmother could fill.

She thought of Floyd, a man so different from Jackson. Yet, he was the most interesting and alluring man, she had ever met. She knew that it would be unwise for her to encourage a romance with him. They were of two different worlds. He was a northerner and laborer and she was a southerner of high breeding. They were of different cultures and lifestyles. How could that relationship last? Would it become a summer fling? How would she face the Rosewillow community and her family after an affair like that? Then, she thought, she had grown to enjoy the wonderful friendship of Floyd's aunt and uncle, and she didn't want to lose them.

She shifted in her seat. She remembered the look Floyd gave

her the first time they met. She could not glance away. He mesmerized her with that twinkle in his eye and deep, penetrating stare. His eyes were like a magnet. She pulled her sweater tighter over her. *What if he says he loves me, and then one day he leaves me? I don't ever want to be hurt again.*

She lifted her head to see if Kat or Spencer was aware of her, but they continued with their conversation, so she laid her head against the back of the seat. She wondered how she was supposed to act on her first date with him. She felt she would be out of touch, almost like a teenager. "Oh, it'll only be a fishing trip," she whispered.

Kat leaned around in her seat and said, "Did you say something, hon? My Lord, we haven't heard a word out of you for miles."

Annah opened her eyes. "I'm talking to myself."

"Hon, we haven't left you out of our conversation. If you want to say something, please jump in."

Annah waved her hand to indicate she was okay. She absolutely could not ask Emily about what to do on a first date. She'd scream, "Mom?" and there would be no end to the questions.

As Spencer pushed the speed limit toward South Carolina, they arrived home in Rosewillow in the late evening. Just as Emily had promised on the phone, she met Annah at the front door. Spencer and Kat told them they would wait for her call to hear the report of Grandma Wilmont and drove away.

"I'll call you as soon as I know what's happening," Annah said to them as they left.

"Mom, you look awful. Your face is still bruised,"

"I'm fine, Emily, just tired from driving all day."

"Charlotte wants to go with you to see Grandma tomorrow morning, but I told her you should visit her without us hanging around. I didn't mention that I was going with you."

Annah picked up her case and started for the stairway. "So, how's your relationship going with Jimmy?"

"Mom, the more I see him, the cuter he becomes. He's always stumbling over his feet and stuttering when he gets nervous. Sometimes I want to just sit and hold him."

Annah thought for a moment, and then said, "I'm happy for you. He's a fine young man."

Annah knew that something had changed in her when she woke the next morning. She no longer wanted to live in her house or in Rosewillow. She lifted her head and sat halfway up, leaning on her elbow. Sunshine beamed through her window casting a brilliant reflection on her bedroom wall, but she longed for the sunshine spreading over the palm trees, sea grapes, and the frothy tides on the

Ionia shores, and wished she were there instead.

She slipped out of bed, dressed, and left her room to walk downstairs and through the hallway toward the French doors in the rear of the house. Outside on the spacious veranda, she ran her hand over the ornate railing and peered out at the ocean and the long stretch of beach interrupted by areas of undeveloped marshlands and minor islands. Swells of sea water pounded the shore, sending thundering echoes up the slope.

She reminisced about the stories her mother told her as a young child of Captain Rupert and his dream of having a plantation and a mansion along the Atlantic shore. She learned how important it was for her to be a Gladstone and to be the one to carry on its legacy.

I once had so many hopes, but now so many uncertainties lie ahead. My life will never be the same again. She lifted her head and stared at the sky. A seagull soared and met several others in the air. Annah wished she could fly away with them. She returned to the house, empty now of voices and laughter and longed for the loneliness to end.

Emily met her at the bottom of the stairs when she was ready to go visit Grandma Wilmont. "Mom, do you want to eat something before we go?"

"No, dear," she said. "I'm sure your grandmother is anxious to see us as soon as possible."

"Then, let's go."

"Annah, I'm so glad you're home," Delsey said, walking up beside them. "We missed you. Charlotte wants you to call immediately. She says it's important."

Annah's composure fell. "Delsey, I'll talk to her later." She walked over to her. "I'm so happy to see you, too," she said. "How was your trip to see your family?"

"Wonderful, Annah. We saw our new great-granddaughter, Ida Ann. She's a year old now."

"Congratulations. I'll bet you'll want to take more trips to see her and your family."

Delsey folded her hands, looked up to the ceiling, and walked away singing to herself.

Annah and Emily drove to Grandma Wilmont's home and parked in front of the gate. As they approached the screen door to her home, Annah peered in and saw Maybelle crocheting. She sat in a cushioned chair beside her grandmother, who lay upon a hospital bed. "Maybelle," Annah whispered through the door. "We're here. Don't wake her."

Maybelle instantly picked her head up and waved for them to come into the house. She walked over and greeted them. "She's dozing. She'll be awake here any minute."

Annah motioned for Emily to sit with her on the sofa, as they watched Maybelle crochet.

"Oh, we have visitors," the nurse said, as she entered the living area. "I'm Gayle, your grandmother's day nurse."

They nodded and introduced themselves.

Annah observed her grandmother's aged and withered face. How quickly she had failed. It couldn't have been more than few weeks ago that she had sat in her home having tea and sharing news.

She remembered the special years she had with her as a small girl and the times they had gardened together. Once, Grandma had prepared a tea party on a small table in her back yard making her feel like a grown-up lady. It was then that she determined to grow up and be like her, a woman of wisdom and grace.

Annah pulled out a tissue to wipe the on-coming tears away. Had she achieved the wisdom her grandmother had? Instead, she thought that she lived a life of pretentiousness, and her life had become shallow.

She remembered the stories her Grandma told her when *she* was little. How she and her brother, Rufus, with their mother, traveled to the island off South Carolina and visited the Gullah village and the relatives of the families that served their plantation for over a century. That's why Grandma took her over to visit the descendants of the same people when she was young. Those trips were the most exciting times of her life because she always felt like part of their family, and they were real people, not like the little girls she played with in her mother's social gatherings.

Annah considered her own mother's behavior. She treated her servants as second-class. Where did she learn this behavior? Certainly, it didn't come from Grandma Wilmont. No. Louisa flaunted her role in the Rosewillow society. Now, that time has passed.

Grandma opened her eyes and squinted. "My darling," she said with a scratchy voice. "You came."

Annah stood and took her hand. "Grandma, how are you doing?"

"Not well, my dear," she said with labored voice. "I want to talk with you and give you something before the good Lord takes me home." She squeezed Annah's hand.

Annah felt her throat swelling, making her unable to speak.

"Maybelle," Grandma Wilmont said, "please lift me up on the pillow."

Maybelle put down her crocheting and walked over to her. Both she and the nurse gently pulled Grandma Wilmont's elderly body up and propped her head on the soft pillow.

"There now, we can talk," she said. "Child, I had a dream

about you while you were in Florida." She coughed and struggled to clear her throat. "I won't tell you the dream, but I will tell you *my* story, and I know you will understand."

Annah and Emily listened, as Maybelle and the nurse slipped from the room.

"When I was a young woman," she said, clearing her throat again, "I was considered the most beautiful lady at the ball. I was an elegant debutante. Many handsome gentlemen wanted my hand, not only for the dance, but for marriage." She closed her eyes and took in a deep breath so she could continue to speak.

"My family expected me to marry Thaddeus Wilmont, the best-heeled young man in all of South Carolina. Oh, yes, he was handsome. All the young ladies flirted with him and," she paused, "he with them."

Annah stared at her curiously. "You married him."

Grandma Wilmont struggled to laugh. "Yes, I married him, but he never kept his eyes off the other young women. I was his porcelain doll, which he put on a pedestal. He boasted about gaining the Gladstone mansion along with me. You see, to the other young men, he won the prize…me, along with the honor of owning the grandest house in Rosewillow."

"But I always thought you were happy?"

Grandma Wilmont drew in a labored breath. "I needed to keep my head high and never let on I was unhappy. I was destined, through my heritage, to live that life. Thaddeus and I only had one child, your mother, while he fathered many others with women who quietly left town for good. Oh, there were rumors, but they were squelched as soon as they emerged."

Annah leaned close to her. "Grandma, I'm so sorry to hear all this."

"What I want you to know is that I fell in love with a young man before I married Thaddeus. I dreamed of running away with him, but I was afraid. He was a man of 'no station', and my family wouldn't allow me to marry him."

Annah saw a tear in her eye.

Grandma Wilmont placed her hands on Annah's cheeks. "My dear child, I lived to regret a love lost, and I don't want you to do the same."

Annah's heart leapt. It was as if her grandmother had foreseen her time with Floyd, even though she had not shared it with her. "Grandma," was all she could say.

Grandma Wilmont looked deep into Annah's eyes, reached her hand out to have Annah hold it. She pulled her face toward her and kissed her forehead. "Now, I want to give you something." She let go, and with her hand trembling, pointed toward the table beside her bed.

Annah was still in shock. How could she have dreamed of her growing affection for Floyd, a man of 'no station'?

"I want you to have my Bible. I've filled the margins with many notes. When I'm gone, you will find all the help you will ever need in there. Now, let the Lord direct your ways," she said, "and your heart."

Annah felt her eyes water, laid her head on her grandmother's knee. Grandma Wilmont gently patted her. She had said all she needed to say.

After a time, Emily stood and picked up the Bible to hand it to Annah. She placed her hand on her mother's back and sat down beside her.

Maybelle and the nurse returned. Maybelle didn't pick up her crochet needle and yarn. She folded her hands together, listening to Grandma Wilmont's strained and intermittent breathing.

The nurse hovered over her and ministered as much as she could, but when all of them heard the quiet rattle, and her breathing stopped, they knew her time had come. The nurse ran her hands over her eyes and closed them. Grandma Wilmont passed peacefully to sleep for eternity with a smile on her face.

At that same moment, Delsey looked up from her work and rushed to her cottage where Jerome was sitting at the kitchen table. "It's time to call the family to come from the islands. Grandma Wilmont has called and the heavenly host has arrived."

Jerome sat up. "Then I'll send Custer to them to tell the news." He pushed his chair back and immediately left the house.

Delsey remained at the table, staring into Jerome's empty chair. "Yes, Sir. It's time to consider the needs," she said. She knew the Gulliver pantry held the necessary food supplies to bake for a large crowd, but this menu would be quite different from the Gulliver's, so she put on her cooking apron and hurried back to the household kitchen to take inventory. Renaldo was not there to help.

She laid cake pans for baking and canisters holding flour, sugar, and various other ingredients on the counter. With floured hands, she drew a circle on the wooden board in front of her, put a hole in the center with her finger, and said, "Gawd, puhtek Annah."

Jerome walked in and stood beside her. "Yes, Mama, God will protect Annah."

CHAPTER TWENTY-FOUR

Custer set out for the islands in his wooden motorboat, which he used for fishing and traveling through the marshes and coastal waters, toward the islands. He preferred the boat to driving their pickup. It would take two hours depending on the tide to reach the south island where their Geechee family lived. He knew even before he left they would expect him.

When he arrived, Aunt Carmita was waiting on the shore for him. She held a large silver cross between the palms of her hands. As he drew closer to her, she called, "Is it time?"

"Yes, Mama, Delsey sees it"

"Well, come on then. I've just boiled up a chicken with beans and rice. You should eat before we gather the people to tell them."

Custer brought his boat up to the beach, leaped out, and pulled the boat farther up the sand bank to tie it to a large root jutting out of a tree. Aunt Carmita took his face in her hands and kissed him lightly on the cheek. He followed her up the sandy path leading to the village.

"I see clouds in the east, and they're swirlin'," she said. "Uh, huh."

Custer nodded. He could hear singing over the hill.

"They're ready," Aunt Carmita said.

Once the news of Grandma Wilmont's passing reached the island people, their Praise Houses rang with the songs of old spirituals as they prayed for her safe passage into heaven.

Over a hundred people came to attend her funeral. They brought sweetgrass baskets filled with rice, black beans, onions, and white corn to be cooked for the family and friends at Gladstone. They also brought sweet potato pies, candied yams, cold shrimp, sausages, and crab cakes to add to the meal after the service.

Annah, aware of the activity in the house when she returned to it after her grandmother passed away, wanted only to hide away in her bedroom and be alone.

Delsey, along with her Geechee family, and Renaldo and Lucia cooked and baked for the reception. Seeing Emily enter the kitchen, she said, "Everything is taken care of Emily, you won't have to help us with the food for tomorrow."

Emily felt relieved. She, too, wanted to be alone to grieve for her great-grandma.

At Georgette Louisa Wilmont's final resting place in the Rosewillow Cemetery the next morning, Pastor Burnham expounded upon a Scriptural discourse and prayer within a circle of family and friends. Soon, the island people began to whisper a song in their Gullah language. The whisper grew into louder voices and eventually into shouts of hallelujah. They clapped and swayed with joy. Several of the ladies laid gifts over the grave.

Annah clutched a moist handkerchief within her hands as she sat in a folding chair in front of her grandmother's grave. Emily, Maybelle, and the families of Charlotte and Morgan sat alongside her. Henry St. James, Randall Spotswood, and Jimmy Nealy stared toward her from the sidelines, and Kat and Spencer stood beside them. Kat glanced up to give Annah a sad look as she wiped tears from her eyes. Finally, Delsey, Jerome, and Custer stood beside them.

Friends from the Rosewillow community stood on one side of the grave and the Geechee villagers stood on the other.

On the villagers' side, she spied her childhood friends, Sallie May and Crystaline, smiling at her from the crowd. Leaning on Clara, Sallie May's mother, was a short, gray-haired lady, Auntie Josie, weeping for her old friend. She coveted the memories of these people. Kindness and friendship were more important than wealth.

She thought, with all these people in her life, why should she feel so alone?

As the company around her began to depart, the tree branches above them began to shake over the grave and a gentle wind blew through the host of mourners. "Uh huh," Clara said, as she raised her hands to the sky. "We see you Georgette. Go peaceably. Go peaceably." Then the island people sang Hallelujah so loud birds flew in all directions.

Everyone but the islanders stood motionless, unable to comprehend the moment. There was utter silence.

At last, Delsey tapped Annah on the shoulder and whispered that the meal was prepared at the house and everyone was invited.

Renaldo and Lucia had stayed behind to spread an abundance of food enough to feed the crowd on long tables set outside on the lawn. Overhead, a canopy of live oaks provided shade for the gathering.

Now, it would be a day of remembrances, old friends meeting after a long time. They ate well and shared stories about Grandma Wilmont until the early evening when the Geechee people headed to their homes and the Rosewillow community people departed to theirs.

Before the people left, Auntie Josie and Clara walked over to Annah to talk with her. Auntie Josie took Annah's hands in hers and said, "Your grandma was a fine lady, and we'll be missin' her visits, but we'll be seein' her spirit all the days comin'. Now you take care of yourself, because that's what she wants you to do. We'll be prayin' for you to have peace."

All Annah could say as they hugged her, with tears streaming down her face was, "Thank you." Peace was what she desperately needed.

Maybelle walked over to Annah to wish her well also.

Annah placed her hand over Maybelle's hand. "Dear, I feel your pain. Grandma Wilmont loved you very much. A while back, she told me to tell you she wanted you to have her house. She said you were a dedicated nurse and companion all the while you lived with her. She also wanted you to know you will inherit her remaining wealth, so you wouldn't have to worry about money."

Maybelle slipped her hands away and held them to her cheeks. "Oh, my. Oh, my."

"I'm happy for you," Annah said. "Let me know if I can help you with anything."

Maybelle left her side, sobbing.

Morgan and Patricia with their daughter left for home right after the food was almost gone and the discussions were, to Morgan, becoming boring. Randall left at the same time as they. He told Emily that Annah was distant and uncaring of his affections for her. Jimmy left after Emily said the activities were over; and Henry hung around a little longer hoping to talk with Annah, but he received only a smile and a wave of her hand as she went into the house and closed the door behind her.

Except for the few times Charlotte had attempted to get Annah aside and have a talk with her, she kept away from Annah and stayed with Bradford watching the children run haplessly around everyone. Annah knew she would have a talk with her in the morning about not letting her go with her to see Grandma Wilmont while she was alive.

—

Annah rose and knocked on Emily's bedroom door the next morning.

Kat and Spencer were waiting for her in their car outside the house. They had planned to leave the day after the funeral. She opened her door slightly and whispered, "Emily, we're leaving for Ionia."

"What? Mom! You're leaving so soon?"

"Yes, we thought it would be best if I left as soon as the funeral was over. We'll be driving all day, so I can be back for the final test at the hospital. We'll be gone for two weeks."

"Two weeks, Mom? Isn't that a bit long?"

"Honey, I need the rest. You can take care of yourself now, and Delsey and the others are here to help."

Emily wrapped her arms around her mother and laid her head on her shoulders. "I'll miss you anyway. Please call me when you get to Ionia."

"Of course I will," Annah responded. "I love you." Before she left the house, she looked for Delsey. "Delsey, please take care of the place while I'm gone. I know I can count on you and the others to do so," she said. "I'll be back in two weeks."

"Two weeks, Annah? Okay, we'll be fine here. You be careful. I'll be thinking about you while you're gone and praying for you."

Annah stopped. "You always do," she said. "By the way, have you seen my pearl earrings and necklace? I was sure I had put it in my jewelry box and it's gone, just like my gold earrings and bracelets."

"No, Annah. Are you sure you put them in there?"

"I'm sure. Well, I don't have time to search for them. If you find them, please put them away."

"Yes. Don't worry about them. I'm sure they'll turn up somewhere. Have a good trip."

When the phone rang, Annah said, sensing that Charlotte was calling. "Delsey, I don't want to answer it." She grabbed her suitcase and hurried down the steps toward the car. "Let's go. Let's go," she said to Spencer, as she hopped in his car."

Delsey shut the front door and walked over to the phone to answer it. "Hello, the Gulliver's residence. May I help you?"

"Delsey," Charlotte said. "Let me talk to my mother."

Delsey paused, holding the receiver away from her ear because of her loud voice. "I'm sorry, Charlotte, but your mother has just left with Mister Spencer and Miss Kat. May I do something for you?"

Charlotte mumbled something Delsey did not understand. "Where's that bratty sister of mine. Is she still in bed?"

She paused again. "Yes, I think she is. May I have her call you back?"

"No!" Charlotte screamed, slamming the phone down in her ear.

Delsey gently laid the receiver back on its bed. "Lord, how

that young woman acts."

___

Spencer drove away from Annah's house and headed toward I-95 on their way to Tampa.

"Why, hon, you look like you just saw a gopher pop its head up raring to go," Kat said, as she stared at Annah over the back seat. "You're sure happy looking. What happened in that house, for mercy sakes?"

"I just dodged canon fire. Charlotte called as I was leaving, so I ran out before I had to talk to her." Annah sat back in her seat. "I'm finally learning how to handle her."

Kat sighed. "Wait a minute. Annie girl, not answering her call is not handling her. You just put her off until you talk to her later."

Annah gave her a look of resignation. "Okay, I'll call her later. Right now, I'm not in the mood to talk to her."

As they drove farther, Annah leaned her head against the window and thought about her grandmother, whom she would surely miss. She remembered the gift she left her. She wondered if she would ever open her Bible. God was too distant for her to care to read it. Why should she? He did not stop Jackson from lying to her. If she could turn the clock back, things would be different. She would try to understand Jackson more, and then maybe he would stay faithful to her. She decided there was nothing she could do now except put those years of her life with Jackson in a lovely imaginary box, wrap it with a crimson ribbon, and place it on her shelf of memories.

CHAPTER TWENTY-FIVE

The drive to Ionia took them until late that evening. Lola and Roy stayed up to hear Annah describe what happened during her grandmother's funeral in Rosewillow. They were especially interested in hearing about the Geechee people and the wonderful abundance of foods they contributed. Lola wanted to know how she could get their recipes, and Roy said he would enjoy going fishing with the men and catching the fish they fried.

The next morning, Spencer and Kat picked Annah up to take her to her appointment at the Tampa Hospital. Annah worried that the test would reveal that she would require surgery.

"This will be nothing," Kat said to Annah as she watched her fill out paperwork. "It'll only be one teeny test, and you'll be fine." Spencer nodded in agreement and returned to reading a magazine.

Finally, Annah heard her name called and rose to follow a lab technician. In twenty minutes, she returned.

"Did everything go okay?" Spencer asked, standing.

"Yes, they told me to wait for the result, and it should be ready in an hour. Let's go have something to eat." The three of them left the sitting room, took the elevator down to the cafeteria and ate a late breakfast. Then, they returned to find that the results were ready.

"Mrs. Gulliver?" the doctor asked, searching the room for her.

Annah stood up. "Yes?"

He sat down beside her. "I was afraid you might have had bleeding between your brain and skull, but you only show a minute sign of it. You're free to go and enjoy your time in Florida, but I want you to return for another test in one week. Sometimes this kind of thing takes time to develop."

Annah looked from Kat to Spencer and back to the doctor. "You mean this is more serious than I thought? I thought I was recovering."

He shifted in his chair. "Yes, you may indeed be recovering, but we want to make sure you will be sufficiently clear of any substantial bleeding." The doctor stood and held his hand out to Annah, ready to leave. "Please schedule your appointment with the office, and I'll see you again at that time." He turned and quickly walked away.

Kat leaned toward her with a look of concern. "Why, hon, you'll be okay. I'm glad you'll be staying here for another week."

Stunned by the doctor's abrupt departure and the possibility that she wasn't completely cured, she said, "Then, I'm going to stay two weeks."

Spencer jumped up. "Good, now let's get out of here."

"Yes," Annah said, as she stood and put her arms between the arms of her two best friends. Time was passing quickly.

As they drove, Annah thought she should call Emily with the news. "Emily, I want you to know the news so you won't worry. My test came out somewhat negative, but I'll be okay. Would you please tell Charlotte and Morgan this so they won't worry either?"

"Oh, Mom, what do you mean somewhat negative?"

"I mean I'm okay, but I have to have another test. I still have some bleeding between my skull and brain. So, I won't be home for another two weeks. You'll be able to reach me at the B&B."

"Oh, my god. Oh, Mom. You've got me scared."

"Don't be scared, dear. I'll be all right."

"By the way, Henry came over to see if you were home."

"Not again. What did he want this time?"

"He wants to tell you something important about fundraising plans."

Annah closed her eyes. "Emily, will you call him and give him my apologies. Tell him that he has Muriel to rely on for anything to do with the museum."

"Mom? You're putting him off again."

"I am." She paused. "Give the others my love. I'll see you in two weeks." She turned off her phone and smiled to herself. She no longer had feelings for Henry, nor any interest in pursuing donors and grants to raise funds for the construction of a Civil War museum, nor being on the board of the Rosewillow Women's Club. She was moving on to new adventures, that is, if she lived.

—

Emily walked into the kitchen to retrieve a soda from the refrigerator. She sat on a kitchen stool, popped open the can lid, and sipped the soda. She shrugged. "I know why Mom doesn't want to think about the museum or Henry anymore. She's falling for this guy Floyd," she said to Delsey.

Delsey poured a cup of hot tea and sat down beside her. "Emily, your mother has changed over this past year in many ways. Things that were important to her before, no longer have her interest."

Emily took another sip.

Jerome came through the door with Custer. "You girls having a talk or two? Can we join you?" They both filled glasses with tea and opened the refrigerator freezer to add ice. Then they sat down across from them.

"So, tell us about your mother," Jerome said.

Emily put her soda can down and folded her hands. "Mom says that her test today came out somewhat negative, so she's going to have stay down there for another test next week. She says she'll be home in two weeks at the latest." She hesitated. "Only...."

After giving her a questioning look, Custer asked, "Only?"

"Only if the results show that the bleeding beneath her skull and brain doesn't get worse."

Jerome placed his cup down hard, making a loud bang. "Bleeding beneath her skull?"

Emily laid her arms across the table. "Well, when Charlotte, Morgan, and I were sitting in the hospital waiting room when we were down there, the doctor came to tell us that he was concerned she might have hit her head so hard blood could begin to form between her brain and skull. I think it's called a hematoma. That's why she went back there to have another scan."

Delsey closed her eyes, Jerome placed his hand on his forehead, and Custer took a long drink of his tea, keeping his eyes on Emily.

Emily looked up at the three of them. "Don't worry. Mom's a strong woman and has overcome other health issues and traumas in her life. I'm sure she'll be okay."

No one spoke. The silence in the room was deafening. Jerome slid off his stool and went to the sink to empty his glass. Custer did the same. Without a word, Delsey rose from her seat and followed the men out of the kitchen. She, too, had nothing more to say.

Emily stayed on her stool, watching them leave, and thinking about her mother. The possibility of her dying suddenly hit her hard. "Oh, my god," she said aloud. She threw away her soda can. *I'm going to take a long walk on the beach. It's been some time since I've prayed, and I'd better start now.*

"Annah, sweetheart, I think we'll be heading over to our hotel. It's been a long day, and we need to get a good night's sleep," Spencer said, as he dropped Annah off at the B&B.

"I know it has," Annah said. "Give me a call tomorrow morning. I'd love to see the inside of your house after you've signed the papers and have the key."

"Our appointment is at two o'clock," Spencer said. "Didn't you say you were going fishing with Floyd?"

"He asked me if I'd like to go, but I'll have to give him a call."

Annah watched them drive off and then walked up the steps. When she entered the house, she saw Floyd sitting in an armchair. Seeing him there was the last thing she expected. "I didn't recognize you. You look wonderful."

He strolled over to her with a grin on his face. "Well, I couldn't wear my work clothes to meet a pretty lady. Now, could I?" Floyd said, as he kissed her cheek. He had on the same outfit he wore to pick her up at the hospital.

"How do you feel? I've been worried about you," he said, examining her face.

Annah seldom showed anyone weakness. "I'm a little headachy once in a while, but I'm all right. My test turned out somewhat okay. The doctor wants to give me another test in a week to make sure everything is still okay, and I'm sure it will be so."

Lola walked over to them. "What do you mean, somewhat okay?"

Annah looked from one to the other. "The doctor is scheduling another test in one week, but I'm going to plan on staying here for two weeks so I can have more time away from home and rest."

"Somewhat okay is not okay," Floyd said. "What's wrong?"

"Nothing. The doctor wants to make sure I don't have excessive bleeding."

They all eyed her with concern. "Don't worry. Just think, I'll have another two weeks here, and I'm looking forward to it."

Floyd took her hand. "Annah, we have a lot of catching up to do. Two weeks sounds like a good thing to me. I'll take you to the hospital for that third test." He let go.

"You'd better do that, Floyd," Lola said, looking glum.

"So, tell me how it went up there," Floyd asked Annah.

"Everything went well." She described the funeral of her grandmother, her reunion with old friends and relatives at the reception afterward, and the special occasion of having the Gullah village people join them. She would tell him of her time growing up and traveling to the islands to visit them with her grandmother later. Floyd interjected that his life had become a daily task of redundancy--working, fishing, and hitting the bar in the afternoons. He looked forward to being with her and visiting her family, her home, and her Geechee friends on the island.

"Is tomorrow a good time for our fishing trip?" Floyd asked,

Annah hesitated. It had been many years since she had been out with any man besides Jackson. "Yes," she said.

"Hey, you'd better be prepared, young lady. The guys around here call Floyd the king of bass fishin'. He's caught more than any fisherman around," Roy said, as he entered the room. "Now, you don't want an alligator to bite you. They're everywhere in the fresh-water channels, just waiting' to eat you up."

Annah gave Roy a silly look and said, "I don't want to miss being eaten up," which brought laughter from everyone.

Floyd put his arm around her shoulders. "Then it's a date, sweetheart. I'll pick you up at eight sharp." He wrapped his arms totally around her and squeezed her so hard she could hardly breathe.

Roy grinned. "Hey, remember we're here."

Embarrassed, she pushed him slightly away. "I have to see if I have the proper clothes to wear. I don't have jeans or sneakers."

Lola popped in. "Annah, you can try on one of my jeans, and I'm sure we can round up a pair of sneakers for you to wear."

"Well, then, I'll pick you up at eight on the dot," Floyd said.

"Ah, you two make me wish I was young again," Roy said.

Lola put her finger to her lips and whispered, "Shhh."

Annah walked Floyd to the door, where he said, "Tomorrow should be a fun day for you. We're going to get rid of those headaches and get you well." He kissed her on the cheek and walked out onto the parking lot.

Tomorrow, she thought, she would come one step closer to being what Kat called a sandpiper, and one more step to being unable to say no to Floyd.

—

Annah knew her euphoria wouldn't last when her cell phone rang, and she saw that Charlotte was calling her.

"Mother, why are you ignoring me?"

"Charlotte, would you please stop screaming into the phone every time you call? I'm not ignoring you. "Is everything okay?"

"Everything's okay here. I'm worried about you traipsing off to Florida again."

Disgusted, Annah said, "Don't you remember I had to be back in Florida for another CAT scan? I had an appointment at the Tampa Hospital early this morning. Spencer and Kat were with me. I am not traipsing off on another vacation. I'll be home in two weeks."

"Two weeks? Why didn't you see if you could have the test here?"

Annah held the phone to her chest momentarily to calm down, and then lifted the phone up to her ear again. "I'll see you in two weeks, dear. Be good." She instantly turned it off.

CHAPTER TWENTY-SIX

Floyd parked his pickup with the trailer and boat in front of the steps at eight sharp the next morning. Annah opened the door as he walked toward her. "Morning," he said, grinning at her. "Ready?"

"Yes and Lola's clothes fit me fine."

"I thought while driving over here that we should take something to drink and a couple of sandwiches to go." He looked at Lola, who was setting up the buffet table for the guests.

"Why, for you Floyd, dear, I will do just that. Sit down while I make your lunches, and I should only be a few minutes."

"Let me help," Annah said, as she followed her into the kitchen area.

Floyd sat in a comfortable chair across from Roy, who put his morning papers aside and smiled at him. "Well, what do you think? Think it's going to rain today?" Floyd asked.

"The paper says it might, but you never know. I don't see a cloud in the sky. Better take sunscreen for the little lady, or she'll burn."

"I have some in my truck, but I think she tans rather than burns."

"Do you think the fish are bitin' today?"

"I hope so, but it'll be a little late when we finally get out on the river. I'm looking more forward to being with her for a day rather than to catch fish."

In the kitchen, Lola pulled lunchmeat and other sandwich makings out of the refrigerator. Annah took slices of the bread that Lola handed her and placed them on a large cutting board.

"So, Annah, what do you think about my Floyd?"

Annah thought about the endearment Lola always used when she referred to Floyd. "Well…," she started, "I like him. He's refreshing."

"Refreshin'? I've heard a lot of people call him names, but never refreshin'. What do you mean?" Lola asked, as she stopped what she was doing and looked at her.

"I mean he's different than the men I've associated with, and very different from my husband." She looked up at her.

Lola picked up her butter knife and began to spread mayonnaise on a slice of bread. "Tell me about your husband. I know you said he died recently."

"Yes, it's been over eight months now. He died of a heart attack at sixty." She paused. "I know what you're thinking. It's too soon for me to become interested in another man."

Lola didn't interrupt her.

"My husband was a neurologist, and I traveled a great deal with him. In our later years, I stopped traveling with him, and we grew distant from each other. I kept myself busy by volunteering in community functions and speaking at women's meetings." She placed cheese and meat on the bread as Lola handed them to her. "What I mean is that toward the end, we didn't have much of a marriage, so the time doesn't matter to me." She stopped. "However, I'm not sure of our relationship yet."

"Not sure of your relationship yet? Honey, I think you're in deeper than you think."

"That's what I'm afraid of." Annah knew she was putting herself in a corner and would have to tell her more. "Lola, I have to tell you the truth if you'll keep it a secret from Floyd."

"Of course I will. We women have our secrets."

She stopped working. "You see, I'm the owner of an historic mansion built after the Civil War. Many generations of our family have lived in it. I have the responsibility to see that it remains with us. From this inheritance, I also have a great deal of wealth."

"My word, you have quite a life." She placed her hands over the jar of pickles and waited for Annah to continue.

"Yes, but here's my dilemma, I don't want him to think I'm better than he is. I would like him to like me for myself. I'm sure I will eventually tell him all about my life in Rosewillow."

Lola reached over and took Annah's hand. "Dear, it's our secret. I won't tell Floyd anythin' that will hurt either one of you. You know that he's fallin' for you, don't you?" She handed her two sandwiches to wrap in plastic. "Let your relationship grow. Things will work out."

"Lola, I don't want either of us to be hurt." She sighed. "I found out that my husband had a mistress, and I'm afraid to trust another man."

Lola stopped. "Sweetie, Floyd is the most trustworthy man you'll ever meet."

She hesitated to go on.

"Annah, if it's to be it will be. I've seen how you react when you're with him. If you're fallin' for him, too, then things will work out. You'll see."

"Lola, I would love to see it work out. My life has been so superficial and empty. Floyd is real and has made me feel whole. I see how you, Roy, and Floyd live and you're so happy. You're so happy doing what you like to do. This is how I want to live from now on, doing what I like and want to do."

"Well, then. Let's see how this goes with Floyd. I have a feelin' you're goin' to do exactly what you want to do." She finished packing a basket for their lunch. "By the way, what happened to that mistress?"

"One day, she showed up at our house and demanded to have the letters back that she wrote to Jackson. I didn't know what to say at first, and then I told her I shredded them, but I lied. I could only bring myself to read one, and it hurt, so I decided to shred them later."

"Dearie, I think you'd better do that as soon as you can to get them off your mind and so no one else reads them."

"She left telling me Jackson never loved me and the entire community knew about their affair."

"How nasty can someone get? Forget about that. She just wanted to hurt you."

Roy opened the kitchen door and peeked in. "Ladies, those sandwiches are takin' forever. The sun is gettin' higher in the sky and the fish won't be bitin'. Floyd wondered if you both took off without him."

"Here goes," she said, as she handed the basket to Annah and pushed her toward the door. "Enjoy your day."

"Hey, ladies, it's about time. Come on, we have fishing to do," Floyd said. He retrieved the cooler from Roy.

As they walked out the door, Annah waved to Lola and saw her wink at her. Yes, this would be an enjoyable day. She hoped there would be many surprising moments.

It took Annah and Floyd over an hour to reach the river. A rundown fishing shack and the bow of a sunken rowboat covered in tangled weeds marked the spot where he always put his boat into the water.

Annah noticed moored yachts of various ages and conditions dotted the river on the other side. "Do people live in those boats?" she asked.

Floyd looked out his window at them. "Yep, you might say that. Local people use those boats. Some use the boats to fish from and some live in them to avoid property taxes. There are no taxes on the river."

Annah couldn't imagine living in those conditions.

"If you'll walk over to the trees, I'll back the boat into the water."

Annah surveyed the area. Nets strung haplessly over a tree branch and discarded pop and beer cans littered the edges of the sandy slope where his boat was to be launched. With caution, she walked away from the truck and over to the edge of the slope.

Once the trailer and boat were down in the water, Floyd left the truck and carried their gear over to the boat.

"Here," he called to her as he threw a rope toward the truck. "Grab this and hang onto it and be careful. I have to release the boat from the trailer."

Annah stepped carefully over to the front of the truck and reached for the rope, but couldn't get it. She placed her hand on the bumper and stretched her arm out to pick up the rope, but slipped and fell.

"Annah, are you hurt?" Floyd yelled.

"Only my pride." She groaned, as she pulled herself up and glanced at him with a sheepish look on her face. Wet sand and algae covered the back of her jeans and shirt.

"Now that you've had your initiation into the world of boating…." he said, laughing.

Annah gave him a sullen look. "Floyd, that wasn't funny."

"I'm sorry, but I couldn't help it. You're covered in slime."

"Oh, God. What am I going to tell Lola? I've ruined her clothes."

Once he parked the truck and trailer, he helped her into the boat. "Let's go, pretty lady, we have fish to catch. Are you ready?"

The warmth of his hand tingled on her shoulder as he climbed into the boat and touched her. "I've never been readier."

Grinning, he revved the motor and backed the boat into the river.

Annah knew this would be a day unlike any other. Lola's clothes were covered in grit. Her sneakers were soaking wet, flies and mosquitoes buzzed around her head, and she had forgotten to bring a hat. Off on the river bank were alligators, sleeping yet ready to slither into the water at a moment's notice. "Floyd, if I make it through this day alive, it'll be a miracle."

"I think I'm already seeing a miracle," he said, as he gunned the motor to take them faster up the river. "Sweetheart," he yelled through the noise, "you're going to love fishing."

They traveled quite a ways until they came to a wider expanse of the river and a deep pool where he shut off the motor and reached for the bait box plus two fishing rods. "I'm going to put some bait on your hook. Here, take the rod."

Annah slapped a mosquito on her face. At home in Rosewillow, she would have covered herself in mosquito repellent. Now she feared their bites and how they would swell on her skin.

"Oh, I forgot to tell you how to avoid mosquitoes. Do you smoke?"

"Do I smoke? No," she said, as she watched Floyd light a cigar.

He blew out a smoke ring. "You see, if you did, I'd give you a cigar to smoke."

She made a grim face. "Don't tell me women smoke cigars."

He waved his cigar around his head and puffed on it again. "Of course, haven't you seen them do it?"

"Not exactly."

Standing up, he leaned over and handed her his cigar. "Make this your first time. It'll keep the flies and mosquitoes off you."

"You're kidding," she said, as she took it and held it straight out in front of her.

"Hold it to your face," he said, watching her. "Come on. I'm not kidding. You might even put it in your mouth."

Annah brought it closer to her head. The end was wet from his chewing. "I'll just hold it, thank you." The smell nauseated her.

"Okay, but it works." He bit off the end of another cigar, placed it between his teeth, lit it, pulled in the smoke, and let it out as he lifted his head to watch the smoke swirl around him.

Annah coughed. "Floyd, the smoke is getting to me."

"Sweetheart, you're going to have to get used to it if you continue to hang around me," he said, as he finished baiting the hooks. "Now, you know how to cast your line into the water, don't you? I'm sure you've seen others do it."

Annah waved the cigar around her face and coughed. "Of course, I do. I mean, no. No, I have never fished before like this. I've only seen people deep-sea fish. What do I do?"

"Here, watch this." Floyd took his rod and cast the line out toward the deep pool. "Did you see what I did?"

Annah laid the cigar on the seat beside her, and tried to imitate him. She held the rod up over her head and swung the line toward his face.

"Hey, not at me." He picked up her line, which was now on

his shoulder, and pulled it in until he found the hook. "At least the bait is still on. Reel your line in and watch me again."

"Okay." In the meantime, the cigar landed at her feet in a small puddle. "Floyd," she said, "I'm sorry. Your cigar is ruined."

He looked at the soggy thing. "Forgetaboutit," he said. "Watch me again." Demonstrating how to toss the line, he repeated what he did the first time.

Annah sat up, lifted her rod to the right of her, and swung it again as hard as she could. This time the line flew so high, it landed on the bank. "Whoops!"

"You're telling me the truth. You've never fished before." As he said that, a fish took his bait, and he fought with it for some time before he reeled it in. "See? This is how you do it." He put his foot on its body and removed the hook. "This one must be at least a pound. Enough for a nice dinner tonight."

Annah didn't answer. She was busy slapping mosquitoes off her arms and face.

"Okay, Annah, you're uncomfortable. Let's stop for the day. We can eat our lunch at the small park we passed on the way to this river."

"Thank you. I think I'd like that." She tried to reel in her line, but it was stuck on a mangrove root.

"Don't pull it too hard or you'll lose the hook. Here, give me your rod." Floyd worked the line loose and reeled in the line. Both the hook and bait had broken off.

Annah saw that he never lost his temper. She remembered times with Jackson when it seemed she could never do anything right. Watching Floyd put away his fish, storing their rods in the boat, and appearing very patient, she felt herself drawn more to him. He was pleasant to be with and certainly a lot of fun.

He knew she was not a sportswoman, but it didn't matter to him. Maybe he was thinking he could teach her to be one, one day, but she shuddered wondering why she so wanted him to do just that.

After he pulled the boat and trailer up out of the water, Annah climbed into Floyd's truck and settled in. "I'm sorry, I should have washed this muck off my clothes before getting into your truck," she said.

"You look fine to me," he said. "I'm more interested in you being with me than worrying about dirty clothes on the seat of my truck."

"But I should have known better."

"I know," he said, grinning. "But you look fine to me. I'm not clean right now either. I have mud over my pant legs and boots. That's what fishing is all about. It's having fun and spending the day getting…ah, bit by mosquitoes and flies." He pointed to her face where a mosquito bite had begun to swell.

"Okay," she said, scratching the bite area.

"We'll have a nice lunch, though. They spray the park with bug repellent. It's a family picnic area, and they want to keep everyone happy."

Floyd helped her out of the truck after they parked and held onto her arms, gazing at her. He slid his hands along her arms and then let go. "Let me get the cooler," he said, as he turned around and headed for the boat.

She couldn't move. The heat from his hands still burned her arms.

Floyd motioned with the cooler toward the nearest picnic table situated below a large palm tree. She followed him over to it and watched him open the cooler. Reaching in, he handed her the sandwiches. As they sat down across from each other, he took the wrapping off his sandwich, lifted it up, and took a large bite.

"Floyd, you make me blush by the way you look at me," she said.

"I'm sorry, Annah, but you are so beautiful I can't keep my eyes off you. I'll try to be more conscious of that."

She looked down while removing the cellophane on her sandwich. When she looked back up at him, he was smiling. "Quit it!" she said. "You're embarrassing me."

"My fisherwoman," he said playfully. "You have some learning to do. You know, of course, this will not be your last experience. You're going to have to stay longer than two weeks. Two weeks in Ionia will never do."

Annah took a bite of her sandwich. With her mouth full of food, she said, "We'll have to see about that," she said, thinking more about extra time than about fishing.

"Annah," Floyd started. "I have something to ask you."

She looked up. "This sounds serious."

"Well, I would like to help you with any hospital expenses you might have to pay. I know you probably have health insurance, but sometimes there's charges that aren't covered and I'd like to help you out with them. When Teresa died, I was surprised at the bills that came afterward. It took me quite a while to pay them off."

Annah put her sandwich down and stared at him. This was unexpected, and she didn't know what to say. She knew the hospital charges would be no sacrifice to her. She had never considered the costs that others like Floyd would have to pay.

"I have quite a bit of savings, and I won't be hurt financially by helping you," he added.

She gripped her hand around her glass, stunned by his unselfishness.

"Please think this over. I don't want you to worry about not being able to pay your bills."

At last, she said, "Floyd, I'm not worried about being burdened with hospital charges, but thank you for your consideration. I appreciate you." She could hardly swallow anymore of her sandwich, so she wrapped the rest of her food in the cellophane and placed it on the table.

They sat for a time watching the breeze sway the palm leaves and listening to the waves washing the shoreline, both of them deep in thought.

Floyd took half of his sandwich and covered it in cellophane. "Annah," he started, "see that family sitting over there?"

She twisted around to look where he was pointing.

"What do you notice about them?"

She turned back to him. "I guess they're wearing clothes too heavy for this heat."

Floyd smiled. "What else?"

She studied their faces. "The children's clothing is dirty; and, I guess, so are the parent's clothes."

Floyd gathered up their uneaten sandwiches, two others from inside the basket, and two apples, and walked over to the family.

Annah watched him and heard him say, "We had extra food and thought you might like to have it." The wife and two children looked up at him and eagerly took the food. The husband stood and shook Floyd's hand. She noticed that the parents divided the sandwiches among the children first and then to themselves.

When Floyd returned, he whispered, "Annah, those people are homeless, and we have so much to share."

Shaken, she glanced over at the woman as their eyes met, and she felt a compassion she had never experienced before. She also felt a deeper respect for Floyd.

"Let's go," he said, as he picked up their basket and headed for his truck. I want to show you my place."

CHAPTER TWENTY-SEVEN

On their way to Floyd's home, Annah asked, "Floyd, what is your biggest dream?"

"Hmm, my biggest dream is to someday own a yacht that I can live on year round and fish to my heart's content. I'd travel down to the Keys and spend all my time finding the best fishing spots. I could also travel around Florida and up the coast and beyond, maybe stopping here and there to tour places I've always wanted to see."

"Would you know how to operate a yacht?"

"Yes. When I was growing up my Dad had a fifty-foot sailboat, and he taught me to navigate. That's when I learned to love the sea. When I married Teresa, her family owned a seventy-foot motor-sailor, which I learned to operate."

She thought about her time with Uncle Rufus. She had sailed once with him along the eastern shores and as far up as Nova Scotia, but that had not been her biggest dream. "I hope you realize your dream someday."

"Someday, my lady, but life is good to me now and I can't ask for more."

"So, tell me about you. Lola said you moved from New York after your wife died. I'm so sorry to hear about your loss, and I know what you're going through, since I lost my husband. It's a sad, lonely, and life-changing experience."

He glanced sideways at her. "You seem to know things about me already, and you've certainly gotten to know a lot more about me in the last few hours." He paused. "Tell you what, I'll tell you even more about myself if you'll tell me more about you. You are my mysterious new friend," he said, rubbing his chin.

Annah shifted her head to stare out the windshield. *What am I going to tell him?* She turned and looked back at him. "I'll try."

"Hmm, that doesn't sound like you're going to tell me your deepest secrets, does it?"

She folded her hands. "Should I?"

"Tell me more about your family. What kind of home do you live in? What's your neighborhood like? How many grandchildren do you have? I've met your adult children already. You know, things like that."

"Okay, you start first."

Floyd put his hand on her shoulder. "First of all, I agree with you. When you lose your spouse, it's devastating. When Teresa died, I almost died with her. I couldn't manage even trying to cook for myself. I made sandwiches for lunch and dinner almost every day. I couldn't find anything in the kitchen, for crying out loud. She did all the cooking, the laundry, cleaned the house, and seemed to do everything for us. Once in a while, she paid a lady to do some deep cleaning, which she didn't have time to do. You know, like dusting high shelves and washing windows. I brought home the big paycheck even though she worked. She worked as a secretary forty hours a week, and I never even considered how much she did for me. She probably worked two jobs a day.

"As for me, I was a general contractor working with developers and built custom homes in a large bedroom community in upstate New York. I sometimes worked seven days a week to meet deadlines, but when we had free time, Teresa and I would take in a few shows downtown and go out to dinner. Occasionally, we'd take trips. That's when we visited Key West, and I grew to love Florida and the Keys.

"We never had children, which was the heartbreak for both of us. My folks died never having the joy of grandchildren. I was their only child. Teresa's parents are still living, but she had two sisters, so they were happy to have six grandchildren from them.

"Let's see. So, we had a good life, but then she died. I decided after a couple of months to come down to Florida and visit my aunt. You know, there's a lot of New Yorkers and people from the north retiring in Florida and, once I visited with them, I decided to move down here. It was okay. The economy was slowing and the jobs were getting fewer and fewer. Now, I still work as a contractor, but I do the work myself."

"You seem to enjoy it. You have several projects going right now."

"Yes, mostly because I can take a job or leave it. If it's too much work, or something I'm not able to do, I don't take it." He looked at her. "By the way, are you still looking for a house down here?"

"Maybe. I keep changing my mind, but I thought if I had more time, I could look around and find a place."

"I'm sorry that the house you looked at didn't work out for you." Floyd watched the traffic slow down. "I'll keep my eye out for something else. You do realize, however, that you could find a house by going through a realtor. You really don't need me to find one for you." He turned his head to face her. "That means you'll have more opportunities to find one."

Annah shifted in her seat. "I know, but it was that first house Kat showed me that caught my eye. It so happened that you were there restoring another house."

"Yeah, imagine that!" he said. "Now, it's your turn."

As she watched the scenery pass by, she scanned the small bait shops, shell stores, and fruit and vegetable stands. She noticed people riding bikes, couples walking hand in hand, and motor homes and campers driving by.

"Annahh," he said, drawing out her name.

She turned her head. "Floyd, I don't know how to tell you about myself."

"Oh, oh. Something tells me you're going to be mysterious again."

"Well, I don't want to hold anything from you. It's just that, at present, I think I should."

"Hmm, at present you think you should keep the truth from me. Now, that doesn't sound very good."

She rocked her foot up and down.

"Okay, I'll tell you what. I would like to take you to my place so you can see where I live. I have to drop off the boat and trailer anyway. It'll be easier to get into the B&B's parking lot. I'm thinking that you'll feel better about me knowing how I live."

Annah felt a chill run through her. She wanted desperately for this day not to end. Nevertheless, should she go to his house? "Floyd, I trust you. It's just that my life is complicated and telling you about it now is not a good time."

"Wow, complicated, huh? Okay, doll, I'll wait until you think it's time to tell me. In the meantime, I'll think you live in an exotic place on an island off South Carolina where you spend the day naked on the beach and run wild with the horses."

"What in the world?" She leaned over laughing. "Okay, you do that."

"So, let me show you my place." He spun the steering wheel with one hand and headed down a sandy road toward his house. Soon, a one-level, brown framed house within a forested area came into view.

Its roof had a green, metallic tile, and its porch had been freshly painted.

"How nice," Annah said. "I like it."

"I thought you would. It's secluded here. I don't like neighbors bothering me, so when I found this place, I knew I could fix it up pretty good. It was run down and hadn't been lived in for years."

Floyd turned the truck in a half circle and backed it and the trailer into a flat spot beside the house. He leapt out, leaving the truck running, and walked around to unhook the trailer. He crawled in, drove the truck a few feet away from the hitch, and shut off the engine. "Come on sweets, I'll show you my palace."

Annah opened her door and slid out onto the damp ground beneath her.

"The density of the trees and the high water table keeps the ground wet. It never seems to dry up," he said, as he took her hand and led her onto the porch and into the house. A small dog ran excitedly toward Floyd, barking and wagging its tail.

"Floyd? You have a dog?"

"Oh, I forgot to tell you. Yes, I do. This is Roscoe." Floyd bent down, rubbed his head. "I found him on my porch one morning, hungry and looking lost. He also had a cut on his back leg. I took him inside and fed him a bowl of cereal. That's all I had in my cabinet that I thought he could eat. When I set a bowl in front of him, he ate as if he hadn't eaten for days. I tried to find the owner, but no one claimed him, so he's mine now."

Annah knelt down and petted him. "I've never owned a dog."

"You haven't?" He watched her with Roscoe. "You've missed a lot of love." He continued. "I treated his leg and bandaged the cut. It wasn't very deep. He may have gotten it snagged on a fence or something. Now, Roscoe and I take long walks together, and he keeps me from being lonely here. I have him to come home to."

She stood up. "What kind of dog is he?"

"I think he's a Jack Russell and Terrier mix. I took him to the Vet to have him checked out. They figured he was five or six years old. "Come on, boy, outside," Floyd said, as he opened the door. "So, you've never had a dog before. Did you have cats? People are either dog lovers or cat lovers."

"I've never had a cat as a pet either."

"You mean you've never had any kind of pet as a child?"

"No. My mother thought pets were dirty, and she didn't want any mess in the house. I've done the same with my family. Besides, never having had a pet I didn't miss one."

"Roscoe, come on," Floyd said, as he held the door open for him to come into the house.

Annah scanned the room as Floyd flipped on the lights. One corner held an overstuffed leather sofa, a small wooden end table with an antique lamp, a braided rug beneath another table, and a television. A hand made bookshelf holding many paperbacks lined the area beneath the one large picture window.

She observed the kitchen with a counter top range, a small refrigerator, a sink with a multi-colored skirt covering the bottom half of it, and white painted cabinets. Next to the kitchen stood a table covered in red and white checkered vinyl tablecloth, and underneath it, two painted chairs.

A doorway with only a floor-length curtain obviously led to the bedroom and probably the bathroom. After she stood from petting Roscoe, he ran to lie down on a patchwork blanket beneath the television. *This is a man's house,* she thought. *Masculine, but inviting.*

"Do you like my castle?"

"Yes. What I'm pleased about is how neat and clean you are."

"Why," he asked. "Do you think I'm messy all the time?"

"Um…seeing your work clothes…. Oh, I'm sorry, I shouldn't have said that."

He walked over to her, put his arm around her, and swept the room with his other arm. "Madam, I am the king of my household. I would hang my servants if they didn't clean up properly."

Without thinking, Annah said, "That's what I tell my help, too."

"Ah ha, so you have servants, my dear. Are you letting me know one of your mysteries?" He embraced her shoulders as he asked that, making her nervous.

"Maybe," she answered.

Floyd leaned his face into hers and pulled her to him, and held her for some time. Annah knew she couldn't resist him and lost the strength to back away. He took his hand, lifted her chin to his, and kissed her on the lips. She froze, but then gave way and let him kiss her, not once but several more times giving into her longing.

"Floyd, we can't do this," she said, pushing him away. "I've only been a widow for eight months, and I have so many things to think about."

Floyd wouldn't let her go. "Madam Butterfly, I've been a widower for over a year. You're never going to forget your husband. I can't forget my wife. But they're gone, and we know the loneliness we both have." He pulled her chin back to his. "Furthermore, Annah, I'm falling in love with you. What are we going to do about that?"

Annah fell again into his warm embrace, giving in to her desire to be loved. Floyd lifted her face to his and kissed her again, this time with more passion. She couldn't resist him. Once again, she pulled away and he let her go.

"Let me get you something," he said, as he walked over to the kitchen and pulled a tissue out of a box. He touched her cheek with the tissue wiped her face. "My lady, you must have something really powerful in your life to stop you from giving in to your desires." He put his hands on her shoulders. "Whether you want to or not, I'm going to see that this obstacle disappears."

She stood back, gripping the tissue. "Floyd, the obstacle is that my husband was unfaithful to me for over ten years, and I'm afraid to trust another man right now. Our love died without me realizing it. I thought he loved his work and research more than he loved me, but he had a mistress. I was a fool and didn't see it."

Floyd held onto her shoulders. "I see. Well, we'll have to work on that."

Annah gazed up at him. She knew she was falling in love with him. How was she going to control her emotions? He was beginning to be all she wanted, and that frightened her.

CHAPTER TWENTY-EIGHT

The first week went by quickly and Floyd and Annah spent time getting to know each other better. They traveled to the Greek town to visit the tourist hang-outs and eat Greek foods. They spent time on the beach feeding the sea gulls with bits of bread from their lunch basket and swimming in the warm, Gulf water. They took a tour on a glass boat to view the sea creatures and fish along the reef, and they went fishing as many times in the river as it took until Annah learned to fish. They also toured the Ionia area looking for homes for sale, but nothing appealed to Annah. In all, they played like two teenagers on their first dates.

During one of those days, Floyd took her to see her car at Ed's Garage. Ed opened the gate to the yard to let them in to view the damage first hand.

Annah shook her head in dismay. They walked around the car. Mud and slime covered the entire car and most of its body appeared scraped and dented from being slammed sideways off the road and rolling into the creek. "We're lucky we made it out alive," she said. "Let me see if I can save any more of my personal items from the glove compartment and trunk."

Ed lit a cigarette and lifted his head to breathe out smoke. "Looks totaled to me, Floyd."

"You can say that again. Annah, you'll have to buy another car."

"My insurance adjuster called and explained that to me, and I'll be receiving a check for its value. But, when I get home to Rosewillow, I can drive my husband's Mercedes," she said. She reached into the console and pulled out what she could save. "I think I have everything."

"Yeah, that adjuster came here about two weeks ago, so I'm sure they'll be pulling it out of here pretty soon."

Ed locked the gate as they walked out of the yard.

"Thanks Ed. We'll be talking with you again," Floyd said, as he led Annah away.

"Hmm," Floyd murmured. "Now I know you own a Mercedes." He looked sideways at her. "Another mystery?"

Annah didn't respond. She had let another secret slip out.

At the end of the week, Floyd drove her to the hospital where she had another CAT scan. As he waited for her, he leaned over and crossed his arms over his knees. He looked at the closed door of the waiting room and let out a long sigh, and then placed his hands over his head for a long while. He had to think about many things. Mostly, he knew he was not going to let her out of his life no matter what the results. He had been through this with Teresa, and he would handle going through it again.

The news had startled both of them and there was not much more they could say after hearing the doctor's report.

—

On the drive back to Ionia, Floyd kept quiet and concentrated on the road ahead of him, while Annah watched the scenery pass by. Once they reached the B&B, Floyd steered his truck into a parking space, and after climbing out, they walked up the steps to the door without speaking.

Lola looked up to see Annah enter the front office. "Annah," she said, surprised to see her expression. "Are you okay?"

She simply waved and kept walking.

She put down her magazine and spied Floyd. "Floyd, is everythin' okay?"

He waited a moment before responding. "Everything's okay. Annah heard some bad news today at the hospital. I'll tell you about it later. Right now, I need to think," he said, as walked back out the door and headed for home.

Lola left the room, rushed up the stairs toward Annah, and knocked on her door. "Honey, you've had two calls today from your daughters. They want you to call as soon as possible. I told them you went to Tampa for your test. One of your daughters, I think it was Charlotte, angrily said that you are never home when she calls, but your other daughter said, I hope she calls to give us the results."

"Thank you, Lola; I'll call them in a minute."

"Okay, then. When you're ready to tell me about your test, please come downstairs."

In her room, Annah sat on a chair facing the open window.

She leaned her elbow on the sill, and stared out at the Gulf. Sail boats passed lazily by each other. She inhaled the fresh ocean air and let her thoughts flow over memories of their week together. *What will this news mean for both of us? Will he still love me after my surgery, without hair and holes in my head, or will he think I'm a freak and never want to see me again?*

Then she remembered she needed to call her daughters to tell them the news.

"Mom," Emily said. "I'm so glad you called. I can't ever get ahold of you. It's so frustrating when you don't even listen to your voicemail."

"Sweetheart, I've had a very busy day."

"Mom, Patricia had her baby early. They needed to take it by C-Section, and we've all been so worried she and the baby would be okay. Morgan was a mess until we learned everything went well, and he's madder than hell at you for not being here."

Annah faced the open window again and wished she could sail away on one of those boats. "Emily, how would I have known that the baby would be early? I was planning on coming home in another week and that should have been around the time the baby was due."

"That's what I mean. You were unavailable all day, and we had no way to contact you." She paused. "The woman at the desk told me you went to Tampa for your test. Mom, you never go out without your cell phone on when you're here."

She watched a pelican land on a post along the dock. "Dear, the doctors read the results to me today, and it looks like I will need surgery to release some blood accumulation between my skull and brain."

Emily screamed. "Mom?"

"Don't worry about it right now. Everything will be all right once they've operated on me. I may have to spend a few days in ICU, but then I'll be okay."

"Mom, when are they going to operate on you?"

"As soon as possible, which means I may have to stay here for some time after that, maybe another week."

"I'm coming right down. I'm going to pack right now and take off."

Annah held onto the phone so tightly her hands hurt. "Emily, you don't have to rush here. The doctor is setting up the appointment, and I'll know tomorrow morning when it will be."

"Will you reserve a room at your place for me to stay?"

Annah knew she wouldn't be able to say no to her. "I'll see what I can do, dear. Maybe you can stay in my room until this is over."

"If I come down there, I'll drive you home when you're ready."

"You might have to do that."

"See you tomorrow. I'll leave real early and be there sometime in the early evening."

"Okay. But, like I said, you may want to wait until I find out just when the surgery is scheduled, and….Oh, I forgot. What does the baby look like and did they call him Curtis like they said?"

"The baby is beautiful. He has blonde hair, and they named him Curtis Jackson."

"Of course," she said. "I like his middle name. Now, what about the house? Everything okay there?"

"Everything else is fine, Mom. Just please come home after all this is over. We need you and you must see the baby. Morgan wants you to help Patricia take care of him. They really need a babysitter since Morgan likes to take Patricia out on his sailboat on the weekends."

Annah held her tongue. He was so much like his father. Shouldn't she have a decision in this? "We'll see," she said.

"Also, Mom, Jimmy and I have something to tell you when we see you. I don't want to talk about it now, but Mom, he's just wonderful. I think I'm in love with him and, well, we'll tell you when you get home."

Annah thought she already knew what they were going to tell her. "I'll be interested in knowing what it is," she said. "Now, Emily, I have to call Charlotte."

"You'll probably get a scolding for not calling her first, so don't tell her I've already told you about the baby."

"Okay, we'll talk later," she said, dreading the next call.

"Charlotte, dear heart, it's Mother."

"Mother, I've been trying to call you forever. Paleez," she said, emphasizing the word. "Please answer your voicemails. I wanted to tell you Patricia had her baby and Morgan was beside himself with worry because she had to have it by C-Section. You should have been here to be with her. For heaven's sakes, Mother, you're needed *here*."

Annah switched the phone to her other ear. "Charlotte, I have been very busy, and I certainly didn't expect the baby to come so early. Are Patricia and the baby doing well?"

"Yes, and they're already home. Morgan says Patricia needs your help, and you should not be fooling around in Florida. He's mad at you for not being at the hospital with us when Patricia delivered the baby. The very thought of cutting open her stomach and pulling out the baby was…oh, just horrible! We all almost threw up just knowing what they were doing to her and the baby."

"The baby came out just fine then and Patricia is fine?"

"Yes, and she decided not to breast feed the baby since Morgan said it would be an inconvenience for them when they want to go sailing. He said it would also be an inconvenience for you, since you had to take care of the baby and may run out of breast milk if they're gone too long, say over a weekend."

Annah held the phone in both hands on her lap. She shuddered at Morgan's inconsideration. Then, she picked up the phone again and said, "Of course, Patricia wouldn't want Morgan to miss his weekend sailing trips," she said with sarcasm. "Charlotte, I have to go right now. I have important things to do. Give Patricia and the baby a big hug for me, and tell Morgan that I'm sure he'll be a good father." She decided the moment wasn't right to share her problem with her. Charlotte would be packing for herself and the children to drive down again and be with her at the hospital. More grief.

"What? Don't hang up on me, Mother. I have something else to talk to you about."

"Can it wait until I see you?"

"No. Bradford and I have started to clean out Father's desk."

Startled, Annah feared they had found the letters. Why hadn't she shredded those letters instead of waiting?

"I knew you didn't have time to do it, so we thought we would help you."

"Charlotte, I've already cleaned out what I could. Is that your responsibility or mine?"

"Mother, it's all of our responsibility to help you. I've been handling your phone calls, which you seem never to answer, and many of Father's business associates have been asking for different research papers. Bradford decided we needed to find them and send them out."

Annah gritted her teeth. "Charlotte, stop what you're doing. *I* will decide what papers to provide them. Please have Bradford stay out of our family affairs."

"Mother! Bradford *is* part of our family. How can you say such a thing?"

Annah's head throbbed. "Never mind. We'll talk about it later."

"Another thing, Mother, Bradford decided you didn't need Father's computer and equipment, so he disconnected it all and brought it to our house. He said he wanted to go through the files on it."

Now, Annah really got angry. She didn't want to lose control, so she turned off her phone. Oh, the impetuousness of him! Annah decided she needed to talk to Spencer and Kat. She needed their advice. They had left a week ago to return home to finalize the paperwork on the sale of their house and finish cleaning the rugs and drapery, but she would try to reach them.

She left her room, stepped down the stairs, and spied Lola

sitting in the comfortable sofa relaxing with a can of soda in her hand.

"Annah," Lola said, as she lifted her head to see her come toward her. "I heard that you have bad news."

Annah sat down beside her. They were alone in the room as it was getting late and the other guests had retired to their rooms or left the building.

Lola twisted sideways to face her. "So, Annah, what's happenin' with you?"

She hesitated for one moment, and then said, "Lola, I have to have surgery. Blood is accumulating between my skull and brain. That's why I've had so many headaches and not feeling well. As the days go by, I'm more and more tired. The doctors read my latest CAT scan and it didn't look good. They're setting up a surgery date at the hospital, and I'll know more in the morning."

"Oh, Annah. I'm so sorry."

"Emily, my daughter, will be here tomorrow evening. Do you have another room available, or should she stay with me in my room?"

"She can stay with you until a room opens up. I have guests leavin' in two days. I'll prepare more towels and such for her." Lola stood up. "I need somethin' stronger to drink. Would you like a glass of wine?"

"Yes. I have more to talk to you about."

"I'm all ears. Go ahead and tell me while I pour the wine."

Annah watched her until she returned to the sofa and handed her a glass. "Lola, you know I'm in love with Floyd," she said. "I've tried not to have this happen, but I haven't been able to control my feelings. I know he loves me, and I don't want him to be hurt if something happens to me, or this surgery goes wrong. What if I don't make it through the surgery?"

Lola sat down cradling her glass. Before she spoke, she took a sip of wine. "Annah, you know he'll be at your side throughout the whole surgery. He's been through this kind of thing before. I don't think anythin' will go wrong."

"I've been thinking that I should go back home after all this and stay there. That will give both of us a chance to forget each other."

"Why, for heaven's sakes? That's crazy talk, Annah. You both love each other and isn't that what love is all about? Stickin' close to each other through thick and thin?"

She wished she could answer. Isn't that what my marriage should have been like? Instead, she responded, "I'm concerned that I haven't told him about my background. I'm afraid he would feel intimidated."

Lola held her glass on her lap holding it with both hands. "I think your background wouldn't make any difference to him. Wealth would be the last thing on his mind."

Annah looked away.

"Annah, we'd love to have you in our family. Roy thinks the world of you." Lola put her arm over the top of the sofa. "Now, dear, you're goin' to have to make up your mind to tell him about your life." She looked steadily at Annah. "How about lettin' him drive you home after the surgery so he will see your home and life for himself?"

"Oh, my. My family would tear him apart."

"Let them try. He's a strong man. Like I said, he's been through this before with Teresa's family and came out fine. None of her family got along with him because they wanted Teresa to marry a different man. They were disappointed in Floyd because he didn't let them control him. Her family was from Philadelphia and his from New York. It was a cultural thing, and they harped about him not bein' of their ancestry, so to speak. To make matters worse, many of her family members were wealthy and his wasn't." She continued. "It looks like he'll be able to handle goin' through this type of problem again. They had a wonderful marriage, and he was faithful to her. She loved him and that's all that mattered to him."

What would he say when she asked him to drive her home? What would he think of her when he sees her elegant home and help? She looked at Lola. "Should I be truthful with him now, or should I ask him to drive me home and let him see my lifestyle for himself like you suggested?"

"Annah, please tell him the truth and let him decide. I don't think it's goin' to make you lose his love. I think he'll enjoy the ride and the excitement. He's been a dull boy since he moved here until he met you."

"My daughter wants to drive me home, but I can explain to her what's happening. She could also follow us there, so she'll feel a part of my request."

"I think it's better that your daughter not follow you. You need time alone with Floyd, and he'll need time to think over what you tell him. Get it all out then because you'll be too weak after your surgery and want to rest." She stopped. "Are you afraid?"

"No." She wished she had an ounce of Grandma Wilmont's strong faith. Would she have been afraid? She decided to read her Bible someday. Sitting back and downing her wine, she said, "Well, Floyd Harrison O'Donnell, sharpen your weapons. Both our lives may change."

Lola slapped her knee. "That's it, Annah my sweet friend, I can't wait to see what happens."

While they were laughing, Roy came in the front door. "Hey, you two, what can't you wait to see what happens?"

"We're just enjoyin' some girl talk," Lola said, as she winked at Annah. "We'll tell you after the battle."

"What battle?"

"Roy, I'll tell you one thing. Annah is goin' into surgery in a day or two."

Annah stood up. "Roy, I had a severe concussion when Kat and I were in that car accident. The doctors are setting up an appointment for surgery for me. It's serious."

Roy froze. "What the heck! Are you goin' be okay?"

"I'm counting on it. I'm not going to think otherwise."

Lola picked up their empty glasses and walked toward the kitchen. Over her shoulder she said, "Roy, we'll talk more later."

Roy gripped his belt with his hands. "Is this something else I should know about now?"

"Nope," she answered, as they both left the room.

CHAPTER TWENTY-NINE

Annah rose the following morning with a sense of apprehension. She picked up her cell phone to call Floyd, but put it down again. Maybe she wouldn't be so nervous to call him once she had breakfast and calmed down.

In the eating area, she spied a spread of breakfast foods. Three couples were engaged in a conversation, and she was glad they didn't notice her. She poured a cup of hot tea with lemon and sugar, picked up a sweet roll, which was all she could eat with the rumbling in her stomach. She thought a good walk down to the beach would also help her quiet down.

Outside, she headed for the beach kicking leaves most of the way down. She scanned the horizon and watched the foamy waves rolling onto the beach. The sand appeared to be too wet to sit upon, so she looked over at a picnic table and bench at the foot of the path and decided to sit there and eat her sweet roll.

Isn't this silly, she thought. *I'm in my fifties, and I'm acting like a teenager.* What would Floyd think about her family? Lola said he had gone through this before.

She watched two men pull a rubber boat up on shore. They looked up and waved, so she waved back. They walked toward her, said hello, and headed up to the B&B, obviously needing a break from their excursion and knowing where they were going. *What a wonderful life this would be, free to go boating whenever and wherever I wanted,* she thought.

What will Floyd think of Bradford and Patricia? He'd be amused by Bradford's bullish behavior. He'll meet Delsey and her husband, as well as the others. Delsey will treat him kindly and so will the rest. There's Morgan and his terrible criticisms of people and

Charlotte with her openly brash mouth. Emily, she knew, would be considerate. She reached out to a bird walking toward her, but it flew away.

Would my family be polite or would they be rude to Floyd? This would hurt her as well as him. Annah rubbed her eyes. The salty wind and bright sun made them burn. She should have thought to bring sunglasses.

Suddenly, she heard a noise behind her. She turned and saw Floyd walking down the path toward her. Her heart raced.

"Annah? I've looked all over for you," Floyd called.

She hoped her voice didn't give away her feelings. "Hi, what brings you here so early?"

He strolled up to her, leaned down, kissed her on the cheek, and sat down beside her. "I've done my thinking, and it looks like you're doing yours," he said, putting his arm around her.

She lifted her head to face him and responded, "Yes, I've been doing a lot of it." She hesitated not knowing how to begin to ask him what had been on her heart all morning.

"What a beautiful view," he said, as he surveyed the blue horizon, the waves washing up the beach, and the choppy waters in the distance. "This is a good place to think." Then, he looked fully into her face. "Well?"

"Well what?" She could smell the aroma of his aftershave mixed with cigar smoke. The scent of his masculinity overwhelmed her. "Floyd, I…."

"Well, what have you been thinking?" He slid closer to her.

Her shoulders sagged as she breathed in the intoxicating air between them. She wondered if Lola had told him about their conversation. "Floyd, have you talked with Lola?"

He leaned his head backward and gazed at her. "Why?"

"Oh, nothing. It seems like you've talked to her either last night or this morning."

"Truthfully, I haven't seen her this morning yet, and I sure didn't talk with her last night. I went to The Albatross for a beer."

Quietly, they sat together for some time watching the seagulls search the beach for dead fish and insects. Finally, she asked, "Floyd, after my surgery and the doctor has released me from the hospital this week, would you like to drive me home to Rosewillow and meet the rest of my family and visit for a few days in my home?" she asked, grateful that her voice did not quiver.

Without hesitation, he said, "Yes. Let's leave as soon as the doctor gives you the okay."

Her heart pounded. "My, you didn't have to think about that one."

"Nope. You've been to my house and met my relatives and now it's my turn to see where you live and meet your folks."

She leaned one elbow on the table and looked at him. "You may be in for a surprise. I want you to see exactly who I am and why my life is complicated right now."

"Madam, I already know who you are. I can sense there is something very special about you that you've been hiding. I won't be surprised. Besides, I can handle complications."

In a moment of relief, she laid her head on his shoulder. He placed his hand over the side of her face and caressed it.

"Have you heard from the doctor when you're surgery will be?"

"I'm waiting for him to call." Then, she added, "Floyd, I'm going to look ugly after it's over. I'm going to lose my hair because they'll shave it to operate, and I'll have at least one hole in my head. Are you sure you want to stay with me through this horrible episode?"

"Lady love, I'm in this for the long haul. I'd love you if your hair never grew back."

"Oh, my god. I hope it grows back and over the hole."

Floyd ran his hand through her shoulder length hair and kissed it. "Sweetheart, it'll be okay. I'll buy you the best wig in town, and you'll be as good as new."

Annah's eyes watered and she brushed the tears away with the back of her hand. The time for worrying was over.

—

Annah went into surgery two days later. Lola, Roy, Floyd, and Emily waited outside the recovery room for news from the doctor. Emily had notified Kat and Spencer in Rosewillow of the operation, and they were on their way to Ionia to be with Annah once she was at the B&B. She also called Charlotte and Morgan, but they said they wouldn't be able to come, but to let them know the results.

"Roy, it's going to be two hours before we learn anythin'. Let's go have lunch in the cafeteria." Looking at Floyd and Emily, Lola said, "Would you two like to come along?"

"I think I'll wait here. I might be down in a little while if I get hungry," Floyd said.

Emily moved to a more comfortable chair next to Floyd. "Me, too," she said, as she opened her backpack and pulled out a novel to read.

He shifted his position in his chair to face her, crossed his arms over the arm of the chair, and smiled.

Emily cocked her head and smiled back. "What are you thinking?"

"I'm just thinking how sweet you are. You're your mother's

daughter."

"Of course, I am," she said, putting her novel unopened on her lap.

"What I mean is that you're different from your older sister. You're considerate and concerned about your mother. I didn't get that feeling about your sister, or your brother."

Emily studied him for a moment. "Well, you met them at an awkward time. They were scared about my Mom's condition even though they didn't seem like it."

"I mean, your sister was rude and your brother ignored me."

"That's them. They're inconsiderate most of the time."

"Emily, I want you to know, if you don't already know, that your mother and I are more than good friends. We love each other, and she's asked me to drive her home to Rosewillow to meet the rest of your family and see your home."

"What? I thought I'd be driving her home."

"I know. That's why I'm telling you this now so you won't be upset."

She leaned back in her chair. "I thought you two had something going between you."

"What do you think about me meeting the rest of your family and staying in your home?"

She scrunched her face. "I think you're asking for problems. Charlotte would have a hissy fit and tell you to get the hell out of our house, and Morgan would tell you off."

"I'm ready for that. Remember, I've already met them."

"And, you'll have to have Delsey's approval. She's my mother's maid and a very, very close confidant."

Floyd moved closer. "Tell me about your mother's life. You just said she has a maid. Does she have other servants?"

"She has five servants, whom she prefers to call domestic help. Delsey is her personal maid, Jerome and Custer are her maintenance men, Renaldo is our Cuban cook, and Lucia, his wife, is our housekeeper."

Floyd scratched his chin. "How big is your house?"

"Big. Very big. It's a mansion."

Floyd reached for a cigar in his upper pocket to twirl in his hands. "A mansion?" he asked, more like a statement than a question.

"Yes. My mother inherited an historic house, which was once on a plantation, when her mother died. My great, great, great grandfather built it after the Civil War in the 1860s. He was a ship captain, and he earned a great amount of wealth during the war. His dream was to build a magnificent house on thousands of acres as a living legacy to his descendants." She paused. "My mother is very influential in the Rosewillow community and well respected because of it and for who she is."

He held the cigar lengthwise over his lip for a few seconds. "That's why she has been so mysterious. She was afraid to tell me all this. Now she wants me to see it."

"That's a good idea. You should visit and see it for yourself. I only know a little about you, so I'd be anxious to know your reaction."

He leaned closer to her. "Emily, whatever will be, will be."

"That sounds like a clique'."

He smiled at her again and leaned closer. "Yes, and it's a good one. I can't wait to see your house."

He looked down at her book. "What are you reading?"

She sighed. "Would you believe, PRIDE AND PREJUDICE by Jane Austen? I read it as a teenager, but I never finished it. I've become interested in it again because of the character, Lizzy. The poor woman can't get it together. She's going to end up a spinster if she doesn't make up her mind who she loves. I want to finish it this time, so I can find out." She flipped the pages. "I guess I feel I'm going through the same confusion. I can't seem to find the man of my dreams."

Floyd leaned back and laughed. "Emily, I hope you know that you're the protagonist in your own life. Get to know yourself, and you'll find a man who'll meet your expectations." He sat up. "I'm glad you're reading it. Take time with that piece of work and study that character. You just may discover yourself through her."

Emily looked at him with curiosity. "Do you like to read?"

"Yes, I love to read. When I start a book, I devour it. I've found that if I look around me, there're plenty of antagonists trying to ruin my life. I've come to recognize them and learn to deal with them."

She sat still and listened to his bit of wisdom. "Floyd, I'm impressed. There's more to you than I thought. My mother has a whole bunch of antagonists in her life, especially from Charlotte and Morgan. Maybe you can help her deal with them."

"I'm already in the process of doing that, my dear Emily."

She shook her head in affirmation, stood up, and said, "Let's go have something to eat."

He lifted himself up, stuffed his unlit cigar in his shirt pocket, and followed her.

Emily decided she liked him. He had a quiet way about him that comforted her, and she was beginning to see why her mother was obviously falling for him.

Within two hours, the four of them returned to the waiting room and the doctor's presence. "I have good news for all of you," he said. "She's come through the surgery well. We've had to shave her head and install tubes to release the pressure from the blood that was forming. We've sent her to the ICU downstairs, and she'll be there for at least three or four days. She's a little groggy right now, so you might want to wait until later or tomorrow morning before you visit her. When she's awake and alert, I'll explain more details to her. Once she's home, she'll need at least a week's rest and quiet time. Then, I'll want her back here for a checkup. For now, be assured she's going to heal properly." With that, he stood, shook hands, and walked away.

Lola sighed relief, and said, "Thank You, Lord." Roy clapped his hands together, Floyd took in a deep breath, and Emily cried.

Tomorrow couldn't come sooner.

—

Floyd climbed into his truck in the hospital parking lot and sat with his head and arms over the steering wheel. He closed his eyes and said a prayerful thank you.

He started his engine and slowly drove away. He had to get home and take care of Roscoe, who needed to eat and go out. Floyd was anxious to go on a long walk with him. He had much to share with him, and Roscoe always understood.

Floyd's head was swimming with thoughts of what the future would bring. She thought he wouldn't love her with the scars on her head from the surgery. He hoped she would have the humbleness to wear a wig after having such beautiful hair. Would she still want him to take her home to Rosewillow? Would she finally tell him about her obvious wealth and inheritance? Would her family approve of him, a simple construction worker? He knew he would love her no matter what, but would she become distant to him just to make it easier for him to let her go?

He would wait and see. He would return in the morning and have a talk with her.

—

Emily drove away from the hospital and south to Ionia. The area was becoming familiar to her. She would enjoy staying in her mother's room at the B&B. It would seem like she was close to her there. She breathed a sigh of relief knowing her mother was going to live.

She thought about Floyd and her mother together. The first time she met him, he put her off, but having that talk with him in the hospital gave her another perspective. He was crude on the outside, but gentle on the inside. She knew he was not after sex or money. *I think he genuinely adores Mom. I'd like to get to know him better.*

"Charlotte?" Emily asked after calling her to tell her about their mother.

"Yes. Well, it's about time you called," Charlotte said. "I've been waiting all day to hear about Mother."

"Charlotte, Mom will be okay. She had to have her head shaved and now her head is wrapped in bandages, two tubes are hanging out of her head, and she'll be in the ICU for three or four days in the hospital."

"What? Tubes hanging out of her head?" she screamed.

"Didn't you know how serious her injury was?"

"Of course not. I thought she just had a concussion, and they were treating her for it."

Emily waited a moment to speak. "She had a concussion, but there was swelling beneath her skull and they had to reduce the swelling by cutting two holes in her head and inserting tubes to release the blood."

"Oh, my god. I'm going to faint."

"Don't. She's going to be all right. She'll have to buy a wig to wear for a couple of months, but her hair will grow back." Emily could hear heavy breathing on the other end. "Are you there?"

"I almost fainted."

"Charlotte, get yourself together. I said she's going to be okay."

"Do you want me to drive down there and see her in the hospital?"

"Please don't. She has friends here and Kat and Spencer are on their way, and I'm sure Kat will be at her side."

"Who are her other friends? That awful man and those two losers at the B&B?"

Irritated, Emily said, "That awful man happens to be very nice and a friend to Mom, and those two 'losers' that you mentioned, happen to be very good people. They are as concerned about Mom as we are."

"I'll call Morgan. You won't have to. I'll talk to you later," Charlotte said, hanging up.

"Morgan, you won't believe what Emily just told me."

"What?" he asked. "What now?"

"Mother has two holes in her head with tubes hanging out of them, no hair, and she's in the ICU of the Tampa Hospital."

Morgan was hosing down the surface of his sailboat with one hand and holding his cell phone to his ear with the other. "That's crap. Emily must be lying."

"No. She was serious. Mother needed surgery for her head injury. I thought she had a concussion, and she was being treated for it."

"Come on, Charlotte. What's the truth?"

"Morgan, I'm telling you the truth. Call Emily yourself."

When he turned off his phone and dropped his hose, he whispered, "You can't believe half the crap women tell you."

"Emily, this is Morgan," he said.

"Oh, good. I'm glad you called me. I just talked with Charlotte."

"I did, too. What's this about Ma in the hospital with holes in her head?"

Emily told him the story. "I'm down here with her, and I'll keep you both informed about her condition. I'm staying at the B&B that Mom stayed at, so I'll be seeing her every day."

"Do you want Patricia and me to drive down?"

"That's up to you, but Kat and Spencer are coming down, and I think she'll be in good hands once she's out of the hospital. By the way, Mom is happy to hear that the C-section turned out well, and gives her love to both of you. She likes the name Curtis Jackson."

"When I see Ma, I'm going to give her a piece of my mind," he said. "Let me know what happens with her."

Floyd visited Annah in the ICU the following morning. He peeked into her room and saw a saline bottle hanging beside her with a tube leading to an IV in her arm. Her head wrapped in bandages had two tubes coming out siphoning blood. She appeared drugged.

He stepped quietly toward her so he wouldn't waken her. He stood over her for a long time, realizing he should have brought her flowers. He would do that later. He pulled up a chair next to her, sat down, and continued to watch her. Beneath her nose, oxygen tubes pumped fresh air into her lungs, and he glanced at the monitor above her to make sure her heart and her breathing were normal. He put his hand on her arm to reassure himself of the life within her. He knew he would not desert her at this time. It only made him love her more.

For the next four days, he visited her, sometimes by himself and sometimes with Emily. Kat and Spencer came also and reassured themselves as well as him that she was recovering. Lola and Roy came to be by her side and bring her little treats that Lola had made.

After they released her from the hospital, Annah spent several days of recuperation at the B&B, and returned to the hospital to have her bandages removed. Kat bought her a scarf to cover her head and told her she would help her pick out a beautiful wig to wear until her hair grew back.

Relieved, Emily drove home, knowing her mother was in safe hands with her friends in Ionia. She accepted Floyd now as a possible future family member after seeing the love they had for each other.

PART III

GLADSTONE

CHAPTER THIRTY

Roy offered his '93 Pontiac for Floyd to drive to Rosewillow. Even though it was an older car, it was dependable and Floyd's truck consumed too much diesel.

Floyd handed Roscoe to Lola to care for him while they were gone. "Now, you be a good boy," he said, petting his head.

"We'll take real good care of him. We'll spoil him rotten, and we might want to keep him," she said, winking at Floyd.

"We have a great day to drive, my dear. It's going to be in the mid-70s today and no rain," Floyd said to Annah. "You're absolutely beautiful," he added after looking at her new wig. She and Kat had shopped for a short, auburn colored wig the day before.

After packing their bags in the trunk of the car, hugging each other, and saying their final words, Annah and Floyd climbed into Roy's car and drove away. Annah was anxious to see Floyd's response to her home in Rosewillow.

"So, my lady, tell me about the house you grew up in. Didn't you say it was a family home for many generations? It must be quite old."

Annah didn't answer right away. She wondered how to begin to describe it. "You'll have to see it," she said.

"Oh, oh. Do I need a cigar to calm me while I listen to the description?" He grinned and patted her knee. "Let me guess, you live in a run-down shanty on a slope so steep you practically slide down the hill every time you step outside."

"No. Of all things, Floyd, I don't live in a run-down shanty on the side of a slope."

"Okay then, let me guess again. You live in a fort surrounded by a mote loaded with alligators and guarded by men in armor ready to shoot arrows at intruders."

"No again." Annah put her hand to her mouth to conceal a smile.

"One more guess. You live on one of those deserted islands off the Carolina coast and have to take a boat to the mainland every time you want to shop for grits and pickles."

Annah bent forward in her seat laughing.

"Okay, let's hear it. This has to be good."

"I can tell you that, architecturally, it is your typical white southern antebellum house. It sits on forty acres overlooking the Atlantic."

"Oh, oh. The kind of house you'd see in the movie GONE WITH THE WIND?"

"Somewhat. My great-great grandfather built it in the 1860s when he retired from being a ship captain. It was once a 4,000 acre plantation, called the Gladstone Plantation after his name, Rupert T. Gladstone."

Floyd stopped her. "Wait! How could he have become rich from just being a captain of a ship? Did he find hidden pirate's treasure?"

"No, but let me tell you. During the mid-1800s, he owned a fleet of six coastal schooners, which hauled freight up and down the Atlantic Coast."

"Ah, that sounds ideal. What a man!"

"Floyd, when the war broke out between the North and South, he used two of his schooners to attack Union cargo ships. They forced one of these ships aground off the Florida shore, which was on its way to Key West. The ship held a substantial sum of money that was to pay the Union troops stationed at Fort Zachary Taylor."

"I've been to Key West and toured that fort. Have you?"

"I've never been to Key West. Anyway, he captured the vessel, took control of the crew, and the government granted him the money."

Astonished, Floyd asked, "Are you telling me a big story to keep me guessing?"

"This isn't a story, it's the truth. Over the years, the house has needed repairs and remodeling to maintain its historical integrity and to continue to make it livable."

"I would assume so. According to my calculations, it's probably 150 years old."

"Succeeding generations deeded portions of the 4,000 acres to their offspring, who in turn sold to developers. The remaining acreage was then donated to the town of Rosewillow and that left the house on 40 acres. The plantation once had fruit trees, rice paddies, and cotton fields, but times have changed, and our family stopped working the land over two generations ago."

Floyd listened and kept his eyes on the road ahead.

"Rupert put the house in a Trust, which states that it is to be conferred to the eldest child of the family living in the home until it would no longer serve the family's interest. At that time, it would be at the discretion of that heir to place it where it would serve the community or the state of South Carolina the best, but not to be sold because of its historical value."

"And that's you, of course."

"Yes." She paused. "Do you see the complexity of my life?"

Floyd took his hand off the steering wheel and pressed her arm. "I'm beginning to."

Annah took a deep breath. "Floyd, I've inherited not only Gladstone, as we call it, but the wealth that comes with it." She waited for his response, which didn't come. "Does this matter to you?" Again, she waited for a response, which didn't come. "Never mind. Would you like to hear my view of it?"

He looked directly at her. "My dear, your wealth does not matter to me; but, yes, I would like to hear your view, and we have plenty of time for you to tell it to me."

"Okay, then…."

He interrupted her. "Just remember I fell in love with the woman who didn't care about the way I looked, the smell of beer and cigars, and kissed me like she had never been kissed before. I knew the moment you threw your fishing line onto shore and almost snagged an alligator that you were special, and I loved you more when you slid down a slippery boat ramp and stood up covered in mud. When you were in that car accident, it scared me; and when you had that horrific surgery, you nearly tore my heart apart, and I knew I could never let you go."

Annah leaned back and closed her eyes.

"All this business about you living in an historical mansion means nothing to me. You are exactly the woman I want to spend the rest of my life with even if we have to travel back and forth from Florida to South Carolina monthly in order for you to manage your affairs there.

"Annah, when the dust settles around your family after they see me bring you home, I'll still be waiting for you to decide what you want to do. I mean, will you stay there with them or come live with me in Florida?" When she didn't answer, Floyd said, "I'm more interested in their reactions towards me than seeing this magnificent house with all its history." He smiled. "I'm really going to enjoy this trip."

Annah relaxed. "Their reactions are what I'm concerned about."

"Besides," Floyd continued, "I have to be honest with you, your daughter already told me about your house and your situation."

"What? Then why did you let me go into such detail?"

"I wanted to hear you tell it to me."

Annah's mouth dropped. "Oh, you big tease."

"Mrs. Gulliver, like I said, I'll be standing beside you all the while you make up your mind about Florida and South Carolina. Now, tell me about your view on all this."

They had traveled for several hours and needed a break.

"I'll tell you after we stop at that rest stop."

Seeing the sign indicating a rest stop, Floyd drove toward it. "Ah, I can't wait to hear another interesting story."

She didn't get the chance to give him her view, since Charlotte called. "Mother, Emily told me you're coming home with that man. Where is he going to stay? In *our* house?"

Annah placed the phone on her lap momentarily, and then picked it back up. "No! In *my* house. If you'll remember *I* live there, not you, and I can invite guests when I please."

She heard the disgust in Charlotte's voice. "I do remember you are living there, Mother, but Father wouldn't approve. He'd have that man stay in a motel or have the servants clean up an unused servant's quarter and make him stay there."

Annah cast a glance again at Floyd and shook her head. "I'm surprised at you. Floyd is a decent, responsible man, and he's my friend; and if I choose to have him stay in my house and in one of my guest bedrooms, you'll have no say in it." Annah heard her gasp. "Is that why you're calling? Is there anything of importance you wanted to speak to me about?"

"Yes. I want to know what time you'll be home tonight."

"I have no idea. We're not rushing. I'll call you tomorrow if you'd like."

"I'll be over early to see you," Charlotte said.

Annah recognized the sound of Charlotte's fingers thumping on a table. She hung up without saying good-bye to her. She knew her first challenge would be with Charlotte the next morning. She leaned her elbow on the window ledge and placed her hand on her forehead.

Floyd passed another car, sped up, and returned the car to the right lane once he was clear of the vehicle. "Well, after listening to that conversation, I have to say I've never had children, but I don't think they would get away with that kind of behavior from me or my wife."

"I tried so many times to correct them as they were growing up, but my husband always reprimanded me. Our children got away with too much, and I couldn't control them."

"Was your husband abusive to you?"

Shocked, Annah waited a moment before answering. "I never thought of him as being abusive. He didn't hit me or do anything that I would call abusive."

"My dear, if you examine what you just told me, I would say you were emotionally abused. He controlled you through your children."

She put her hands to her face. How could she have never seen that? She closed her eyes.

Floyd brushed his hand against her cheek. "Are you feeling okay?"

Annah opened her eyes. "You've just made me understand my life."

Floyd pulled her shoulders toward him. "I'm sorry if I was too bold, but I felt you should be aware of that possibility."

"Don't be sorry. I needed to hear what you said." She looked out the side window, and thought about her mother, Louisa. She was a stern and cold toward her. Did Grandma Wilmont unconsciously treat her coldly out of bitterness toward Thaddeus? Was I cold-hearted to my children because of Jackson's lack of discipline and my inability to control their behavior?"

"You're shivering. Do you want me to stop so you can put on a sweater?"

"No. I've been thinking a lot of things over right now and understanding a few more."

"Well, I don't want you to think I'm interfering with you and you're adult children."

"Floyd," she said. "I've just realized that I am to blame as much as Jackson. Yes, he controlled me through the children, but I let him. I distanced myself from all of them and lacked being the caring, loving mother I should have been." She paused. "You and I have something many people never have, truthfulness, and I'm grateful to you for your observation."

"Don't be too hard on yourself. You're quite a gal in my eyes."

She glanced at him. "What I appreciate most about you is your honesty and open friendship. You're not controlling, you're easy to be with, and I feel free to be myself."

He grinned, "Lady love, we can't ask for more!"

Floyd drove north without saying much else for several miles, turning occasionally to look at Annah. Coming upon a small town, he said, "Our fuel is low. Let's stop and get gas. It'll give us a good break, and then we can find a small park to stop and eat that good lunch Lola made for us."

"That's a good idea. I'm getting hungry."

After they gassed up, they found a picnic table under shade

trees next to a school playground and pulled the car over next to it.

While they ate, Annah asked him, "Have you ever eaten Gullah food?"

He put his sandwich down and wiped his mouth with a napkin. "Yes, as a matter of fact I have. I used to stop at a restaurant on my way down from New York and through the Carolinas. They served Gullah food. I guess some of the people there also called it Geechee. I enjoyed it."

"I wanted to tell you the rest of the story I started when I came home after the funeral. When I was a child, my grandmother took me to the islands off the coast from our home. I have wonderful memories of my times there, and I ate many foods that my mother did not like. Delsey, my mother's maid, has family there and over many years, I learned how to make some of their crafts. Over a hundred island people attended my grandmother's funeral. They brought the food for the reception. My grandmother would have been blessed knowing this."

"I remember eating shrimp, rice, and potato salad, which was mixed with onions, celery, pickles, and I think an egg or two."

Annah picked up a spoon full of the potato salad Lola made. "Like this?"

He humorously studied the spoonful of salad. "Yeah, like that."

"I think I'd like you to visit Delsey's family with me when we're home so you can meet some old friends of mine and experience their culture."

"I'd like to do that."

Finishing their lunch, they packed up and continued on their way.

—

After Annah informed Emily when they would be arriving, Emily swung the door open to the laundry room to look for Delsey. "Delsey, Mom called and she's on her way home. Says she's bringing Floyd, the man I talked to you about."

Delsey put her hand over freshly washed and folded clothes. "I know. She called me to get things ready for them. She didn't have a car and didn't want the hassle of flying." Walking toward Emily with a handful of towels, Delsey continued. "I've already asked Lucia to help me clean the guest cottage for him and bring in fresh towels and sheets."

Emily stepped aside to let her pass. "What if she wants him to stay upstairs in Morgan's old bedroom?"

"We'll wait and see," Delsey said, as she left her to find Jerome, who was sitting on the front porch of their cottage in his wicker chair.

She sat down next to him.

"Annah is on her way home and bringing Floyd with her."

Jerome leaned forward and put his elbows on his knees.

She gazed up at the house. "I see that we'll be leaving soon and moving to the islands."

"Yes, I see that, too."

"Annah wouldn't bring a man home to us unless she wanted our approval."

Jerome leaned back in his chair and Delsey scanned the back of the house looking especially at the windows. Jerome peered up to see what she was looking at.

"The house will survive when the Gullivers are gone," she mused. "Now, it's time for us to go to the islands with Custer and talk with Aunt Carmita. She'll know what we are to do."

"I'll get the truck ready. We can leave as soon as our chores are done."

"They'll be here late tonight."

"We'll be back."

He leaned forward in his chair again and Delsey rocked in hers for a long while. She hummed her familiar praise song and Jerome slapped his knees to the rhythm. Their lives would survive, too. They would be returning to their ancestral islands.

Emily expressed her concerns about Annah to Jimmy that evening. "Don't worry about your mother; she's quite capable of making the right decisions. If she thinks it won't be appropriate to have him spend the night in your house, then she'll tell him so. If she thinks it doesn't matter, let her decide where he should sleep. You said she doesn't approve of unmarried people staying overnight together." Jimmy stopped a moment. "However, in this case, they're mature adults, been married before, and it's up to them what they do."

"Jimmy, I didn't say they were going to sleep together. That would be against Mom's principles and our wishes."

"You're wishes? How about theirs?"

Charlotte called and interrupted their discussion. "Emily, I'm beside myself with worry. I talked with Mother, and I won't have her let that man stay in our house."

Emily hesitated to speak to her.

"She didn't ask us if it would be okay."

"Charlotte, Mom is a grown woman and can make these decisions by herself. Besides, you don't live here anymore, and she can invite whom she pleases to stay here."

"Oh, for God sakes!"

"God has nothing to do with it. Get used to it. She likes the guy."

"I'm going to give her a piece of my mind when I see her."

"You can't do that."

Charlotte's voice grew louder. "I can if I want to. Wait till Morgan hears about this."

Emily hung up. "Jimmy, when I first met Floyd I thought he was a crude man, but I've come to like him. He's devoted to my Mom, and I feel that she's falling in love with the guy."

"Then what's the beef? Whose side are you on? Charlotte's or your mother's?"

"Charlotte wants to dominate her. I just want her to be the Mom I'm used to."

Jimmy pulled her to him. "Honey, your Mom is going to have to handle this herself. She's a big girl. Just relax and let things work out."

Emily laid her head on his chest and sighed. "I hope it does."

"Morgan," Charlotte said. "Mother is coming home with that man. You know…the one you met at the hospital. The one who wore dirty overalls."

"How do you know that?" he asked, as he pulled off a white, cashmere sweater and leaned his head into the phone on his shoulder.

"I talked with Emily and told her not to have that man stay in our house."

"Good. We don't need that kind of trash there." He paused as he threw his sweater across a chair. "I'll talk with her in the morning. Maybe I'll even go over there early and let her know I disapprove of her lack of consideration to us."

"I think I'll join you," she said. "We want to see what's going on. Emily is staying the night with Jimmy, so she won't be there overnight, but we have Delsey to take care of things."

"Hmm, Delsey is too soft on her. She won't tell Ma what to do. We'll just have to assume Ma knows how to take care of herself. Maybe she told Lucia and Delsey to clean out one of the vacant quarters for him to sleep the night, or maybe she'll send him off to a motel. We'll see. Don't worry about it. I'll have a word with her tomorrow."

"We both will. I'll see you about eight-thirty. Okay?"

"Yeah, that's a good time. See you then, Pudge."

"Morgan! How many times have I asked you to stop calling me that horrible name?"

CHAPTER THIRTY-ONE

Floyd slowed the Pontiac as he turned through the open, iron gates leading to the Gladstone mansion. It was late. Overhanging trees caused an eerie darkness as they made their way along the driveway. A full moon cast a ghostly light over the fountain, revealing its antiquated and grandiose features. Spellbound at the sight of the massive, antebellum structure in front of him, he turned to face Annah, unable to speak.

"We're here," she said, seeing his amazement.

He turned off the engine and gazed at her.

"Come on. I have much to show you. This is only the beginning."

Annah turned her key in the bronze lock and pushed the heavy front door open. The crystal chandelier swayed from the breeze as they entered, and Floyd watched it change colors from white to pink and blue over their heads. He looked around to view the long elegant hall leading toward another ornate, wooden door at the back entrance.

Quietly, Annah led him into her home. She understood his amazement as she observed him stand in awe of what he saw before him.

"Delsey did not expect us home this early or she would have answered the door. She lives with her husband, Jerome, in a cottage in the back. We'll have to assume she'll be here to welcome us tomorrow morning."

Floyd studied the polished spiral staircase leading to the second floor and the antique furniture placed strategically throughout the hallway. An old-fashioned phone placed next to a bouquet of fresh flowers suddenly rang making him jump.

"Don't worry about that. I seldom answer it. We have it for display, but it's connected to our regular phones to let us know someone is calling."

Delsey opened the back door and walked toward them. "Why, Annah, I'm glad to see you made it home safely. I came in to see if that was you calling."

"Yes, we're home safely," Annah said and turned to Floyd. "I want you to meet my friend Floyd. He was kind enough to drive me home."

Floyd walked toward her holding his hand out to shake hers. "Hello, Delsey, I've heard wonderful stories about you."

Delsey gave Annah a pleased look. "I'm happy to meet you, too," she said, as she reached to take his hand. "Annah, would you like me to make something for you to eat?"

"Thank you, but no, we ate a little while ago. Would you have Jerome or Custer take our things upstairs? Floyd can use the guest room, since Emily is using hers."

"Emily is staying the night with Jimmy. She said she'll be home early tomorrow."

Annah wasn't surprised. "Then, after we get our suitcases, I'll take him up to his room."

"Yes, I'll get Jerome," Delsey said. As she turned away, Annah thought she saw a glimmer of humor on her face.

Floyd glanced at Annah. "I can get the suitcases."

"You could if you'd like, but I'd like to give you a quick tour of the house." She showed him through the house, turning lights on and off in room after room, and noticed that he didn't make any comments. When she opened the door to Jackson's office, she gave a shout. Jackson's computer was missing just as Charlotte had said; his office shelves were bare of books, and his desktop lay empty of his papers. She quickly walked over to the desk and opened several drawers. They were empty, too. Angry, she slammed the drawers shut and walked out into the hallway.

"Delsey? Delsey? Are you still in the house?"

Delsey came out of the kitchen. "Yes, Annah."

"Were you here when Charlotte cleaned out Jackson's office?"

"Yes. Charlotte and Bradford came over while you were gone this last week and did it."

"I told her to leave his office alone. It was none of their business what's in there."

"I told her that, but she said she was his daughter, and she was taking care of matters while you were away."

Floyd came to Annah's side.

She looked up at him. "I'm sorry for shouting, but my

daughter has gone too far. I want to know what she did with Jackson's papers and books. My son-in-law also took his computer and all the files on it. I was going to donate Jackson's books and research papers to the Neurological Society." She faced Delsey. "Do you know where they put the books and papers?"

"No. Charlotte and Bradford boxed them up when I wasn't here."

Perturbed, she said, "The nerve!"

"Annah, calm down," Floyd said. "You know your daughter's behavior. Talk to her in the morning. Maybe they stored them for later when you decide what to do with them."

Annah put her head on his chest and took a deep breath to calm down.

"Delsey, Annah will be all right," Floyd said. "If you'd like to return to your home, we'll continue the tour tomorrow. It's been a long day, and we're both tired."

Delsey nodded and stifled a smile. "If you want me for anything more, please call me," she said, as she began to leave.

"How do I do that?"

"There's a buzzer on every wall in the house, just press one and I'll hear it."

"Great. I'll do that," he said, holding Annah close.

"Floyd, let me show you the guest room." Annah walked over to the hallway switch and turned the chandelier lights lower, checked the front door, and led Floyd up the stairway toward their rooms. He followed her to the upper landing until she opened the door to Morgan's room, now a guest room. Jerome had put the luggage in the center of the room. "I'll take my things over to my room," she said.

"No, let me help you."

She hesitated. "Thank you, but I can take it with me." She felt him watching her as she picked up her case and started out the bedroom door.

"Wait. Don't I get a good night kiss?" He walked toward her, took her case, set it down beside him, and pulled her to him. He lifted her chin to his and kissed her.

"Good night, Floyd," she said, as she struggled to turn away.

With one swift motion, he pulled her back to him, enclosed her in his arms, and kissed her again, this time long and lovingly.

"Good night," she said again, turning away. She made her way to her bedroom, opened her door, and closed it without looking back, but then she remembered she had left her suitcase in his room. How was she going to get it?

She heard him knock on her door. With her heart pounding, she opened it and saw him standing there with her case. "Oh, I forgot it," she said, trembling.

Floyd handed it to her, but when she reached for it, he wouldn't let it go.

"May I have my bag?" she asked, feeling her face flush.

"Only on one condition."

She tried to laugh. "What one condition?"

"To thank me with another kiss," he said, as he bent over her. Once again, he encircled her in his arms and dropped her case. This time, his kisses were hot and intense. Then he kissed her again, and again, until she gave in to his passion and longing.

Floyd backed her into her room, shut the door, and continued to embrace her as he found the bed and carried her onto it. This time his kisses and hands were all over her, and she was unable to stop the craving within her.

It was at this moment, she knew, she wanted him as badly as he wanted her. She was in love with him, and he was everything she needed. She had missed so much for so long. Giving into her lust, she let him undress her and in a matter of moments, they consummated their love.

—

Emily spotted the Pontiac near the fountain as she and Jimmy returned home the next morning. They drove around the fountain and parked. It was too early for Delsey to be up, so Emily took out her keys and unlocked the front door. "Come on; let's surprise Mom with a cup of hot tea. I'll bet she's sleeping in from the long drive home."

"Looks like her friend stayed the night also," he whispered.

Emily looked around the hallway and tip-toed toward the kitchen. "Yes, I'm sure she must have put him in Morgan's old bedroom. We use it as a guest room now. Let's get the teapot started," she said quietly.

Jimmy followed. They walked around the small table in the breakfast room, entered the kitchen, and Emily switched on the lights. She filled the tea kettle with water, heated it, and reached for the tea bags in the upper cabinet. She also brought down three cups and the sugar bowl, placed them on the counter, and opened the refrigerator to take out the pitcher of cream.

"Don't you think you should bring down another cup for her friend?"

"I didn't think to do that. Thanks for reminding me."

Jimmy and Emily sat on the stools placed along the table and talked while they waited. "I'm really impressed with your kitchen, Emily. Your family must have entertained crowds of people to have so many copper pots and pans hanging above this cook's table. You have two commercial refrigerators and a stove that has six burners. How many parties did your family have?"

Emily surveyed the kitchen with curiosity. "Yes, I guess we did. My parents always had company. My father was well known in his field of work, and he often invited groups of people here to discuss his latest research in neurology. My mother also planned great parties on holidays and the community counted on her to host a number of events. At one time, we had three cooks and six servants year round."

"Wow, what happened?"

"Oh, you know. Times change and when my father died, the big parties stopped and my mother let two of the cooks go and three of the servants."

"It must have been fun growing up here."

"Sometimes."

They heard the tea kettle whistle and Emily stepped down from her stool and took it off the stove. She remembered to bring down another cup for Floyd.

"You know, Mom thinks a lot of this guy. He's rough and crude, but she wouldn't have let him drive her up here if she didn't approve of him."

He cleared his throat. "I've been thinking about that, and I want to bring something up with you. Is it possible they slept together last night?"

Astounded, she turned from the stove and held the cup in front of her. "Of course not. My mother's too prudish. She wouldn't even think of sleeping with that man, especially in this house. Anyway, I don't think she knows him *that* well."

"How do you know, and what's the house got to do with it?"

"Well, it's not proper here. I mean, I kind of agreed with her when she wouldn't let Michael spend the night here. I'll bet that if that man is not in the guest room, he's sleeping in one of our cottages outside."

"It's a thought I had, but what would you do if they *were* sleeping together?"

"Stop it, Jimmy, you're making me think less of my mother."

"I'm sorry." He paused. "I just had thought maybe you ought to think about that."

She gave an exasperated sigh. "Just for that, I'm going to go up and knock on Mom's door. I want to prove to you that she's a fine, respectable woman. She has high morals. You'll see."

"Okay, I'll stay down here. I don't want to see the fireworks."

"Darn it, Jimmy, I'm going up there right now." She saw him grin, lean his elbow on the counter, and watch her storm away.

"You'll see," she said, as she walked quickly toward the stairway. "He'll see," she whispered. "My Mom would never do such a thing!"

Floyd yawned and stretched his arms across the bed. He rolled sideways, gently moving Annah's head with his hand to view her face, and smiled at her. "You're beautiful, even in the dim light of this room." He leaned over and kissed her.

Annah returned his kiss with passion, and then couldn't resist teasing him. "You're just saying that. I couldn't keep my wig on through the night."

"Ho there," he responded. Lady love, you're beautiful even without hair. It'll grow back fast, you'll see."

Annah rolled closer and gazed at him with a mischievous smile on her face. "Hmm," she murmured. "Thank you. I'm always afraid you'll think I'm frightful."

He gently rubbed her head. "I would love you even if your hair never grew back."

"You only say that to make me feel good." She curled her head into his chest. "I wish I could stay right here all day."

"You can."

"No. My children will be coming over and, who knows, I have to face their bad tempers and explain you to them."

"Me?" he asked. "I know you have to face them with a few major decisions, but I can get out of your way if you'd like."

"Please don't. I need your support, and I have to be honest with them."

He lifted her face to him and kissed her on the cheek. "Madam, I will support you to the ends of the earth."

Annah closed her eyes and enjoyed his closeness. "I hope you will."

They were quiet until they heard a knock on the bedroom door. Annah sat up quickly as Floyd slid sideways from her. She covered Floyd's head and body.

"Yes?"

"Mom, may I come in?"

"No, dear. I'm not dressed, and I'd prefer to have privacy right now."

"Please, Mom. I have to talk to you about a few things before everyone comes over. Jimmy's here, and I don't want him to hear what I have to say."

Annah pulled her covers up to her neck. "I'll be dressed and out as soon as I can. Just wait," she called as she saw the door opening.

"Mom," Emily said. She saw Floyd's form in the bed and yelled, "Mom?"

"Emily, I told you to wait until I was dressed," Annah yelled.

"We can talk then."

Emily screamed again. "Mom! You're not doing what I think you're doing?"

"Out, young lady, right now!" Annah pointed to the door.

Emily abruptly turned around and slammed the door on her way out. She ran down the stairs and back to the kitchen. "Jimmy, you were right."

"See," he said. "Your mother is a grown woman and, if they were up there doing it, it's her business."

"I can't believe it. I can't believe Mom would do such a thing. Why, she's old."

Jimmy slid off the stool and came near her. "Your mother is not old. She's in her fifties. Women still make love at that age."

"But, she could have waited until they were married at least!"

"Yeah. I can't wait to meet that man. He must be something for her to give in to him. I couldn't stop being a world's clumsiest nerd around her when I first met her because she's so…well, perfect."

Emily stomped her foot. "Well, she's not perfect now."

Jimmy gave her a comical look. "Are you disgusted at us? We go to bed together."

She punched him with her fist. "We're different. I'm not the Mrs. Gulliver of the Rosewillow high society class. I'm her daughter, who's going to college."

He put his hands in his jeans pockets. "What makes you think high society broads aren't jumping in and out of every man's beds?"

Emily screamed. "Oh, you're just horrible!"

Annah and Floyd heard her words. They left the bed and Floyd rushed to his room as Annah dressed quickly. Right now, she needed to confront Emily without Floyd being with her.

CHAPTER THIRTY-TWO

Charlotte lumbered into the house with her children. "Delsey, are you here? It's eight thirty," she called. She walked to the kitchen where she thought Delsey would be and spied Emily and Jimmy.

"Well, you didn't waste any time getting over here, did you?" Emily said with a scornful expression on her face.

"Of course not. I want to talk to Mother about a few things."

"Mom is getting dressed."

Bradford came in behind them. "Any coffee made?"

"No, sir," Jimmy said. "We made hot water for tea. Would you like some?"

"Tea? Where's Delsey or Renaldo? They usually have a pot of coffee made every mornin', and I need some right now."

"They're probably sleeping in," Emily said.

"That's unacceptable. Servants don't have that luxury," Charlotte said.

"Of course they don't. We pay for service, not luxury," Morgan said, as he entered the kitchen. Patricia, Mandy, and the new baby, Curtis, came through the door after him. "Where's Ma? Who owns that sorry Pontiac out there?"

Emily shook her head in annoyance. "Floyd stayed here last night."

"Holy crap. What's he doing here? She could have found a flophouse for him to stay in."

"I hope she hurries getting dressed," Patricia said, as she removed the baby blanket away from Curtis's face. I want her to see him awake. He's so sleepy right now."

"I'm *sure* she will hurry," Emily said through bared teeth.

"Do you want me to make the coffee, Bradford?" Jimmy asked.

"You make the coffee? It'll end up bein' mud."

"What? There's no coffee?" Morgan asked. "What the hell's going on here? Where's Renaldo? Where's Delsey?"

"Renaldo and Lucia are probably sleeping in. They drove all the way from Miami yesterday. I'm sure they're pretty tired and Delsey hasn't come in yet," Emily answered.

Delsey entered the kitchen from the outside door just as she spoke. "My, oh my, is everything okay? Why is everyone yelling and standing in the kitchen?"

The twins started fighting. Douglas tried to hit Daphne. Cherry squealed as he knocked her down.

"Stop it right now or I'll spank you," Charlotte yelled.

"Delsey, please make coffee for my crabby brother and brother-in-law," Emily said.

"Yes, Emily. I came in to make the coffee and bring out breakfast rolls."

"It's about time," Bradford said. "I'm hungry. My wife didn't think to make us breakfast this mornin'."

"Shush," Charlotte said to him. "Delsey, we're all here to see Mother and talk her out of that asinine idea of buying a house in Florida for a get-away. Heavens, we all know she has too much to do here."

"Charlotte, I get tired of your bossiness," Morgan said, as he flopped down on a kitchen stool. "We're here to discuss our inheritance as well as to tell her to stay home."

"Well, I get tired of you trying to usurp my place in this family. I'm the one who's going to inherit this house when Mother's gone. I'm the oldest."

"Over my dead body. We all have a stake in this house. I'm the only son of Jackson Gulliver, and in my mind, I should be the first to inherit it. This house has belonged to three women before us, and it's beginning to look like it. Now it's time for a man to take over."

"*You* say. What about me? Jimmy and I are going to be married, and we don't have a place to live. We should live here. Besides, when I graduate from college I'll have the right to come back here and stay."

"There you go again being spoiled and getting your own way. Why should you get the house?" Charlotte asked.

"Because…because I'm pregnant."

Everyone stared at Emily, except Jimmy, who looked proud.

"Don't tell me you're pregnant with this guy who's just a journalist? He has no culture," Morgan said.

Suddenly, everyone turned around to see Annah standing in the doorway. She looked flushed and angry. "Excuse me, but I have a say in all this. No one will make decisions about the house except me."

"Mother, we're only watching to make sure you don't do something foolish."

"Like what?"

"Like, even thinking about going back to Florida. You have plenty to do here, like taking care of Curtis and Mandy when we want to go sailing for a weekend or a week," Morgan said, now standing up. "And what are you doing bringing that twerp here to stay in our house?"

Patricia walked over to Annah to show her the baby. "Isn't he just precious?"

Annah glanced at the baby. "Yes." She turned back to the others. "Morgan, you have not even asked me if I want to take care of your children while you go off sailing. I may have plans of my own. Another thing, I raised my children. You can raise yours. That is your job in life. If you need a babysitter, get yourself a nanny. In addition, don't you ever call my friend any name but Floyd."

"Oh, yeah, Mom, he sure is your friend," Emily said, jabbing her index finger at her.

"What do you mean by that," Charlotte said, seeing Emily's gesture.

"Nothing."

"Nothing? How much of a good friend is he to you, Mother?"

Emily glared at Annah. "A *very* good friend."

Annah glared back at her.

"What the hell is going on here?" Morgan asked. "How good of a friend is he?"

"Mother, you have good friends here. You've lived here all your life. Everyone relies on you to entertain as you did when Father was alive. They all hope you'll have your annual Christmas Ball here."

Fed up, Annah said, "I have a surprise for all of you. I'm not going to have large dinner parties and social occasions anymore. I'm going to relinquish my role as the one and only person in this community who can put on these events."

"Mother, you can't. We all expect it of you. That's who you are. What are my children going to do at Christmas time? Santa Claus always comes here so they can sit on his lap and ask for presents. You just can't stop all that."

Annah felt a headache coming on. "Yes, I can."

"No, you can't," Morgan said, as he walked over to her. "You are expected to do those things even with Dad gone. Now, straighten up!"

"Don't talk to me like that!"

Morgan stood taller to tower over her. "Ma, you look like a frump with that ugly wig on. At least you could have brushed it before you came down here."

Cherry and the twins cried. "Mama," Cherry said. "Isn't Santa Claus coming this year?"

"Yes, dear, and at Grandmama's house."

Annah reached over and put her arm around Cherry. "Sweetheart, Santa is coming this year, but not at Grandmama's house. He's coming to your house."

"Mother, where are you going to be? In Florida?"

"I just might be."

Jimmy attempted to sneak out of the kitchen. "Jimmy, don't you leave me. This is my family, and you're going to be a part of it," Emily said. He stopped and walked back to her side.

Jerome and Custer came into the kitchen. "What's all the noise," Jerome said, as he looked around. "Is something wrong?"

"No. Annah is talking with her family," Delsey said. "Annah, we'll leave and let you go on." She gently pushed the two men out the back door and closed it behind them.

Morgan put his hand on Annah's shoulder. "Ma, I think it's best that one of us move in with you to take care of you. Who do you want here, Pat and me with the kids, or Charlotte and her brats?"

Charlotte punched his arm. "Brats?"

"Or, me and Jimmy, with our new baby?" Emily added.

Annah looked at her with surprise and then continued. "Morgan, I'm beginning to lose respect for you. I'm tired of your mouth and trying to control me." Annah swept her arm over his to remove it, and waved it over everyone in the kitchen. "Also, I'm tired of all of you trying to control me. I'm going to buy a house in Florida whether you like it or not, and I'm going to continue seeing Floyd for as long as I want to. I'm also going to take as many trips to Florida as I please. Another thing, what happened to Jackson's books and papers?" she asked, staring at Charlotte.

"Bradford and I decided…."

"Bradford and you decided?" She gritted her teeth. "Who gave you both the right to clean out his office and go through his papers? I told you not to; and, Bradford, I did not give you permission to take Jackson's computer, printer, and all his files to your house. You stole them."

"What? Who the hell do you think you are?" Morgan asked. "You stole my Dad's computer? I ought to call the police."

"Morgan, Mother wasn't here, and we wanted to make sure Father's books and papers were taken care of," Charlotte said, as she put her hand on Bradford's back. "Besides, Mother, we found letters that you should know about."

"Now what? I ought to punch your eyes out," Morgan responded.

Annah's anger rose higher. "And just what did you two do with those letters, Charlotte?"

"Well…," Charlotte said. "Well, Mother…"

"When is that coffee goin' to be done?" Bradford asked, leaving her side and walking over to the coffee pot. He poured a cup of coffee.

"Bradford and I boxed Father's books and papers up and stored them in the upper level of the carriage house."

"I asked you what you did with those letters, Charlotte."

"What's so important about some letters?" Morgan asked.

"I'll tell you later," Emily said.

"No, you won't!" Annah said, steamed.

"Morgan, it's none of your business," Charlotte responded. "Mother, we were only trying to help. We all want to help you make good decisions. You're going off to Florida is not a good decision. Who's going to take care of the house while you're gone? See? This is why Bradford and I should move in with our children."

"I'll make my own decisions whether it's good or not and all of you should stay out of my affairs. Now, answer me, Charlotte. Where are those letters?"

Charlotte protruded her lips. "If you really want to know, then I'll tell you."

Annah waited until she wanted to explode. "Then tell me!"

"Okay. That woman called again and asked for her letters back. I told her I found them; and, so…."

Annah fumed. "So? I've had it with you, Charlotte; you have no right to do with my things as you please. So what did you do? I want to shred them, but I just haven't had the time."

"Why does it matter to you, Mother? Father is gone and those letters were not yours."

"For crying out loud, what letters?" Morgan asked again.

"None of your business, Morgan. This is between Charlotte and me."

"And me," Emily said, glaring at Charlotte.

"Emily, you stay out of this. Mother, since you're spending your time gallivanting all over kingdom come, I've taken charge of matters here."

"We're going to talk about this later, Charlotte. From now on, you keep your hands out of my personal effects and your father's business affairs."

"Uh huh," Emily said, glaring at Charlotte. "Mom, getting back to this issue of moving in here, you wouldn't be able to have a minute's peace with Charlotte's kids hanging around you all day, and Morgan would just as well hand over his for you to take care of twenty-four hours a day. Jimmy and I would be quieter."

"Ha, you won't take care of the house or our mother. Your cigarette smoke would kill everyone who comes into it," Morgan said.

"Thanks, Jerk," Emily said.

Annah put her hands on her forehead. "This is too much. You're all acting like little children. Please leave this house at once."

"I'm not leaving. Remember, I live here," Emily said, as she grabbed Jimmy's arm to hold him there.

"Bradford, will you go catch the twins and bring them back," Charlotte said. "We're not leaving either. These matters have to be settled."

"We're not leaving either," Morgan said, as he saw Patricia turn around and walk out with the baby crying. "Stay here."

Annah felt a heavy hand on her shoulder and looked up to see Floyd stand beside her with a grim look on his face.

Suddenly, everyone froze. They watched as he placed his arm around her shoulder and he peered around the room. One by one, they left the kitchen and slowly walked toward the front door and out of the house. There was nothing more to say. Somehow, they knew *he* was now in charge.

CHAPTER THIRTY-THREE

Alone in the house, Annah stepped up the stairs to her bedroom, she turned and scanned the great hallway below. There were so many memories, but why should she continue to live in Gladstone for the sake of her ancestors? They were long gone and the house had passed on through history fulfilling the dream of Rupert T. Gladstone. The time had come for the family to let go of it.

Charlotte and Emily had never quite fit into the Rosewillow society as she did. Neither had Morgan filled Jackson's place in the community. Jackson wanted them to grow up to choose their own ways. *Well,* she thought, *they did just that.* It was futile to think that her children would ever get along or come to any agreement over the use of Gladstone.

When she reached the upper floor, she held her hand on the banister and didn't move. Suddenly, she knew that giving up her the house and her heritage would be the best thing to do.

"Ma'am, can I talk to you for a minute or two," Renaldo called, seeing her on the upper level.

Annah looked down. "Yes, Renaldo, what would you like to talk about?" she asked as she walked back down.

"Lucia is upset. She overheard you talking to Delsey about missing pieces of your jewelry. She's afraid you think she's been stealing them."

Annah hadn't addressed this with anyone besides Delsey. Taken aback with this revelation about Lucia, she said, "I'm sorry, Renaldo. I have asked everyone else if they've seen them, but no one has, and I have no one else to suspect."

His shoulders slouched. "Lucia didn't take them. She's been crying about it. She doesn't wear jewelry, and where would she go to pawn them? She only leaves the house when the both of us go grocery shopping or out for one reason or another."

Annah watched as Lucia came to his side. "I'm sorry, Lucia, I don't want to hurt your feelings. I've asked everyone to look for the missing pieces, but no one's been able to find them. Please forgive me if you think I suspected you."

She held onto Renaldo's arm. "Gracias, Senora," she answered.

"Lucia…," Annah started to say as they turned to leave. Her heart went out to her as she observed her clearly for the first time. Here was a small, humble woman, devoted to her husband and a servant anyone of her socialite ladies would honor to have in their home. All she could finally say was, "You're welcome."

When they left, Delsey spied her. "Annah, is everything okay?"

"Yes, for now. Did Floyd go outside with Jerome and Custer?"

"They asked him to help fix the alternator on Jerome's pickup."

"Good. Then that gives me the opportunity to ask Renaldo and Lucia to help me get rid of Jackson's files, which are in several boxes in the carriage house. Delsey, please catch them and bring them back here."

"I'll go find them," she said, as she turned and headed for the kitchen.

When they came, Lucia said, "Senora, how do we help?"

"Lucia, I would like you and Renaldo to go with me out to the carriage house. Renaldo, would you bring a book of matches please?"

"Yes, ma'am," he said. He headed for the fireplace in the parlor to retrieve a box of matches from the mantel.

They walked to the carriage house and climbed a set of stairs to reach the storage area above. Once they were standing on the wooden floor, Annah saw the boxes. She hoped the letters from his mistress were in them. If so, they would be destroyed. The damage is done she realized. Charlotte and Bradford know about Jackson's infidelity. What she was going to donate to the neurological society would be on Jackson's computer, and she could print them out when Bradford returned the computer and she had more time.

"Would you please carry these boxes down for me? I'll help you so you don't fall."

Once down, Annah directed them to take the boxes out to the barrel far beyond their cottages and burn them. She also asked them to stay until the fire destroyed every bit of them. She wanted no remnants left. They nodded and walked out carrying the boxes.

Now the evidence would be gone, as well as her hatred for Jackson's mistress. The only thing left for her to deal with was Charlotte and her impudence.

Annah returned to the house and met Delsey. She folded her hands. "Delsey, I'm going to let Renaldo and Lucia go, so they'll be free to return home to their families in Miami. I know they miss them and would like to move there." She unfolded her hands and placed one on Delsey's shoulder. "You see, we won't be having large dinners and people visiting here anymore. I won't need their services."

Delsey shook her head in agreement. "I know. Annah, will you let the rest of us know when we can go home to our families, too?"

Annah's mouth dropped. "Oh, my. Everything's changing, isn't it? All of you have been so faithful to us all our lives. I would never let you go, but you're right, the house will be empty if and when I leave."

Delsey continued. "When we visited Aunt Carmita and Ruthie Ann, they showed us that their island is being developed into hotels and commercial centers, so she suggested we could go and help them preserve our culture and whatever is left of their village."

Annah felt sad. "I know how important that is to you. I've been concerned about that for a long time. Look at Hilton Head and the other islands like Edisto and Fripp. They're so populated and overrun with hotels and high-end restaurants that the old ways are becoming lost."

"Yes, and also Jerome and Custer feel that they can help repair the old elementary schools that our children are still using. The people can't afford new schools for the children, and there's no money to build them. The older children travel to Buford for high school and then they hope to go to college somewhere in South Carolina, but we all know they have no money for that either. The people could sell their land, but the families would have to permanently move to the mainland." She paused. Her voice sounded sorrowful. "Our ancestors have lived there for over two hundred years. That's our home and the families don't want to leave it."

Annah thought about her own children and how they were able to go to the best schools and the best colleges without any regard for what it cost Jackson. Here were her island friends, unable to send their small children to decent schools. "Delsey, don't worry about it now. I'm sure there will be a resolution to those problems."

"Yes. Ruthie Ann told me she could give me a job helping her cook Gullah foods in her small restaurant. She's beginning to see more tourists coming in looking to eat local foods, and she needs help. Jerome and Custer will have jobs. They will help in the restaurant."

"Will you have a place to live?"

Delsey shook her head in affirmation. "She said we could live with her temporarily, since she's all alone. Eventually we'll find our own homes. Annah, I'm very happy about this. We would be with our daughter and our grandbabies. All these years, we've only been able to visit with our families when we take a day or two off work here."

Annah reached out and hugged her. Delsey's face beamed giving Annah a sense of peace. She knew everything would work out well for the three of them, as well as for Renaldo and Lucia.

"Oh, Annah, just one more thing."

"Yes?" Annah waited for her to go on.

"I've wanted to tell you that I had a dream last night." She paused. "Annah, you're going to go through travails soon that will hurt you deeply. I want you to know that you can always count on me to help."

Stunned, Annah asked. "Travails? You mean troubles? Can you tell me what you dreamed?"

Delsey folded her hands, "No, but what I heard from your children this morning upset me very much. They're relentless and selfish. You saw their true natures. Don't let them destroy your relationship with Floyd or you."

Annah felt her heart sinking. What more was she going to go through? She held her breath. This may be the reason she should leave Rosewillow.

—

Annah's children did not return that day.

Having finished helping Jerome and Custer work on Jerome's truck, Floyd walked up to Annah. "Lady love, you've had your fill today, how about a drink on the veranda?"

Annah took his hand. "That's the best thing I've heard all day."

Floyd took a bottle of beer for himself and a glass of wine for Annah and led her onto the veranda. After they dried off a hanging swing on the ocean side of the house, they sat down to rest. They were quiet as they pushed the seat and viewed the roiling white caps on the ocean. Seagulls darted along the beach looking for washed up fish, and pelicans sat perched on posts. Lightening flashed up the coast, while dark storm clouds moved north.

Annah could not get Delsey's words out of her head. She stopped the chair with her foot. "Floyd, do you think our relationship will last? Delsey said there will be travails ahead."

"Travails? Does she foresee the future?"

"I don't know how she does it, but when she predicts something, it happens."

"Huh." He took a sip of his beer.

"Delsey has a way of knowing things. I think she talks to the spirits."

"Come on. That sounds like heebie jeebies to me."

Annah pushed the chair with her foot, and let it swing slowly.

"This morning I thought your kids were all going to pounce on you until I came down and stopped them. That seems like trouble to me."

Annah pushed the chair harder. "I'm sorry about that argument this morning. You shouldn't have had to hear it."

"I think I was supposed to hear it. They're very rude to you, like I've said, and I see that you've let it go on for years."

Annah sipped her wine. "Yes."

"Are you going to let that continue or are you going to take a stand against it?"

Annah laid her head on Floyd's shoulder. "What can I do about it? They're all adults now. We didn't discipline them while they were growing up. They don't know any better." She looked up at him. "I can't blame Jackson for it all though, like I said before, I was just as much at fault. I spent too much time away from them. My help were their surrogate parents, and you can see how much they listened to them."

Floyd drew his arm around her shoulders letting her head rest on his chest. "Annah, we all make mistakes in life. I have many regrets. Don't blame yourself now. Your kids are all grown up and raising their own families and you should let them go. They'll reap what they sow." He patted her head. "I won't put up with their rudeness to you. If you'll let me, I'll step in and say something when they act that way."

"I think you've already established that fact with them. They'll probably act differently around you when we're together."

CHAPTER THIRTY-FOUR

"This is the Gulliver house. May I help you?" Delsey asked, after picking up the phone. "Annah," she said, turning to look at her. "Mr. St. James is on the phone for you."

Annah shook her head, hoping not to have to answer. "Oh, for goodness sakes," she said, taking the phone. "Yes, Henry, what can I do for you?"

"Annah, I'm so glad you're back. Now you can get to work on the fund-raising. May I come over and show you our plans? The committee has had several meetings since you've been gone, and we have some great ideas I'd like to share with you."

Annah's feelings for him were over, and how would she tell him she wanted to drop out of the committee? At one time, she had put her whole heart into the project, but now it was oppressive to think about it.

"Henry, I'm sorry, this is not a good time. I have company and have much to catch up with here before I consider thinking about the museum." She paused. "I thought Muriel took over the fundraising?"

"She did, but we asked her kindly to step down. She really wasn't much help." He continued. "It will only take fifteen minutes, sweetheart, and I'd like to see you. It's been over a month or so since we've talked."

"Henry, I said this is not a good time for you to visit with me. Please understand." She heard Henry's heavy sigh and knew he was not going to give up.

"Annah, I'll be right over," he said, as she heard him hang up.

Upset by his call, she slammed the phone down just as Floyd entered with Jerome and Custer. They had driven Jerome's truck around the area to make sure their repair worked. They were laughing with Floyd as if they had known him all their lives.

"Annah, love, what's wrong?" he asked.

"I just received a call from an old friend, Henry St. James, who is involved in the planning of the Civil War Museum downtown and, without my permission, he's coming over. I was in charge of the fund-raising committee, and he wants me to look over the committee's reports. I really don't want to talk with him today and look at reports, but now it looks like I have to." She gazed up at him. "It's another burden in my life."

"Then don't do it."

She put her hand to her cheek. "How can I stop him from coming over?"

"Say you're no longer interested in doing it."

"Floyd, that sounds easier than you think."

"I mean it. Your life is changing and you're moving on to newer things. Just tell him that since your husband died, all the commitments you had before died with him." He led her away from the door, and Jerome and Custer, who had stopped to listen, left them to be by themselves.

She knew it was true. "I don't know how to tell him that."

"I could tell him, but it's important that you stand up for yourself. Annah, you've been so controlled by everyone. You have to learn to let people know what you think and not let them dominate you," Floyd said.

"I know, but telling him that won't be easy."

"I'll leave you alone with him. Jerome asked me to look at the plumbing in their sink. He's been having difficulty with it. The pipes are rusting, and I'll try to fix or replace it."

"Okay, thank you for doing that. If it's too much of a problem, I'll have my property manager call for a plumber."

"You have a property manager?"

"Yes, I pay him to oversee any maintenance problems the house may need. He's in charge of not only the house, but the acreage and all the needs of the outer cottages."

He rubbed his chin. "I guess you would need someone to do that." When he started to leave, he said, "I'll take a look at that plumbing job anyway. I can probably fix it with Jerome and Custer's help. Enjoy talking with your friend."

—

Annah was not happy that Henry didn't take no for an answer. She went into the kitchen and heated a pot of water to make tea. "The nerve of him to not listen to me." She heard the doorbell ring and knew Delsey was not there to answer it. Delsey had finished her work and left to go to her house out back. Annah turned off the tea pot and walked to the front door trying to think of a way to tell Henry to leave.

"Annah, sweetheart," Henry said, as she opened the door. "I've missed you." He raised his arms to give her a bear hug, but she moved out of his way.

"Henry," she said. "What did I tell you before you rudely slammed the receiver down?"

"What? Me, slam the receiver down while talking to you? Annah, I would never do that." He held a two-inch thick folder in front of her face. "Here's our plan. I'm excited to show it to you."

She cleared her throat and gently pushed the folder away. "I'm not interested."

"What? You've been the main person in this whole project, and you're not interested?"

"That's what I said. I'm not interested in the committee's reports anymore. Henry, since Jackson died, my life has changed. I want to start doing things differently and begin anew."

He placed the folder against his chest and frowned. "This is probably only a passing phase, Annah. You'll finish grieving for Jackson and find yourself bored with nothing to pass the time. You'll be looking for responsibilities and involvements all over again. I know you."

Annah cocked her head and looked up at him. "You don't know me. You never have really cared to know the real me," she said. "Well, it's over. My responsibilities to this committee and the Rosewillow community are over. I'm moving on to do what I've always wanted to do and be who I've also wanted to be."

"That's ridiculous. You can't shake off who and what you are. Now that your mother and grandmother are gone, we all expect you to carry on your role as the matriarch of your heritage."

She defiantly crossed her arms. "Well, I have a surprise for you and everyone else here. I'm not going to carry on that role."

Behind her, she heard a cough and turned to see Floyd. He clapped and walked toward them, putting his arm around Annah and smiling at Henry.

"Who's this?" Henry asked, with a look of shock on his face. Floyd's shirt bore the grease from working on Jerome's truck and helping with the plumbing.

"Henry, meet Floyd,...my fiancé."

Henry's mouth dropped open, and he eye-balled him.

"Glad to meet you," Floyd said. He held his hand out to shake Henry's, who didn't reciprocate.

Henry took in a deep breath and leaned backward. "Well, that answers that." He swung around to leave, but stopped and turned back to Annah. "Mrs. Gulliver, you will eventually be very sorry for shirking your responsibilities." Then, he swung around again and walked out.

Floyd grinned. "Mrs. Gulliver, I'm proud of you. You're learning fast. And, you know what else?"

"What?"

"Thank you for calling me your fiancé. I was going to ask you, but I was waiting for the right time."

She turned to him, laughing. "Well, you have time right now."

"Will you be my fiancé?" he asked, kneeling before her.

"I'll think about it," she said, not able to control her laughter. "When is a good date to get married? We're getting older by the minute."

"Let's see. Let me see. Hmm," he said, rubbing his chin and standing up. "How about September?"

CHAPTER THIRTY-FIVE

It had been two days since Annah had seen Emily after the argument. She heard her call up the stairs and walked over to lean on the railing. "I'm up here, Emily."

"Mom," she said, walking up toward her. "Since Jimmy and I will be married after I graduate, I've decided to clean out my room and move in with him now. We're here to do that."

Annah turned to greet her. "I'm glad to see you're making that decision, and now is a good time for you to move."

"Mom, I'm sorry about that argument we all had. I hope you're doing okay."

"I'm fine and I'm sorry, too."

Emily hesitated. "I know you like Floyd very much. I was shocked you would do what I never thought you would do, especially in our house. I mean, you were angry when I invited Michael to stay here with me, and you went and did what you got mad at me for."

"We're all adults, aren't we?"

They momentarily held each other's eyes. "It's okay with me, but I'm not sure Charlotte and Morgan would be happy if they knew about you and him."

"I no longer care what they think. I have a life of my own now. Charlotte and Morgan have no say in what I do."

Jimmy walked into Emily's room to let them to talk. He closed the door to begin packing small items of hers in a box he carried up with him.

"You're right, Mom. It's none of our business. Are you going back to Florida to live with Floyd?"

"Yes, dear, as soon as I finish packing and taking care of some personal matters."

"What about the house?"

Annah changed the subject. "Do you have extra boxes? I'm going to pack some personal things to take with me."

"Yes, Jimmy borrowed a truck from a friend and went around to the stores in town and picked up enough. I don't have that much to pack. I'm not taking my furniture."

"Good. If you have any extra boxes, I'd like to have them."

"Mom? You didn't answer me. Who's going to take care of the house?"

She paused. "I have to think things over, and I'll let you know what I decide to do." She took Emily's arm and led her into her room. "I'd like to talk to you about something else."

Annah closed her bedroom door and stood in front of her without speaking for a moment.

"What is it, Mom?"

"How do you know you're pregnant with Jimmy's baby? You haven't known him that long. Could the baby be Michael's?"

"Mom, it couldn't be Michael's. I haven't seen him in months."

Annah placed her hand on Emily's shoulder. "Have you seen a doctor yet?" She dropped her hand and gazed at her.

"I saw him three days ago, and he said I should wait until I've missed a second period. He said it was too soon to know, but I feel sure I'm pregnant." She wrapped her arms around her stomach.

"Well, then. Call me in Florida when you learn more."

"You bet I will. Mom, I'm so happy."

"I love you and I'm happy, too. You're a young woman now, and I can't treat you like a teenager any more. Another thing. Why are you waiting until you graduate to get married if you think you might be pregnant?"

Emily dropped her arms. "I guess I thought we should."

"Well, if you decide to marry before then, let me know, and we'll be up for your wedding."

"Mom, I keep forgetting to ask you how you like your wig. It's so natural. I don't think anyone can tell it's not real."

"That's because it is real hair and I paid a pretty price for it. Kat helped me choose it." She smiled, but then said, "Morgan made a rude remark about it, but I'll deal with him later.

"As far as the house goes, Emily, like I said, I need time to think. For now, it's going to stand empty. I'm letting Renaldo and Lucia go, which is what they want. They miss their families in Miami. Renaldo said he could always find a position as a cook, and Lucia told me she could go to work as a housekeeper. Her English is not very good, but she knows she won't have trouble getting a job. I wish them well.

"As for Delsey and the others, they're happy to go also. They've never had the opportunity to live on the islands and be close to their families."

"Mom, you mean there's going to be no one here to take care of the house? Won't you worry about someone breaking in and stealing or vandalizing it?"

"I'll ask Louis, my property manager, to look after it while I'm away."

"Emily," Jimmy called, "I need your help."

"I'll be right there." Emily stared at Annah. "Mom, I just can't believe this is happening."

—

Annah wanted to see Patricia and the baby that afternoon. She didn't give enough attention to the new baby when Patricia showed him to her, and she didn't want Morgan and Patricia to think she didn't love him like the rest of the grandchildren.

She asked Floyd if she could drive the Pontiac. "Of course," he said. That was fine with him since he and Jerome were driving into town in Jerome's truck to buy a new faucet and plumbing parts. She also mentioned she would like to leave for Ionia in the morning. "Sounds good to me," he answered. They would have to visit the islands at a later time.

Driving away, she glanced up at the rear view mirror and viewed her house. It suddenly looked different to her. She knew that all she could take away with her were memories and that the house didn't matter anymore. She turned her eyes to look through the car's windshield. Now, an incredible future loomed ahead.

On her way, Annah stopped to buy a baby gift and a card, and once she reached the Patricia and Morgan's house, she pulled into the driveway and let the car idle for another minute. Morgan spent most of his time sailing, horseback riding, and golfing and was seldom home to enjoy it. She wondered if Patricia shared his interests or if she was just as lonely as *she* had been many times when Jackson was gone. She saw Patricia wave from the doorway, then holding the baby in one arm, and opening the door with the other. She had called her to tell her she was on her way.

"Hi," Patricia said, as Annah entered the house knowing she would have a warm reception. Patricia decorated her home with country colors, patchwork quilts spread over the backs of chairs, pictures of farms, cute caricatures of animals, and old-fashioned lamps and tables. Annah often wondered if Morgan wished there were pictures of sailboats, horses, and decorated in a more modern décor.

"Hello, dear. I wanted to visit with you and Curtis. He is

precious and I didn't have much time to look and hold him when you were at our house."

"That's okay, Annah. I knew there was too much quarreling going on, and I'm sorry about that. You know Morgan when he gets upset. He lets his mouth run and hurts people."

"Yes," Annah said, as she walked through the living room. "I'm sorry about that, too. How are you?"

"I'm fine, and I'm glad you came over. Please sit down and we'll have tea. I brought out some cookies for us to eat, too."

"That's nice, dear. Annah gave her the gifts, took the baby from her, and sat down in a comfortable chair. Patricia went into the kitchen to gather the tea and cookies. Alone with the baby, Annah cuddled him in her arms. He looked more like Patricia than Morgan, she thought.

For almost an hour, they talked about the baby, Morgan's sports, and his hopes to have another boy, since Mandy is now five going on six, and she would soon be in first grade. He thought boys would be more fun. He could take them sailing and horseback riding and teach them how to be men.

Annah asked about Mandy and Patricia told her she was playing at a neighbor's house with a little girl her age. Annah wouldn't be able to say goodbye to her.

Soon, their time together ended. Annah took a last sip of tea and rose from her seat. She felt a tinge of regret. It would be a long while before they would see each other again; and, somehow, Patricia was more like a daughter to her than Morgan was a son. Then, they said their farewells and Annah left in her car. Annah felt pleased. Her son's house was a home in which a mother's heart was evident.

—

Once she left there, she thought she would drive to the nursing home and see her Aunt Beatrice and Uncle Rufus, since she hadn't visited with them for over a year. She knew Grandma Wilmont had wanted her to do so. Aunt Beatrice and Uncle Rufus still occupied a room together. Aunt Beatrice at eighty five suffered from Alzheimer's and Uncle Rufus at ninety-one lay flat on his back unable to move because of a stroke.

She drove around the Rosewillow town square and parked on the street in front of the nursing home, a structure reminiscent of old southern architecture. She knew her time there would only take a few minutes, but it would take away the guilt she felt for being so uncaring.

She reminisced on the time she visited with them at their home years ago. She always liked hearing Uncle Rufus's stories of when he was in the navy. He had such a hearty laugh, and she couldn't help laughing with him. Now, she thought, he couldn't even talk.

The last time she saw Aunt Beatrice, she called Annah a terrible name, but maybe, just maybe, she would be nicer this time.

Annah entered and went straight to the information desk, signed the visitor's book, and walked down the hallway toward their room. As she lingered at the door, she could see they were sleeping, and she scolded herself for not visiting them more often. She moved from one to the other, kissed them on their foreheads, and listened to their breathing. "Grandma Wilmont, I kissed them for you," she whispered, as she turned to leave, knowing she'd never see them again.

—

On her way through town, she stopped at the Rosewillow Cemetery. She walked through the old wrought iron gate, hearing the metal scrape as it moved. The sound was eerily loud, giving her an uneasy feeling. She headed for Jackson's grave. She found a headstone, which read Jackson Morgan Gulliver 1945-2005. On the same stone, she read her name engraved, Annah Elisabeth Gladstone Gulliver 1955-, with no ending date.

Annah stared at the grave. The finality of it shook her. *God, not here, not if I have anything to say about it.* Over Jackson's grave, she laid several small wild flowers, which she had picked from the grounds on her way to the gravesite.

"Jackson, I'm sorry for all the years we had together that caused you to be so unhappy. I hope you're at peace now," she whispered. Then, she added. "I'm only going to remember the good times we had and forget the past. You should know that I've found a man who will love me unconditionally for the rest of my life, through good times and bad, and I'm happier now than I've ever been before." With that, she turned and walked away.

She had one more grave to visit. She strolled over to Grandma Wilmont's. "Grandma, oh, how I miss you. I want you to know that I've fallen in love with a wonderful man, and I've heeded your words. He may be a man of 'no station', but I love him and I won't let him go. I won't let my family sway me to forget him. He's not rich in money, but he's rich in wisdom, and I know he'll be faithful to me." She wiped her eyes. "Thank you for being my friend all my life and being the mother I needed. May God rest your soul," she said, with tears streaming down her face. As she turned to leave, she thought she heard a bird sing right above her grave, but she didn't see one.

—

Annah had one more thing to do before returning to Ionia. She had to settle her ire with Charlotte. "Charlotte," Annah said. "Are you free to have me come visit you right now?"

"Of course, Mother. You're always free to visit me. I just finished helping Cherry with her bath. Come over and I'll make coffee."

Annah drove to her house and parked in her driveway. Charlotte met her at the door scowling as she looked at the old Pontiac sitting in front of her garage, but Annah ignored her behavior.

"Mother, it's good to see you. I was afraid you weren't talking to me since the argument the other day," she said, as she opened the door to let her inside.

"We can't let arguments tear our family apart, Charlotte. It's essential that we talk them over, which is why I came."

Charlotte led her into the parlor. "Let me get you a cup of coffee," she said, as Annah sat down and she walked away. As with Patricia's home, Annah surveyed the room. This is just like her personality, she thought. It's cold and unwelcoming. The colors are bland and the furniture presumptuous.

Cherry ran up to Annah. "Grandmama, see the new doll Mama gave me? Isn't she pretty?"

Annah took the doll in her hand and examined it. "Yes, dear, she's very lovely."

"Here, Mother, it's hot, so don't scald yourself." Charlotte sat down beside her on the sofa. "Cherry, go play. Grandmama and I have something to talk about." Cherry ran happily away from them.

"Where are the twins?"

"They're outside playing."

Annah set her cup down. "Charlotte, the main reason I didn't want you to go through your father's papers was because of those letters you found. How much did you read?"

"Mother," she groaned. "I never knew Father was being unfaithful to you."

"That's what I thought. Your father's mistress asked for them back. That's when I discovered that he had been unfaithful for over ten years. I didn't want anyone else to know, and I intended to shred them as soon as I had time to clean out his desk. Now, tell me. Did you give those letters to that woman?"

"Bradford and I thought we were helping you."

"Answer me," Annah demanded.

"No. She never showed up."

Annah felt relief. "Do you see that it's very important for you to stay out of my business?" She leaned toward her. "I told you not to touch anything more in his office, and you both ignored me. In doing what you did, you not only hurt me twice but yourself and Bradford. "Now, I want you to tell me that you'll never, and I mean never, tell anyone else. That means Morgan or anyone. Emily has already found out about him."

Charlotte didn't answer. She lifted her cup and drank some

coffee.

"Did you hear me?"

"Yes, Mother, I'll keep my mouth shut."

"Good! I had the boxes with your father's files burned so if there's any more evidence of their affair, it's gone." She drew in a deep breath. "Now! You stay out of my bedroom, too. I know you've been rummaging in it. There are a few things missing."

Charlotte stood to look out the window to see the twins playing in the front yard.

"Did you hear me? I said there are a few things missing."

Charlotte sat down again and picked up her coffee cup to take a sip and put it down again. "Well, I can't imagine what they are. Have you asked your servants about it?"

"I'm missing some jewelry."

"Mother, jewelry doesn't just stand up and walk away. Maybe you misplaced whatever you're looking for."

Annah calmed down. "Charlotte," she started. "I'm going to ask you again in another way. Did you take my jewelry?"

She gave her a look of contempt. "Well, okay. I took your jewelry home and put it in my jewelry box. I figured you wouldn't need such expensive things since you're hanging around with a worthless handyman in Florida." She smirked.

Annah lifted her arm and slapped her hard.

Charlotte's hand flew to her face, and she stared at her in shock.

"Now, I have something more to say. Floyd and I will be driving back to Florida tomorrow. I don't want you back in the house. I have many things to consider and decisions to make. Can I trust you to stay out?"

Charlotte still held her hand to her face. "Mother, we were just helping you."

Annah felt the sting on her hand. "Let's forget about the jewelry. I want you to know I love you and your family. I must go back to Florida for a follow-up on my surgery and to get away from everything for a while."

"Why do you say you must go back there, Mother? You have the house to yourself most of the time, and your servants handle everything for you. I don't understand it."

Annah stared at her empty cup. "Because I've been a bundle of nerves with all the paperwork I've had to complete over these last few months because of your father dying. I've spent too much time meeting with my attorney, who's helping me transfer our assets, investments, and bank accounts into my name. That's only some of the problems." She looked up at her. "I want that computer back,

Charlotte. What makes you think I don't need it? Bradford had no right to take it out of the house."

"We'll return it to you then, Mother, since you need it so much."

Annah was ready to slap her again, but restrained herself. "I could go on and on, Charlotte, but I want you to understand that I am a woman alone now, and I need time to figure out a few things without the pressure of my commitments here and without my place beside your father."

Charlotte straightened. "I've wanted to talk to you, and don't get mad at me again. Don't you know that we're all upset that it hasn't even been a year since Father died, and you're hanging onto to him like a lover? Is he your lover, Mother?"

Daphne and Douglas came barging through the front door. "Grandmama," they said as they ran to her and fought over her.

Annah held them at arm's length. "Did you two have fun playing outside?"

"Yes," they said in unison, and then ran away to their bedrooms.

"They always come in excited after they've played with their friends. I'll be glad when summer is over, and they're back in school," Charlotte said.

Angry, Annah stood. "Charlotte you have no right to ask me that. That man, as you call him, is a good friend, and it's none of your business what we do together. I am not ashamed of my relationship with him. You, however, should be ashamed of your bigotry and insolent behavior toward me. I'm leaving." She walked straight to the front door without looking back and slammed it.

Cherry ran back to the room. "Grandmama didn't see the new dress I put on my dolly."

Charlotte turned to her. "Grandma doesn't see much of anything anymore."

—

Before Floyd and Annah left for Florida, she met with her help. Annah explained to Renaldo and Lucia that she appreciated the years they had served her family. She said she would have her accountant give them a substantial sum to see them on their way, and she hoped they would enjoy returning to live near their families in Miami.

"Yes, ma'am," Renaldo said. "I'm sure I can get a job in a Cuban restaurant. Tourists love our Cuban cooking and I'll be glad to return to that."

Relieved, Annah said, "That's good news, Renaldo. I didn't want you to feel we had to let you go for other reasons, and I know how you love Miami. You've talked so much about it over the years."

"Gracias Senora, por todas cocas," Lucia said, as she reached to hold her hand.

"Thank you, Lucia, you're welcome for everything. I have enjoyed knowing you."

"Bueno, we'll pack and be gone as soon as we can," Renaldo said.

Sadly, Annah watched them walk away and out the back door. "Yes, they were good help for Jackson and me," she said to herself.

Floyd came to her side and scratched his chin. "What are you going to do with all the boxes stacked around your bedroom?"

Annah wrapped her arms around his waist. "My love, we'll figure that out later."

"Let's go. The hours are passing, and we should get on the road."

Annah couldn't hold down her joy. "Just wait a minute. I have to say goodbye to Delsey, Jerome, and Custer. I have to tell them to turn off all the lights and lock all the doors and windows after everyone's gone and before they leave for the island. Delsey said it should take them a couple of days to clear their things out of their two homes. I'm going to have my property manager take care of the house until we return, and I'm not sure how long that will be."

When she left Delsey standing on the porch of her home in back, Annah felt overwhelmed with the loss of her good friend. She had known her all her life. Delsey's final words to her were that she knew Floyd would take good care of her. He is a good man.

As they drove away from Rosewillow, Annah told Floyd about her talk with Emily and her visits with Patricia and Charlotte.

"You know, Charlotte's going to find a way to get into the house, don't you?"

"It'll be locked up, and she doesn't own a key. Delsey will handle it."

"Okay, let's go. We have miles to go before we sleep...what's the rest of that line?"

Annah whispered, "Just thinking of the miles to go before we sleep is satisfying enough."

CHAPTER THIRTY-SIX

Floyd turned south on I-95 toward their destination in Florida. Annah settled back in her seat, glad to be leaving the problems at home. She had called Spencer and Kat that they were on their way. Spencer said he wanted to discuss something important with her when they had time. It had to do with her Rosewillow house.

"So, Annah," Floyd began, "you never told me about your view of living in your beautiful home, having servants, never having to worry about money issues, and being a high-society gal. I'm still interested in hearing about it."

Annah turned sideways. "You mean you haven't figured that out yet?"

"No, ma'am. I have a couple of serious things I'd like to talk to you about, but I want to hear what you're thinking."

She stayed quiet for a few moments to gather her thoughts and wondered how she would explain the way she felt. She swung her head around to look out the side window. "I feel I've lived a shallow life, always having to appear perfectly dressed, always having to conduct myself with proper etiquette, and always being known as the grande dame of Gladstone."

"That goes with the expectations of your role. You shouldn't expect less."

As they left Rosewillow, Annah considered her role. She observed other grand mansions pass by. She knew many of the women living in them. Were they stuck in roles they could not escape from, like her? "I'd like you to know that when I was growing up I envied the young girls who could run around in ratty jeans and get dirty without being scolded," she answered.

"Ha, so you wanted to be a tomboy?"

"No silly, I just wanted to have fun. My mother took me to ballet school to learn to be graceful. I went to afternoon teas at twelve years old, so I could learn etiquette. At eighteen, I became a debutante and groomed to follow in my mother's footsteps."

"Your mother did a hell of a job."

"Thank you, but instead of being excited about it all, I was bored," she said, sighing. "I was schooled in the arts. I traveled to Europe to experience different cultures, and I learned to speak French and Spanish."

"Your life sounds like a fairy tale. I don't mean in a mystical sense, I mean like a dream. I'm sure many women would trade places with you."

"You could call it a fairy tale, but I think I would have liked to trade places with them."

"Well, your upbringing didn't do you any harm. You've turned out to be a very elegant and graceful woman." He glanced at her and winked.

"Thank you again," She watched as they sped past flowering mimosa bushes, foliage so familiar of her life in South Carolina. Would she miss them when she moved to Florida? "I feel I've missed being a child. If it wasn't for my grandmother and our trips to the island, I wouldn't have enjoyed life."

"Your life is what you make it, and you can adapt to whatever you do and wherever you are. It has to do with attitude. If you only look on the negative side, you will be unhappy. If you look on the positive side to every experience, you'll be happy."

She thought about his comment. "So, you want more of my view? It's that I don't want to live in a stuffy mansion anymore. I want to go fishing like you do and enjoy life without pretense and formality."

Floyd slowed the car as another passed him on the left. "I understand your disillusionment, but I had the opposite experience, and I'm satisfied with it. I grew up in a blue collar neighborhood. My Pop was a union man and my Mom a seamstress. My wife's family came from the Philadelphia aristocracy. I felt that I never quite fit in with their society, and they didn't think I was fit for their daughter. We were married for thirty years, and I don't think they ever accepted me." He paused. "Teresa and I fell in love the first time we met, and she rebuked her family for their prejudice. She embraced life for what it was, and we never had a problem. She enjoyed being with her family and mine without regard to class."

"See? Then you know how I feel. Like Teresa's family, my family doesn't think you're fit for me. Well, I have something to say to them, and it's that they are not fit for you. Their behavior stinks.

You're a gentleman who's kind and caring, and not like my son, who's rude and snobbish. My daughter Charlotte is brash and controlling, and Emily may be all right most of the time, but she has her bad moods, too."

Floyd took out a cigar. He chewed the end of it without lighting it. "I believe people are all the same, whether they're rich or poor. We have a God that loves us all equally and wants us to get along."

Annah turned away. *God, why am I always reminded of You?*

"Now, let me tell you what's on my mind."

"Yes, please do."

"Do you realize that since I came along, your children have been fighting and tearing you apart to keep me away from you?"

"Yes," Annah said, "but Floyd, I won't let them. I don't want you to see them as a hindrance to our relationship. I make my own decisions, and I won't let them stop me from seeing you."

He returned his cigar to his shirt pocket. "Look what's happened, you've let your servants go, and you've closed up your house. When I met your friend Henry, I realized that every bit of your life before me has been turned upside down." He looked directly at her. "Annah, you're throwing away everything for me."

She put her hand on his shoulder. "I don't want you to think that way. For heaven's sakes, the breakup of our family started long before I met you. I went to Florida with Kat on a short vacation and, when I saw the beauty of the area, I decided to look for a house as a place where I could go for a refuge and get away from it all."

"Then you met me."

"Yes. You were restoring a house that I thought I could buy. I did not intend to fall in love with you. My children are angry at me for even thinking of buying a house in Florida. It's not because of you."

Floyd kept his eyes on the road for quite a while before speaking. Annah looked from him to the road ahead and then back to him, waiting for a response.

"Annah, let me ask you this." He didn't look at her. "Would you like me to get out of the way so you can restore your relationships with them?"

Annah couldn't believe what she was hearing. His question was too serious. "I don't want you to get out of the way," she said. "Floyd, don't say that again."

Floyd watched the traffic slow down in front of his car, so he slowed with it. "Well, I want you to know I feel responsible for the breakup of your family." He sped up when the other cars did. "If I've caused your family to get at each other's throats and blame you for everything that's happened, then I'll go away."

"No you won't. I have a right to do what I want to do with my life and, right now, it's being with you." She felt her throat closing and coughed. "The problems with my children did not start with you coming into our lives. Right after Jackson's funeral, they planned a dinner for us to get together so they could talk me into letting Charlotte and her family or Morgan and his family live with me. They wanted, are you ready for this? They wanted to 'take care of me'." She cleared her throat as her words rushed out. "Can you believe that? They wanted to take care of me," she reiterated. "Am I going to roll over and die soon?"

Floyd looked at her with concern. "Annah, I want the best for you. You decide what you want to do now." He turned back to view the road. "I also feel responsible for you letting your help go. They've been loyal to you and your family for all your lives." He sat straight up and flexed his shoulders.

Stunned by his words, Annah couldn't answer. She couldn't stop the choking feeling in her throat. His words were too disturbing for her to bear.

They drove along the highway for over an hour without speaking. Floyd took his cigar from his pocket and put it in the ashtray, played with the radio to find a good station, and turned the volume up when he found classical music.

Annah nervously watched him hoping he would understand that he was not the reason for everything falling apart in her life. She couldn't speak. The lump in her throat choked her and the pounding of her heart filled her with dread. Was he saying good-bye? Didn't he hear what she said? Didn't he understand she loved him? All she heard over the music was silence.

—

Upon arriving late at the B&B, Floyd parked Roy's car in his usual spot. The house was dark except for the front porch light and one light in the living room. The remaining trip home had continued to be tense and quiet. Their conversations focused on the scenery and the fact that it was mid-August and soon it would be fall.

Floyd opened the trunk to retrieve Annah's suitcase and handed her the other items one at a time. "Thank you, Annah, for a very interesting trip to Rosewillow and South Carolina. I enjoyed seeing your magnificent home and meeting your friends and family. You have a nice life up there." He lingered. "Annah, I've made my decision. You need to make yours." He continued. "Don't make a mistake and lose everything over a summer romance."

Annah gasped.

He walked toward his truck, climbed in, started the engine,

backed up, and drove off.

She thought if she said anything, she'd cry. Her throat tightened as if she had been strangled. He didn't even kiss her good-bye. She could only watch him drive away. Shaking, she picked up her case and with great effort walked up to the front steps. She had never felt so alone in all her life. She opened the door without looking back, feeling her heart beat so fast she couldn't breathe. She hoped that by tomorrow he'd call her and say he changed his mind.

Annah didn't want to face Lola and Roy the next morning. They would ask too many questions, and she wouldn't know how to tell them Floyd's mood had suddenly changed. During most of the trip down, he was detached and emotionless, keeping his eyes on the road and looking sullen. She tried to make conversation, but his responses were stiff.

She slipped out of bed and looked in the mirror at her haggard face, swollen from a night of sobbing. "Who do you think you are?" she asked. "You're just another woman, who made the wrong choice. You gave in to your lust with a man you thought loved you."

She sat down, putting her hands over her face, and letting the tears wash over them. Her shoulders shook, and she trembled thinking of how she could have fallen so low as to let a beer drinking, cigar smoking man rob her of her dignity. She chastised herself for her foolishness. "I'm no different than a prostitute."

Not only that, she knew he was right, she had thrown everything away for him. Since he came into her life, nothing else mattered.

She reached for a tissue and blew her nose. "What a mess you've made. You've lost your friends, family, house, and heritage over a man who made a joke of you."

Annah heard knocking at her door. "Annah? Are you okay in there? I hear you talkin' to yourself and you don't sound good," Lola said.

Annah quickly wiped her face. "I'm okay. I'm getting ready to take a shower, and then I'll be down to see you." She moved away from the mirror and opened her suitcase to pick out clothes for the day.

"Okay, I'll meet you downstairs when you're through," Lola said.

As she showered, she thought about calling Spencer and Kat. Spencer always had good advice for her. She would ask them to take her to the hospital for her follow-up, and then drop her off at the airport to fly home. Emily could pick her up in Charleston.

After she dressed, she walked downstairs and spied Lola. She waved hello and decided to pour a strong cup of black coffee before talking to her. Tea would not be strong enough this morning.

Lola came over to Annah, and they both sat down on the parlor sofa.

"Well, tell me about it. Did Floyd meet your family and see your house?"

Annah sipped her coffee, nervously holding the cup with both hands. "Yes, he did."

"Well, what happened?"

She put her cup on her lap and covered it with one hand. "Lola, I don't know what to say or do about what's happened." She stared at her hand.

Lola looked at her curiously. "Tell me what happened."

"Lola, everything went beautifully up there. Floyd and I had a wonderful time together. He met my family and understood my concerns about their behavior. He enjoyed working with my help and meeting Delsey, my maid. He met my friend Henry and realized I had quite a busy life before Jackson died. Lola, he toured the house like a man who couldn't believe his eyes at the sight of it. He loved it."

"Then, what's the matter?"

Annah put her hand over her eyes. "I don't know what happened. On the drive here, he became distant. He said, since I met him, I threw away everything for him."

"What did you throw away?"

"He said everything--my family, my help, my house, and my heritage. Everything."

Lola leaned her elbow against the arm of the sofa.

"Then he asked me if I would like him to get out of the way. He feels responsible for the breakup of my family and by his leaving me I would be able to restore that." Annah sighed. "Lola, I haven't lost a thing. It's all there if I want to go back home. I just have to patch things up and work things out." Annah knew that would be the most difficult thing she'd ever have to do. She really had lost everything. "I don't want him to leave me. I love him, and I know he loves me, but now he said I should make up my mind what I want to do." She reached for a tissue from the box on the coffee table. "Then, he said he had already made his decision."

Lola listened intently, staring at her. "Annah, remember why you came to Ionia with your friend in the first place. Didn't you want to have a short vacation and look for a small house as a get-away from your home up there?"

"Yes. That was my initial desire. My children demand so much of me. Their behavior makes me angry, and I've told them so. I wanted to get away and find some peace. I never imagined that I would meet Floyd and fall in love with him."

"Annah, you can still find a place to live down here. Maybe in time Floyd will come to understand that it's not his fault and that you didn't throw it all away for him."

Annah lifted her cup and sipped the last of her coffee. "Lola, I've decided to have Spencer and Kat drive me to my final check-up in Tampa and then fly home. I may never come back here again."

Lola stood and walked over to the coffee pot to pour a cup of coffee. "I need somethin' strong to drink right now, too." Returning to her side, she said, "Annah, I'm goin' to have a talk with him."

"Don't. I think it's all over between us. I wish I had known this would happen. I thought we had real love, but I guess it was just another summer romance, like he said."

"That's bullshit."

Annah raised her eyes and looked at Lola.

"You and Floyd are meant for each other. I'm goin' to talk to that man and speak my mind, and I don't want you to stop me."

"Please don't. I don't want him to think I asked you to talk to him."

Lola drank her coffee in one gulp. "Yes, I will!"

CHAPTER THIRTY-SEVEN

Floyd didn't call Lola and Roy because he didn't want them to ask questions. He knew he had to pick up Roscoe, but he needed time to think. Annah's lifestyle was beyond what he ever expected. Never in his imagination did he consider the magnitude of her position and wealth. She had been mysterious about her home and now he understood why. Her family heritage went back to the 1800s. How could he expect her to live with him in his humble shack and be happy?

He had lived a similar circumstance with Teresa. She, too, came from a wealthy family, but not to the extreme of what he experienced with Annah's situation. He and Teresa were able to manage their differences when dealing with her family's snootiness, but she did not run away from them or them from her.

Annah was different. She said she was tired of her aristocratic life. Was she really? Was she using him to run away from something else? The death of her husband? His infidelity? The inconsideration of her children? Was her affection for him simply a distraction to cover the real reason? Floyd rolled these thoughts in his mind until he couldn't handle them anymore. He missed his dog, his solitude, and his simple life before Annah.

When he returned to Packard and The Albatross, his friends cheered. "Clark Gable returns," one man yelled. "Here comes the ladies' man," another man said. "Did you get some?" another asked.

"Shut up, you guys," Floyd said, as he walked over to the bar and sat down. "My usual," he told Hank.

"Welcome back, man. We missed you," Hank said, as he wiped the bottle and placed it on the bar with a thud. "What's South Carolina like? I've never been there."

"Beautiful," Floyd said, as he slugged down the beer. "Just beautiful."

One of his friends came over and sat down beside him. "Why do you look like you've just eaten a skunk?"

Floyd swirled the froth around in his bottle and downed the remaining beer in one swallow.

"What happened?" he asked, moving closer to him and leaning one elbow on the bar.

"Same old crap. You meet a woman that you think, for the second time, you might have met the love of your life, and then you realize you wouldn't be good for her."

"Why so?"

"Well, look at me. I'm fat, ugly, low-class, and I stink of cigars and beer. What woman would want that in her life when she lives like a queen in a castle loaded with servants to wait on her and money pouring out of her ears?"

"Hey, man, you knew she was class when you started dating her."

"Yeah, what a stupe I was. I fell head over heels for that dame, hoping she felt the same about me."

"Doesn't she?"

Floyd lit a cigar. "Yes," he said, as he drew in a long drag.

"Well?"

Hank took his empty bottle and placed another in front of him.

"I want to get out of her way. She's given up everything for me, her house, her family, her life, and her…." He was going to say her self-esteem, but stopped.

"Hey, Charlie, give me a shot of whiskey," his friend said, looking at Floyd. "Are you sure you're distancing yourself from her for her sake or for yours?"

Crushing his half-smoked cigar into an ashtray, he asked. "What do you mean for my sake?"

His friend lifted his drink and downed it. "Just a thought," he said, as he slid off the stool. "You're the one who called yourself names, not her."

Floyd gripped his beer bottle and glared at him.

"See you later, man."

He sat staring into the mirror above the back bar and then stood up, threw a couple of bucks on the counter, and walked out.

He decided to go fishing. At home, he backed his pickup to the boat trailer and hitched it up. He needed time to think about what his friend had said to him. *What the hell did he mean by saying, "Are you sure you're distancing yourself from her for her sake or for yours?"* "Why would I want to distance her for *my* sake?"

The words bothered him the entire drive to the river, and by the time he got there, he was so distraught, he jumped from the truck, stooped down to pick up rocks, and threw them as far as he could into the river. As each one hit the water, he yelled, "Crap!"

His anger didn't subside as he backed the boat and trailer onto the concrete ramp and pushed the boat off. All he could think of was their time together and her mud-covered clothes.

Once he parked the truck, he threw one leg into the boat and pushed it off with the other foot. His foot slid on the slimy edge, and he had to grab the rope to keep both him and the boat from rushing into the river. Covered in mud up to his knees, he plucked a cigar from his shirt pocket, bit the end off, and lit it. The smoke swirled around his head and, once more, all he could think about was Annah smoking a cigar.

"You're a jerk, Floyd. How can you let that gorgeous woman get away?" he asked himself.

He took a long drag and let the smoke rise above his head. "You led her on, you know that?" He stuck the cigar back in his mouth and chewed on it. "Whatever made you think she would love a slob like you?" He ran the boat upstream to his fishing spot.

He picked up his fishing rod, put a lure on the line, and cast the line out. It snagged on a mangrove root, just where Annah had snagged her line.

"Geez!" He put his rod down on his lap, bent his head, and sighed. "You big fool, you're so damn lonely, and you let the love of your life get away just because you thought you were doing it for her sake. Do you want to know the truth? You don't think you're good enough for her. Well, would she have said she loved you and given up everything if you weren't?"

"Thank God, I have Roscoe," he said, letting the river current send him downstream.

He took a pocket knife cut the line where it snagged, and reeled it in. He didn't feel like fishing anymore.

After he left the river, he drove to his house, dropped off his boat and trailer, and headed for the B&B. He had to tell Lola and Roy that he was home. He wanted to pick up Roscoe, and the only way to get him was to answer their concerns.

Once there, Lola asked, "Floyd, we've been waiting for you to call. What happened up north?"

Roy motioned for him to sit down on one of the chairs. "Hey, buddy, tell us about it."

He sat down across from them, petted Roscoe and said, "Well, it's like this. It's like this. Annah lives in a magnificent mansion on forty acres off the coast of South Carolina. It was once a plantation, and her family has owned it since the 1800s." He stopped, scratched Roscoe's ears, and continued. "She's class. She has servants, wealth, and influence."

Roy listened without comment, but Lola said, "So what."

"So, I told her to think things over. She would give up everything for me, but I'm not going to let her. I'd never fit in with her family or friends."

"Floyd! Annah confided in me and told me she was tired of that lifestyle. She wanted a change so she could live a quiet life down here with you and said she loved you."

Floyd leaned down and cuddled his dog.

"So, what did you do? Just up and drive away? Didn't you give her a chance to explain this to you?"

"Of course I let her tell me that, but like I said, I told her to think things over and then I drove her here and left so I wouldn't have to explain anything more."

"Explain anythin' more? I'm goin' to swat you!"

Instantly, he stood. "I'm sorry, Lola, I'm going home. Thank you for taking care of my dog. Come on, Roscoe, let's go," he said, as Roscoe followed him out, leaped into Floyd's truck, and curled up on the passenger seat. Floyd couldn't wait to get home, close the door, and shut out all the voices knocking around in his head.

—

At a nearby restaurant, Annah, Kat, and Spencer chose a small corner table away from other diners so they could speak confidentially. A waiter delivered their order of chardonnay.

While they waited for him to fill their glasses, Annah tried to think of how to tell her friends about the trip to Rosewillow. She folded her hands and glanced from one to the other.

"Annah? What happened?" Kat asked.

"It's all over between Floyd and me. After meeting my family and help, seeing the house, and learning about my life up there, he has changed his mind about our relationship. I've made a big mistake, and I'm very sorry." She sipped her wine. "I was so sure that he and I were going to get married that, out of impulse, I let my help go, closed up the house, and said my good-byes to my children."

Kat reached out to cover Annah's hands. "Oh, no."

"Oh, yes. I'm afraid I made a poor decision taking him up there. It intimidated him. I thought he would know that I was telling the truth. I told him I was tired of the superficiality and wanted a change, but I don't think he understood. He told me that I had given everything up for him and that I should rethink our relationship."

"Hon, you did the right thing. He had to know about where

you came from. That's something you couldn't hide from him."

"Well, right now, I'm at a loss. I've packed my personal items in boxes and told my children that I'm going to make a decision soon about what to do with the house, all because I thought I was going to live in Ionia with Floyd." She felt her throat tighten. "He called our relationship a summer romance."

Kat and Spencer stared at her. "Annah, I'm sure he thought more of your time together than that," Spencer said.

"I don't think so. He's so cold to me now that I don't think he'll change his mind."

"Hon, I agree with Spencer. Give him more time. If he truly loves you, he'll come around. You'll see."

"For now, I have to make a serious decision. "Would you two drive me to the hospital in Tampa for my check-up, and then drive me to the airport? I'm going home to try to forget about Floyd and finding a retreat here."

"Annah, I'm so sorry for you," Spencer said. "Of course, we will, but don't be so hasty. Maybe you two can patch things up."

The waiter served their food and replenished their wine.

"Hon, after lunch I'd like you to see our new home," Kat said. "And, you know what? You don't have to see Floyd anymore, if that's what you want, or if that's what you think he wants. We'd love to help you find a home here. You'll be away from Rosewillow, like you said, and you won't have to deal with your house and children every day. You can visit them occasionally up there, or they can come down once in a while and visit you here."

Spencer added. "I have a suggestion for you regarding Gladstone if you do move out of it permanently."

Annah stopped her fork midway between her salad and her mouth and looked from one to the other. Actually moving to Ionia gave her hope.

"We love you, Annah. "I think you would have a wonderful life living in Florida."

"I love you, too."

"Let us know what your air schedule and your appointment at the hospital will be and we'll take you to Tampa," Spencer said.

Annah lifted her glass, clinked it with theirs, and Spencer asked the waiter for another round of drinks.

—

Kat and Spencer took Annah to see their new home when they left the restaurant. Annah toured the rooms as Kat pointed out her décor and explained how pleased they were that the builders did such splendid work on the house. Then, they drove her back to the B&B.

Annah decided to change into her swimsuit and lie on the

beach when she returned. She didn't want to think about anything. She was happy for her friends, but it depressed her. Their dream of a retirement and a change of lifestyle would not be for her.

Once downstairs, she met Lola. "Annah, a man called you. He said his name is Louis Harrelson, and he wants you to call back."

"Thank you, Lola. I'll call him later. He's my property manager, and I don't want to deal with possible problems about the house right now. I want to lie on the beach for a little while and soak up some sunshine." She poured herself a tall glass of ice tea to take down with her.

"Aren't you hungry, Sweetie? I just made a platter of cookies. Would you like one or two to take with you?"

"No thanks. We had lunch. Just this tea will be fine." She saw her hand shake as she carried the glass out the sliding door with her. She strolled down to the beach, scanning the area for a good spot to lie upon, and stopped where she thought she would be away from others. She put the glass in the sand, spread a long beach towel out, and then sat down. Looking at the rolling waves pounding the beach and watching the seagulls fly overhead, she thought, *Nature has a way of freeing us from life's anxieties. I wish I could stay here forever.*

Lola was out on the back patio watering flowers when Annah came up from the beach. Immediately, she stopped watering and met her.

"My nephew!" Lola exclaimed. "I didn't want to tell you this before you went down to the beach, but all he said was he wanted you to think things over. He didn't go into specifics."

Annah didn't answer. She walked into the house, climbed the stairs to her bedroom, and lay down on the bed. *He wants me to think things over,* she thought. *He didn't go into specifics. How can I overcome a broken heart?* Right now, she didn't care if she died.

She slept the rest of the afternoon, and woke realizing it must be close to dinner time. She wondered what to do. Her first chore was to schedule a flight home to Charleston after her time at the hospital. She would call Emily to meet her there. She didn't know what she was going to do once she got home. The house would be empty, and all she'd have left would be memories.

She slipped off the bed, walked over to the window, and observed the horizon. What would Grandma Wilmont have done? What were those words she said? Something about the Lord knowing the plans He has for me and giving me a future and a hope. Well, now I have no hope and no good future. She thought about the Bible her grandmother gave her. Maybe she'd find answers scribbled in the margins.

CHAPTER THIRTY-EIGHT

Charlotte wasn't aware that Annah had closed the house and sent away her help. She shut off the engine in front of Annah's house and had an eerie sense that something was wrong. She knew Annah planned to leave for Florida again, but she didn't expect the shock of seeing the empty and lifeless house. She walked up to the front door to open it, but found it locked, which had never happened before. She rang the bell several times. No one answered. She stomped her foot, irritated that her mother had not given her a key to the house. Morgan and Emily had theirs, where was hers?

She left the front porch and walked around the house to the back. Jerome had finished packing the final boxes into the bed of his pick-up. "Jerome? Where's everybody?"

He wiped his sweaty hands on a rag he had hung from his front pocket. "Miss Charlotte, we're all leaving."

She surveyed the surrounding area. Renaldo's and Lucia' cottage stood vacant. "Where did they go? Why are you leaving?"

"Renaldo and his wife left for Miami yesterday, and we're moving to the islands to be with our family."

"Why? Jerome, you're not making sense. What do you mean?"

Delsey heard them speaking and came out on her porch. "Charlotte, your mother has let all of us go. She went with Floyd back to Florida, and Emily moved out to live with her boyfriend."

Charlotte placed her fists on her hips. "So, no one's here to take care of the house?"

"No one's living here anymore."

Charlotte's mouth dropped. "Oh, for heaven's sakes! Delsey, give me your key so I can get into the house."

She hesitated. "No. Your mother told me to lock up the

house and let no one in. Her property manager is taking care of it for now."

Shaking, Charlotte said, "Her property manager is taking care of it?" She felt herself hyperventilating. "Give me your key!"

Delsey looked from Jerome to Charlotte and back.

"Miss Charlotte, Delsey has her orders," Jerome said.

"Damn it, give me that key right now before I have to come over and force it from you."

Jerome stepped toward her ready to block her from doing so, and Delsey placed her hands over her chest. "Charlotte, I don't like your behavior, and I don't want you to talk to me like that. I don't want to get in trouble with your mother." She reached into her apron pocket and pulled out a ring of keys used to open different doors, including the garage and carriage house, while Jerome stood between them.

Charlotte pushed Jerome away and grabbed the keys from her. "I can't believe what I'm hearing. This is intolerable," she screamed back at them.

She hurried up the steps to the back entrance, fumbled with the keys, and unlocked the door. Once inside, she rushed around the rooms, horrified by the void of people and hearing her footsteps echoing across the wooden floors. She ran up the stairway to the upper rooms and opened them one by one. Annah's room held boxes of her possessions. *She must be coming back or she would have taken all this,* she thought.

She opened her old bedroom door and noticed that the furniture was still in place. She ran over to Emily's room and saw it emptied of her belongings, and finally she opened Morgan's door and saw that no one been in the room for a long time. Dust had settled on the tables and dresser.

Finally, she peered over the banister to the downstairs level. Her heart beat fast. "Well, you see?" she asked to no one. "I'm going home right now. It's time for us to move in and take over. It's our right."

Later that day, Charlotte and Bradford and their children returned to the house and made a grand tour of it. "As soon as Mother returns and takes her boxes out of her bedroom, we can start moving our things in here," she said to Bradford. "Mother said she would be gone for two weeks, so that will give us time to move in."

"Ha! No way! We don't have to wait two weeks. We can move her boxes into the ballroom, and she can haul them all away from there. We can start packin' now."

Charlotte ran her hands through her short, curly hair. "Oh,

why didn't I think of that? I'll call a moving company and get an estimate."

As they walked around the property, the children played hide and go seek between the magnolia shrubs, breaking the branches. Charlotte noticed that Delsey and the men had moved out. She was glad they were gone. She didn't want to return the key to Delsey anyway.

"Have y'all talked to Emily about this?" Bradford asked.

"No, she's busy getting ready to go back to school, and I don't care to talk to her. She'd tell me to mind my own business and not move into the house."

"Well, someone should know. How about Morgan?"

"No, he'd say he had the right to be here and not us. If we don't tell him until we've moved in, there's nothing he could do about it except scream at me."

"Okay, let's get packin'."

As they piled into their car, a pick-up truck pulled up behind them.

"Who's that?" Bradford asked, looking in the rear view mirror.

Charlotte twisted her head around. "I'll check," she said, leaving the car. A dark-haired gentleman walked toward her. "Excuse me. Who are you?"

Louis Harrelson, Annah's property manager, walked toward her. "Who might you be?"

She looked him over. "I'm Charlotte, Annah Gulliver's daughter. I asked you who you are."

"I'm glad to meet you. I'm your mother's property manager. I came over to inspect the house and see what work I may have to do here."

Charlotte gave him an uncertain look. She knew Annah hired a property manager after her father died to take care of the house, but she had never met him.

"Am I interrupting something here?" he asked.

"Just what work did my mother tell you to assess?"

Bradford stepped out of the car and came toward them.

"Your mother called me and said she was leaving Rosewillow and would move out of her home shortly. I am here to determine if there's any property damage or jobs that to be done if she decides to put it up for sale."

Charlotte screeched, "Put it up for sale?"

"Put it up for sale?" Bradford asked, walking right up to him. "She can't do that. This has been in the family for over a century. She doesn't have the right to do that."

Louis put his hands in his jeans pockets. "Please understand

I'm only here to do my job. I've worked for your mother since last November, and we've had a good relationship. What do I tell your mother in regards to this?"

Charlotte became hysterical. "Tell her I'm the next in line to inherit this house, and she has no business trying to sell it. If she does, we'll get an attorney to stop her."

Louis pulled his hands out of his pockets and jiggled his keys. "Okay," he said. He held his hands up as if to ward them off. "But I'll have to discuss this with your mother." He walked to his truck, started it, and backed away.

"How dare her!" Charlotte wailed.

"Mommy, you're scaring us," Daphne said.

Cherry cried, and Douglas knocked her with his arm. "Baby!"

Bradford took Charlotte in his arms. "Hey, the house is yours and there's nothin' your mother can do about it."

"Mother, how could you? How could you be so mean?" Charlotte asked on the phone to her. "That property manager of yours told us you wanted to sell the house. How could you want to sell it when you know Bradford and I want to live in it? If you don't want it anymore, it's our right as the next generation to move into it."

Annah thought about the word "right." *Who has rights anymore?* She still had the right as owner of the estate to do anything she wanted with it. That was *her* right. "Charlotte, I don't know what I'm going to do with the house. Certainly, I will let all of you know when I decide."

"Mother, Bradford and I want to move in as soon as we can. We'll put your boxes in the ballroom. It's empty, and it will hold everything you want us to store in there. We're ready to start packing today."

Annah did not respond.

"Mother, make up your mind."

Still, Annah did not answer. She needed time to think.

"We're ready to pack, and you know we want to live in our home. I grew up there, and it's our heritage as well as it was yours."

Finally Annah said, "Don't do anything until I tell you what my plans are." Then, she turned off her phone, knowing anything she said to Charlotte would only create more trouble.

Annah knew she would never feel the same about her house in Rosewillow. Delsey predicted it would happen and Henry was right, someday she would be sorry for shirking her responsibilities. She had never felt so sorry in all her life.

"Can you imagine the mess I'm in?" she asked Kat the next day at her home. "I talked with Louis. He told me that Charlotte and her family were in the house and apologized for not stopping them. Somehow, she got hold of a key."

"Hon, you're not surprised are you? She can connive her way into anything. She probably got it from Delsey. How else could she have gotten it?"

"You're right. Poor Delsey. I asked her to take the keys with her to the islands and I would get them later. I should have known Charlotte would ask her for them before they left." Annah sat down on a chair on Kat's patio. Kat sat next to her. "I've had enough of her belligerence," she said. "I can't have her and her family living there. They wouldn't take care of it, and the grandchildren would break everything in sight. We have too many antiques and collectibles, and there is too much history in that old house for them to destroy it."

"In other words, you have to go back home and restart your life there again?"

"Yes. I don't want to go back, but I should anyway. I don't have anywhere else to go. I don't have a house here, and I'm responsible for the care of that estate."

Spencer walked toward them, having heard their conversation. He pulled up a folding chair and faced them. "Annah, has Floyd called you today?" Spencer asked.

"No, like I said, it's over between us."

"I was hoping you two would patch things up by now," Spencer said, as he folded his hands and leaned toward her. "Why don't you go visit your friend Delsey on the island? That may give you a different perspective on things, and you'll have time to stay away from your house and think things over."

She thought a moment and then said, "I might just do that."

"What a good idea," Kat added. "Delsey has always been a good friend of yours. I wish we could visit with you."

"Annah, cheer up. You're not yourself today. Things will work out," Spencer said.

"We'll see," she responded, but her heart was not hopeful.

That afternoon, Spencer and Kat took Annah for her hospital appointment. Within an hour, the doctor told her that the final CAT scan showed that the hematoma had receded, and that she should watch for the next two to three years for any complications.

"Thank God," she said, taking a deep breath.

"See, hon, you're going to be all right."

"Now, let's go to the airport. I called Emily last night, and she'll meet me in Charleston and take me home."

"Go ahead and visit Delsey. She may have some advice for you," Spencer said.

"I will, and maybe I'll find that peace and quiet I so desire there."

As they dropped her off at the departure area of the airport, Kat said, "Now, you keep us informed of what you decide to do. We can help you with your plans for Gladstone, and you know you're always welcome to stay with us here if you decide to come back."

"I'll let you know."

"You'd better or I'll wring your neck," Kat said. "All you ever do is make me worry about you."

Annah rolled her suitcase away from the car and waved. *Worry is becoming my second name,* she thought.

CHAPTER THIRTY-NINE

It was nearing midnight when Annah's plane touched down in Charleston. Her flight had been delayed by strong winds. Emily and Jimmy met her at the gate and drove her home. On their way, Annah relayed the good news of her final test.

As they drove closer to Rosewillow, Emily asked, "Mom, do you really want to go home this late at night?" Emily asked. "That empty house would give me the creeps."

It had been a long day. She could find a motel for the night, but the thought depressed her. "Honey, I've lived there all my life. Why would I be afraid of anything? Just drive me home and drop me off. You two can go home, too, and not worry about me."

"Okay, but I think I'll go in the house with you to make sure."

Annah nodded. "Thank you…just to make sure."

As they pulled into the driveway, Annah experienced a sense of loss so great she had to catch her breath. Seeing the dark house without lights matched the heaviness that overcame her. Would she really be able to stay in it tonight? She had asked Louis to keep a few lights on so the house wouldn't look abandoned and vandals wouldn't try to get into it, but something must have happened.

With the headlights of the car left on to light up the porch, Annah and Emily walked up to the front door and turned the key in the lock to open it. As they entered, they were sure they heard voices.

"Do you hear that, Mom?" Emily whispered. "What if there are ghosts in here?"

"Don't be silly. You probably heard our footsteps echoing down the hallway."

The sound of their shoes walking in the entryway matched her response. Annah flipped the switch to light the chandeliers, and in the dim light, the house appeared ghostly.

Emily put her finger to her lips. "Hush, Mom, someone's here. I'm still hearing voices."

"I think you're right, but it might be our imaginations. Let's listen."

"Are our ancestors talking to us?" Emily asked, trying to make a joke.

Annah gave her a wry smile. "I don't hear anything now. Let's have a look around."

As they peered up the shadowy stairway, they heard movement.

"Mom, I'm sure there is something or someone in the house."

"Well, there shouldn't be anything or anyone moving around. The house was locked."

Then they heard voices again.

"Oh, no. It can't be," Annah said. "If it's Charlotte, I'll wring her neck."

While they talked, Charlotte turned on the upstairs hallway lights and peered over the banister. "Mother, I'm surprised to see you," she said, as she descended the stairs.

Motionless, Annah asked, "What are you doing here? Did Delsey give you the key?"

"Mother, I made her hand over her keys. The house was empty, so Bradford and I decided to move in; and since you said you didn't want to stay here anymore, I felt I had the right to move my family into it, especially so you wouldn't sell it. I'm the oldest child and I am the first to inherit this house. You have no right to do so."

"Oh, my god," Annah said. "Didn't I tell you not to move in and that I was making plans for the house?" She turned to Emily. "Let's go. I'll find a place to stay tonight, and I'll have a talk with her in the morning." She turned and stormed out the door.

Charlotte called after her. "Mother, come back here. We have a lot to talk about."

Annah was not in the mood to discuss anything with Charlotte now. She would have a lot to talk to her about when the rage inside her calmed down.

Emily helped Annah back to Jimmy's car and they drove away. "Mom, you can stay with us. We don't have a guest room, but we could make a bed for you on our sofa. We have extra blankets and pillows."

"Thank you, Emily. It will only be for tonight. Tomorrow, I'm going back to the house and taking a few things of mine and have a talk with Charlotte. Then I'm going to drive the Mercedes over to the island to see Delsey, and I may be there a long while."

Jimmy left early for work the next morning and Emily stayed at home to spend time with Annah and then drive her back to the house.

"Good morning," Annah said, coming out of the bathroom after dressing. "I smell coffee, and I'd like a cup of it."

"Did you sleep well?" Emily asked, pouring two cups of coffee. She walked over to the kitchen table and set them down as Annah pulled up a chair to sit.

"Yes, dear. I had a good sleep. I'm sorry I'm putting you two through all this."

"Mom, you're not putting us through anything. Charlotte does whatever she likes without regard to others." Annah lifted her cup to take a sip. "Watch it, it's hot," Emily said. "So, what are you going to say to her?"

"I'm going to tell her to move her family out of the house. I decided last night that I'm the owner and I've come back, so there's no need for her to think she's going to take the house over. If she doesn't listen to me, I'll have my lawyer give her some ultimatums."

Emily put her cup down on the table and stood. "Would you like a sweet roll?"

"Yes, thank you." She surveyed several in small box and chose a white frosted one.

"Mom, how are you going to live in that big house alone? It's too big for you to take care of without some help."

She took another sip of her steaming coffee and took a bite of the roll. "I'm not sure yet. I can't ask Delsey and the others to come back. I'll have to hire new help, but I'll be okay there. I've lived there a long time, so I know what to expect, and I can teach the new people the same jobs I'm used to." She added, "But, I'll never be able to replace Delsey. She was more of a friend than my help."

"I'm going to miss her and Jerome and Custer, too. I didn't know Renaldo and Lucia that well, since you and Papa hired them after I went to college."

"Renaldo and Lucia worked out very well. I'm sure I can replace them with people as capable as them."

Emily finished her sweet roll and drank the last drop of her coffee. "I'm so sorry things didn't work out with you and Floyd. I kind of liked him after I got to know him."

Annah put her cup down. "I'm sorry, too. But it's over, and I have to move on…again."

Emily put her hand on Annah's arm. "Are you okay with it?"

She didn't answer at first. "I will be as soon as my life returns to normal."

"Nothing's normal, Mom. We only live one day at a time trying to keep our heads straight and keeping focused because before you know it, everything changes."

Annah studied Emily's face. "That was a bit of wisdom."

"Come on, Mom, let's get dressed, and go see Charlotte."

"Yes. Let's get this over with."

—

Annah didn't knock on the door as she and Emily entered the house. It was quiet and she could not hear the voices. It was mid-morning and, possibly, they had gone out somewhere.

"Let's have a look around, Emily," Annah said. They walked through the house peering into every room. Charlotte and her family had moved all their furniture into the rooms, and it was obvious that they planned to remain there. Annah stepped upstairs to see her bedroom and discovered that all her boxes were gone and Charlotte and Bradford had taken over the room.

"Well, what did you expect, Mom? Charlotte needed the room and your boxes were in her way. Who knows what she did with them?"

"I guess I was naïve. I didn't expect her to go this far, nor this fast. I don't know what I'll do now to get her out quickly. It'll take two truckloads to move all their stuff."

"What kind of ultimatums are you going to give her?"

"I'll have to ask my lawyer, but I'll make sure they do move out even if I have to get a court order to evict them. Right now, I'm going to look around to see where they put my boxes."

They checked the remaining bedrooms and found the children's furniture and clothing. The vacant guest rooms were left untouched.

"Let's look downstairs." When they entered the ballroom, Annah found her boxes stacked against one corner. "There they are, piled like trash. They didn't have the decency to take care to see if there was anything fragile in them."

"Charlotte is meaner than I thought she was. Look at all the antique furniture they brought in here to make room for their stuff."

"I'm glad they did. The children would have ruined them."

"Let me take a look through my boxes. There are a couple of things I want out of them." They walked over to the stack of boxes and opened a few. Annah found her grandmother's Bible, held it for a moment, and said, "This is something I want to take with me to the island."

"Oh, I remember when Grandma gave that to you. That's special."

As they searched several other boxes, Annah found articles of clothing and essential toiletry needs. "Emily, I know who took my jewelry. It was Charlotte."

"Well, I'm not surprised. She's selfish and thoughtless, and she's proven herself to be a thief on top of everything else."

"I told Charlotte to return it, and all this time, I questioned if Lucia was the one taking pieces of it a few at a time. They opened more boxes. "Let's go before I get so angry I'll do something I'll regret."

They headed for the door with armloads of Annah's possessions.

"Mother, you're back," Charlotte said, holding two bags of groceries as she entered through the front door. "Where did you stay last night? With Emily?"

Annah put her items on the floor and closed her hands into tight fists. "Yes. Where else could I have stayed? You've taken over my house like I told you not to."

"Let me bring in my groceries and we'll talk."

"You bet you will," Emily said.

Charlotte gave her a scornful look and went outside to her car to bring in the rest of her bags. She carried them to the kitchen and began to empty the items. Annah and Emily followed and sat down on stools waiting for her to finish. The air grew tense with no one speaking.

Finally, Annah said, "Charlotte, I'm going to give you one week to move out of this house. I did not give you permission to move in."

Charlotte wadded a plastic bag into a ball and threw it toward the garbage can in the corner. "One week, Mother? That's impossible. Besides, you said you were moving to Florida and the house would be empty until you decided what to do with it. Your property manager told us you might want to sell it. Well, Bradford and I won't let you sell it. It's now ours."

Annah seethed. "Regardless of my moving to Florida, this house is still mine and in my name. I have the right to sell it. I also have the right to move back in it without you here."

Charlotte's face reddened. "How can you move back in when you've packed all your personal belongings in boxes and let all your help go. You have nothing left here."

"I'm here to tell you that I'm not moving to Florida. I'm moving back into this house. You, however, will be moving out; and if you don't, I'll have my lawyer take care of this. In addition, I asked you to return every piece of my jewelry that you've stolen and you haven't done so yet."

Charlotte slammed her fist on the counter. "Wait until I talk to Bradford."

"Charlotte, you're rude and inconsiderate," Emily yelled.

"Keep out of this Emily. This is between Mother and me."

"No, it isn't. This involves all of us. I picked Mom up at the airport last night because she and Floyd split up, and now she needs to move back into this house and hire new help. You have to get out because she doesn't want you and your bratty kids staying here."

Charlotte looked from one to the other with defiance. "Well, Mother, I'm glad you broke up with that fat, filthy man; and, Emily, don't call my kids 'bratty'."

"They are, and Floyd is not a fat, filthy man. Who are you to talk about being fat? You waddle when you walk."

"What?" She screamed, "I ought to knock your head off. You can't criticize me. I can talk about you going to bed with one man after another."

"Shut up. I can't stand you anymore. I'm ashamed to be your sister."

Annah held her breath. Her head started to swim. She had never felt so angry in her entire life. "That does it, Charlotte. I'm disgusted with you. Come on, Emily, if we don't go now I may do something else to Charlotte I'll regret." Turning to her, she said, "This is not over. I'm going to visit Delsey for a week. When I return, you'd better be out of here because I'm moving back in."

Charlotte tightened her grip on the edge of the counter and seethed. "It's not legal to give us only a week to move out. You will have to wait thirty days."

"Let's go," Annah said, leading Emily toward the door.

As they left, they picked up the boxes Annah had chosen to take with her and carried them to the carriage house. They put them in the back of Jackson's Mercedes SUV. The key hung on the wall beside it. Annah slid in and closed the door, and rolled down the window to speak to Emily.

"Morgan is as nasty as Charlotte, Mom. He took Papa's Corvette, and he takes whatever he wants without consideration for you."

"I know, and I've told him about that."

She started the engine. "Thank you for helping me, dear. I'm going to spend time with Delsey and her family. I haven't had a chance to call them yet, but I know I'll be welcome, and I'll call you when I return. Don't let Charlotte or Morgan get to you. I'll take care of everything."

Emily leaned on the car door. "Mom, take your time and, by the way, you're getting skinnier all the time. Go eat some Gullah foods and fatten yourself up."

"Uh, fatten myself up? That's the last thing on my mind right now, but I will enjoy my time there."

"Love you, Mom."

"Love you, too," she said, as she backed the car out of its spot to drive away.

As she cleared the trees hanging over the driveway and headed toward the highway, she felt sick. Her argument with Charlotte was just another episode to break her heart. She turned north toward the road leading to the islands and tried to calm herself. She would visit with Delsey's people and fill her time reminiscing about her childhood with Grandma Wilmont. Maybe she would be able to find that rock she used to sit on as a child to look over the marshes and tall grasses, a place to be alone and remember good times. There, she would be able to think. There, she would make decisions; and, there, she would rest.

PART IV

THE ISLANDS

CHAPTER FORTY

Sea Island Parkway, U.S. 21, paved the way to Delsey's ancestral home, and to one of the few villages retaining its Gullah heritage. Condominiums and gated communities now consumed many of the larger islands, such as Hilton Head. Development had eaten away the rich African-American culture that had endured since the 1700s when planters imported laborers from West Africa to work the cotton, rice, and indigo plantations on the islands. Because of their isolation, still today, many speak a mix of English and Creole languages, called Gullah, and maintain their African folktales and handicrafts, such as sweetgrass baskets and carved walking sticks. The people call themselves Geechee, and their culture Gullah.

Annah grew more excited the closer she came to Delsey's village home. Small wooden houses and fishing shacks lined the road as she drove, giving her a sense of anticipation. What would she say to Delsey? Floyd changed his mind about their relationship. Annah felt a pain pierce her heart. Jackson betrayed her and became distant. Now, Floyd had led her to believe he loved her, but suddenly changed his mind. What advice would Delsey give her?

As she headed into town, she stopped the car in front of a small restaurant, gripped the steering wheel, and felt happy for the first time in a long time. The town had not changed except for the parked cars and lighted signs appealing to tourists to buy in their stores and eat in their restaurant.

She left the car and walked through the screen door of the restaurant. Sounds of people talking and laughing were like music to her. Several people looked her way, but she didn't recognize anyone. She headed for a table covered in a blue and white checkered tablecloth along one side of the room, pulled out a chair and sat down. In a few minutes, a short, plump black lady with a pleasing smile held a menu out to her.

"Good day, ma'am," she said. "What would you like to drink? Sweet tea?"

Annah smiled back at her and took the menu. She decided she was hungry and would certainly want something to eat. "Please bring me a glass of water while I look over the menu," she said, and added. "Would you know where a lady named Delsey lives?"

"Yes, ma'am, about five minutes from here." She mused. "But I can get her for you right now." She turned and walked into the kitchen.

Two minutes later, Delsey came walking out wiping her hands on a dishtowel. "Annah? What are you doing here?"

Annah moved her chair back and stood. "Delsey, I'm so glad to see you." They hugged quickly, and then sat across from each other at the table.

"I thought you were in Florida? Where's Floyd?"

Annah put her elbows on the table and her hands on her forehead and looked down. She sighed. "Delsey, what can I say? I never told Floyd about Gladstone. That's why I had him drive me home to see my house and meet the rest of my family and all of you, but I made a mistake. It was too overwhelming for him."

Delsey looked surprised. "Too overwhelming for him? He seemed to enjoy being with you there and working with the men." She paused. "I know he was in love with you."

Annah shook her head. "That's what I thought. Then Floyd told me to think things over between us and became aloof. Delsey, that's not the end of the story. I left the house in the hands of Louis when I went back to Ionia. I wanted time to decide what to do with it, which is selling it, since I thought I was going to live with Floyd." She leaned toward her. "I flew back home and Charlotte and her family had moved into our house thinking I was gone for good. She didn't have the right to do so, since I told her to stay out."

"That girl. I could spank her sometimes. I knew she was up to no good when she took my keys; and, Annah, I tried not to give them to her since you told me not to."

"Who's this pretty lady with you?" a woman asked.

Annah looked up to see a tall, slim black lady with rich black hair tied in a tight bun standing over them.

"This is Annah, the lady I've lived with and worked for, for many years," Delsey said. "Annah, this is Ruthie Ann. Jerome and I are staying with her right now, and she's the owner of this restaurant."

Ruthie Ann moved Delsey over into the next chair and sat down facing Annah. "Why, I swear. I've heard so much about you,

I'm so glad to meet you."

They both studied Annah's face, making her wonder what they were thinking.

"Uh huh, pretty lady you need some fattenin' up. Let me get you a plate of good-home cookin'. Right Delsey? This lady needs some comfort foods, some greens, chicken, and crab fried rice," she said, sliding out of her chair and standing. "Now, you don't go away. I'll be right back."

"You've lost weight, Annah. You look ill."

She held back tears. She knew she had lost weight, mostly from not wanting to eat. "I'm hoping you can find a place for me to stay here for a week so I can get myself together and rest. I have a lot of thinking to do, and I've always been able to talk to you." She paused. "I don't know what to do or where else to go. If I go back to Ionia, I could probably stay at the B&B or with Kat for a little while, but I don't want Floyd to think I'm there to pressure him to change his mind."

Ruthie Ann returned with two plates of food and set them in front of her. "You eat now," she said, sitting down again.

Annah looked at all the food. "My, I must really look skinny."

"Yes, ma'am."

Delsey explained Annah's situation to Ruthie Ann as Annah ate her food.

"Uh huh," she said, studying Annah. She began to hum like Delsey always did.

Annah stopped with her fork in mid-air. "What does it mean when you two hum like that? Are you singing to yourself?"

They looked at each other and back to Annah.

"We're talkin' to the Lord. We're askin' Him to carry on His work in you. Your problems are hangin' all around you and shoutin' at us."

She put her fork down on the plate, wiped her mouth on her napkin, and stared at them. "Ruthie Ann, am I that transparent?"

"Yes, ma'am. But we're going to heal those hurts with His power, and we won't let you go until you're well."

Annah laid her arms beside her plates and looked from Delsey to Ruthie Ann. She couldn't stop the tears from rolling down her cheeks.

"Honey lady, when you finish your food, I'll take you back to my house. You can stay with us, but you'll have to sleep on the couch since we don't have another bedroom," Ruthie Ann said.

Annah wiped her face with her napkin and picked her fork back up. Her words consoled her. "Thank you, both of you. I knew I could ask you for your help."

During her time on the island, Annah walked the beach thinking about Floyd and trying to find answers to why he changed his mind about her. He said he wanted her to think about their relationship. Did this mean he didn't really love her after all, and this was his way of saying goodbye? A way out? She grappled with the hurt she felt. She had never loved before as she loved Floyd. When she met Jackson, their relationship had been one of respect and admiration for each other and not much else. *How I miss Floyd,* she thought.

On one of her walks, Annah found a log bench near a fishing pier to sit upon, and opened Grandma Wilmont's Bible. She was glad she had thought to bring it. Her grandmother told her she had written in the margins and that someday, she might read them. She opened the book without knowing where to read and found a verse with her Grandmother's tiny writing on the side.

"Be anxious for nothing, but in everything by prayer and supplication, with thanksgiving, let your requests be made known to God; and the peace of God, which surpasses all understanding, will guard your hearts and minds through Christ Jesus."

In the note on the side, her grandmother wrote, "And God's peace will be with you."

She put her hand on the book and looked up. "God, how I need Your peace," she said. "I've never really talked to You much, so You'll have to have patience with me. I don't know how to begin." She spent time reading more verses and talking to Him. Until finally, she stood and walked slowly through the grass, stepping over mud puddles, until she reached the dirt road and headed back to town.

As the week passed, Ruthie Ann gave her responsibilities in the restaurant, which Annah came to enjoy. It kept her mind off what she knew she would face when she returned to Rosewillow. She gave her the job of welcoming visitors, handing them menus, and setting the tables. She watched Delsey cook several dishes of Gullah foods, especially turkey wings, collards, and rice dishes with crumbled bacon, garlic powder, and fried fish.

Jerome swept the floors, took care of any maintenance, and took out the trash. Custer's job consisted of running the commercial dishwasher and stacking the dishes on the kitchen shelves, and Delsey helped Ruthie Ann cook. Tourists filled the tables daily and their loud chatter and laughter made it a happy place for her to heal.

One day, she asked Jerome to drive her around the island so she could see the condition of the schools that Delsey said needed rebuilding. She was astounded by the weathered structures. She had him stop so she could walk up to the window of one and look in. The tables were old and many had cracked corners and braced legs. The chalkboard needed replacing and the books were tattered. She thought how sad they were in comparison to the schools she and her family had attended as children.

"Delsey, why hasn't the state rebuilt your schools?" she asked her after they returned to the house.

"They forget we exist."

"What? Your island is part of the state of South Carolina. Why wouldn't they provide you with better buildings and classrooms?"

Delsey attempted a smile and said, "Uh huh."

Annah said no more.

—

Reluctant to leave Delsey and her island friends, Annah knew it was time to return to Rosewillow and confront Charlotte with leaving if she hadn't already done so.

"Miss Annie, you listen to me. That man you talk about is losin' a fine lady if I don't say so. I've been watchin' you and seein' your achin' heart. My advice to you is to go and talk it out," Ruthie Ann said.

"I think she's right, Annah, I think Floyd is looking more after your welfare than his. Why don't you call him?" Delsey asked.

Annah didn't answer. She didn't want him to think she was pressuring him. He had lost interest in her and it was final, and she was too depressed to think about it.

Jerome came up beside them. "Miss Annah, your bags are in your car. You sure you want to leave so soon? You've only been here a week. We like having you around helping us."

"I think I've overstayed my welcome."

"Hush, don't you even think that. You're family. Why, everyone's goin' to miss you greetin' the folks comin' in to eat and settin' the tables," Ruthie Ann added.

"Annah, we understand. Let us know what happens with your house and what you are going to do after you've talked to Floyd. We'll be praying for you," Delsey said.

She wished she could stay longer. "I need all the prayers you can give me. Now, I have to go. You all have a special place in my heart, and I won't forget you or my time here."

Annah climbed in her car and slowly drove away, as they watched her leave. She really did wish she could stay longer.

"My, my," Ruthie Ann said. "She's a good woman. She gained weight on our good cookin', huh Delsey?"

"Yes. And, her face is shining with the peace of the Lord."

—

When Annah returned home, she parked her car and thought that if Charlotte and her family had not moved out, she would pack more clothes in her car and decide where to go for the night. If they were gone, she would try to regain some semblance of order back in her life.

She walked up the steps and turned the knob on the front door. It was locked. She fumbled for her key and opened the door. The house appeared empty. She walked down the hallway and peered into the family room. It looked like Charlotte had moved out. The room was orderly and the children's toys were gone. She walked up to her bedroom. No, they had not moved out. She saw Charlotte's family pictures placed strategically on her dresser and her clothes hanging in the closet. In anger, she opened Charlotte's top dresser drawer and gathered her own jewelry, and then picked up the box on top. *She is not getting away with stealing my personal things.* She pulled a pillow case off a pillow and filled it with her possessions.

Annah placed her hand on her forehead. *God, what do I do now?* She left the room to find a telephone to call her lawyer and explain the difficulty. He said he would take care of it and have Charlotte and her family out within the next thirty days. "Thirty days?" she asked. "Yes, legally it would take that much time, unless you want to press criminal charges for trespassing," he said. She hung up, sat down on the bed, and shook her head. She certainly didn't want to do that to her own daughter.

Where could she go for a month? She didn't know any lady in the Rosewillow Women's Club well enough to stay with for a month, nor did she want to explain her predicament. Kat's invitation to visit would be her answer and that's just what she had to do. That meant she would have to drive to Ionia again, and this time by herself.

She found the boxes in the ballroom and again sorted through them to take what she needed. She would call Kat. She was sure she and Spencer would let her visit. She was also sure Lola would find a room for her; but then, Floyd would find out.

She packed the Mercedes with as much as she could, filled the tank with gas at the nearest station, and bought snacks and drinks to take along with her. First, she thought, she had better drive to the bank and store her jewelry in her safety deposit box in the vault, but where did she put the key? She remembered she had hidden it in a corner in the bottom drawer of her jewelry box. She would be all right. Once done, she returned to her car and headed for Ionia. It was late in the afternoon, but she could drive all night.

"Why, hon, of course you can stay with us," Kat said, when she talked with Annah on the phone. "Y'all can stay as long as you'd like. Just knock on the door when you get here. I'll wake up and help you bring your suitcases in."

With a sigh of relief, Annah stepped on the gas pedal to increase her speed and counted the hours to figure out when she would arrive. It was four o'clock, and she would pull up to her house around two or three in the morning.

Her anger with Charlotte had not subsided while she drove on. She thought about how she could have raised such a selfish, arrogant child. As an adult, Charlotte is a disappointment and a disgrace, she thought. Annah watched the highway signs and continued driving I-95 toward Florida. She had not eaten dinner and reached for a rolled nut bar she purchased at the gas station. With one hand, she opened the wrapper and bit into it.

She knew she chastised herself too much. Jackson was just as much at fault for the way their children turned out. She took another bite. Well, she thought, Charlotte and Morgan are adults, and she would have to set down new rules so that they could no longer control her life.

For goodness sakes, I've spent my life in a museum, always being in fear of breaking the antiques and heirlooms, and yelling at the children to stay away from them. She thought that when she moved back in, she would put the display cases and pictures in storage.

She finished her nut bar, crushed the wrapper, and threw it in a plastic bag. *Oh, Floyd, I would have loved you until the day I died. I'm so sorry this happened to us.* She knew wealth could be intimidating, but she had hoped Floyd would not have cared. Isn't that what Lola said? She wished she could give all her money away, but she needed to provide for herself now that she was on her own.

She reached for a water bottle, opened it, and drank from it. She thought about her time on the island with Delsey and her family. It was there she came to find the peace she so craved; and, it was there she found God. As she studied the highway signs, she felt her life brighten. *He* was now in control.

During her drive, she stopped at a rest stop for a few minutes. Bright lights led her safely to and from the building guiding her away from semis and large motor homes.

She felt sleepy, but kept on until she reached Ionia and pulled into Kat's driveway. She shut off the engine and stretched. Her shoulders ached from tension and from sitting for hours behind the wheel. She yawned. Kat had left the front door light on for her, but she didn't want to wake them, so she pushed the lever to let her seat lay back and fell quickly to sleep in the car. She had made the drive without incident, had stopped again for gas, another snack, and to relieve herself, and now it was time to sleep.

"Hon, what are you doing sleeping in your car?" Kat asked, knocking on the window early that morning. "You come in the house right this minute."

Annah looked out and saw Kat staring at her. "I didn't want to wake you."

"Well, I never! Y'all get your buns in my house. I made up the guest room for you as soon as you called." She opened the car door and helped her out.

She returned her seat upright and slid out of the car. "Good morning."

"It sure is a good morning. Come on in and have breakfast," Kat said, as she led the way into their home. "Spencer," she called. "Annah's been sleeping in her car. I just can't believe it."

Spencer walked toward her. "Why did you do that, Annah? We were ready for you."

"I didn't want to disturb you. It was too early, and I thought I'd wake you."

"Come on in. You're just in time for breakfast."

Annah spent the morning sitting with them at their kitchen table and telling them about Floyd, the house, Charlotte, and her time on the island with Delsey and her family.

"Now, what have you decided to do?" Spencer asked, sipping the last of his coffee.

"That's just it. I had hours to think about that while driving here. I called my lawyer and he's going to have Charlotte and her family removed from the house in thirty days, but I have mixed feelings. I really don't want to move back into the house, but I probably should."

"Are you going to talk to Floyd?" Kat questioned.

Annah knotted her napkin and laid it on the table. "Just as I said, it's over between us."

Kat put her hand on Annah's arm. "Well, you know we're here for you. Whatever happens, you can count on us."

Spencer excused himself from the table. "Ladies, I have some paperwork to do. You can go on with your discussion."

"Annie girl," Kat said, releasing her hand. "You needed that time here to get away from everything--your family, the ladies club, the museum committee, just everything, so you could think things out. Maybe Floyd is the man for you and maybe not. Let things work out."

"Kat, I also needed time alone on the island. I found something I never expected. I've been frantically searching for peace in every place but with God. I thought I'd find it in a change of environment, or a change from the lifestyle I grew up in, or leaving my house, or even finding a man that would truly love me so I could forget Jackson, but that was not the answer."

"Well, silly, of course you couldn't find quiet and peace by making all those changes."

"Peace and quiet, Kat, not quiet and peace. People say 'peace and quiet'."

"Humph. Annah, there you go again correcting my words."

"I'm sorry. Say it the way you want."

"I will. Peace and quiet or quiet and peace mean the same thing. I'm just happy that you've found it with the Lord. I could have told you that years ago. Do you know what I think? It's really Floyd that has screwed up your life. You've been hurt again, and you think you're over him, but you're not."

"I'll get over him. It'll just be a matter of time. I've lost so many people in my life; this one won't be any different."

"Sure you will. This time you're stronger."

"Hey, ladies, let's all go into the Florida room. Annah, I think it's time for me to tell you my idea for what you can do with Gladstone."

They left the table and followed Spencer into the room. The discussion lasted over an hour, and Annah made a significant decision, one that *would* change her life.

CHAPTER FORTY-ONE

Spencer's suggestions prompted Annah to spend time the next day on the phone contacting her legal and financial advisors to work out the details of his suggestion. She also called Louis, to relay information regarding Charlotte.

In addition, she had to find a reputable moving company to pack up her small furnishings and move them to the storage unit in Ionia. She had already boxed up her personal items, so all they would have to move in addition to them were specific pieces of furniture that she would list on the forms they would send her. Louis would help when she returned home.

She needed to call Henry to tell him the news so he wouldn't be surprised. When she told him her plans, it took several minutes for him to respond.

"Annah," he said. "I would have never dreamed of you doing that. I only hope you never regret it."

"I won't regret it, Henry. This is the right decision."

One final call needed to be made. "Randall, how are you?" Annah asked without explaining that she was calling from Florida.

"Annah, my dearest. I've waited quite a while for you to contact me. Are you ready for our little dinner party?"

She held the receiver with both hands. "Randall, I'm sorry. I won't be able to make it. I called to tell you that I'm moving to Florida." She heard silence, and then he hung up. She was not surprised. She had hurt him again, but she could not have given him any other answer.

Annah knew that once she told Charlotte the news, she would scream. Morgan would scold her, and Emily would cry, but what else could she do?

While Annah continued working on her plans, Emily called. "Mom! Jimmy wrote an award-winning article about our house and its history. You should read it. I'm going to give you a copy of the newspaper. He said his editor was so pleased he had to give him a raise and a better position. Can you believe it? I'm so proud of him."

"That's wonderful, dear. Please do give me a copy of it."

"Since the article hit the papers, people are driving up to the house to view it and take pictures. Mom, what should we do? Charlotte is disgusted and says they're trespassing, and she's going to put up a barricade in front of the driveway to stop them from gawking."

Annah thought, *That's so like Charlotte.* "Emily, please tell Jimmy that I'm impressed with his writing and knowledge of our home. He has interested many people."

"Just what are your plans, Mom?"

"I can't tell you right now. You should know that I'm staying at Kat's house in Florida. We'll talk later when I'm home."

"Mom? You drove to Florida? I thought you were still visiting Delsey on the island."

"I was there for a week and went home, but Charlotte and her family were still there. I had no other choice but to drive back to Florida. Kat and Spencer offered to let me stay with them for a day or two while I figured out what to do with this mess." She paused. "Emily, I contacted my lawyer to have Charlotte and her family removed from the house, and he's given her thirty days."

"She's not going to be happy about this."

"I could care less. I can't return until then, so call me at the B&B if you have to reach me. Now, let's change the subject. Have you found out if you're pregnant yet?"

"Yes. The baby is due the end of March."

"Well, I'm happy for you and Jimmy. Have you set a date for your wedding?"

"Not yet. I want to finish my senior year, and we'll get married after I graduate."

Annah shook her head. This generation was so different. When she was young, she would have been pressured to get married immediately. "Okay, dear. We'll talk when I get home to take care of matters."

—

Annah stayed with Kat and Spencer for one week, and then she felt it was time to leave. She left them with the knowledge that she would stay with Lola for another three weeks and would be in touch. She drove away hoping Lola would not question her sudden return.

Lola met her at the door of the B&B and welcomed her back. After she settled in, she told Lola about her problems with Charlotte and all that transpired while she was home. She explained she didn't want her to tell Floyd about her being at the B&B. She didn't want him to think she was there to make him change his mind.

Lola looked squarely at her. "Dearie, put on your walkin' shoes. We need to talk."

Annah knew this would become more than just a talk. "Okay. Give me a minute." Once she changed into her sandals, she returned and followed her out the sliding glass door, heading for the beach. She kicked sand as she walked and waited for Lola to start the conversation.

"Annah, you're goin' to have to stop cryin' to everyone about your problems and be the strong woman everyone thinks you are. You've been soundin' like a broken record, for Pete's sakes. I have a mind to shake you. You're only makin' yourself more and more depressed."

Lola sat down on the beach and patted the sand for her to sit beside her. "What do you really want? You say you're tired of your life of wealth and status, and you want peace and a simpler life, which is why you came down here in the first place. It seems to me you're torn between who you are and who you think you are."

Annah emptied her sandals of sand of crushed shells. "What do you mean?"

"What are you *really* lookin' for?"

She didn't know how to answer.

"You've had a full life accordin' to what you told me. People can find peace in the comfort of familiarity. They can also create a simpler life by just changin' their expectations. The life you've described to me is all you've ever known. Surely, with your wealth you shouldn't have any worries, so maybe you need to go back home and reevaluate what you already have. The way I see it, you have to take control of your adult children and not put up with their crap. They don't respect you, and it's up to you to change that."

Annah shuffled her feet in the sand, wrapped her arms around her knees, and looked at Lola. "Lola, I know I have to accept who I am because of my inheritance. I've already come to terms with that."

"Okay, then go back home and change whatever you need to and quite lookin' like the world has done you no favors. You can always start over. People do it every day. That's life. Pick yourself up and begin to look to the future as a new chapter in your life, and like I said, for gosh sakes, stand up to your adult children. They'll handle it and realize they can't walk over you anymore."

She slipped her feet into her sandals. "Lola, I've talked with my two friends about all this, and they suggested that I make other plans. They think I would be happier in Ionia away from the troubles up there. I really don't want to live there anymore. Spencer has given me an idea of what to do with Gladstone. I've discussed it with my lawyer, and he's preparing for me to make the required changes." She paused. "I want to be free of my responsibilities to that house."

Lola stood up. "Well, I'll be danged!"

Annah stood up with her. "I feel it's the right thing to do."

Lola stared long and hard at her, and then said, "Another thing. How do you know for sure that Floyd doesn't care for you anymore? He hasn't expressed that to me."

"I'm sure. I haven't heard from him since he told me to think things over. He thinks I'm giving everything up for him, and I don't think he wants to be responsible for a bad decision on my part."

Lola put her hands on her hips. "Well, sweetie, you're right. I'm sure he wants you to be sure you're makin' the right decision because it looks like you're runnin' away instead of facin' your problems head on. Anyone who has the easy life you've had would be nuts to throw it all away."

She didn't answer. She stared past Lola at the seaweed awash on the beach, and it reminded her of Delsey's island. "Lola, I spent a week visiting Delsey on her family's island off South Carolina. I read a few notes written by my grandmother in the margins of her Bible. Delsey's family is praying for me."

Lola listened and then frowned. "Sweetheart, you can talk to me until you're blue in the face about others praying for you. You have to do some of it, too."

She couldn't get the words out for the lump in her throat.

"Did you pray for His plans for your life?"

She cleared her throat. "Yes."

"Then, you may be in for a big surprise." Lola turned and started to walk up the path to the house. "But, before you make any drastic changes you'll regret, you'd better get you buns into that car of yours and go now. Your daughter needs to know you won't back down from them movin' out, and that you won't wait thirty days for them to do it. Forget about that letter your lawyer wrote to them. You said they moved into your house in a few days. Okay, they can move out in a few days, too, and then you can do what you want with the house. Then, and only then, can you make definite plans about your house and life."

Annah followed her. She really didn't want to face Charlotte right now. She was tired of the whole situation. "If you don't mind, I'll stay here until the end of August."

Lola sped up and didn't answer.

Annah stopped and took a deep breath, letting the wind blow

through her hair. Then, she followed her to the house.

Once inside the house, Lola stood behind the counter reviewing charge slips and ignored her as she entered.

"I'm sorry, Lola, if you want me to leave, I'll get my things and go."

"Dang it, Annah," Lola said, slamming her fist on the counter. "I don't want you to leave. We all know why you're really upset, and we know just who's causin' it."

Annah sat down on the edge of an armchair. "Lola, I know…it's Floyd. I'm getting used to the fact that he doesn't love me anymore. I just have to get over it."

She walked around the counter. "Annah, he's miserable, too. He's tryin' to get on with his life, and he's walkin' around like a sad puppy dog."

"He's the one that walked away from me."

"Well, sweetie, you're both tearin' each other apart by not talkin' this out. Let me tell you that Floyd is a good man, and if he distanced himself from you, he thinks he has a good reason to do so, and I think he thinks he's not good enough for you."

"That's nonsense. I've told and shown him in many ways that I love him and our backgrounds don't matter to me."

"Tell me honestly, do you think you're too good for him?"

Annah felt a tug at her heart. "No, Lola, Floyd knows who he is and there's no pretense. I've been living a lie for most of my life." She moved to sit down on the chair. "I'm telling the truth when I say I want to have a different kind of life. You asked me if I'm running away. Well, I think I'm running from being a doormat to my family and the responsibilities of taking care of my ancestor's expectations."

Lola let her talk.

"My mother used to say, 'Always hold your head high. Be a pillar of the community. You have a reputation to keep for all of us.' Well, I'm not so sure anymore. Right now, my reputation is ruined in Rosewillow. They all know of my affair with Floyd, my letting go of all our help, and possibly selling my historic home. I've become a scandal, and it would take many years to restore my position in society."

"So what," Lola said. "Some people have nothin' else to do but gossip." Slapping the back of Annah's chair, she turned and walked away.

Annah watched her go. She stood and walked toward the steps and up toward her room. Once in her room, she sat down on the edge of the bed and stared at her unopened suitcase. *God, what do I do now?* There were places she could go, a local motel, or one in Tampa. She peered around the room. She felt she couldn't return to Kat's because she'd overstayed her welcome. She didn't want to drive home as Lola suggested. Where would she stay there? Fly to Charleston and find a hotel? She didn't want to impose on Emily, nor go back to Ruthie Ann's home, even though that thought was appealing. She knew of a friend from the Women's Club in Rosewillow that had moved to Palm Beach. She could drive over there and find a hotel. Maybe she could find her name in the phone book.

She leaned over and rocked. She felt very alone. Lola was her best friend beside Kat, but now she had angered her. She listened to her heart beating and her head pounding. The silence in the room was deafening. She looked around, searching for something to hang onto. *Lord, what should I do?*

Getting up from the bed, she picked up her suitcase and packed the few things she had taken out, like her sandals that she wore down to the beach and her toiletries. Her thoughts were now on the boxes stored in her car. Where could she go so that someone wouldn't steal them out of her car? A mere look at her car would tempt a robber to steal from it. Look what happened to Morgan. She would have to haul the boxes in and out of any hotel. She decided to call Kat and explain her dilemma.

"Kat," Annah said, as she answered her call. "I need your help."

"Why, hon, what's the matter?"

She felt her throat tighten and could barely speak. "Dear, I thought I could stay here with Lola, but I've angered her because I asked her not to tell Floyd that I was here. Now, I don't know where to go. I could find a motel in Tampa, but I need somewhere to store the boxes that I took from my home."

"Yes, hon. I know you brought them into our house for safekeeping when you were here. My gosh, I don't know how you stashed all that in your little car."

"Do you mind if I bring them back over and have you store them again?"

"Annah! You bring your little bottom over here and set yourself down in my house. You hear? I'm not having my best friend run from one place to another while her daughter has shown herself to be a selfish, spoiled brat by taking over her house."

Annah sat back down on the bed and sighed relief. "Thank you. You don't know how good it is to hear you say that. I don't know what else to do right now. I was afraid I would be in your way."

"What? Now, you listen to me. I'm going to be waiting at the door with a wooden spoon to swat your butt when you get here. I don't ever want to hear such talk like that again."

Annah couldn't help but laugh. "I'm on my way over. Give me twenty minutes."

Suddenly, she heard a pounding on her door. "Annah, open up."

Startled, Annah walked to the door and opened it. Lola stood there with her hands on her hips.

"Let's go. We have a job to do." She pulled Annah's arm and led her downstairs. "We're goin' for a drive."

"Lola, please. I've arranged with Kat to stay with her. I'm sorry I made you angry."

Lola dropped her arm. "Misses, I have a mind to shake you. "You're comin' with me."

They traveled in Lola's car without speaking. Annah stared straight ahead knowing the direction they were going and fearful of what she was about to do.

"Lola, I have to call Kat. She's waiting for me to be there in twenty minutes, and I'm not going to make it."

"Then call her," she said, staring ahead at the truck driver in front of her that was going too slow and calling him names.

Annah called Kat and explained what was happening, just as Lola pulled her car into a spot between two pickups close to The Albatross.

"Now, young lady, you go in there and talk to him," Lola demanded.

Annah felt like her heart was ready to burst. "Lola, he doesn't want to see me. Please turn around and go back."

Lola leaned on the door and glared at her. "I didn't bring you here to turn around and take you back."

"What can I say to him? I'm sorry things didn't work out for us?"

Lola wouldn't budge. "You'll figure it out," she said. "I'll wait here for fifteen minutes. If you don't come out, I'll leave you and let Floyd take you home."

Annah hesitated and then reached for the handle to her door. "Be ready to see me walking out crying." She left the car, slipped her purse under her arm, and anxiously made her way to the black wooden door in front of her. She knew that when she turned the knob and pulled the door open that the hinges would squeak and everyone would turn to look at her when she entered.

"God, don't let me lose courage," she whispered, as she reached for the door handle. She swung the door open and the odor of stale liquor and smoke wafted out. She spotted Floyd in the dim light sitting alone at the bar drinking a beer. She hesitated and then walked over to the stool next to him, sat down, and looked up at the bartender. Her heart pounded inside her like a drum beating. She held her head straight and prayed that she could get the words out without stuttering.

"Beer, please, the same as his," she said, as she pointed to Floyd's bottle without looking at him.

Instantly, she felt Floyd sit up straight and felt his gaze on her. "Hello, Floyd," she said, whispering and turning to face him.

He was quiet for a few minutes, making her panic and ready to flee.

He swung around in his stool. "Hello," he said without emotion.

Annah's beer was set in front of her with an empty mug next to it. She lifted the bottle and knew her hand was shaking, and she knew she wouldn't be able to pour the beer into the mug without trembling, so she drank the beer from the bottle and set it back down on the bar.

For a long while, they gazed at one another without speaking. Finally, Annah leaned toward him hoping her words would come out right. "I'd like to go fishing tomorrow."

Floyd took in a deep breath, closed his eyes, and moved his body closer to hers. He put his arm around her and said, "Me, too." He ordered another beer for the two of them, and placed his face close to hers. "I'm sorry."

Annah laid her head on his chest and whispered, "Me, too."

After Floyd waved from the bar door for Lola to go home, they stayed for a couple of hours talking and drinking, and then he took her to his house.

The next morning, Floyd scrambled eggs, fried bacon, toast, and made coffee.

"I might keep you as my personal cook," Annah said. "Everything is scrumptious."

"Hmm, we'll see about that. You might get tired of bologna sandwiches every day."

She shook her head. "Guess what? I haven't cooked a full meal in my entire life."

Floyd raised his eyebrows. "Then we're both in trouble."

When they finished breakfast, they drove to the B&B. Roy sat reading a newspaper, and Lola was in the kitchen cleaning up as they entered.

"Well, I wondered what happened to the two of you." Roy said, putting down his paper.

Lola peeked around the kitchen door frame and caught Annah's eye. She walked into the parlor to be with them. "I'm glad you two patched things up. I was so worried."

Annah gave her a knowing smile.

Roy smirked at Floyd. "Yep, and I'm glad you didn't do

somethin' stupid like lettin' her go."

Lola held a straight face and returned to the kitchen, where she quietly sang to herself.

Annah left the men and walked up to shower and change into the jeans and t-shirt Lola had previously given her to go fishing. When she was ready, they drove over to Spencer and Kat's home. Annah wanted Floyd to hear Spencer's plans for her Rosewillow home as he had offered, and, afterward, she and Floyd would go fishing.

Kat met them at the door and reached out to hug them. "I'm so glad you're here," she squealed. "Come in, come in." She led them into the Florida room and waved her hand around it. "Sit where you'd like. Spencer will be right with us."

Floyd squeezed Annah's hand and pointed to the most comfortable looking chair in the room. Finding a chair next to hers, they sat down.

"Would you like coffee? Ice tea? Beer?" Spencer asked.

Annah shook her head. "I think I've had enough beer. We must have drank every beer in the bar last night."

"I'll have coffee," Floyd said. He shifted in his chair to make himself more comfortable. "And I'll have coffee, too," Annah agreed.

Kat left them to prepare the drinks.

"So, Annah, as we discussed last week, I have an idea for you to free yourself of your estate, but I'd like to hear what your plans are first," Spencer said, as he took a seat next to a small, round table.

Annah quickly moved her head to eye Floyd and back to Spencer. I haven't told Floyd yet what you suggested to me. We discussed the possibility of selling it, but I have to say that I feel guilty about doing so."

She leaned forward. "As you all know, I have a dilemma. My children would not be able to manage the estate. Charlotte and Bradford will not take care of it, and I hate to see it ruined because of them. Neither would Morgan take care of it. His passion is to sail. In addition, he would rather be deep-sea fishing than staying around his home. Patricia is a wonderful wife and mother, but she has no experience running a house with domestic help.

"Finally, there's Emily. Emily is currently finishing her college degree and plans to marry Jimmy after she graduates. I don't know what their plans are for the future. You see, I'm really at a loss." She stopped, leaned back, and took a sip of coffee.

Spencer thought a moment. "Okay then. Floyd, here's what Annah and I discussed. He elaborated on the details for twenty minutes. After he finished and each one was in full agreement with his thoughts, Annah and Floyd left knowing they had another trip to Rosewillow ahead of them. Today, however, they would go fishing.

"How many fish did you catch," Roy asked, seeing them come in through the door.

"Would you believe six? This should make a nice dinner for all of us," he said, proudly holding up a zip lock bag filled with fish. He continued. "Before we went fishing, we stopped to see Annah's friends. Spencer had a good idea about what she can do with her house, and Annah wanted me to hear it."

"Now what?" Lola asked, looking at Floyd and wiping her hands on a towel as she walked out of the kitchen.

"Annah has started the dissolution of ownership of her estate, so it's important that we take another trip up north to finalize the paperwork. We're leaving tomorrow morning."

"Oh, my word," Lola said, looking surprised.

"I have to explain to my children what I'm going to do. I want Floyd to be with me to support me. I'm afraid there will be fireworks, and they won't like what I'm going to tell them."

Lola came to Annah's side. "So you've made a final decision to move down here permanently. I'm happy for you and Floyd."

"Hey! I can't wait to hear what happens," Roy said.

"I really can't wait to get this over. I've been tied up in knots for the last month."

Lola pointed her finger at Floyd, "For more reasons than one," she said.

CHAPTER FORTY-TWO

Charlotte discovered Annah's jewelry and box gone out of the dresser in Annah's room. Angry, she called Emily. "Where did mother go? I haven't heard from her in over a week. Did she come back to the house?"

"Charlotte," Emily said. "Mom doesn't steal. Besides, I know that jewelry was not yours, and you stole it from her; and, yes, she spent a week visiting Delsey and came back to the house. When she found out you were still there, she took Dad's Mercedes and drove to Ionia to stay with her friends at their bed and breakfast."

Infuriated, she said. "I told her we were not moving. I'm going to call down there and tell her that again." With that she hung up.

"Lola," Charlotte said. "Is my mother there?"

Lola leaned across the counter and winked at Roy. "Is this Charlotte?"

"Yes! Is my mother there?"

Lola hesitated. "Here?" she asked.

"Yes. I asked you if my mother was there with you."

Since Annah was not standing beside her, she honestly answered, "No, Charlotte, you mother is not here with me."

Charlotte swore and said, "Emily told me she drove down there to stay with you people. She's been gone for over a week, and she hasn't called here. Is she with Kat?"

Lola tapped the back of her phone with one finger to kill time. "Dearie, I really don't know. She could be anywhere. Why don't you wait until she calls you?"

Charlotte slammed the receiver down. "I know where she is,

probably with that awful man again. I'm going to call the Ionia police to watch for my father's Mercedes."

—

The road to Rosewillow became a familiar route to Annah now. She and Floyd had much to talk about regarding the possible loss of one another. It was refreshing to have restored their relationship and love. The heartbreak had become unbearable.

"Floyd," Annah began. "We've never talked about religion, have we?"

He lifted his eyebrows. "No. I didn't think it was necessary to talk about it."

She turned in her seat to face him. "Well, for years, I longed for something or somebody to fill the emptiness I felt, but nothing or nobody seemed to satisfy. I've told you how I filled my calendar with what I thought were worthwhile activities, volunteering here and there, etc. My life seemed to be an endless pursuit for fulfillment. Isn't that laughable?" she asked, waiting for his response, which didn't come.

"Since Jackson died, I've felt only loneliness. We were distant to each other, but his physical presence at least gave me someone to talk to in the evenings. There seemed to be a purpose being married." She breathed deeply and continued.

"So, as you know, I felt I needed to get away for a while and take a vacation, which Kat and I took to Ionia. That's when I realized I was searching for peace. I found myself embroiled in one problem after another and unhappy with my life." Still, Floyd did not interrupt her.

"My grandmother told me that God had plans for me and they would be good. That I should go on my vacation, and I would find the peace I was looking for. When I fell in love with you, I thought God was there in the midst of my cry, but then we had that falling out, and I didn't believe you or God cared about me."

Floyd took her hand and held it.

"I have to tell you that God has never been important in my life. Lola asked me what I was really looking for. Now I realize I was looking for Him."

"So, you found religion."

She waited a moment to respond. His comment seemed harsh. "No, I didn't find religion." She hesitated. "I found the Lord."

Floyd looked over at her, took his hand away, and smiled. "Good for you."

For a moment, she thought his words were insincere. "When I visited Delsey, I took my grandmother's Bible with me to read some of the notes she wrote on the pages. I asked God that if He was real, would he make himself known to me."

Floyd looked like he was about to laugh. "And?"

She tightened her arms around her. "He did."

Floyd looked at her with a twinkle in his eyes. "Don't tell me you're going to start quoting scripture to me?"

Now, she felt foolish. Would he understand or would he tease her? "I want you to know that I actually felt a ton of weight lift off my shoulders." She held back tears. "And, I found such a moment of peace that I knew God answered me. I know He is real now, and I can trust Him to help me through all my troubles."

He took a hold of her hand and kissed it. "Lady love, I've always trusted God. I just don't make a big deal about it."

She felt a sense of relief.

"Hey," he said, smiling at her. "I'm here and that's an answer to your grandmother's advice. He has plans for us, and they're going to turn out pretty good."

She sensed his humor. "It looks like God let me meet you for this time."

—

The Ionia police returned Charlotte's call to look for Annah's car and told her they had searched the area and didn't find it. Angry for not knowing where Annah had gone, she threw the dishtowel against the kitchen wall where she was standing. "Just wait until I find out where she is. I'm going to give her a piece of my mind!"

—

Annah phoned Emily to ask her to tell Morgan and Charlotte that she and Floyd would be home the next morning and would like to speak with all of them together at ten o'clock at her house. She had something very important to say.

Emily relayed the message.

"Mother wants us to meet her at the house tomorrow?" Charlotte asked. "This is our house now. She should have called me first."

"Well, she didn't. I'm relaying her message. We are all to meet tomorrow at ten at *her* house. You're there, so it shouldn't be any problem."

Charlotte fumed. "And I'll be the first one to chew her out, too."

—

Annah and Floyd drove over to the house at eight the next morning and found that Charlotte and the children were not at home. They decided to take the time to pack up boxes of kitchen utensils, pots and pans, dishes, and a few appliances to give to Delsey and Ruth Ann for their restaurant. These were the items she had specifically left off the mover's list when her boxes were shipped to Ionia.

"I think we have enough for now. If they need anything more, we can always come back and get them."

After the last box was loaded onto Floyd's truck, he covered the bed with a large tarp and secured it with bungee cords.

Charlotte drove up to the house just as Floyd finished, climbed out of her car and yelled. "Mother, where in hell have you been, and what's this man doing? Are you taking things out of the house that we need?"

Annah rested her arm against the side of the truck. "Charlotte, where I've been is none of your business. Didn't my lawyer send you a letter telling you that I want you and your family out of the house? He was to give you thirty days to do so."

Charlotte stared with her face turning bright red. "We're not moving, Mother. We are not going to let you sell this house. It belongs to the family, and I'm the next heir in line to take it. Bradford and I decided to get our own lawyer to fight this."

"It won't do you any good. I've already signed papers to dispose of the house and everything in it. You have no choice but to move out as soon as possible."

Charlotte clenched her fists. "No, we won't."

"What's this? What do you mean you've signed papers to dispose of the house? What are you doing, selling it?" Morgan asked after exiting the car with his family and hearing Charlotte.

"Yes, she is, but we're going to make sure whatever she did is reversed. Bradford and I have already moved into it."

"Damn. What's going on, Charlotte? What gives you the right to live here? Maybe we want to live here, too."

Floyd leaned his back against the truck door and put his hands in his jean pockets. It was obvious he didn't want to interfere.

"Come. Let's all go into the house and parlor and discuss this like adults," Annah said.

"Does Emily know about this?" Morgan asked, as he followed Annah.

"Know about what?" Emily asked, as she and Jimmy joined them as they walked into the house and into the parlor.

Morgan explained the situation and pointed at Charlotte. "She thinks she's the owner of this house now, and she and her bratty kids and fat husband are going to live here."

"Stop it, Morgan, you numbskull," Charlotte shrieked.

"Mom, what have you decided to do about the house?" Emily asked, ignoring both of them. "And, what's all that stuff in the pickup?"

"Calm down everyone. Let's sit and talk about this," Annah said, motioning to Floyd to sit beside her on the loveseat. He walked over from the door and sat down.

"I know," Morgan said, pointing at Floyd. "He's the instigator. He wants the cash from this house just as I thought. He's after you're money, Ma."

"No! Stop this right now. Floyd has nothing to do with my decision. Listen to me, all of you. Let me explain what I've decided to do."

Daphne and Douglas came running into the parlor screaming and tripping over an ottoman. "Mama, Dougie won't play with me."

"Twins! Go play in the family room. We're busy in here," Charlotte yelled. They jumped up, pushed the ottoman out of their way, and ran out.

Annah's nerves were rattled. "Now, everyone hold your voices. I'm going to tell you something very serious, and we'll have a discussion when I'm through."

"Oh, here we go. Our mother is going to lecture us like kids," Morgan said.

Annah took a deep breath, while giving Morgan a stern look. "All of you listen to me. I gathered you here to tell you that I'm donating the house to the State Historical Society for a Civil War museum. None of you will inherit it."

Charlotte's mouth dropped in astonishment, Emily broke down in sobs, and Morgan abruptly stood up with his hands clenched, ready to fight.

"What a great idea," Jimmy said to Annah. "Emily, just think of the great historical value this place holds, not only for South Carolina, but our nation."

Morgan stormed over to Annah. "I'm going to fight this. Wait until I talk to my attorney. You're not going to do this to us."

Defiant, Annah stood up and faced him. "Yes, I can. I own this property, and I can do whatever I wish with it. All of you will be getting your final inheritance. That should be enough to let you live comfortably and happy for the rest of your lives."

Floyd watched as Morgan's face turned a blotchy red, Charlotte dropped her head into her lap and held her face with both hands, and Emily sobbed louder.

"It's settled. I have talked to my lawyer and worked out the arrangements. Your money is in a trust, and it will be doled out to each of you on a monthly basis. Morgan, there's nothing your attorney can do. I have a clause in the documents that if you dispute my actions, you will lose everything." She paused to catch her breath. "I am giving you enough money to pay off your boat and home. Charlotte, you haven't sold your house yet, so you can pay off the mortgage and move back into it. Emily and Jimmy, you will have enough money to purchase a home for yourselves and your family.

"Also, Jimmy, I have told Henry St. James I think you would make a wonderful museum curator, as well as Emily, after she graduates, to work along with you as a photo-journalist and docent. Your interest in the history of this place and her memories of it will be helpful in keeping the legacy alive. In addition, Jimmy, I'd like you to put a notice in the paper to announce my intentions."

"Yes, ma'am."

For a minute, the depth of the silence held Annah's three adult children in a state of shock.

It was then that Emily remembered that elderly lady's joy knowing her family was together for the first time in fifteen years and finally getting along. *What is it going to take for my family to ever get along? This news will tear us apart forever.*

Finally, Charlotte said, "Mother, I'm ashamed of you, letting this…this man, control you and make you do this."

Annah fumed. "If you only knew the truth. Floyd never once told me to do this. It's been my decision from the start. Not one of you has ever asked me if I've been happy here. You've only thought of yourselves. Well, it's my turn to think of myself."

"Mother, you've never told us you were unhappy living in this house. I've been in and out of the house almost daily to check on you because I thought you were depressed over Father's death. You know that."

"Yes, you rush in and rush out. You haven't spent one minute considering what I want, it's always been about you, your children, and their activities." She leaned forward. "I want you all to know that I do not need you to take care of me. I'm a healthy, educated, mature woman. I can take care of myself, thank you, and I'm ready to move on from being your aging mother to start a new life." She turned to Floyd and back to them. "I have an announcement."

"What else?" Morgan said, looking disdainful.

"Floyd and I are getting married."

Stunned by the announcement, no one spoke except Charlotte.

"Mother, you've lost your mind. How can you marry a man like him?"

"Stop it, you're prejudice is too much to bear. Floyd has more decency in his little finger than all of you combined, except Emily who's admitted she's happy that I met him. Charlotte, I'm sick of your criticisms."

Morgan stormed from the parlor and headed for the door. "Ma, don't expect me to be at your wedding. I'm still going to talk to my attorney," he yelled, slamming it as he left.

Charlotte pouted, looked at Floyd, stood, and ran upstairs to what would no longer be her bedroom.

"Mrs. Gulliver, I wish you well," Jimmy said. "I'll be looking for your letter to include in the paper." He took Emily by the elbow and led her out the front door.

Floyd stood put his hand on Annah's shoulder. "Annah, it'll be okay. They're hurt, but they'll get over it."

"Yes, when they receive their money," Annah said.

Annah sat back down in her parlor seat. The angry storm of her children's reactions grieved her, but she knew she had made the best decision. Gladstone would remain in better hands than with her family, especially considering the next generation, her grandchildren, who would never be able to maintain its integrity.

Floyd sat back down beside her and put his arm around her. She leaned her head on his chest and sighed with exhaustion. It was finished. Spencer had the best idea, and she appreciated his counsel. The committee would soon begin new plans to convert the house into the Civil War museum for the public to appreciate. *Thank you, Lord, for answering my prayers. Please take care of my children in their sorrow,* she thought.

Walking down to the truck, Floyd suggested they have brunch at a nice restaurant and talk, which Annah agreed to. She looked around to appraise the house where she had spent her entire life, a life of duty self-indulgence.

CHAPTER FORTY-THREE

They found a quaint restaurant on the outskirts of town. Annah perused her menu while Floyd sipped ice water and skimmed the selections with his finger.

"So, my lady, are all your legal matters finished, or are you still working on them?"

"I'm still waiting on a few things, but my lawyer is efficient, and I'm sure everything will work out with the transfer of the house to the State Historical Society."

"I knew you were smart," he said, as he chose his meal.

Annah made her choice from the menu and put it down. "Floyd, let's go after lunch and take the kitchen cookware to Delsey and Ruthie Ann. I want to tell them that I'm also going to donate funds for their school."

"You betcha', sweetheart."

—

They took off for the island on Highway 21 after she called Delsey to tell her they were on their way. Arriving at the village area where Delsey said they would all be waiting, Annah and Floyd climbed out and embraced them. Ruthie Ann grabbed Annah by the arm and swung her around in a joyful dance.

Then, Jerome slapped Floyd on his upper arm and grinned. He turned to face Delsey and Custer. "I think Miss Annah's going be okay. He's going get her out of the dumps," he said.

Floyd lifted his cap and ran his hand through his hair. "The dumps? I hope so."

Annah left the ladies and walked up to them. "Jerome, I heard what you said."

Jerome and Custer let out a howl.

"Annah, what did I tell you? You weren't the same after

Jackson died. You had us all worried, and now you're happy. We can see that you've changed," Delsey said. "Your grandmother would be proud of you, and so are we."

Floyd put his arm around Annah's shoulders. "I'm proud of her, too."

"Can't you see, Annah? Your children had you trapped. They wanted you to stay put, in your home, in your affairs, and to be continually in their lives, but Floyd came along and took everyone by surprise."

"Yes, ma'am," Floyd said. "It took some doing, though."

Annah playfully poked his side.

Then he turned to the men. "Come on, men, let's take my truck over to the restaurant and you can help me unload the kitchen items.

Eagerly, Jerome and Custer hopped into the truck and directed Floyd to the back of the restaurant. Annah and the ladies followed them on foot. Once the cookware was stored, they walked toward Aunt Carmita's home to have a meal. There, they feasted on a Low Country boil of rice, potatoes, sausage, onions, corn, shrimp, and crab claws spread out on newspaper over a long table. Floyd ate two helpings of it, while telling Ruthie Ann how delicious it was.

"Why, Mr. Floyd, you're surely welcome. Now, I want you to know you're family. You can visit us with Miss Annah whenever you like."

He grinned. "Thank you," he said. "I'll be at my wife's side whenever she visits."

"Your wife?" they responded together.

"Yes. Floyd and I are getting married," Annah said.

Ruthie Ann came up to Annah, put her face in hers, and said, "Didn't I tell you we would be praying for you?"

She returned the gesture. "Thank you for your prayers and making me feel a part of your family."

Once they finished eating, Annah said that she would provide funds to build an elementary school and a high school, everyone cheered. She said they would also be furnishing and supplying textbooks and materials needed in the classrooms.

Ruthie Ann leaned forward and said, "Thank *you* for all you've done for us. The good Lord has blessed us with your gifts."

Annah could say no more.

Once they said their good-byes, they drove back to Rosewillow and their hotel for the night. It had been an exceptional day.

"We have something to do today, don't we?" Floyd said the next morning.

"If it's what I think it is, then let's do it."

They left the hotel and parked in front of the courthouse to sign papers for a marriage license. Then they drove to the church where Pastor Burnham agreed to marry them with his janitor and secretary as witnesses. After signing the proper paperwork, they proceeded to the sanctuary and altar where the pastor recited the wedding vows. After the three wished them well, Floyd and Annah left the church to return to Ionia.

"Before we get on the road, Annah, let's go for a drink to celebrate at that small bar across from the courthouse.

"Let's do," she answered.

"As soon as we get back to Ionia," Floyd said, lifting his beer mug. "I have a little gift for you. I want you to have my mother's wedding ring. I know you'll love it, and we can get it sized if it doesn't fit."

"Why, Floyd, how wonderful. I'd love it wear it. Didn't you give it to Teresa to wear?"

He put down his beer. "No, she wanted something different, so I bought a ring for her. This is special, and I want you to have it."

Annah sipped her wine. "Floyd, I have something for you, too, but I won't be able to give it to you until we get back to Florida because you'll have to pick it out."

"Great! I get to pick out my own wedding gift."

"It's…large."

He held on to the handle of his mug. "How large?"

"Real large."

"Real large? Just how large is it?"

She hesitated, rotated her glass with her hands, and said, "About seventy feet long."

Floyd put his mug down, sat back, and held the table with his hands.

"It's about seventy feet long and over a one or two hundred feet high. I'm not sure exactly." She paused. "And, you'll have to think of a name for it."

Floyd slid forward. He stared at her with a look of shock and swigged his beer. "Annah, what in the world are you talking about?"

She bent her head and said quietly, "It's a motor sailer."

His mouth dropped in shock. "Annah?"

"Well, you said you wanted to one day own a yacht so you could fish the Keys and travel around the coast to places you've always wanted to visit."

"Yes, but…." He shook his head. "That was only a dream."

She folded her hands over the table. "Sometimes, dreams come true. My accountant is aware of my purchase and has it ready for me to order or buy the boat when we've made our decision." She paused. "I asked Roy and Spencer if they would help me select a yacht broker in Tampa, and they found one. Floyd, this can be our home for as long as we wish to live on it."

He caught his breath for a second, put his head down between his hands, and closed his eyes. Then he looked up. "Annah, in all my imagination, I never thought it would happen." He continued to study her face.

Annah picked up her wine glass and, shaking, laid it back down.

Awed, Floyd could only look at her with surprise.

—

Charlotte and Bradford reluctantly prepared to move out of the Gladstone mansion. Bradford angrily conceded and Charlotte and the children cried. At least, they could return to their home. Out of indignation, he insisted on hauling away specific antique furniture and pictures that belonged in the house. He left the computer and equipment uninstalled. Charlotte agreed with it all.

After Morgan left the house upon Annah's announcement, he went directly to his attorney, who told him there was nothing he could do. If his mother had prepared her directives so that if he challenged her will, he would lose everything, then he should forget about it. Once he heard that, he stormed out of his office, sought solace on his sailboat, and got drunk.

Emily accepted her mother's desires and told Jimmy that they were blessed to still be able to continue being in the house as caretakers, he as the curator and she being able to use her college degree as a photo-journalist as well as a docent.

When Annah and Floyd left the bar, she wanted to take a final look at Gladstone. "Good-bye," she whispered, as they drove under the live oak trees gracing her mansion. They circled the fountain now overflowing with fading geraniums and stopped beside her magnolia shrubs, which had lost their blossoms because it was nearing fall. She reminisced about her life there, remembering years of ballroom dances, family get-togethers, parties with Jackson's peers and their wives, and the quiet times while growing up. Nevertheless, she said, she knew she would have no regrets.

"We have one thing more to do here, Floyd. I have to drop my note off to Jimmy at his office and mail a letter."

"Yes, ma'am," he said. "Show me how to get there."

On the way, Annah said, "I'll just be a minute." She climbed out and slipped her letter to the Rosewillow Women's Club into the blue mail receptacle on the side of a public lot. In her mind, she recalled what she had written to her friends. *It's better this way*, she thought, *I don't have to face them and answer any questions.*

The letter thanked the ladies for their years of friendship, and she told them about her desire to make a dramatic change in her circumstances. She was remarrying and moving to Florida. She wished them well. She explained that she was donating Gladstone to the South Carolina State Historical Society to preserve it for future generations.

As she climbed back into the truck, she felt an overwhelming sense of freedom. "Now, let's hurry to the newspaper office."

Annah could see Jimmy typing on his computer when she entered the office area.

"That was fast," he said, when she entered.

"Here it is, Jimmy. This is a personal note from me to the community. I appreciate your putting this in the paper. It will explain what I intend to do with Gladstone." The note would answer everything. She knew there would be gossip, but it no longer mattered to her.

He took the note and said, "Mrs. Gulliver, thank you for giving me the opportunity to be the curator. Henry St. James called me and said you talked with him, and he offered me the job."

"We'll be back sometime to see the museum when everything's taken care of. I should also tell you that I'm very pleased to know you'll be my son-in-law. Emily needs a man with a head on his shoulders. I'll be here for your wedding as soon as you let me know the date, and I'll come to see my new grandchild, too."

"That would be great. I wish you well in your new life," he said. "Um, Mrs. Gulliver, may I call you Annah?"

"Of course, you may call me Annah. Just so you know, my last name is now O'Donnell."

"Why, is this Mrs. Gulliver?" Jimmy's editor said, seeing her as he came out of his office. "Madam, you've taken away my best journalist." He patted Jimmy on the head.

"Ah, Mrs. Gulliver. I mean Annah. No, I mean Mrs. O'Donnell, meet my editor," Jimmy said. "I've given him notice already that when the museum is completed, I'll be leaving here."

The editor leaned back and put his fingers into the loops on his pants. "Yep, he's been my best writer. How am I ever going to replace him?"

Annah smiled. "Mr., Jimmy, what did you say his name was?"

"I didn't. This is Mr. Mansfield." He turned to him. "Mrs. Gulliver got married. Her new name is O'Donnell."

"Well, congratulations, Mrs. O'Donnell. You've done a wonderful thing for our community. I wouldn't want to lose Jimmy to any other enterprise."

"I know I'm leaving the house in good hands."

Jimmy smiled sheepishly.

"It's nice to meet you," Annah said. "I have to run now. We're driving to Florida today."

"Be careful driving. I hope Jimmy will still contribute articles for our paper. He's topnotch."

Jimmy added, "My wife will be a great help writing articles, too."

Annah began to walk out the door, but turned around to face Jimmy again. "Oh, one more thing, Jimmy. Would you do me a big favor? Would you reinstall Jackson's computer and copy all his research materials on neurology onto CDs. There may be hundreds of files and then send them to the Institute of Neurology in Washington, D.C. It's important that these files be saved for future research."

"Certainly."

Then, Annah turned and walked out the door, knowing that Jimmy was a responsible young man and the files would be saved.

"Come on, Mr. O'Donnell, let's go." Annah said, as she climbed back into the truck.

"Yes, Mrs. O'Donnell. Let's go."

Jimmy opened Annah's note and read it. It didn't say what he expected it to say, but he understood. He would place the piece at the bottom of the article he would write about Gladstone being donated to the South Carolina Historical Society.

It read,

To the Rosewillow community,

After careful consideration and several years of work on the committee of the Rosewillow Civil War Museum and as heiress to Gladstone, I have come to the decision to donate Gladstone to the State Historical Society with the knowledge that you and your descendants will remember a time in history when our world and our values changed forever. May the Rosewillow Civil War Museum bring unity, not only to your community, but also to the nation, so that we will continue to live in peace remembering that we are all God's children, of every race and creed, and war is never the right solution.

Mrs. Annah Gladstone Gulliver O'Donnell

CHAPTER FORTY-FOUR

As Floyd and Annah approached the yacht brokerage in Tampa on their return trip to Ionia, sleek yachts, sailboats, motor sailers, and various shapes and sizes of boats loomed before them. Floyd was speechless.

He glanced at Annah. "You're sure about this?"

"I'm sure," Annah said, excited at the prospect of seeing what Floyd would think of the boat that Roy and Spencer had chosen for them.

He spied Spencer's car by the sales office and parked his truck next to it. Spencer stood next to Roy and a gray-haired salesman, while Kat and Lola wandered around the enormous watercrafts.

Spencer introduced Floyd and Annah to Tom, the yacht broker. "He'll show you the motor sailer Roy and I thought you would like to see."

"It's nice to meet you, Floyd. We think we've found what you and Annah would like. It's a seventy-foot motor sailer. You can sail as well as use motor power to operate it. It has all the new technology, sonar, self-furling sails, computerized control panel, etc. It will be easy for two people to navigate. I'll show you when we go up to the cockpit. In addition, it has a kitchen with a nice size galley and eating area, a living room, a queen-sized bed in the master bedroom, a decent bathroom with a shower, a sitting area with a bar, and all the amenities, plus one other sleeping room."

"Let's take a look," Spencer said, as they followed Tom toward it.

Floyd looked up at the tall masts and sails, the white body glimmering in the water, and the extreme length of the yacht. "Right now, I'm in shock that I would ever own something like this." He placed his hand on Annah's shoulder. "I mean us."

"This can be our home for a while," she said. "It has everything we need."

"Annah, are you sure we can afford this? You *do* realize this will be expensive to operate, and we may have to hire a captain to take over for a time or two. We'll also have to pay for docking privileges whenever we enter a port."

"I have it all covered. My accountant will take care of the purchase price and set aside the amount of money to take care of the expenses." In her will, she had signed Floyd as the beneficiary if anything happened to her, and he would have enough resources to maintain it for the rest of his life. Her remaining funds were to go to the museum, her grandchildren, as well as a sum to her Geechee friends for their schools and Ruthie Ann's restaurant. Her adult children had their inheritance already.

Floyd scratched his head. "Let's tour the yacht." They followed the salesman up a ladder into the stern of the boat.

The others joined them. "I've got to hand it to you, big fella, you sure are a damn lucky man," Roy said. He slapped Lola on her bottom as he followed her up the steps.

She swatted him. "Now, you stop that."

"Feel free to take a tour," the salesman said. "I'll point out the features as we go."

"Annah, hon, I'm amazed. This is the finest thing I've ever seen, and here y'all were going to buy a little cottage to get away from your kids for a while. Now, you're going to be traveling the world. They'll never catch up with you," Kat said.

"That's the idea," Annah said, as she turned to her. "Now, I can do what I want to do and go where I want to go." She glanced at Floyd. "I mean the both of us can."

"Lola," Roy called after her. "Did you hear that? Let's sell the Bed & Breakfast and follow them in our dingy so we can accompany them wherever they go."

"What in the world?" Lola asked, giving him a scornful look. "Roy, go buy yourself a bigger rowboat and go fishin'. I'm stayin' at our B&B."

Floyd and Annah toured the interior of the yacht. "One room is as beautiful as the next," Annah said. "Spencer and Roy, you both made a wonderful choice. Do you like it, Floyd?"

He pulled her to him. "I'm astounded."

"If you purchase the yacht today, we'll throw in two weeks of training to sail and operate it. If you're interested in operating it yourself, you may want to hire a captain the first month, so you can get the hang of running it with his guidance."

Still holding Annah, he whispered, "Lady love, I need to talk to you in confidence."

She looked at him for quite a while, noticing his serious expression. "Okay."

They walked a distance away from the salesman. "Babe, I will only let you buy this on one condition."

Uncertain about the condition, she responded. "What is it?"

He let her go and looked her directly in the face. "The price of this yacht is so great that I feel unworthy, and it's really too much for you to spend on just the two of us. I will let you buy it for us on the condition that we only live on it for two or three years, as you said, and then we will sell it and give the money to help others. There are people so poor, they can't feed or clothe their families. We could donate to soup kitchens, homeless shelters, community health centers, disaster relief agencies, you name it. Being rich, we have a responsibility beyond ourselves."

Annah stepped back, unable to speak. All she had ever known was wealth. Her travels to the islands were light-hearted fun times with her grandmother. Her intentions were good to help Delsey's island families, but she had never thought beyond them. What was that she had read in Grandma Wilmont's notes? "*One thing thou lackest: go thy way, sell whatsoever thou hast, and give to the poor, and thou shalt have treasure in heaven....*"

"Love, after we come home here, we'll look for a beautiful home for us to live in for the rest of our lives. I promise that."

She couldn't say no. What he was saying was good. "Floyd, I've never met a man so concerned about everyone and so unselfish. Thank you for letting me to see through your eyes and heart. I accept your condition."

Floyd nodded and walked back to the salesman. "That might be a good idea. We'll see how our two weeks of training go. I sailed a fifty-foot motor sailer years ago, but a refresher course would be helpful for me and important for my wife."

"Floyd, I didn't tell you this, but I have experience sailing a yacht. Like you, I learned to sail with my Uncle Rufus when I was a teenager. He owned a smaller sailboat, and he taught me to operate it. He also taught Morgan to sail when he reached thirteen. That's why Morgan loves to sail now."

"Annah, did I hear right? You got married? When and where?" Kat asked.

"We were married on the sly, and we haven't told our children yet. They know we had plans, but they don't know we actually did it. We were married in Pastor Burnham's church with his staff as witnesses." She leaned closer to Floyd.

"This is an answer to my prayers," Lola said. "Floyd, I just knew you two would tie the knot."

"So, what do you think?" Tom asked, looking at Floyd.

Turning to Annah, Floyd asked, "What do *you* think?"

"We'll buy it," Annah said, seeing the grin on his face.

After touring the entire yacht, Annah and Floyd saw the others off and walked with the salesman over to his office to sign papers and make a call to her accountant. They would soon become proud owners of a motor sailer and their new home.

They spent the next two weeks learning how to operate the yacht. Floyd knew quite a bit about how to handle a fifty-footer, but one this large would take some time. He also needed to learn the new technology in the control center in the cockpit, the sonar, and the computerized navigation equipment. Annah attempted to learn these operations, but her focus was on how to run the appliances and electronics within the galley.

During that time, they lived in Floyd's small house and waited for Annah's furnishings and personal effects to arrive in the moving truck from Rosewillow. Once it arrived, they led the driver to their storage unit on the outskirts of Ionia and supervised him and his helper to unload everything into the unit. It would be a long time before she would unpack it. Their honeymoon and new house would be on their yacht, sailing down the Keys.

Finally, when they had everything taken care of, Floyd and Annah took the time to visit Kat and Spencer to say they were leaving. "But we'll be back. We'll be traveling along the coast of Florida, down the Keys, and stopping at Key West for some time. Then we plan to travel up the east coast," Floyd said.

Kat handed Annah a wedding card and a bouquet of roses. "Hon, I couldn't think of anything else you'd need, so put these flowers in a vase on your new kitchen table, and make sure they don't slide off."

"Thank you. How lovely," Annah said, smelling the fragrant flowers. "I'll make sure they stay pinned to the table."

Annah held back tears. "Kat and Spencer, I owe you two a lot. You take care of yourselves, too. We'll keep in touch by postcards and phone calls, so you'll know where we are."

"Oh, I can't wait to hear what you two will be doing and where you'll be going. Take many pictures and send them to us. Maybe we can meet you some place to spend some time together along the way," Kat said.

"Yes, let's do that."

"I want to call Renaldo and Lucia when we pass Miami,"

Annah said. "I want to hear if they're okay and have found jobs, since I haven't heard from them; and then I'd like to go on to visit with Delsey and Ruthie Ann at her restaurant on the island. We've given them kitchen equipment from Gladstone, and I want to make sure they have enough funds to keep the restaurant going." She winked at Floyd. "Besides, Floyd wants to eat another meal of Low Country Boil." She continued. "In addition, I want to see if they've finished building the new schools by the time we get there."

"Annah, are you going to visit your children and grandchildren while you're in the area?" Kat asked. "Your trip around Florida will take some time."

"I plan to do that, too, and visit Maybelle to see how she's fairing. I also have to check with my lawyer and with Henry on the progress of Gladstone as a museum."

"Let us know the date Emily and Jimmy plan to marry, and we'll be there," Spencer said.

"Good. They would love to have you attend."

"After that, I think we should travel north to put flowers on my wife's grave," Floyd said. "I would like to do this for the last time."

Annah remembered her visit at Jackson and Grandma Wilmont's graves. That was her last time for them also. "That's thoughtful of you, Floyd."

"Well, it sounds like you two have your travel plans all worked out," Spencer said. "You two be careful on the high seas. Watch those storms and pull ashore when the waves get too high."

"You bet," Floyd said. He shook Spencer's hand and hugged Kat.

Once they left, they headed for their boat. It sat in the water tied up along the pier. Annah surveyed the area as they approached. She closed her eyes, listened to the water slapping the sides of several boats, and watched pelicans flying overhead. "This is music to my ears. I'm going to enjoy being a seafaring sailor with you."

"You've really taken to the water, huh? You've gone from fishing in a river to sailing a yacht on the high seas. I'm impressed," Floyd said.

She handed him the bags of food she was carrying while he climbed up the ladder and into the boat.

"My dear, I bought you the finest of wines and the best of beers for me," Floyd said, as pointed to several boxes he had hauled from his truck and set on the pier. Annah handed them up to him one by one.

After the supplies and personal items were stored, Floyd called Roy to have him pick up Annah's car and park it next to the B&B.

"I'll be right there with Lola, so she'll drive our car back home," he said. "Give us an hour or so to get there."

"Great. We'll be in the boat." As he helped Annah into it, he said, "Let's celebrate. I've opened a bottle of champagne." He took the bottle and two stemmed glasses outside the cabin and sat down on the seat beside Annah. He poured champagne and they tipped their glasses in celebration.

"Floyd, I have something very important to do right now." She stood up, reached into her pocket, and pulled out her cell phone. She walked to the edge of the boat, swung her arm, and threw her phone hundreds of feet in the air and into the ocean.

"Annah, won't you need that?" Floyd asked.

"No, I've been bothered with calls for months on end, and I'm not going to be tied to it any longer. If anyone wants to get a hold of us, we have yours and that's enough."

"Well then, I have something to do also." He stood up beside her, pulled his cigar out of his shirt pocket, threw it high into the air, and watched it fall into the ocean.

Surprised, Annah said, "You didn't have to throw your cigar away. I'm getting used to the aroma."

"I didn't have to, but I did." As he said that, he reached into his pocket and grabbed a pipe and a pouch of tobacco. "Lady love, since we're now proud owners of a ship, the ship's captain needs a pipe to smoke."

She leaned back and laughed. "Where's your captain's hat."

"We'll get one in Key West."

She took another sip of champagne. "Tell me about Key West. You're always mentioning it, but I know very little about it."

He leaned back. "Key West is an old town, but quite the tourist area today. It's a fun place to visit. Ernest Hemingway made it famous in the thirties and forties because of the novels he wrote and his reputation. You can visit and take a tour of his home. Harry Truman had his southern white house there, which you can also tour. Mel Fisher found millions of dollars of gold coins, trinkets, and jewelry on the bottom of the ocean close by. It was a Spanish treasure. You can actually hold a gold bar and try to pull it out of a glass case in his museum. If you can, you'll be rich. There are fine restaurants and dingy bars throughout the town. Sloppy Joe's was Hemingway's favorite bar and Jimmy Buffet's Cheeseburgers in Paradise restaurant is a fun place to eat. Shall I go on?"

"What happened to Fort Zachary Taylor?"

"Oh, that's off the beach on the southern side of the island. Key West is an island unto itself, just like all the other keys. We can tour that if you'd like. That should be of interest to you, especially because of your story about Captain Gladstone being rewarded the money he received from capturing that union vessel."

She finished her champagne and set it down on the table beside them. "It certainly would. I don't know why Jackson and I never thought to visit there."

"Okay," he said. "I have another thing to do." Out of the other pocket, he withdrew a small, velvet covered box. "For you, Madam."

"Oh." Annah opened it and saw his mother's wedding ring. He removed it from the box and slipped it on her left ring finger. "It's lovely, Floyd. I don't think we'll have to size it, it fits my finger."

"Mrs. O'Donnell, when Roy and Lola leave, I want you to read the name I had them paint on the bow," Floyd said.

"What did you call it?"

Before he could answer, Roy and Lola walked up to the boat with Roscoe on a leash. "Hey, you lovebirds, let us up," Roy called.

"Come on," Floyd said, as he reached down to pick up Roscoe and help Lola up. Roy followed.

"Hi, boy," Floyd said, cuddling him. He put him down and Roscoe took off exploring.

Lola and Roy stepped into the boat.

"Annah, I made these for you. They're pecan cookies. Floyd's favorite."

"Oh, mine, too. Thank you, Lola."

"Yeah, and don't forget you're on your honeymoon. You've got to get it on," Roy added.

Lola slapped his arm. "Roy!" Then she pulled a letter out of her pocket. "Annah, this is for you," she said. "It's from Jimmy."

Annah opened it and read that the Board of Directors appointed him as the museum curator and that Emily was placed in charge of the volunteer docents. He said his interest in history was greater than his desire to be a journalist; so, as soon as the museum was completed, he would quit his job at the newspaper. In the meantime, he would be involved with the museum committee preparing its opening.

She also read that they were planning their wedding during Emily's spring break from school and that their baby boy would be due the beginning of March. They plan to name him, Thomas James Nealy. They hoped she would be at the wedding and the arrival of their son.

She folded the letter, put it in her pocket, and said to everyone, "It's amazing how everything is working out."

"It seems so," Lola said, as she sat beside Annah. "You have a beautiful new home,"

"Lola, so do you. You have a lovely Bed & Breakfast."

"Would you take the key to our house and keep a watch on it

while we're gone," Floyd said, as he took two keys off a ring. "If you need anything out of the house, help yourself; and, Roy, consider my truck yours. Otherwise, it'll sit there for at least two years and rust out."

"Thanks! I've wanted another pickup since my other one crapped out," Roy said.

Lola huffed. "Roy, you made it unfixable when you tried to fix it yourself. You don't know a hoot about fixin' engines."

"And Lola," Annah said. "You may drive my car. I don't want it to sit and rust out as Floyd said. We plan on sailing for two years, maybe three years, and return here to buy a custom home."

Lola's hands flew to her face. "Annah? Me drive your Mercedes?"

"I want you to enjoy it."

"Oh, Annah, can you just see me drivin' it? Why, I'll be the talk of the town."

"I hope it's all good talk," Annah said, handing her the key.

Roy smirked. "Can I drive it home?"

"No sir. I'm drivin' my new car home," she said, laughing with Annah.

For a little while, they talked about the trip Floyd and Annah were about to embark upon and their plans to settle down in Ionia when they returned. Then it was time for Roy and Lola to leave.

"Hey Floyd, are you going to have a captain on board for a couple of weeks?"

"We talked about it, but I think we'll try to sail it ourselves. If it's too much to handle, we'll hire a man in Key West. It's not too far to sail from here, and there's plenty of them down there."

Floyd picked up Roscoe and held him tightly to his chest. He rubbed his face into his furry back for quite a while. "Buddy," he said, choking, "I have to leave you to go live with Roy and Lola. You know I love you, but where we're going, you can't go."

Everyone watched the two of them and understood. Roscoe had been Floyd's faithful companion for a couple of years and now they had to part.

"You'll have a good home with my family. You'll be okay, and I know you'll be taken care of." He coughed and turned around so no one could see him. "I'll be back and maybe we'll be together again," he whispered into his ear. Then he turned around again and handed him to Roy.

Roy held him for a moment and finally said, "We'll take good care of him, Floyd, you old coot, and love him just like you do."

Roscoe wiggled in Roy's arms and wanted to get down.

"Now, you two be good," Lola said, as she climbed down the

steps. "Don't you worry about your precious dog. We love him to pieces."

"Have a good trip you two. I wish we were goin' with you," Roy said. Floyd and Annah waved and watched them walk up the pier, and Roscoe barked as they walked away.

"Well? Are you going to read the name of our yacht?" Floyd asked.

"Yes, let's see it." She crept down the steps as Floyd helped her balance and follow behind her. They walked around to the back of the yacht for Annah to get a good look at the name. She stopped and studied the writing. It read, "September Song." Turning to face him, she asked, "Did you name it that because it's September?"

"That and for another reason," he said, and then began to sing parts of *September Song* in a rich baritone.

Oh, it's a long, long while from May to December,
But the days grow short when you reach September.
When the autumn weather turns the leaves to flame,
One hasn't got time for the waiting game....
And these few precious days I'll spend with you.
These few precious days I'll spend with you.

As Annah listened, her eyes watered. The words left her speechless. She remembered Delsey's words, *Sectembtuh com' yuh, September is coming.* They were prophetic. She shook her head in amusement thinking about Delsey's mysterious way of knowing the unknown and Grandma Wilmont's prediction through scripture that God had plans for her to give her a future and a hope. *The Lord has plans for our future, and they will surely be precious*, she thought.

She looked up at Floyd and wrapped her arms around his big belly. Laying her head on his chest, she said, "Mr. Romantic, let's hope the days are many."

Floyd lifted her face to his, and whispered, "Let's go then, we have the wind in our sails, time on our hands, there's not a cloud in the sky, and Key West is calling."

THE END